Praise for
The Raines of Wind Canyon

Against the Wind
"This is definitely a page-turner full of compassion and love
shared by two unlikely souls. This is a 'don't miss' read…
Kat Martin is a very gifted writer who takes you from the
beginning to the end in total suspense."
—*Fresh Fiction*

Against the Fire
"After reading the first book about the Raine brothers,
I knew Kat Martin would have to do something pretty amazing
to make her second book as much of a joy to read. As soon as
I opened the book, I realized that she has succeeded.…"
—*Suspense Romance Writers*

"There's something irresistible about a bad boy.…
This sexy page-turner is a perfect blend of romance,
mystery and action."
—*RT Book Reviews*

Against the Law
"Once you start *Against the Law,* be prepared not to stop
until you've reached the end. With its nonstop action,
nail-biting episodes mixed with some sizzling love scenes,
this is one I highly recommend."
—*Romance Reviews Today*

"4 ½ quills! Ms. Martin has struck the motherlode…
Against the Law is by far the most powerfully intense
romantic suspense with its charismatic characters,
[and] a story line that defies gravity."
—*Romantic Crush Junkies*

AGAINST THE
ODDS

KAT MARTIN

AGAINST THE ODDS

HARLEQUIN®

entertain, enrich, inspire™

ISBN-13: 978-1-62090-798-6

AGAINST THE ODDS

To my great friends in Bakersfield, California, who know what that scorching desert heat can feel like. Miss you all.

One

"Mr. Justice! Mr. Justice, can you give us a moment of your time?"

Sabrina Eckhart stared at the news broadcast on KTRK-TV. She had watched the segment run on an earlier edition, but found herself watching it again.

The reporter, a small man with dark hair and a determined expression, hurried to keep up with Alex Justice's long strides as he walked out of the downtown Houston Police Department building. "Mr. Justice!" At the sight of several TV cameras, Alex's steps reluctantly slowed.

"Everyone in the city is grateful for what you did," the reporter said. "People are calling you a hero. What do you think about that?" The man thrust a microphone into Alex's handsome face. Six two, dark blond hair and blue eyes, always dressed as if he'd just stepped out of a *GQ* magazine, Alex Justice was an amazing-looking man.

"I'm a private investigator," Alex said. "I did what I was paid to do—find evidence that would identify the killer of a ten-year-old girl. I was lucky enough to make that happen. There's nothing heroic about it."

"It's been said you'll do anything to catch your man. Is that true?"

Alex just kept walking. There wasn't a glimpse of the deep dimples bracketing his mouth that Rina remembered so well. She hadn't seen him in more than six months, not since the day her best friend, Sage Dumont, married Jake Cantrell, one of Alex's best friends.

Rina watched him stride away until he disappeared offscreen, then the camera cut to the reporter, who relayed the story of the little girl who had been abducted, sexually abused and murdered three years ago. Ten-year-old Carrie Wiseman's killer had never been found—not until Alex Justice had come up with DNA evidence that directly linked the girl to a neighbor who lived down the street from her home.

Two days ago, the neighbor, Edward Bagley, was arrested, which took at least one killer off the streets.

As the newscast came to an end, Rina hit the button on the remote, turning off the TV. She crossed her living room to the delicate antique French writing desk in the corner. Her apartment was a mixture of comfortable contemporary furniture and French antiques: rosewood armoires, gilt mirrors and marble-topped tables, many pieces from the sixteenth century.

The apartment was softly feminine but not crowded, and it suited her personality perfectly.

Reaching down, she picked up the pile of bills from the desk, began to sift through the stack. In the six months since she had last seen the handsome private investigator with the amazing dimples, a lot had changed.

She had broken up with her live-in boyfriend, Ryan Gosford, and moved back into her own apartment. She had liked Ryan; she just hadn't loved him, and things were beginning to get sticky.

During those months, her finances had dropped sharply. The stock market had taken another dive and this time wiped out the last of the money she had invested in her retirement account. Her job as a stockbroker at Smith Barney Morgan Stanley had become more and more difficult as her clients pulled their money out of the market and put it into gold and silver, real estate bargains and anything else they considered a safer bet than wildly fluctuating stocks.

Alex's image popped back into her head as she sorted through the bills—utilities that would start to soar as summer approached and the heat rose into the hundreds in Houston, the tax payment on her mother's small house in Uvalde that Rina had taken over paying several years back; miscellaneous bills just to pay the costs of living in Houston. In a week, the rent would be due on her uptown apartment.

At the bottom of the pile was a white nine-by-twelve envelope from Delaney, Dennison and Smith, Attorneys at Law, the contents of which she had examined a dozen times. Papers finalizing an inheritance from her late uncle Walter, the probate settled and the estate officially hers: three thousand acres of dry, barren land in the middle of nowhere—or, more accurately, the middle of somewhere in the West Texas desert.

It was probably worthless, as her mother and the rest of her family kept telling her, and yet...

The land was the reason she kept thinking of Alex Justice, and seeing him on TV had finally been the catalyst she needed to push her into taking action. Alex was a former navy pilot, a jet jockey with a cocky attitude and an ego that was out of control. Also, like his friend Jake Cantrell and the rest of the men at the Atlas Security office, Alex was a typical macho man who exuded testosterone and buckets of male sexual appeal.

He was the kind of man females lusted after.

All except Rina. Or at least she did her very best not to.

Still, there was one thing about Alex Justice she couldn't deny. The man was good at his job.

Beyond that, and for reasons she couldn't completely explain, she trusted him.

A knock sounded at the door. It was the moment she had been dreading all morning. The man standing on the porch was wearing an expensive suit, his light brown hair combed straight back. He was in his thirties, a man most women would find attractive, but he looked a little too slick for her.

"Ms. Eckhart? I'm Nathan Billings. I'm here about the car?"

"Of course. I've been expecting you, Mr. Billings."

He gave her a winning smile. "It's nice to meet you, Ms. Eckhart, and it's just Nate."

Rina slung the strap of her handbag over her shoulder. "Fine, just Nate, let's get this done." Walking him outside, she pointed to the little red, two-passenger Mercedes SLK convertible that was her pride and joy. A car she had worked sixty hours a week since she'd started her job as a stockbroker to earn. Six years of hard labor and counting, and now even her car was gone.

She handed Nate Billings the keys. "It's all yours. I hope you enjoy the car as much as I have."

Billings smiled and looked covetously at the Mercedes. "I'm sure I will." His gaze returned to her, took in her jeans and a lemon-yellow sweater that showed a hint of cleavage. He opened his mouth to pursue a conversation, but Rina impolitely stared down at her wristwatch—not the ladies' Rolex she had sold last month, but a nice, practical Timex—hoping he would get the drift that she wasn't interested.

He cleared his throat. "Well, then, thanks" was all he said. She watched him climb into her car and start the powerful engine, a smooth, throaty purr that always made her heart beat faster.

She waited until the car drove away, then walked over to the light blue 2007 Toyota Corolla she had purchased last week with most of the money from the sale of the watch. Sliding behind the wheel, she cranked up the much smaller engine and drove out of her apartment complex onto Post Oak Park. From there, she wound her way through the streets till she reached the single-story brick building in the University District that housed Atlas Security.

She knew where it was. Jake Cantrell, her best friend's husband, worked there. As she pulled into the lot in front, she spotted Alex Justice's dark blue BMW M3 coupe in one of the parking spaces, a gorgeous car that reminded her how much she had loved driving her flashy red Mercedes and gave her a soft little pang.

At least he was there. Hiring him wouldn't be cheap, she knew, but she had the rest of the money from the assets she had liquidated, a little savings left in the bank, and she was willing to take the risk that in the end it would be worth it.

She grimaced at the thought, since it was that kind of thinking that had caused her to lose most of her retirement fund.

Now came the hard part.

She and Alex had never really gotten along. Alex was always baiting her and she was always trying to dodge the unwanted physical attraction she refused to admit she felt for him. At the moment none of that mattered.

Rina took a deep breath, squared her shoulders and headed for the front door of the office.

Alex ended his phone call and settled back in the chair behind his desk. The office was busy, considering it was getting close to noon and things had usually slowed down a little by now. Annie Mayberry sat behind the front desk, a once-blonde, now gray-blonde woman in her mid-sixties with the personality of an overprotective bulldog. She was the office manager and receptionist, currently fielding unwelcome phone calls from the media that had been hounding him all morning.

Sol Greenway, the Atlas Security computer whiz kid, sat behind an oversize monitor in his glass-enclosed office. Trace Rawlins, the owner of the company and one of Alex's closest friends, worked in the glass-windowed office next to Sol's.

The office decor was masculine, with heavy oak desks, dark green carpet and photos of Texas ranches hanging on the walls. Alex sat at a desk in the main room of the office, a place to return phone calls and keep a few supplies. Most of the work he did was in the field.

A few feet away, dark-haired and blue-eyed ex-SEAL Ben Slocum, another freelance investigator, sat with a phone pressed against his ear. The other P.I., Jake Cantrell, was out on a protection detail for the next few days.

Alex checked his gold wristwatch. He was almost

ready to take off for an early lunch when the bell above the front door started jingling. He glanced up to see a petite redhead in a pair of jeans and a sleeveless yellow knit sweater talking to Annie. Great body, he thought, nice full breasts and a round little derriere.

He was smiling when she turned and started toward him, a smile that turned into a flat-out grin.

Alex rose as she drew near. "Hey, Red. Haven't seen you in a while."

Her pretty mouth tightened a little at the nickname, which he'd given her because she reminded him of a little red fox—though he'd never told her that.

She paused in front of his desk. "I saw you on TV this morning. That was a good thing you did."

His smile slid away. "I would have taken that case for free." And practically had. Finding the evidence to put away a murdering pervert was something he'd enjoyed doing. Besides, money wasn't something he needed. Alex's family was East Coast, old-money rich, and his grandfather had left him a bundle. It was the work he loved, doing something productive. He liked it almost as much as flying.

"I know I should have called," she said, "but I was...I was hoping you might have a minute to talk."

"You don't need an appointment, Sabrina. You want a cup of coffee or something?"

"No, thanks, I'm fine." She sat down in the chair next to his desk and he returned to his seat.

"So...what have you been doing with yourself for the last six months? Besides keeping good ol' Ryan entertained."

One of her dark red eyebrows arched up. "'Good ol' Ryan' and I broke up. It was a mutual decision."

He doubted it. Ryan Gosford was pretty well gone over the feisty little redhead. He was a computer geek, a good-looking guy but dull as dirt, while Sabrina was anything but. It was hardly a match made in heaven.

"Who's the lucky guy taking his place?" he couldn't resist asking.

"Nobody. I needed a break for a while. I'm not seeing anyone." She eyed him with a hint of challenge. "How about you? I doubt you're sitting home alone at night."

"I'm not a eunuch. I'm seeing a couple of people. No one in particular."

"Of course not," she said, as if she could have guessed.

His grin returned. "So you're not dating anyone. Does that mean you came by to see me because you're lonely?"

Sabrina stiffened. "Your ego never ceases to amaze me." She came up out of her chair. "I knew this was a bad idea. I should never have come." She started to walk away, but Alex caught her arm.

"Take it easy, Red. I was only kidding. I promise I'll behave myself." He tugged her back to his desk and she reluctantly sat back down in her chair. "So tell me why you're here."

Sabrina smoothed the front of her crisp blue jeans. "Well…the thing is I…umm…inherited this land out in West Texas. I'm not really sure what's there or what it's worth, so I want to take a look. I figured you could fly me out and help me locate the property, take a look around."

He leaned back in his chair, giving himself a little time to assess the situation. "Your hair's longer." His gaze ran over the shiny red locks that now curled softly along her jawline.

Trace had always been drawn to redheads. Alex had never understood the attraction, but looking at those heavy curls his fingers itched to touch, for the first time he thought maybe he did.

A little self-consciously, Sabrina smoothed the tempting strands back from her face. "A good salon costs a fortune these days. It was cheaper just to let it grow."

He noted the remark, thought it was an odd thing for her to say, considering what a successful stockbroker she was.

"I mean, I just thought I'd try it this way," she corrected, making him wonder again.

"Looks really good," he said, and a hint of color washed beneath the faint spray of freckles across her cheeks.

He cleared his throat. "Okay, so you want to see this property you inherited. Why don't you just fly commercial and rent a car when you get there?"

"Because the closest town is Rio Gordo and it's miles from an airport that handles commercial flights."

"Rio Gordo? Hell, that's five hundred miles away."

"That's right. And even after I get there, I'm not exactly sure where the property is. I mean, I know where it is on Google Maps. I've located the land on satellite photos, and I've got county plat maps of the property, but I can't find a road. There's a place to rent a helicopter in Rio Gordo. I was thinking once we get there, we could rent the chopper and you could fly me around the area until we locate the site."

"The site of what?"

"The...umm...the mine."

He was beginning to get it. Sabrina Eckhart was a

businesswoman, first, last and always. "What kind of mine?"

"I'm not exactly sure. Silver, maybe." She sat up a little straighter in the chair. "It's a long story, Alex. The point is, my uncle Walter left me the property. It was all he had in the world. It may be valuable. It may be worthless. But I need to find out. Can you take me or not?"

Not a chance in hell he was going to say no. Aside from the fact Sabrina was Sage Cantrell's best friend and Jake Cantrell was one of Alex's best friends, she was a fox. He'd been attracted to Sabrina Eckhart from the day he'd met her. And though every look, every word she said told him that attraction was not returned, he wasn't convinced.

"I'll take you."

Sabrina smiled, seemed to relax. "Great. I've already started making the arrangements. I figured you'd know the best place here to rent a plane. I've called about the helicopter. I remember you saying you could fly one, so we're almost set."

"You done any checking, tried to find out if anyone in Rio Gordo knows where the mine is?"

"My uncle was a hermit and extremely secretive. He never even told me. No way would he tell anyone else."

"When do you want to go?"

"The sooner the better."

He didn't ask how she could get away from her job so easily. She'd always been a workaholic. Maybe she was due some time off. "How about day after tomorrow?"

"That'd be really great. You get the plane lined up and I can reserve the chopper."

"I'll do you one better. We'll use my plane." The Twin Beechcraft Baron he'd bought a couple months ago. Any excuse to fly it was a good one. "And I'll need to make the call on the chopper myself, make sure it's something I'm checked out in."

"Okay." She stood up from her chair and stuck out a small hand. "Thanks, Alex."

Alex rose and took her hand but didn't let go. "Only one question."

"What's that?"

"Why me?"

She eased her hand from his. "Because, whatever our differences, you're good at your job. I saw how well you worked with Jake to protect Sage." Jake had served as Sage's bodyguard. They'd ended up married. "You proved it again when you found the evidence the police needed to arrest the man who killed little Carrie Wiseman."

"Go on," he pressed, figuring there was more.

She looked like she didn't want to say it. "All right— because I trust you. It's as simple as that."

But she probably shouldn't. Just seeing her standing there looking like a hungry man's dessert made him want to take her to bed. "I'll need to do some recon on the area. I'll need those maps and whatever information you have on the property."

"I'll make copies and drop them off here at the office."

"Good enough. I'll pick you up Wednesday morning."

"All right. My address is—"

"I know your address. I'm a detective, remember?"

She eyed him with suspicion. "What about my cell number?"

He grinned. "Same number you had before?"

"Yes."

"I'll pick you up Wednesday. Eight o'clock okay?"

"I'll be ready." She started to leave, then turned back. "Thanks, Alex."

"You haven't asked my fee. You may not thank me when you hear what it is."

It was her turn to grin. "I know your fee. I may not be a detective, but I have my sources."

He laughed. "Come on, I'll walk you out." She didn't object as he kept pace with her to the front desk. He reminded himself he preferred tall, svelte blondes, not petite, curvy redheads. Still, there was something about this particular redhead that had him looking forward to the flight to Rio Gordo.

He pushed open the glass front door. Unfortunately, instead of Sabrina walking out, Melissa Carlyle walked in.

"Alex! I was hoping you'd be here." She threw her arms around his neck and gave him a smacking kiss on the lips. Alex inwardly groaned. Unwinding her arms, he eased her back a couple of paces.

"I'll see you Wednesday," Rina said, flicking him a smug, knowing glance over her shoulder. "Unless you get too busy." She walked past them out the door, the bell jingling as it shut behind her.

Damn. He looked over at the woman eagerly awaiting his attention. Melissa was tall, blonde and svelte, just the way he liked. She also had a brain that rattled around like a marble inside her head.

"I thought maybe we could go to lunch," she said. "Not that I dare eat all that much. I have to watch my weight, you know."

Alex looked past her, saw Sabrina getting into a little blue Corolla instead of her sexy red Mercedes and frowned.

"Did you hear me? I said I thought we might—"

"I heard you. I thought we decided to take a break from each other."

"Did we? I must have forgot."

"Did you also forget your ex-boyfriend is in town? You said the two of you were thinking about getting back together."

She shrugged. "Well, maybe."

"Look, Melissa. I'm really busy. I think you should call your ex, see if he wants to go to lunch."

She just nodded, smiled. "Okay." She turned and started walking toward the door. "See you later."

Alex made no reply. He was hoping he never saw the airheaded blonde again and couldn't understand how he'd gone out with her a second time.

He shook his head. As he walked back to his desk, Sabrina's image swept into his mind, a breath of fresh air blowing back into his life. Sitting down behind his desk, he began to make the arrangements for a trip to Rio Gordo.

Two

Those dimples. *Oh, my God!* Be better for the female population if the man never smiled. As she drove back toward her apartment, Rina sighed. She must have been insane to get Alex Justice involved in this.

Except that she needed his help. What she'd said was true. She trusted him. She had met him when her friend Sage Dumont, a VP at Marine Drilling International, had needed protection. Well, actually, Sage had introduced Rina to Jake Cantrell, her bodyguard, and Jake had brought Alex in to help with the job.

She'd seen him in action enough to realize how good he was at what he did.

And there was no way she was going out to some remote location in the desert with just anyone. The mere thought of hiring some overweight, muscle-headed helicopter pilot from a nowhere town like Rio Gordo sent a shiver down her spine.

Clearly, Alex was a man with a strong sexual appetite, but he wasn't the kind of guy who would ever force himself on a woman. And since he sometimes worked as a bodyguard, he had to be a lot tougher than his blond, blue-eyed, cover-model appearance made him look. She would be safe with Alex Justice—even in the middle of God only knew where.

Since she was on a leave of absence from her job at Morgan Stanley, which, considering her customer base had shrunk to almost zilch, wasn't a problem, she went straight back to her apartment to make the necessary calls and start packing an overnight bag for the trip. She hadn't mentioned it to Alex, but she might need to stay an extra day, depending on what she found on the property.

Excitement trickled through her. She reminded herself not to get her hopes up, but she couldn't help herself. During the past six months of market ups and downs, she had decided she was ready to make a change. If the land had any sort of mining potential, she was going to jump in and see if she couldn't make it work, see if she could make some money.

Silver prices had spiked to more than thirty dollars an ounce. Her research told her that historically there wasn't much silver in Texas, and mining for the ore had stopped in 1994. But recently, with the cost of silver climbing, the Desert Mine had reopened, and it wasn't that many miles away from her uncle's property.

Rina couldn't wait to find out if Uncle Walter's ramblings over the years might have been right. She couldn't wait to see if there was actually something there.

Rina was dressed in a pair of jeans, sneakers and a sleeveless turquoise blouse when Alex arrived to pick her up on Wednesday morning. It was only the first of May, but an early heat wave had arrived in Houston, and it was going to be even hotter out in the dry West Texas desert, reaching a possible high of ninety-five degrees. According to weather.com, it would also be extremely cold at night.

Aside from a change of clothes, her makeup bag and a toothbrush in case they needed to stay an extra day, she had a warm, fleece-lined jacket in her flowered tapestry satchel.

Alex didn't say much as he drove her to the airpark southwest of the city where he kept his plane. By the time they arrived, it had been towed out of its hangar and was waiting for them on the tarmac.

"It's a beautiful airplane," she said, admiring the sleek blue-and-white twin-engine aircraft that looked extremely expensive.

"Beechcraft Baron," he said. "I've only had it a couple of months." He looked at it with the same covetous expression Nate Billings had when he'd eyed her little red Mercedes, and also a hint of pride.

Rina studied the Baron, a much larger plane than she had thought he would rent. "It's more than I figured we'd need. How much is this going to cost me?"

Alex grinned and his dimples popped up. "You're in luck, sweetheart. I was going to take her up anyway. Might as well go to Rio Gordo as anywhere else." There was something in his eyes, like maybe he knew the truth—that she didn't have the kind of money she'd had a year ago. He was a detective, after all, as he had reminded her.

But Alex had no reason to be digging up information on her so she was probably wrong. She certainly hoped so. She didn't want Alex Justice's charity. She didn't want anything from him except a ride out to the property she now owned.

Still, fueling planes like this one didn't come cheap. "Are you sure?"

"Not a problem. I'm just anxious to get her in the air." She worked not to sag in relief. "Great. Me, too."

Alex made an exterior equipment check, wandering around the plane, checking the tires, whatever pilots did before takeoff, then tossed her satchel and a bag of his own into the luggage compartment and helped her climb up on the wing.

Once they were both inside, Alex in the pilot's seat, Rina riding copilot, he began his preflight check. The cabin was first-class, with club seating for four in back in butter-soft blue-gray leather, and immaculately clean.

"You ready?" he asked when he'd finished and both engines were running smoothly.

She didn't tell him she'd never flown in a plane smaller than a commercial airliner. Didn't mention the butterflies swirling in her stomach. She didn't want him to know what a small-town girl she really was.

Uvalde, Texas, where she was raised, wasn't Houston. Her mother, Florence, had been a homemaker, her father, Big Mike Eckhart, a truck driver. She'd studied hard to get a partial scholarship to the University of Houston. Uncle Walter had sent her some money on occasion, and she'd worked part-time to earn the rest, enough to get through college.

She gave him a saucy smile. "I'm ready." And actually, she was looking forward to the flight. She was always up for a new adventure. Seeing new country, trying new things. Besides, Sage had told her that Alex had flown planes off a carrier. This had to be a piece of cake for him.

The engine hummed as they taxied down the runway, then built to a roar as the plane picked up speed. In seconds they were lifting into the air, the ground falling away beneath them, becoming a collage of miniature houses and high-rise buildings, then tiny blue lakes in a landscape of green. She jumped at the crack that echoed through the cabin as the wheels rose and locked into place, then sat back and relaxed, beginning to enjoy herself.

Instead of dreading the flight when she flew commercial, jammed in between two other people, trying to see out the tiny cabin window, she watched the land give way to a patchwork of fields and prairie, delighted by the view from up so high.

"You like to fly?" Alex asked.

She gazed out at the beautiful blue sky and white puffy clouds Alex was careful to avoid. "I guess I do."

He flicked her a sideways glance. "You haven't done this much?"

She hated to admit it but she wasn't about to lie. "I've only flown commercial."

Alex grinned. "Then you're in for a treat. Just sit back and enjoy the ride."

So she did. According to Alex, the plane cruised at two-hundred thirty miles an hour so it wouldn't take long to reach Rio Gordo, a little less than five hundred miles away.

"Now that we're on our way, you want to tell me what's going on with this? You said you got an inheritance, but you don't really know what it is. How does that work?"

She talked over the engine noise, which wasn't as bad as she had expected. Probably because it was such a well-built plane.

"It's kind of hard to know where to start."

"How about starting with the guy who left you the property? You said he was your uncle. He didn't have any other relatives?"

"Uncle Walter was my father's older brother and he and his wife had three kids. But Aunt Marlene divorced him and married someone else, and Walter and his kids never got along." She looked over, caught Alex studying her profile. "Maybe I should start by telling you Uncle Walter was extremely eccentric."

"Eccentric how?"

"From the time I was old enough to remember him, my uncle was mostly off on some adventure. My mom said when he hit forty, he went into his second childhood. He quit his job as an accountant and left town in search of buried treasure. He was never around, always off somewhere digging in the dirt. After a couple of years, my aunt divorced him and his kids all turned against him. They blamed him for their mother's unhappiness—and they were pretty much right."

"So he left the property to you instead of his kids."

"I loved Uncle Walter. I was adopted when I was a baby so I was the youngest of all the kids. As I grew older, the fact he had the courage to go and do exactly what he wanted seemed really cool to me."

"So he was out in West Texas hunting for treasure?"

"Not exactly. Earlier, when Walter didn't find any buried treasure, he started prospecting...you know... looking for gold and silver."

"I can see why you called him eccentric. Sounds like a character right out of an old Western movie."

"Oh, he was. He had snow-white hair and a scruffy white beard, the whole bit. But Walter wasn't a fool."

"That why you think there might be silver on the land?"

"That, and because he told me there was. He always came home for Christmas, back to Uvalde where he was born. Christmas was a big deal to my family so I always went back, too. We all knew he'd been working this mine he owned out in West Texas. The Christmas before he died, he told me he hadn't found the mother lode yet but he was really close. He believed it completely."

"How long was he out there?"

"He bought the property about seven years ago. Before that, he was in Nevada for a while. I think he owned a mining claim there, but he sold it and moved up to South Dakota. He had a couple of gold claims there that came to nothing."

"So he wound up prospecting for silver in Texas."

"That's right. He died right before Christmas, almost six months ago. Car accident on his way to our house. My mom and I were devastated. My dad had died six years earlier. When Walter died, Christmas pretty much died with him, at least for Mom and me. I don't think it'll ever be fun for either of us again."

Alex made no reply, but a muscle faintly tightened in his cheek. Sabrina was glad he'd stopped asking questions. Stirring up painful memories of her father's death and then her uncle's was making her heart hurt. She knew why Walter had left her the property, knew it was because no one had ever had any faith in him but her.

As a kid, she had always been sure he would find the treasure he'd been seeking.

She couldn't let him down without at least taking a look, finding out if what he had told her might be true.

Alex made an easy landing at the Rio Gordo airport, which sat at the edge of a town of less than two thousand inhabitants. There were a couple of fleabag motels, three gas stations, a post office, town hall, a Mexican restaurant and the Rio Gordo Café. He taxied the plane over to a pair of concrete tie-downs and shut off the engine.

They'd made good time from Houston, mostly clear skies so the trip was smooth and easy. He could tell Sabrina had enjoyed herself. She had an adventurous spirit he had admired from the first day he'd met her on a shopping trip to the Galleria with the daughter of a Saudi sheik and her entourage. He had been helping Jake Cantrell with the protection detail, and Sabrina had been there to help her friend Sage keep the Saudi women occupied.

Rina was feisty and smart.

And she flat-out hated any man she thought might have more than an ounce of testosterone. She didn't like macho men, she'd said, and she didn't like smart-ass jet jockeys.

He smiled at the memory.

She didn't want anything to do with a guy like him, yet she was here with him in Rio Gordo because she wanted a man who could protect her. She hadn't come right out and said that, but both of them knew it was true. As he spotted the tough-looking characters hanging around the helicopter sitting on the tarmac fifty yards away, he thought she'd done the smart thing.

"Let me get the plane tied down then we'll go into the office." He grabbed Sabrina's pink-flowered satchel out of the luggage compartment along with his gear bag, then finished securing the plane and guided her inside a metal-roofed wooden building.

The interior was spartan, with only two worn green leather chairs and a table stacked with dog-eared magazines. A gray-haired man stood behind the Formica-topped counter, a pencil perched above his right ear.

"We're here for the chopper," Alex said. "I spoke to someone about it. This is Sabrina Eckhart, she phoned a couple of days earlier."

Sabrina smiled and the old man smiled back as if he'd known her for years instead of only through a single phone call.

"Why, yes, I surely do recall."

"Hello, Mr. Woodard, it's nice to meet you in person."

"You, too, Ms. Eckhart. Don't get a lot of folks out here from the big city."

"I'm from Uvalde originally. It's not all that big."

"Uvalde, huh? You wouldn't know a guy named Leonard Jenkins out there?"

"Jenkins...? I'm afraid not. I've been gone for a while."

Woodard looked as if he had another dozen names he wanted to run past her, but instead took the file Alex handed him containing his pilot-helicopter credentials and forms he'd pulled off the internet. In exchange, Woodard handed him the service records he'd asked for on the helo.

"Your lady said you was a navy pilot."

She wasn't his lady, not even close, but he didn't bother to correct the guy. "That's right."

"I guess you've got plenty of experience," the older man said, reviewing the file he'd brought with him.

"I've been at it awhile."

"You fly into Afghanistan?"

Alex nodded. "Air Wing One off the *Teddy Roosevelt*. Iraq off the *Enterprise*."

The creases in the old man's weathered face went deeper. "Lost a boy over there. Appreciate the work you fellas do for our country." He looked up, seemed to shove the memories aside. "You don't have to worry about the chopper. We take real good care of her."

Alex handed back the maintenance record. "Let's take a look." Setting a hand at Sabrina's waist, he guided her outside and they crossed the tarmac to the helicopter. The woman he had spoken to on the phone had told him it was a two-passenger Schweitzer 300C, a well-performing little chopper, and not as expensive to rent by the hour as some of the bigger machines.

He knew Sabrina's finances were tight. When he'd seen the Toyota she was driving instead of her Mercedes, he'd done some digging. According to Sol Greenway, the office computer geek, her retirement fund had turned to worms, her clients were on the run from the bad market and Sabrina had taken a leave of absence from work. That he'd found out by calling her office.

No wonder she was hoping to find silver on her uncle's land.

Alex fixed his attention on the chopper, made a careful inspection, determined it to be in good condition. Shoving his gear bag behind the seat, he tossed in the flowered satchel and climbed aboard.

Sabrina stood by as the old man climbed in beside him for the flight check. Alex performed the required takeoff and landing, enjoying the feel of the stick in his hands, the lift, the mobility that was different than flying a plane. He circled once, then returned the chopper to the tarmac.

Satisfied with the demonstration of his skills, Woodard nodded and Alex turned off the engine, letting the rotor blades slow to a stop. The old man climbed out, turned and helped Sabrina aboard.

"Have a good trip!" Mr. Woodard called out from a safe distance as Alex restarted the helo and the blades once more began to spin.

"You ready?" Since there were no doors, he made sure she was safely buckled in.

He caught her nod and grin. "I'm ready."

She was looking forward to this. He was glad he was the one giving her her first ride, but pulled his mind from where that thought took him, and lifted off gently. The chopper rose into the air, moving higher and higher, rising gracefully away from the ground. When Sabrina grinned wider, he laughed and picked up speed, swung the chopper away from the airport and headed in the direction they had pinpointed on the map.

He knew where her land was located, knew the coordinates, at any rate. He had no idea what they would find when they got there.

Rina's adrenaline was pumping. The thrill of being so high in an open-air helicopter was a rush unlike anything she had ever felt before. Add to that flying with Alex Justice, watching his long fingers work the controls, seeing the capable way he handled the machine, made her heart rate soar even higher. There was something about a man taking charge, a man who was good at what he did, that turned her on.

Not that she would ever admit it.

Alex wasn't her type and she wasn't his and both of them knew it. Still, she wasn't dead and Alex was definitely eye candy and more.

She forced herself to concentrate on the search they were making. They'd been flying for more than an hour and had located the property but not the mine itself— assuming there was one. There'd been nothing in the will to indicate its location or anything about it. Just the legal description of the land itself: three thousand acres—five square miles—of what appeared to be nothing but dirt, rocks and cactus.

Her gaze followed the contours of the property. Ravines scarred the landscape. Ridges of granite rose out of the sloping desert floor. Chaparral, mesquite and scrub brush dotted endless stretches of rocks and sand.

"Not much out there," Alex said above the sound of the rotors.

"We haven't covered that much area yet. Maybe we'll find something that marks the mine."

"If there is one," Alex said, reminding her there might not be anything more than exactly what they were seeing—miles and miles of vast, empty desert.

The hours began to blur together. Once they had reached the property location, Alex had begun searching in a grid pattern to cover as much of the area as possible. The temperature was rising, the heat building inside the chopper, the afternoon slipping away. Rina yawned and rubbed her eyes, which felt gritty from the wind and heat.

An odd noise caught her attention. The *whop, whop,*

whop had been so regular she'd been trying not to fall asleep. This sound was different, a kind of grinding that had her gaze shooting to Alex, whose features suddenly looked grim.

Sabrina's heart stalled and, a few seconds later, so did the engine.

Three

━━━◦❍◦❍◦◦❍◦━━━

"Alex, what's happening?"

Alex heard the fear in Sabrina's voice. There wasn't time to answer. Instead, his years of training and experience kicked in and he did what he had been trained to do—slamming the collective down to neutral, taking the pitch out of the blade. The chopper fell like a stone.

"Oh, my God!" Sabrina's voice rose even higher as she realized they were in trouble.

The blades were flat now, the wind whistling up between them, making them spin even faster than the engine, which had gone deadly silent.

"Just hold on!" he shouted. "We'll autorotate down! We'll be fine!" He'd done it dozens of times, knew without thinking exactly how to make it happen. As the inertia built, he began to search the ground for a place to land, but something didn't feel right, something was altering their approach while they were still too high to make a safe landing.

It was the blades, he realized. Instead of moving at the speed they should have, they were sticking and slowing, jerking instead of spinning smoothly. They were going to hit the ground hard. Way too hard.

At the last minute, he flared the chopper, hoping to slow it as much as possible, hit a little softer, keep the helo in one piece, but the chopper was coming in too fast and the ground rushed up.

Sabrina screamed as the windshield shattered and he leaned over her, tried to cover her as much as he could with his body. The rotor blades tore free and spun away, shattering into jagged pieces that flew like deadly knives into the desert.

The chopper shook and continued to disintegrate. After what seemed like minutes but was only seconds, the machine finally started to settle. Alex popped his seat belt and reached for Sabrina, eased her back in the seat and saw blood trickling down her forehead. She was moaning, conscious, but barely. From the corner of his eye, he spotted the lick of orange flames behind them, rushing up from what was left of the engine.

The fuel tank was going to blow. They had to get out and fast. Reaching behind his seat, he grabbed his emergency gear bag, slung the strap over his shoulder, then reached for Sabrina, popped her belt and started to pull her out of the chopper from the pilot's side.

The effort had him hissing in pain, his body telling him he had injured a couple of ribs, but there wasn't time to worry about that now. Ignoring the sharp stab in his side, he pulled Sabrina free of the wreckage, half dragging, half carrying her over to an outcropping of rock, settled her behind it.

There was just enough time to throw himself over her, protecting her as much as he could, before the helo exploded into a ball of thick black smoke and searing flames. The blazing inferno shot into the sky, and a barrage of shrapnel sliced through the air around them.

Alex felt a sharp sting as a jagged piece of metal cut through his shirt and sliced into his back. A second explosion ripped through the air, then the only sound he heard was the crackle of flames.

He took a quick look over the rock to make sure it was safe, then turned his attention to the woman on the ground. Her face was as pale as the sand under her head, and a thin line of blood trickled from her forehead to her left temple.

She moved her head a little and groaned. Then her pretty blue eyes cracked open and she looked up at him. "Alex…?"

The pain and fear in her voice made his chest clamp down. She was lucky to be alive. They both were. Lucky he'd been able to make any kind of landing at all.

"It's all right, you're safe. I need to take a look, see where you're injured."

She reached a shaky hand up to her forehead. "My head…hurts." She swiped at the trickle of blood. "I think I cut myself."

His jaw hardened. She had hired him to protect her. But he couldn't protect her from this. "Are you hurt anywhere else?"

"No, I don't…don't think so."

Jerking the strap of the canvas bag off his shoulder, he set the bag aside and made a cursory check for broken bones, felt her legs and arms, which seemed to be okay. He checked for neck or spinal injuries, didn't find anything obvious. There were nicks and cuts from the crash on her neck and arms, but aside from that she seemed to be okay. Alex breathed a sigh of relief that she hadn't been hurt a lot worse.

"I'm kind of dizzy."

"You probably have a slight concussion." He held up three fingers. "How many do you see?"

"Three."

He checked her pupils. They looked normal. "You remember what happened?"

"We crashed. I remember how scared I was, how fast the ground seemed to come up from beneath us. Then I blacked out."

"We hit pretty hard." *To say the least.*

"Can we...can we radio for help?"

"Chopper exploded. No time to call it in and now the radio's gone."

Her eyes widened at the news. She sat up a little too quickly and hissed in pain.

"Take it easy." He tried to ease her back down, but she moved his hand away and managed to prop herself against the rock to look over at the slow-burning chunk of metal, all that was left of the helo. "What... what caused the crash?"

A muscle tightened in his jaw. "I don't know. Something went wrong with the engine. We should have been able to autorotate down safely, but the rotors jammed. We're lucky we fared as well as we did."

Her eyes remained on the chopper, then swung to his face. "You saved me. You got me out of there. I never would have made it on my own."

He thought of how close they'd both come. "You'd have made it if you hadn't hit your head. It's no big deal." He could see by the set of her chin that she didn't believe him, but she didn't say more.

He pulled his cell phone out of a pocket in his jeans, noticed a burn hole in his pant leg, felt the sting where the hot metal had struck. He had the same nicks and cuts she had, a few more, maybe. His back was bleeding, but he didn't think the cut was that bad. He was just grateful to be alive.

Flipping open the phone, he saw there wasn't any service, as he had expected. There weren't any cell towers this far out in the middle of nowhere.

Sabrina silently watched him. Tentatively, she touched the growing knot on her forehead next to her hairline. "God, Alex, what are we going to do?"

He grabbed his bag and unzipped it. He never went anywhere without his emergency gear. Now he was damned glad to have it.

"The bleeding's stopped. If you've got a concussion, it looks like it's pretty mild, but we'll take precautions until we know for sure. That means no aspirin or ibuprofen, at least for a while."

He found a gauze pad and tore it open, located a bottle of alcohol, poured some on the pad and wiped away the blood on her forehead, but didn't touch the wound. Instead, he put a Band-Aid over it, being careful not to touch the injury itself. He had a couple of bottles of water in the pack. He cracked one open and handed it over. Sabrina took a sip and handed it back.

"Thanks."

He went to work pulling bits of glass out of her arms and used the alcohol to clean the injured area. He pulled a sharp piece of glass out of the back of his neck and some out of his arms, dabbed alcohol on the cuts and put a Band-Aid on his neck. His back needed tending, but now wasn't the time. He needed to find some shelter, get Sabrina out of the sun.

She glanced around, taking in the barren landscape, the dry earth and mesquite trees. "Okay," she said, "how do we get out of here?"

"We don't. We're going to stay right here, close to the wreckage until they find us. When we don't get back by dark, they'll try to contact us on the radio. When that doesn't work and we don't show up, they'll start looking for us."

Sabrina stared down at the hands in her lap. "They might not, Alex." She gazed up at him. "I told them when I reserved the chopper, we might need it for two days instead of just one."

He frowned. "You were planning to spend the night out here?"

"I thought we'd go back and get a motel room, go out again in the morning."

He couldn't resist the chance to put a little color back in her cheeks, take away some of the worry. He grinned. "So you were planning to spend the night with me?"

Those pretty blue eyes widened in outrage. "Of course not! I was planning on us getting separate rooms." She poked him in the ribs and he released a grunt of pain.

"You're hurt! Oh, my God, what is it?"

"Cracked a couple of ribs. They aren't dislocated, so in time I'll be fine. Got a few cuts and bruises, just like you. The important thing, in case you haven't noticed, it's hotter than a West Texas stripper out here. We need to find some shelter."

He eased her back down on the sand, dragged a silver emergency blanket out of his pack and tented it over her head. "I'll be right back."

Sabrina opened her mouth to say something, then closed it again. He could see she didn't want him to leave her. But she was smart enough to know there were things he needed to do.

He reached down and touched her cheek. "I won't be gone long." Just long enough to find a place for them to spend the night, because it damned well looked like that was going to happen.

Alex swore softly as he hoisted his gear bag over his shoulder. They'd get out of there, even if they had to walk. There was a road out there, due west according to the map, but it was at least fifteen miles away from their last charted location. And the road wasn't traveled that often. He hoped to hell it didn't come to that.

By the time Alex returned, Sabrina's mind had cleared. The ache in her head still pounded away, but it was a little less violent now. The bad news was, her ankle had begun to throb.

She'd thought about taking off the Reebok she was wearing, but her ankle was swelling and if she did, she was afraid she wouldn't be able to get the shoe back on.

She looked up at the sound of heavy footsteps muffled by the hot, deep sand. True to his word, Alex hadn't been gone very long. Being alone out there just made it seem that way.

"You feeling well enough to get in out of the heat?"

"I'm feeling better, but I...umm...I think I sprained my ankle."

He frowned as he knelt in the sand beside her. "I should have noticed. Damn."

"It's not your fault. It didn't start hurting right away. Can you help me up?" She reached out to him. Alex ignored her, handed her the foil blanket and scooped her up in his arms. She caught a faint grunt of pain.

"I'm hurting you," she said. "I can make it on my own. You don't have to carry me."

Alex just kept striding across the sand. Sabrina looped her arms around his neck to keep her balance, felt the muscles tighten in his shoulders. The ground firmed a little as the desert floor sloped upward and he lengthened his strides. She spotted a ridge of granite set in a windswept hillside, saw that Alex had cleared away some of the brush, leveled the dirt and spread a layer of dry grass on the ground, making a place for them beneath an overhanging ledge that provided shade.

He had also dug a fire pit and stacked dry mesquite and whatever wood he'd managed to collect beside it. He set her down gently on the dry grass, then eased himself carefully down beside her.

"Are you okay?" she asked.

"I'm all right. It'll take time for the ribs to mend." Removing her sneaker and sock, he took a look at her ankle. It was swollen and turning purple. He moved it a little, caught her intake of breath, but it didn't appear to be broken. But there was no way to know for sure until she got it x-rayed. He eased the sock back over her foot but didn't replace the shoe.

"Too bad we don't have any ice." Instead, he wound an adhesive bandage around the ankle to keep it immobile.

"Maybe you should tape yourself up, too," Rina suggested, tipping her head toward his pack. "You seem to have just about everything in there you need."

"People used to do that. Found out it didn't make a damn difference for cracked ribs. In fact, it can make things worse." He zipped his pack open, took out a bottle of Advil and poured four tablets into his hand. He twisted the lid on the plastic water bottle and took a small sip, just enough to wash down the pills.

"We haven't got much water so we need to be careful. I've got what I need to pull a little liquid out of that dry wash down there, but it takes a while to work and you don't get all that much. I'm hoping they'll find us before it comes to that."

Reaching into the pack, he lifted out a couple of items and stuffed them into his pockets, pulled out a compact piece of canvas that unfolded into a small backpack, then drew out something she hadn't expected.

"Smith & Wesson .45," he said, turning a little to show her the heavy weapon. "If we're going to be out here for any length of time, we're going to get hungry."

She was already hungry. They hadn't eaten since they left the airport.

Next he pulled out what looked like a hunting knife and strapped the sheath onto his thigh. He handed her an energy bar. "We've only got two, so make it last." Sabrina clutched the bar against her chest, wishing it were a corned beef sandwich but grateful to have anything at all.

Rising a little stiffly, Alex shoved his arms into the canvas pack and stuffed the gun into the back of his jeans.

"I spotted some javelina tracks while I was looking for shelter. They're fresh and they're close. With any luck we'll have roast pig for supper."

He started to walk away.

"Alex, wait! How...how long will you be gone?"

"Long enough to get us something to eat. Don't worry, there's nothing out here that's going to hurt you."

Nothing but coyotes and bobcats, snakes and wild pigs, and God only knew what else. She'd be fine, she told herself and wished she believed it. "Do you have a compass?"

He dug into his pocket, came up with one and held it up for her to see. He smiled. "I won't get lost, I promise."

She nodded but instead of leaving, he walked back and knelt beside her. "You'll be all right, love. If you need me, just shout. Sound travels a long way out here."

She thought of being alone in the middle of the desert, remembered the crash and felt like crying. Instead, she managed to smile. "I hope you're a good cook."

Alex smiled back. "I can't cook for spit, but I can barbecue like crazy. Try to stay awake for a while, just till we know for sure your head is okay. I'll see you soon."

She watched him walk away and wondered what would happen to her if he didn't return. What if he fell into one of the hundreds of ravines they had spotted from the air? What if he got lost in spite of the compass? What if he got bit by a snake or—

She closed her eyes, forcing away the thoughts. For long moments, she just sat there, her back propped against the rock in the shade beneath the ledge. The heat was still fierce, though the sun was moving toward the horizon and pretty soon it would start getting dark.

And cold.

She remembered the forecast she had seen on weather.com and wished she had the fleece jacket she had stuffed into her satchel, wished she had the lipstick, Kleenex, hairbrush and all the other miscellaneous feminine necessities she kept in her purse.

The heat made her eyelids feel heavy and she yawned. Her head was still booming, her ankle throbbing, and she was tired clear to the bone. Propping her foot up on a stone, she leaned back against the rock and closed her eyes. But she didn't let herself fall asleep. She had no idea what might creep up on her if she did.

Or at least that was her plan.

It was the cold that awakened her. By the position of the sun, she hadn't been asleep more than an hour, but it was almost dark and Alex hadn't returned. Icy fear crawled down her spine. She had no idea how to survive out here, or the vaguest notion of how to get back to Rio Gordo. If Alex didn't return…

Dear God, she had never imagined her very life might depend on Alex Justice. But clearly it did.

Four

Though the air had begun to grow cold, Alex was sweating. The javelina had evaded him, driven him deeper into the desert than he had meant to go. The pig had gotten away—for the moment.

Tonight's supper would have to be something a little more exotic than free-range pork chops.

He grinned, thinking of the long white strip of meat he had skinned and stuffed into his backpack. Fortunately, he had spotted the rattlesnake sunning on a rock before he'd stepped on it. Fortunate for him. Not so fortunate for the snake.

He caught sight of the rocky ledge up ahead that would serve as their home for the night. Saw the moment Sabrina spotted him walking toward her and stood up from the thick grass pallet he had made for her, balancing on her uninjured foot.

She was shaking, he saw, and there was just enough sunlight left to see that her face was pale. He had stripped off his short-sleeved blue chambray shirt an hour ago and was carrying it in his hand. He lengthened his strides until he reached her. He didn't say a word, just draped the shirt around her shoulders and thought how tiny she looked with it hanging nearly to her knees, how glad he was she had come to him for help instead of trusting someone else.

Sabrina caught the front of the shirt and pulled it a little tighter around her shoulders. Her shaking eased and a little color washed back into her cheeks. It took a couple of seconds for him to realize that instead of looking up at him, she was staring at his chest.

"What is it? Your head? Your ankle? Are you all right?"

Her eyes moved over his bare torso, all the way down to the jeans that rode low on his hips.

"What is it?" he asked again when she still didn't speak, beginning to get even more worried.

"It's nothing…I'm fine. It's just… I didn't realize you were…you were…" She pointed at his naked chest. "All those muscles right there under your clothes. I didn't realize you were so…so…" She looked up. "Ripped."

He laughed. He couldn't help it. "I'm glad you like what you see. I've liked looking at you since the first time I saw you."

She jerked her gaze away from his body and back to his face. "You have?"

"What did you think? I didn't notice?"

"I'm hardly your type. I'm small and I'm…well, curvy. I figured you for the type I saw in your office the other day—blonde and thin and gorgeous."

"Might be nice if she also had a brain."

She looked past him, searching for the pig, didn't offer to return his shirt. "I guess you couldn't get us any supper."

"Actually, I did. Though it tastes more like chicken than pork." He urged her back down on the pallet. Checked her pupils again, saw they still looked normal. Carrying his pack over to the pit, he set to work building a fire. He'd stacked dry wood next to the circle of stones. Digging waterproof matches out of his pack, he used dry leaves and grass to get the flames going.

"I meant to get back earlier," he said as he worked. "I was so close to the boar it was hard to give up the hunt."

"I don't imagine you like to fail."

"Not much."

He continued working, taking a deep breath now and then to ease the ache in his ribs, using the knife he'd used to kill and skin the snake to whittle a makeshift spit. The fire was blazing, lighting their campsite with a nice golden glow when he pulled the snake out of his backpack. He heard Sabrina's sharp intake of breath, and his gaze swung to where she sat once more on the pallet.

"We're eating a snake?" she said.

"Rattlesnake. The two of us had a little face-off. I won. It actually tastes pretty good."

She surprised him with a grin. "I know. I've had the rattlesnake version of a crab cake at The Grill. It was delicious."

He smiled. "I doubt my cooking skills compare to the chef at The Grill, but it beats going to sleep on an empty stomach." *Sleep.* Not likely. He'd imagined taking Sabrina Eckhart to bed a dozen times. The thought of sleeping next to her had his sex drive kicking into gear. This wasn't the way his fantasy went, but still...

"How are you feeling?" he asked, figuring he had better change the subject.

"Better. My head isn't hurting the way it was. My

ankle's still swollen. I put it up on a rock and fell asleep for about an hour. It still hurts but at least I feel rested. How about you?" She frowned, then shoved to her feet and hobbled toward him, reached out and gently touched his bare shoulder.

"You've got a nasty gash on your back. You should have said something. The blood's dried but you need to let me clean it."

He nodded. "After we eat." He tugged her down beside him. "You need to keep the weight off that ankle."

"I know." To his amazement, she had pretty much been doing what he said. As independent as she was, he wondered how long that would last.

"How're the ribs?" she asked.

"Sore as hell, but I've had worse."

"When you were a pilot?"

"Survival training. Took a fall into a rocky gorge. I was pretty banged up when I walked out. Parachute training wasn't any snap, either. And a couple of cases I was working went south and ended up in a slugfest. Seems like there's always something."

"Survival training," she repeated, watching him as he worked the snake onto the length of mesquite branch he'd stripped smooth with his knife. "That's how you know all this stuff?"

"It's required for navy pilots."

"I guess if you have to bail out of a plane it only makes sense to know what to do after you land somewhere." Her gaze slid away from his and went toward the darkness, a curtain of black outside the glow of the fire. "They might not find us for days."

"Days we can handle. Longer than that, we may have to figure on walking out."

"Out to where? We don't even know where we are."

"I know our last location. I know there's a road west of us that runs from Rio Gordo to the border. It's not much, but it's a road."

"If we have to walk…I don't think I can make it, Alex." And the fear in her eyes said she was afraid she couldn't handle it if he left her there and went to get help.

"Let's not get ahead of ourselves, okay? Whether they think we decided to spend the night out here or not, it's going to alert them when they can't reach us on the radio. Likely, they'll be sending out search parties tomorrow, day after at the latest."

"There's a lot of desert out there."

A helluva lot. But he didn't say that. He turned back to the meat roasting over the fire. "Smells good, doesn't it?" Succulent juices dripped into the flames and his stomach growled.

Sabrina surprised him with a smile. "Just like dining at The Grill."

She was doing her best to keep her spirits up. He appreciated that. So far she'd been a trouper. Hadn't complained, hadn't cried. And even with her soft red curls drooping into her eyes and her makeup mostly gone, she looked sexy as hell. Alex wondered what she'd do if he leaned over and kissed her.

He didn't. She had made it clear she wanted nothing to do with him in that way, and even if she was physically attracted to him, it wouldn't be fair to take advantage of her when she was scared and vulnerable.

Or at least that's what he told himself.

They ate the snake, which wasn't as easy to do as Rina pretended. It was still a snake. Eating it all chopped up and mixed with breadcrumbs and onions at The Grill wasn't the same as eating it in chunks torn off a stick.

Still, it wasn't bad tasting. It was just the idea of eating a reptile that made those lumps of meat hard to swallow. Afterward, she tended to the cut on Alex's back, being careful to remove the pieces of fabric, sand and debris that were buried in the wound, trying to avoid starting the bleeding again, intrigued by the feel of his smooth bare skin beneath her hands.

God, he had the most incredible body. Since it had been hidden beneath his designer clothes, she had never really noticed.

"Didn't anyone tell you a suntan is bad for your skin?" she teased, noting the warm brown color and wondering if there was any sort of tan line. Knowing Alex, she figured there wasn't.

"I've got a pool at my house. Swimming's a good way to stay in shape."

"And working out at the gym. That's what I do."

His gaze slid over her breasts, and she would have sworn there was heat in those blue eyes.

He glanced away. "I've got a gym in one of the downstairs bedrooms," he said. "I use it a lot and I practice Tai Chi with a trainer whenever I get the chance."

Tai Chi. That was Bruce Lee stuff. She figured he must have a pretty big place and was only a little surprised. The clothes he wore were expensive. So was the BMW he drove and the airplane he flew. Sage had told her he'd graduated from Yale.

"Sage said you were raised in Connecticut. How did you get to Houston?"

He tossed a stick into the fire. Orange flames curled around it, licked up over the wood. "A guy named Joe

McCauley lived there. We met when I was flying missions off the *Enterprise.* Joe was an officer on the maintenance crew. We got to be good friends."

"So Joe convinced you to come to Houston."

He shrugged. "There was nothing for me in Connecticut. Joe got out of the service a few weeks before I did. He thought I should come to Houston and I figured it was as good a place to start as any. I met Trace through Joe's dad, who was a friend of Trace's father."

He looked up at her and smiled. "I got my P.I.'s license and went to work for Trace. The rest, as they say, is history."

Rina finished cleaning the last of the dirt out of the gash on his back and he hissed in a breath as she poured alcohol into the wound. "Hey, watch it!"

"You've got cuts and bruises all over, and a couple of injured ribs and you complain about a little alcohol? Big baby." But of course he was nothing of the sort. He was strong and tough and at the same time oddly gentle, and he had saved her life.

Rina put a gauze pad over the six-inch gash that probably should have had stitches and would definitely leave a scar on that smooth, tanned skin. She taped it in place, then took off his chambray shirt and held it out for him to put back on.

"Keep it," he said. "It's getting pretty cold."

"What about you?"

He just shrugged. "I'll be fine. But we'll have to share the blanket. We don't have any other choice."

A little tremor went through her that had nothing to do with the cold. "If we have to then we have to." Her eyes met his. How blue eyes could possibly look hot she had no idea, but they did.

They slept huddled together beneath the silver foil blanket, which helped them generate a surprising amount of warmth. That and Alex's half-naked body. He refused to take his shirt back and as the temperature dropped, Rina was glad. It was the only thing warm she had to wear, and besides, she liked the way he looked with his chest bare.

Beneath those conservative pants and shirts he wore was a body that was all lean muscle, wide shoulders and six-pack abs. Six foot two inches of virile male, dark blond hair and blue eyes, and a movie star face to wrap up the package. It didn't seem fair that one man should look so good.

And she had stupidly blurted it out, which, as cocky as Alex was, surely gave his ego a boost, something he most certainly didn't need. He'd surprised her when he had said he liked the way she looked, too.

But maybe that was only because they were out here alone and he was trying to make her feel better.

As the fire burned down, they sat beneath the ledge and curled up together beneath the blanket. As tired as she was, it didn't take long to fall asleep. She wasn't sure how long she slept but a slice of moon hung over the desert by the time she awakened with her ankle throbbing and her body chilled. She was nestled against Alex's side, his arm around her, his head back against the rock.

His skin was hot, she realized as she snuggled deeper into his heat, his breaths coming a little too fast. Dear God, maybe the wound she had cleaned after supper was infected.

She reached up to feel his forehead, see if he had a temperature, and her breasts pressed into his chest. Alex grunted in pain.

"Oh, Alex, I'm so sorry. Did I hurt you? You were so hot I was afraid you were running a fever." She tried to reach up again, but Alex caught her wrist.

"The fever I'm running is a lot lower down. If you don't quit wiggling, I'm going to show you exactly how hot I am."

Her eyes widened in shock and her face flushed. He didn't have a fever; he was aroused. "Oh…"

"Look, Sabrina, we're stuck out here. We're sleeping together—sort of. I'm a man. It's only natural for a guy to get turned on when he's half-naked and pressed up against a beautiful woman."

Her heart was thumping. None of it registered except the last few words. "You think I'm beautiful?"

The muscles across his chest tightened. "For chrissake, what do you think? Don't you ever look in the mirror?"

A soft warmth slipped through her, driving away the chill. Alex Justice thought she was beautiful. In the two years she had lived with Ryan Gosford, he had never said anything remotely similar to that.

"Thank you."

"Thank you? That's it? Do you have any idea how hard it is for me to keep my hands off you? For that matter, how hard I am just sitting here beside you?"

She swallowed, forced down the urge to lean over and press her mouth against his just to see what he would do. "It's only…only the circumstances. You don't even like me. And I don't like you."

This last was said in an effort to convince herself. Alex was exactly the kind of macho, take-charge, steal-your-heart-and-walk-away kind of man she refused to allow into her life.

She'd been down that road a few years back when she had dated a pro-football quarterback. She had fallen head over heels for Caleb Redmond, and he had said he loved her, too. They had planned to get married, even talked about having children.

Then he'd dumped her six months later and taken up with one of the Dallas Cowboys cheerleaders, leaving her heart in tatters.

She'd known better. She'd fallen for a West Point grad when she was in college, a soldier headed for the Middle East. That relationship had crashed and burned, as well.

Macho men were all alike, all just interested in making a conquest or sleeping with you until something better came along. Alex was no different.

She eased a little away from him, trying to put some distance between them, ignoring the rush of cold that slipped beneath the foil blanket.

The arm around her tightened, drawing her back against his side. "Just stay put. If you don't, both of us are going to freeze our asses off."

She ignored a shot of irritation, forced herself to relax and settle back against him, absorbing his warmth. By the way he was scowling he didn't like the situation any better than she did. It seemed unlikely that either of them would get any sleep.

She must have dozed off. When she awakened again it was morning. The sun was up, a fire started, and Alex was nowhere in sight.

A shiver went through her. *He'll be back,* she told herself. He wouldn't just leave her—not even to go for help.

Would he?

Rina pulled the foil blanket around her shoulders, forced her stiff muscles into action and shoved to her feet—or foot, as it were. Her head immediately started pounding, she ached all over and her ankle throbbed. But the flames beckoned, promising their warmth.

Limping in that direction, she sat down near the fire beside the pile of dry branches, which appeared to have been replenished, and began to feed the flames, determined not to let them burn out until the desert air grew warmer.

By then Alex would surely be back.

Rina searched the horizon for any sign of him, but didn't see a thing.

Five

As he made his way back to camp, Alex checked his wristwatch. It wasn't quite noon but he'd accomplished a lot. There was a huge SOS made of rocks in an open area on the other side of an outcropping a hundred yards from the burned-out chopper. Using a sheet of plastic, a plastic container and a few heavy rocks, he had set up a still for making water in the dry streambed not far from their makeshift camp.

Next he planned to build a stack of firewood to light at the first sign of a search plane in the area. He walked into camp expecting to see the little redhead, wishing he wasn't quite so eager to get there.

She wasn't sitting beneath the ledge out of the sun with her foot propped up as she should have been. The fire had burned down to embers, but the pile of dry branches had mostly been fed into the flames so he knew that wherever she was, she hadn't been gone very long.

A pit stop, he told himself, which was the only reason he didn't chase off to find her. He'd give her a few minutes of privacy before he took off in search of her. By then she would probably be back.

He set down the pair of makeshift crutches he had made for her that might need to be shortened, and started collecting wood for the signal fire. All the while, he was listening for sounds of her return. When five minutes passed and he didn't hear footsteps, his worry ratcheted up, and he started calling her name.

"Sabrina! Sabrina, where are you?"

He checked for small, female footprints, found a hop-skip pattern that moved off down a trail leading toward a rocky ridge not far from the campsite.

He had almost reached the pile of boulders when a bloodcurdling scream sliced through the quiet desert air. A jolt of adrenaline hit him and Alex shot down the path, his heart practically exploding as he raced toward the rocks, nearly running over Sabrina as she hobbled as fast as she could in the opposite direction.

To avoid a collision, he caught her around the waist and swung her away from him before she could impact his aching ribs.

"Alex! Oh, my God! Oh, my God, it bit me!"

Fear kicked his heartbeat up a couple more notches. "Rattlesnake? Show me. Show me where it bit you."

She was shaking her head, red curls flying around her face. "Not...not a snake." She wheezed in a breath. "Scorpion," she said, shaking all over as she pointed toward the rocks behind her.

Crawling into a crevice was a big, black, nasty-looking scorpion about five inches long. It disappeared into the shadowy depths of the rock, and Alex relaxed a little.

"It's all right, love. They sting like bloody hell but a

scorpion bite won't kill you." Her arms tightened around his waist and when she looked up at him, he read the terror in a face that was rapidly turning blue.

"Can't breathe…"

"Oh, shit, you're allergic."

She nodded, wheezed in a breath. "Bee…stings."

For the second time in two days, he gritted his teeth against the ache in his side and lifted her into his arms. Alex started running, heading back to camp.

Her eyes were closed, her breathing ragged as he laid her on the grass pallet, raced over to retrieve his pack, set the bag down beside her and unzipped the top.

"Listen to me, Sabrina. You're going to be okay. One of my sister's friends was allergic to bee stings. I had to take her to the hospital once. Scared the hell out of me. After that, I've always carried an EpiPen in my gear bag."

She nodded, tried to smile. His chest squeezed at her bravado. He knew Sabrina was a woman who liked to be in control, one who had a hard-on for men she couldn't walk on. But now he knew she was also sweet, and tough when it counted.

Determined to do it right, he unzipped her jeans and tugged them down over her hips, ignored the pretty little pink lace panties she was wearing, took the cap off the needle and jammed it into her thigh. He flinched a little at her faint whimper of pain.

"Just take it easy. Lie still and let the medicine go to work." He checked her pulse and waited for her heartbeat to slow. A few more minutes ticked past. "How are you doing?"

Sabrina swallowed and opened her eyes. She was

breathing much easier, some of the color back in her face. A little of his tension eased.

"I...umm...always carry a Pen...in my purse," she said, "but..."

"But your purse went up in flames when the chopper exploded. It's all right. Things happen out here." He wanted to rail at her, yell at her for leaving the camp and scaring him half to death, but he held himself back as much as he could and helped her slide the jeans back up when he wanted to pull them all the way off instead.

"What the hell were you doing out there?"

A blush crept into her cheeks. "What do you think? I'm human, you know."

His mouth edged up. And female. No question of that. "Feeling any better?"

She moistened her lips, which were pink and plump and made him think about last night and how much he'd wanted her.

"I could use a drink of water. I know we don't have very much."

He pulled the plastic water bottle out of his pack. It was the last of the first bottle, just enough for a couple of sips. He took the lid off, handed it over, and she pressed it against her lips. Sabrina held the wetness in her mouth for a couple of seconds before she swallowed.

"Thanks." She handed him back the now-empty bottle and tried to sit up but he pressed her back down.

"Give yourself a few minutes."

"I think I'm okay. I'm a little dizzy but I think that's normal."

"You ever had a reaction to epinephrine?"

"No. I've only had to use it one other time, but I remember it worked pretty fast."

His sister's friend had been nauseous and light-headed, but without the drug she could well have been dead.

"You're getting sunburned," Alex said. Capping the needle, he disposed of it back in its case and stuck it in the pack. Withdrawing a tube of sunscreen, he smeared it over her forehead, cheeks and nose.

"I swear you have everything in there but the kitchen sink."

"Actually, I've about exhausted my bag of tricks."

"You…umm…mentioned you have a sister. Does she live in Connecticut?"

"Used to. Six months ago, Rebecca and her daughter, Ginny, moved to Houston."

"That sounds nice. The two of you must be close."

He nodded. He loved Becca and her little girl. When he found out his sister's husband was abusing her, he had flown back to New Haven and confronted the bastard. It wasn't much of a fight, just enough to show the guy what it felt like to have someone beat the crap out of him the way he had done to Rebecca.

"Her husband was knocking her around," he said, keeping it simple. "She left him and came to Houston with her daughter to start over."

Sabrina's eyes remained on his face. They were a different shade of blue than his own, more vibrant somehow, more a sapphire, while his were the color of the sky.

"You know, Alex, you're different than I thought."

He grinned. "You mean I'm not the cocky jet jockey you thought I was?"

She laughed and he felt a sweep of relief. She was going to be okay.

"Oh, you're cocky, all right. But you have a tiny, itty-bitty hidden nice streak I missed seeing before."

He smiled. He *was* a decent guy, and now he knew that Sabrina Eckhart was a really decent girl. The kind you took home to meet your family—if you had a normal family—which he didn't.

A nice girl like Sabrina was the last thing he needed. He wasn't ready to get involved with a woman. He had no idea what he wanted out of life, had been trying to figure it out since the day he graduated from Yale and signed up to become a naval aviator. He'd loved the job, but after a while he'd learned it wasn't what he wanted for the rest of his life.

He liked what he was doing now, but it didn't seem to be enough. Nothing did.

Her eyes searched his face. "Saving my life is kind of getting old, don't you think?"

"You could have done it yourself if you'd had your purse."

Something shifted in her features and the softness disappeared from her voice. "Is that bit of humility actually coming from the great Alex Justice?"

Irritation slipped through him. She had always seen him as arrogant and self-centered. Apparently, that hadn't changed. "You're right. I saved your ass so now you owe me. As soon as we get back, I intend to collect."

Fire flashed in her eyes. "You're on the payroll. I'll be sure to give you a bonus."

"Sorry, sweetheart, money isn't what I had in mind." Turning he stormed off, leaving her sitting there fuming. Maybe it was better this way. He didn't need a pain-in-the-ass redhead in his life.

"I'm going to build a signal fire," he called over his

shoulder. "There's a chance they'll send up a search plane today and if they do, I want them to see the smoke."

Alex stalked away.

Sabrina watched him go, wishing she could call back the hateful words. Alex hadn't deserved that. It was a defense mechanism she had used against him since the day they'd first met. She'd been physically attracted to Alex Justice from the moment Sage had introduced them.

She knew the kind of man he was, knew he wasn't a one-woman man. Alex dated some of the most beautiful women in the world. He was the last man on earth she wanted to get involved with.

From the shadows beneath the ledge, she watched him head off to work on the bonfire. It took a while, but eventually he had enough dry branches stacked up to send a decent signal, and twigs and leaves in position to get it started.

It was hot now, the sun beating down, sweat glistening on his bare torso. She shoved to her feet and started hobbling toward him.

"Alex!" He turned, saw her limping in his direction and swore something she couldn't quite catch.

He strode toward her, stopped directly in front of her. "I thought I told you to keep your weight off that ankle."

"I just… I'm sorry. You didn't deserve that. I don't know why I said it. I'm grateful for everything you've done and there is no amount of money or anything else that could ever repay you."

Some of the tightness in his features slipped away. He reached out and touched her cheek. "I don't expect any payment, Sabrina."

"I know."

Then he smiled. "But if you're offering, well who am I to refuse?"

She laughed. He was teasing her, no longer angry. "Forget it, flyboy."

His mouth curved. "I was afraid you'd say that."

She was still smiling as she looked past him to the pile of dry branches and wood he had collected.

"I wish I could help you with some of this. Dammit, I hate having to just sit there and do nothing."

"That reminds me. I made you a present."

"A present?" She felt a jolt of excitement. Out here where she had nothing, anything at all was appreciated. "What kind of present?"

Alex walked over and picked up what looked like two pieces of wood and carried them back to her. "I had to guess on the height."

It was a makeshift pair of crutches. They were no more than sturdy branches stripped bare and fitted into a cross piece that tucked under her arms. Another cross-piece fit through a hole partway down the shaft to provide a handhold. Rina reached for them, eager to try them out.

Fitting them beneath her arms, she gripped the handles, took a couple of tentative steps and grinned. "I love them! They're a great present. Thank you, Alex." She swung over a couple of steps and stopped right in front of him, leaned up as far as she could and pressed a kiss on his lips.

A flash of heat hit her that went all the way to her toes. Alex's mouth opened under hers and for an instant the kiss went deeper. But when he reached for her, Sabrina pulled away.

She stared into his handsome face, her fingers trembling as they came up to touch her lips. "Oh, my…"

Alex's eyes looked dark and turbulent. He seemed to be replaying the mind-blowing kiss that hadn't even gotten off the ground.

"I was afraid of that" was all he said.

No plane came that day. Alex hunted that afternoon, retraced his steps and brought back the feral pig. He roasted it that night, and as hungry as both of them were, it was delicious. By the morning of the third day, they were down to half a bottle of water and half of the first plastic bottle refilled with the condensation he'd been able to collect from the greenery living in the dry streambed.

It was early, still chilly but beginning to warm. They were sitting beside the fire, sharing a few more chunks of roast meat.

"I think we should try to walk out," Sabrina said. "My crutches are working great. It's early. We can cover a lot of ground if we leave right away."

"It's not a good idea. Best thing is always to stay with the downed aircraft."

"Yes, but even if they're looking for us they might not find us for days. Maybe not at all. There are thousands of acres of desert out there. Remember that guy who got lost in the mountains outside Las Vegas? They didn't find him or his plane until years after he was dead, and he was some famous CEO or something. Imagine how many people in Rio Gordo will be looking for us."

In a way, he agreed. If he was by himself, he'd already be gone, but Sabrina had a sprained ankle, and no matter how game she was, the territory between here and the road was brutal.

"It isn't all flat, you know. You saw what it looks like from the air. Hundreds of ravines, miles of cactus, hot sand, scrub brush, rattlesnakes and more of those damnable scorpions. And those crutches won't be easy to handle."

"I can do it." She grabbed the crutches and made a show of using them just to prove her point. It reminded him of the first time she'd tried them, of the hot kiss they'd shared that wasn't really a kiss at all and had turned him inside out. He'd hardly been able to sleep last night just thinking about it. Aching to do a lot more of what they'd started.

"Let's go, Alex. We're almost out of water and I'm tired of just sitting here roasting in the heat."

Well, hell, if she was game, so was he. "All right, but if we do this, we do it my way. We walk during the morning, rest and sleep during the hot part of the day, then walk again in the evening as it starts to cool off. I figure we can make it in two days if we don't run into problems."

"All right!" She grinned. "I'm already packed and ready to leave."

"Very funny." All she had was the clothes on her back. He walked over to where he'd rested his gear bag. He was sporting a three-day growth of beard and wearing his shirt again, magnanimously handed back to him as soon as it had warmed a little this morning.

"I've got a couple of things to do, then we'll leave. We'll walk for a couple of hours, rest, walk again before we make camp for the night."

"Sounds good to me."

He left her sitting there while he collected a few more rocks and made an arrow pointing due west in the sand not far from the burned-out chopper. If anyone was looking for them, they'd see the arrow and know they were walking toward the road. The crutches were going to be a problem. As soon as the ground turned to sand, the ends would sink into the soft soil. He'd wind up carrying her but there was no use telling her that and she was too bullheaded to believe him if he did.

Alex checked the wrapping on Sabrina's ankle, then shouldered his pack. Since her head had apparently stopped hurting but her ankle hadn't, they each swallowed a handful of Advil and started off across the desert.

Alex took it slow, giving Sabrina the chance to keep up on those ridiculous crutches he had made with no intention of her using them beyond the camp. They weren't making much time and the sun was getting higher, the temperature rising. By the end of the third hour, it was obvious this was going to be just as tough as he'd imagined.

Sabrina was hot and tired, the underside of her arms chafed from the wooden crutches and pulling the tips out of the sand was exhausting. So far she hadn't complained.

He was letting her go as far as she could before he told her he was going to have to carry her. It wouldn't sit well, he knew, but sooner or later, she wouldn't have any other choice.

By the time he called for the third rest stop of the day, even after using sunscreen, Sabrina's cheeks were red, and her good leg was shaking with fatigue. She sat down in the sand beneath a mesquite tree and drew her knees up beneath her chin, used them to pillow her head.

When Alex sat down beside her, she looked up at him, her expression so weary it made his chest ache.

"Alex?"

"What is it?"

"I think I'm going to cry." Her eyes welled, and his chest squeezed. He reached over, eased her into his arms and just held her.

"Go ahead, love. You've earned it."

She let out a sob and her body started shaking; he could feel the wetness against the side of his neck. He ran a hand over her back, hoping it would soothe her, wishing there was a way to make all of this easier.

Just as suddenly as it had started, it was over. Sabrina clung to him for another couple of seconds before she eased away.

She wiped the wetness from her cheeks. "Thank you."

"We're gonna be okay. You believe that, right?"

She swallowed, nodded. "I'm glad I chose you, Alex."

He knew what she meant. "So am I."

"I didn't want to like you. I tried really hard not to."

He caught her chin. "Too late," he said and then he kissed her.

Six

As kisses go, it didn't last long. But what started as a tender, gentle kiss, expanded into a deep, greedy exploration of mouths and tongues that had her shaking with need, her arms winding up around his neck. She could feel Alex fighting for control against the hunger burning through him. The same hunger that burned through her. It had her skin tingling and heat flaring in the pit of her stomach.

Alex ended the kiss long before she wanted him to. Breathing hard, he came to his feet and ran a hand through his hair. "I didn't mean for that to happen."

Rina licked her lips, tasted him there. "I know. It just did."

He took a couple deep breaths. "We need to keep going." His voice was gruff as he reached down, grabbed her hand and hauled her to her feet. The hunger was still in his eyes, but it was guarded now. Whatever was happening between them wasn't something he wanted any more than she did.

That was good, she told herself, still working to catch her breath. Certainly better for her.

She gazed across the barren expanse of desert that seemed to go on forever, and exhaustion washed over her. Her ankle was killing her and the strength in her good leg was almost gone.

"Stand still," Alex said.

"Why? What are you doing?"

"You're wearing the pack."

"What?"

"I'm going to carry you. We'll be able to make better time."

"No way! You can't carry me *and* the gear all the way to Rio Gordo!"

"We aren't going to Rio Gordo. We're going to the road. We've covered some ground this morning. It's probably no more than ten or twelve miles away. It might take us a while, but I can carry you there without a problem."

"What about your ribs? You're going to make them worse."

"Let me worry about my ribs. We made the decision to leave. Now we need to get where we're going."

Her good leg trembled. Her mouth was as dry as cotton. A drink of water sounded better than a glass of Dom Pérignon. "I can make it a little farther."

Alex ignored her. The next thing she knew the pack was securely in place across her shoulders and she was riding piggyback style, clinging to Alex's strong neck while he held on to the legs she wrapped around his waist.

He started walking. "It's getting hot. We'll be stopping pretty soon. Just hang on and let me do the work."

She looked back over her shoulder. "What about my crutches!"

"Sorry, love. I'll have to make you a new pair."

Her heart sank. The last of her independence was gone. As Alex started over the rugged landscape, she clung to his broad back and prayed he could get them out of the desert safely.

Another hour passed. Alex was sweating, his jaw set against the pain in his side. Even though she knew he was tired, he kept going, trudging over the burning landscape, doggedly setting one foot in front of the other.

"We need to stop, Alex. You said we would rest in the middle of the day." Rina was as hot and sweaty as he was, her ankle throbbing.

He took a few more steps, then blew out a breath, clearly wishing he could continue. "All right. We'll rest until it cools off."

She held on tightly as he crossed a deep ravine, making his way to the opposite side, headed for a patch of shade beneath an overhanging rock.

That's when she heard it. The *whop, whop, whop* of a chopper. Alex set her down and shot out into the open, madly waving his arms. The chopper circled, spotted Alex and swooped lower, then began a slow descent.

For the second time that day, Sabrina started crying.

The Rio Gordo County Sheriff's helicopter settled into the desert, blowing dust and sand and hot air around them. The two EMTs aboard made a cursory check of Rina's ankle and Alex's ribs, pronounced the two of them stable enough to make the ride back to the airport. Sabrina refused a stretcher and instead let Alex help her aboard the chopper.

For a moment as she glanced around the interior, she forgot about her ankle. She was too busy remembering the crash that had nearly killed them and praying they would make it safely back to Rio Gordo.

As soon as everyone was back aboard and she and Alex were strapped into their seats, the helo lifted off the desert floor and swung away, heading back in a different direction from the route they had originally taken.

Rina had just ended her quick prayer when she looked down and spotted the parallel lines of a tiny dirt road cutting through the desert, a two-track path they hadn't seen when they were searching from the air before. At the end of the road was a cluster of wooden buildings and what looked like a hole in the side of a cactus-covered hill.

"Alex! There it is! It's the mine!"

Sitting next to her, Alex leaned forward, spotted the buildings and the mine and let out a hearty laugh. He grinned at her, his gorgeous dimples popping out, and just shook his head.

Seven

The helicopter flew them to a clinic in Rio Gordo where an older Hispanic doctor named Navarro had Alex's ribs and Sabrina's ankle x-rayed. The doctor grumbled about the stitches Alex should have had in his back, but said neither of them had any broken bones. They were dehydrated and a little sunburned, but they were alive. A miracle in itself.

"We'll be going over the chopper," the sheriff told Alex as he sat outside the emergency room, waiting for Dr. Navarro to finish with Sabrina. "It might take a while, but we'll do our best to find the cause of the crash."

Sheriff Beau Dickens, a heavyset man with a leonine main of silver hair and a thick Texas drawl spoke with a sincerity that made Alex believe he would do his best to find out what had gone wrong.

"Not much left to work with," Alex told him, thinking of the pile of burned-up metal sitting in the middle of the desert.

"We'll be bringin' in an aviation forensic expert. Dan Baldwin's one of the best."

"I'll want to know what he comes up with."

"No problem."

He and Sabrina were both released that day. That night, they took two rooms at the Eazy Eight Motel near the airport. In the room next to his Sabrina slept twelve hours straight before they headed for his plane late the next morning and the flight back to Houston.

That had been two weeks ago. He was home now, back at work in his office. Sabrina was recovering in her apartment while she waited for her ankle to heal. Her mother had driven down from Uvalde and spent a couple of days fussing over her, or at least that's what Sage had told him. He'd sent flowers and a get-well note, but hadn't seen her since he'd flown her back from Rio Gordo.

Staying away from her was better for both of them—which was clear from the moment he had kissed her. He wanted her, but with a girl like Sabrina, a one- or two-night stand was out of the question, and more than that was out of the question for him.

Instead, he was determined to focus on work, to find another case that interested him. He had begun to thumb through the messages on his desk when the bell rang above the door and his sister and her five-year-old daughter walked into the office.

Grinning, Alex stood up from behind his desk and opened his arms. Little Ginny ran straight into them.

"Uncle Alex!"

"Hi, sweetheart!" He planted a smacking kiss on her cheek. Ginny Wyatt was a towheaded little imp with the same blue eyes Alex had inherited from his father.

She was smart and sweet, and he was flat-out crazy about her.

"Me and Mommy went shopping," Ginny said. "Mommy said we could come by and see if you wanted to go to lunch."

Alex thought of Melissa Carlyle, the last woman who'd come to the office and asked him to lunch. He had dodged that bullet. But there was no one he'd rather spend time with than the two most important people in his life.

Well, maybe there was one other person he'd like to include, but that wasn't going to happen.

He hoisted Ginny up on his shoulder, leaned over and kissed his sister's cheek.

"Hi, big brother." Rebecca was a pretty young woman with long, straight blond hair, brown eyes and a slender figure. She was tall, like their dad, but she looked more like his mother, with high cheekbones and a slim, straight nose.

"I'd love to take you to lunch," he said. "I have to be back here in an hour, but we can go someplace close. Maybe Prego? Great Italian food over there."

"Ginny was hoping for the Texas Café. She loves the fries and chocolate shakes."

"Good idea. Great burgers, too." It wasn't quite as healthy as salad and pasta, but Becca was good about watching what Ginny ate and staying away from fast-food restaurants. The café was a local favorite, the place Trace had first met his wife, Maggie.

As they headed for the door, he waved to Annie, who sat behind the receptionist desk.

"We're off to the Texas Café," he said. "I'll be back in an hour."

"How 'bout bringing me a chocolate shake?" Annie asked.

"You got it."

Annie winked at Ginny, her penciled blond eyebrows going up and down. "Don't let your uncle forget, okay?"

Ginny grinned, showing a hole where one of her bottom teeth should have been. "Okay."

The bell rang again as they walked outside. "How's the house coming along?" Alex asked Rebecca. His friend, Joe McCauley, the guy who'd been responsible for his move to Houston, had become a contractor after he'd left the navy. Alex had recommended him for his sister's remodel job. She'd bought a beautiful old Victorian in the Heights District, already partially remodeled. Joe was continuing the work.

Becca's eyes cut away for an instant. "Joe's good. He's doing a great job so far."

There was something in her face. Joe McCauley was a good-looking guy, and solid as a rock. "You like him," Alex said, opening the door to the backseat of Rebecca's Ford Explorer. Since his sister's car had a booster seat, they were taking her vehicle instead of his. He settled Ginny in the seat, took the keys from Becca's hand and slid behind the wheel.

"Joe's a nice guy," she said, picking up the thread of conversation once they were inside the car.

"That's it? Nothing more exciting than nice?"

She shrugged. "I'm not ready for another relationship, Alex. I'm not sure I ever will be."

He wanted to say she needed to think of Ginny. That she had to learn to trust again sometime. But since, for different reasons, he wasn't ready for a relationship either, he kept his mouth shut.

He glanced at Ginny in the mirror. "We're off to shakes and burgers," he said with a grin, and little Ginny giggled.

Alex's thoughts strayed to the woman who wasn't going with them, the person he would have liked Becca and Ginny to meet. He shoved her image from his mind and started the engine.

Rina opened the door and stepped back to let her best friend into the apartment. Sage Cantrell's wavy dark hair swung forward as she leaned over to give Sabrina a hug.

"How are you feeling?" Sage was about five inches taller that Rina's petite five-foot-one-inch frame, but the spike heels Sage always wore pushed her up to nearly six feet. Which was probably good, since her husband, Jake, was six foot five.

"I'm good," Rina said. "Bored, but good." On a pair of crutches made of aluminum instead of wood and not nearly so dear as the ones Alex had made for her, Sabrina led her friend into the living room. "Want a cup of coffee or a Coke or something?"

"I can't stay long. I've got a staff meeting this afternoon." Sage was the Vice President of Marketing and Acquisitions for Marine Drilling International. She was a dedicated career woman in line for the presidency of the company. "So the ankle is doing okay?"

"The sprain is pretty much healed," Rina said as they sat down on the cream sofa in front of a low, gilt, French table. "I'll be off these crutches in a few more days."

She'd been back from Rio Gordo for a little over two weeks. She was bored to tears and eager to be doing something instead of just sitting around the apartment friending people on Facebook and playing solitaire on her iPad.

And strange as it might seem, the *something* she was itching to do was get back to Rio Gordo. Now that she knew where the mine was located and had seen the two-track road that would get her there, she wanted to finish what she had started. She wanted to know if Uncle Walter had found silver on his land.

Land that now belonged to her.

"I hope you had a good visit with your mom," Sage said.

Her mother had stayed nearly a week. They'd always gotten along great, so it was fun. "It was nice to catch up. And her cooking is terrific. I'm sure I put on five pounds."

"That's okay, you lost that much out in the desert."

"Snake and javelina aren't big favorites."

Sage laughed. "So when are you going back to work? You've never been much for sitting around the house."

"I...umm...guess I didn't mention that my leave of absence is open-ended. I may not be going back at all."

Sage knew all about the land Rina had inherited, knew that was the reason she had hired Alex to fly her out to Rio Gordo. In fact, it was Sage and Jake who had demanded the sheriff's department start a search when Rina failed to call Sage the first night she was away as she had promised to do.

When Sage couldn't reach her the next day and Jake couldn't reach Alex, Jake had called the airport and discovered the chopper hadn't made radio contact for two full days. It wasn't until after a lengthy search that the sheriff had spotted Alex stumbling toward the highway.

"So what will you do if you don't go back to work?"

Sage asked. "You aren't thinking about that mine again, are you?"

"I never *stopped* thinking about it. I need to know if Uncle Walter found silver. If he did, there's no reason I can't find a company to work with to help me mine it. I'm tired of working for somebody else. And look where it's gotten me. In the last twelve months, I've lost most of what I worked for years to earn."

"I guess you've thought this through."

"I have. If it doesn't work out, then I'll find something else to do."

"Whatever you do, I know you'll be successful. It's just the way you are."

Rina smiled. "Thanks for the vote of confidence."

Sage's gaze moved around the apartment, taking in the soft curves of the rosewood tables, gilt-edged chairs and the Persian rug beneath the coffee table. There were still a few vases of get-well flowers that had arrived after she'd come back from Rio Gordo. One of them, a bouquet of yellow roses, was pretty much wilted, but it had come from Alex and she couldn't quite make herself toss it away.

"So, have you heard from Alex lately?" Sage asked, her gaze on the wilted bouquet she knew he had sent.

"I'm sure he's busy. I hope his ribs are mending."

"He's back at work so he must be feeling okay. I'm surprised he hasn't called."

Rina glanced away. "I gave him enough trouble on that trip to last him a lifetime. I imagine he's glad to be rid of me."

"Jake said Alex told him you were amazing out there."

Her interest sharpened. "He did?"

"He said you were tough when you needed to be."

Sage smiled. "He said he wouldn't have wanted to crash with anyone else."

Rina's heart pinched. She didn't want to like Alex Justice, let alone be attracted to him. She didn't need that kind of trouble. Unfortunately, she couldn't seem to get him out of her head. "He was really sweet out there."

Sage's dark eyebrows went up. "Sweet? Somehow that isn't a word I would think of to describe Alex. Tough, smart, loyal. Definitely good-looking. I'm not sure the women he usually dates would think he was sweet."

Rina didn't want to think about the women Alex dated. The ones he was probably seeing right now. "I'm going back out there," she said instead. "I've already made arrangements to fly commercial into Odessa and rent a car. I'll drive to Rio Gordo and go south from there."

The narrow dirt trail to the mine came off the highway between Rio Gordo and the border, she now knew. On the flight back out of the desert, she'd asked the helicopter pilot to mark the location when they were in the air. It was south of town about thirty miles. "I'm going back next week."

"Wait a minute—you aren't planning to go out there by yourself?"

"I'm meeting a mining expert from Presidio, a man named Arturo Hernandez. He'll be joining me out at the mine."

"I don't think that's a good idea, Sabrina."

"Look, I'm not going to be flying around in a helicopter again. Once I get to the mine and Mr. Hernandez and I take a look around, I'll drive back to Odessa and fly home."

Sage glanced over at the wilted yellow roses. "What

about taking Alex with you? I'm sure he'd be willing to go again."

Rina shook her head. Spending more time with Alex was exactly what she didn't want to do. "The last time I nearly got him killed. I'm not asking him to go out there again."

"But—"

"I can handle it, Sage. It's important for me to find out what I've got. If there's silver in that mine, I'm going to find a way to get it out."

Sage bit her lip, but didn't continue to argue. They respected each other's judgment. At least for the most part. Not that either was afraid to speak her mind.

Sabrina changed the subject and they talked about the houses Sage and Jake had been looking at, hoping to find something to buy.

"Jake's going crazy in my apartment. He needs a yard, a place he can get outdoors. We saw a house yesterday that might work. We're going back to look again to-night."

They talked about the offer she and Jake were going to make if they decided the house was what they wanted, but Sabrina's mind kept drifting to the trip she would be making early next week.

She wasn't looking forward to going back into the desert, but what little money she had was being stretched thinner and thinner. It was time for her to make her next move.

Eight

Alex rapped on the door to Sabrina's uptown apartment. When she didn't answer right away, he pounded harder. When the door swung open, he took one look at the petite woman with a headful of soft red curls, ignored the kick he felt in his gut and stormed past her into the entry.

Alex slammed the door behind him. "Have you lost your mind?"

"Well, hello to you, too."

"Sage tells me you're going back to Rio Gordo—alone. That's bullshit, Sabrina. You nearly got killed the first time. What the hell is the matter with you?"

She crossed her arms over her chest and for the first time he noticed she was wearing only a short pink silk robe.

"Do you know what time it is?" she asked, forcing him to tear his gaze away from her bare legs and small feet, the toenails that were painted a bright shade of pink.

"So it's a little early."

"It's six o'clock in the morning. I'm barely out of bed."

The image that conjured made his groin tighten. He'd been so damned mad he hadn't noticed that her face was void of makeup, all that fiery hair temptingly mussed. She looked a lot like she had when she'd been sleeping beside him in the desert. Which reminded him of the crash and made him mad all over again.

"I don't care what time it is. You can't go out there alone."

"I can do whatever I please, Alex Justice. And you don't have a damned thing to say about it."

He caught her shoulders and hauled her close, forcing her to tip her head back to look at him. "Don't I? I'm the guy who dragged you out of that chopper. I'm the guy who kept you alive out there and I'm not about to stand by and let you do something that could wind up with you hurt or dead."

She didn't back down. "I'm driving out to the mine and I'm meeting a mining engineer there. I'm not going to be in any kind of danger."

Reluctantly, he let her go. Running a hand through his hair, he fought to hold on to his temper. He didn't have any say in what Sabrina Eckhart did or didn't do, but he sure as hell wasn't letting her go back there alone.

"Fine, you want to go back, I'll go with you. You don't even have to pay me. I'll just go along as a friend."

She stared up at him, tried to read his face. "Why?"

"Why what?"

"Why do you want to go?"

"Because I…because I feel responsible for you. And because Sage would never forgive me if I let something happen to you."

She glanced away. "Oh."

"When are you going?"

"Day after tomorrow. I've booked a commercial flight out of Hobby to Odessa. I'll be renting a car to drive the rest of the way."

"I'll fly you. It'll be faster. Change the rental car location to Rio Gordo."

"But—"

"You need me, Sabrina, and you know it. You remember those guys at the airport? A woman who looks like you shouldn't be going off to a place like that alone."

She frowned. "A woman who looks like me?"

"That's right. You saw those guys. They'll be drooling all over you. No telling how far they'd be willing to go to have you."

For the first time she smiled. "I think there was a compliment in there somewhere."

"Are you listening, dammit?"

"All right, fine. But I almost got you killed before. If something happens, don't you dare blame me."

He felt the pull of a smile. "You didn't almost get me killed. The helicopter did that."

"Whatever you say."

He relaxed a little. "What time is your meeting with the mining engineer?"

"Noon."

"All right, I'll pick you up at seven. That should give us plenty of time."

"Fine."

She just stood there with her arms crossed and her legs bare. He wanted to eat her up. He wanted to kiss her so badly his jaw ached. Ever since they'd gotten back, he'd done his best not to think about her. He'd considered calling one of his old flames just to get rid of some of his frustration, but couldn't work up the least bit of enthusiasm. Now he was here, the last place he should be, and he had no desire to leave.

She looked up at him. He could tell she was trying to brazen it out, not let him know how uncomfortable she felt standing there in only a swatch of pink silk and probably not a damned thing on underneath.

Inwardly he groaned.

"I need to take a shower," she said.

He tried not to imagine peeling off the robe and joining her under the warm, wet spray, but his body had a mind of its own and he started getting hard.

"Want some company?" he said with a grin, just to be annoying. He hadn't felt such a jolt of heat since she'd been sleeping next to him in the desert.

Sabrina rolled her eyes. "There's a box of powdered doughnuts and some coffee in the kitchen. Help yourself."

Dammit, he didn't want coffee. He wanted her. And coming here had just made it worse.

You had no damn choice, he told himself. He sure as hell couldn't let her go back to the desert by herself. Sage and Jake had both agreed with him on that. And the truth was, he cared about Sabrina Eckhart. He might not want to, but he did.

"Thanks, I'll grab a doughnut on my way out. I'll see you Wednesday morning." He thought of the hours they'd be spending together, the torture he would be putting himself through. With a long-suffering sigh, he went in to get a doughnut, which would satisfy at least one of his appetites.

The pounding of a hammer somewhere downstairs forced Rebecca's eyes slowly open. She swung her long legs to the side of the bed, stood up and walked to the window. Joe McCauley, the carpenter Alex had recommended, was already at work, hammering away in her kitchen, adding a window with a flower box that looked out into the big backyard, knocking out a wall to make the space larger.

From her position at the upstairs bedroom window, she watched him walk from the house to his white pickup truck, shoulder another piece of plywood and start back to the kitchen. Though it was still fairly early, it was already getting hot and Joe was working with his shirt off. He was as solid as the slab of wood he carried and as tough as the nails he pounded into the walls.

Hard work had given Joe the kind of powerful build her brother had. Joe was beefier than Alex, with bigger arms and thighs. Joe was shorter, maybe five-eleven, with dark hair and dark brown eyes. With heels on, Rebecca was taller than he was.

Not that Joe seemed to notice. Well, there *was* the occasional male glance in her direction, but mostly where she was concerned, Joe was all business. It was Ginny who won his smiles, Ginny he seemed completely at ease with. He liked kids, he'd once told her. Said he hoped to have a couple of his own someday.

Clearly, Ginny liked Joe. The two shared such a feeling of camaraderie that Rebecca felt a little left out when the three of them were together. Which wasn't very often, since Joe mostly worked and kept to himself.

Exactly what Rebecca wanted. She had no interest in men. At least not right now. Been there, done that. Though she'd been separated from her ex-husband for more than two years, her divorce was only final six months ago. She was starting over in Houston, had come because she had family here, an older brother she could count on if she needed help.

Unlike her wealthy parents back in Connecticut, whose only concern was their highly esteemed position in society, Alex loved her and Ginny. The only thing Spencer and Virginia Justice cared about was making sure their children did exactly what they were told.

It hadn't worked on Alex, who'd refused to continue his Yale education and attend law school, then go into politics. Instead, he'd signed up for navy flight school. He'd been a crackerjack pilot and now he was a successful private investigator. But no matter what Alex accomplished, their parents considered him a total failure.

Rebecca was the one who had done exactly what her parents wanted. She'd yearned for the approval they doled out in rare bits and pieces. Wanted it so badly she had married a man she didn't love just to please them. Jeremy Wyatt had turned out to be both verbally and physically abusive, but even that wasn't enough to convince her parents she should divorce him.

It had taken a while to build the courage to go against their wishes. She might never have left Jeremy if Alex hadn't been there when she needed him. Just as he had been since they were kids. He was only two years older, but he had always been her strength, the one person she could count on.

He still was.

Rebecca looked out the window and caught another glimpse of Joe. Reminding herself she wasn't interested in having a man in her life, she headed for the bathroom to shower and dress for the day. Ginny would be up soon, Rebecca's whole world.

She didn't need a man. She had figured that out the hard way.

Cloudy skies hung over the airpark as the plane rose into the early-morning sky over Houston. A passing spring storm was moving through, the turbulence making the ride a little bumpy. Alex glanced over at the woman riding next to him in the copilot's seat. Where Sabrina had relaxed and enjoyed herself before, this time as the plane dropped and jolted, her fingers dug into the leather seat.

He flashed her a glance. "Everything's okay, you know. This is nothing like what happened with the chopper. This is just a little turbulence. Nothing out of the ordinary. We should smooth out in a few more minutes."

She swallowed, looked up at him and nodded, but her face was a little too pale. He was glad when the turbulence lessened and she finally leaned back in her seat.

The rest of the ride went smoothly and they landed at the Rio Gordo airport right on time. Alex retrieved her bag, which was bigger than before. He didn't have to ask what was in it. He figured she'd had to make do with nothing on her last trip. She wasn't taking any chances this time.

He took care of securing the plane then checked in at the office. Sabrina said hello to Mr. Woodard, who seemed relieved to see her all in one piece.

"You got some good friends out there," the old man told her. "Seemed like they was calling every five minutes. Had the sheriff jumpin', said somethin' must have happened or you would have phoned."

Sabrina smiled at him. "We kind of look out for each other."

Woodard nodded his approval, handed her the keys to the rental car, a four-wheel drive Jeep Cherokee. "Thank you," she said.

"You be careful out there. Desert can be a real nasty place…but then I guess you know that already."

"I'll make sure she gets back safely," Alex said, hoping to hell the rental car was more reliable than the chopper.

As they walked out of the office, he took the keys from Sabrina's hand. "We've got a little time. Let's stop at the market and pick up some lunch meat and cheese, stuff to make sandwiches to take out there with us."

Sabrina grinned and tapped her canvas bag. "Already got 'em. Along with some water and a few other goodies."

His mouth edged up. "I guess you're playing it safe this time."

"I'd just as soon not have to eat any more snake." She slung the strap of the bag over her shoulder. "You brought your emergency gear. I brought mine. I'm a fast learner, Alex."

He thought of the lessons he'd like to teach her that had nothing to do with survival. "So I've noticed." She'd done just fine out there in the desert. Better than he ever would have guessed. The courage she had shown only made him want her more.

They made their way over to the rental car pickup area, located the dark green Jeep, and he tossed their bags into the back. Sabrina went around and climbed in the passenger side. He was getting ready to slide behind the wheel when the roar of a jet plane signaled the ringing of his iPhone. He pulled it out of his jeans pocket but didn't recognize the number.

"Justice."

"Sheriff Beau Dickens here. I've got some information regardin' the helicopter crash."

"I'm listening."

"The aviation expert says the wrong kind of oil was added to the engine. Says the same thing happened with the rotor blades. Wrong lubricant used. Human error caused the chopper to crash."

Alex mulled that over, tried to understand how that could have happened. "Who's responsible?"

"That's the funny thing. Guy named Dexter Phillips is the mechanic on the helo. He's been taking care of her for the last five years. Dex swears he used the right oil."

"Maybe he was drunk or drugged-up or something."

"Man's a teetotaler. Family man all the way round. He claims someone must have tampered with the chopper after he did the maintenance work."

Alex didn't like the sound of that. "You're saying the crash wasn't an accident."

"We aren't sure yet, but it's startin' to look that way."

"Who else would have access besides Phillips?"

"This is Rio Gordo. We've only got one security camera out at the airport."

"I assume you've checked it."

"We've been goin' over the images. Be pretty easy for somebody to get in and out without being seen. We aren't sure, but we may have found somethin'. Too soon to say."

"What about Phillips? You're convinced he's telling the truth?"

"Dex's real good at his job. Takes pride in his work. So yeah, I think it's likely someone else did it."

"You have any idea who that might be or why?"

"As I said, we're followin' a lead. Too soon to tell if it's gonna pan out."

Alex's mind ran through a scenario that was unlikely, but he couldn't afford to overlook. "Listen, Sheriff, Ms. Eckhart and I just got back to Rio Gordo. My plane's out here at the airport. We'll only be away for a few hours. Think you could post a deputy to watch it? I'll pay for his time."

Silence fell on the other end of the line.

"Is there somethin' you aren't telling me? Like a reason someone might want to bring that chopper down with you and the lady aboard?"

"Just being careful. Until we know for sure what happened, I don't want to take any chances."

"I'll see to it," the sheriff said. "You don't need to worry."

"And keep me posted on that lead."

Dickens agreed and the call ended. Alex shoved the phone back into his pocket, but instead of climbing into the Jeep, he leaned down and took a look at the undercarriage. Maybe he was being paranoid, but until the sheriff came up with something concrete, part of his job—whether he was being paid or not—was to protect Sabrina.

He took a good look, saw nothing, checked beneath the hood, then slammed it closed. Sliding behind the wheel, he started the engine and caught Sabrina watching him.

"What was that all about?"

"That was Sheriff Dickens. They figured out what happened to the chopper."

"So what happened?"

"He thinks someone may have tampered with the engine and the rotor blades. Fouled the oil. It clogged the hydraulics and caused the blades to jam."

Her eyes widened. They looked bigger and bluer than they usually did. "That doesn't make sense. Why would someone do that?"

He thought of her uncle and the silver that might or might not be in the mine. Maybe Walter wasn't quite as secretive as Sabrina believed. Maybe someone figured to benefit with the new owner out of the picture. It was a long shot, but unless the sheriff nailed down the perp, it was a possibility he couldn't ignore.

"Looks like that's something we're going to need to find out."

Nine

"I don't understand, Alex. Why would someone purposely cause the crash?"

"Could be any number of reasons," he said.

"Is that why you were checking the car? You were afraid someone might have tampered with it?" A faint shiver ran through her as a memory arose of Sage and the bomb that had been planted in her limo. She'd been entertaining a Saudi sheik and his family. The bomb was one of the reasons Alex had been brought in to work with Jake.

Things like that happened, she knew—just not to her.

"We've had one problem," Alex said. "I don't want another."

"You aren't thinking someone was targeting one of us?" She kept her eyes on Alex's profile, saw a muscle tighten in his cheek.

"Until the sheriff tells us otherwise, it's a possibility we can't ignore."

"But—"

"I'm not expecting trouble, Sabrina." He drove the

Jeep out of the parking lot toward Highway 67, the road leading south. "I'm just being careful."

Just being careful. Alex was a professional. Of course he would be careful. "But no one even knows we're here."

"No one except the people who arranged the rental car and whoever they might have told. Now Woodard knows we're here."

It all seemed so unlikely. "What else did the sheriff say?"

"He says they have a lead they're following. He says he'll let us know."

"That sounds promising."

"Maybe. But it's better to be safe than sorry."

True enough. And if the sheriff suspected someone had purposely caused the helicopter engine to fail and one of them was the target, that someone might find another way to make them dead.

On the other hand... "But it could have happened accidentally, right? The oil problem? It could have just been human error...a mistake."

"*Two* mistakes," he said. "Engine and rotors. It's a little hard to believe."

She thought of how close they had come to dying, thought of the freezing nights and burning days in the desert, and a chill crept down the back of her neck.

"Maybe it was someone who just wanted to cause trouble, just a case of malicious vandalism. Maybe the person was trying to destroy the chopper, and we were just collateral damage."

"Could be. Definitely an angle to check. That may be where the sheriff's investigation is headed, but until we know for sure, we have to explore every possibility.

What would have happened to the mine if you'd been killed?"

"What? Oh, my God, you aren't thinking that was the motive? We don't even know if there's anything of value in the mine."

"We don't know. Maybe someone else does."

She couldn't make it fit. The crash couldn't possibly have anything to do with her. "I don't believe it. Even if Uncle Walter found silver, he wouldn't have told anyone."

"He told you. Maybe there was someone else he trusted."

He trusted her mother. And her mom, as sweet as she was, wasn't good at keeping secrets.

"He told my mother the same thing he told me—that he was very close to finding silver. Mom would hardly arrange for me to be killed in a helicopter crash. And even if I died, she wouldn't have gotten the mine."

"Who would have?"

She frowned, trying to think of what it had said in the will. "I'm not sure. Someone else in the family. I know there was a clause about survivorship, but I wasn't paying attention. I didn't really care who got the mine if I was dead."

Alex shot her a glance. "We'll find out. Besides, it's all just conjecture until we take a look, see what your uncle might have discovered."

"And till we know what the sheriff comes up with."

"That's right."

The whole thing seemed incredible. And yet Sheriff Dickens believed someone had purposely sabotaged the helicopter. For several miles, Sabrina allowed her mind to absorb that news while the Jeep roared along the highway.

It was little more than a black asphalt strip that rolled south out of Rio Gordo toward the town of Presidio on the Mexican border, a distance of about sixty miles. Outside the window, the desert floor rose toward a range of jagged, rocky hills in the distance. Her mind went back to the miles of barren emptiness she and Alex had struggled to survive and a different thought occurred.

She looked over at Alex. "Who knew you were flying me out here?" His blue gaze swung back to hers. "You have enemies, right?"

"You're thinking maybe I was the target?"

She shrugged. "How many people have you pissed off lately? As I recall, I saw one of them on TV not long ago." The pervert who had murdered little Carrie Wiseman. "Maybe someone wants *you* dead instead of me."

As the miles ticked away, Alex started slowing the vehicle. "It's possible. I'm a private investigator. I work closely with the police. And as you say, sometimes I piss people off."

Rina looked down at the speedometer. They had traveled twenty-eight miles. "It makes as much sense as anything else."

"For now, let's see if there's anything out here worth killing for, then we'll know more." He checked the odometer. "The turn should be right around here. Keep your eyes open."

Alex slowed a little more and Rina fixed her gaze on the east side of the highway, looking for the faint dirt track that led to the mine.

"There it is! That has to be it."

He braked. "Looks like it. Not much else out here."

And if a person didn't know where to look, he would miss the slight indentations marking the parallel ruts that indicated a road leading into the desert.

Alex turned onto the road, slipped the Jeep into four-wheel drive, and they headed off. Sabrina ignored a feeling of déjà vu, a memory of the last time she had been out there.

And the trace of uncertainty crawling down her spine.

The mine was little more than a hole dug into the side of a mountain. A black spot in a low ridge of rock that stretched for miles, north to south, through the desert. Alex counted half a dozen old wooden buildings clustered nearby, battered by the years, wind and sand.

"It's a ghost town," Sabrina said, her gaze following his to what was left out there, just the worn-out bones of the structures they had once been.

"Not much of a town, but there were definitely people living out here at one time."

"Working the mine, you think?"

"Be my guess." One of the cabins looked like it had been restored, the wooden sides reinforced, the roof repaired. There was an old rock fireplace against one side of the building, the chimney rising a few feet above the top. A rocking chair sat forlornly beneath the covered front porch as if waiting for someone to come out and sit in it.

"That must be Walter's cabin," Sabrina said. "He talked about it when I saw him that last Christmas. He died a week before Christmas this year."

They headed toward the cabin, their hiking boots crunching in the sand. Both of them were wearing jeans, but today Sabrina wore low-topped leather boots instead of the sneakers she had worn before. How a woman could look sexy in jeans and hiking boots, he couldn't imagine. But desire settled low in his groin, making it clear this one did.

Maybe it was her hair. Longer now, it curled in soft, fiery waves around her face. And those full pink lips. He remembered exactly how they tasted, how perfectly they fit with his, and fought his unwanted arousal.

They crossed the wooden porch and he opened the door, which wasn't locked. The inside of the structure was as simple as the outside. Just a cot covered by a pair of flannel sheets and a red-and-black-striped wool blanket. An old-fashioned dry sink ran along the wall, a wooden table and two sturdy wooden chairs sitting next to it. A coffeepot sat on an old cast-iron woodstove that must have been used for cooking and also for heat.

"He lived a modest life," Sabrina said. "At least after he and Aunt Marlene got divorced."

"What about before?" he asked.

"Walter was an accountant. He owned a very successful firm. Marlene enjoyed the high life but Walter never did."

Alex prowled the cabin, saw Sabrina doing the same. She picked up a little wooden box that sat on a low pine table next to the bed. The box was made of polished rosewood, the top inlaid with mother-of-pearl.

Her small hand stroked lovingly over the lid. "I gave this to Uncle Walter one Christmas. I brought it back with me from France."

The morning Alex had stormed in and confronted Sabrina about this trip to the desert, he had noticed the French antiques in her apartment, had appreciated the way she had blended the beautiful French pieces with a comfortable modern decor. At the time, he'd been too damned angry to mention it.

Sabrina ran her fingers over the box, then slowly opened the lid. "Oh, my God. Alex, there's an envelope in here with my name on it."

So the old man had expected her to come. "Go ahead...open it."

Her hand trembled as she removed the letter, stared down at the envelope in her hand. Alex watched as she carefully broke the seal and pulled out a single sheet of paper.

"What's it say?"

She took a deep breath as she stared down at the letter. "'If you are reading this, my dear sweet girl, then something has happened and I am dead.'" She swallowed, took a moment then started reading again. "'If that's true, you are now the owner of the Sabrina Belle.'" Her eyes filled as she looked up, and Alex's chest tightened at the sadness in her face.

"Oh, Alex, he named the mine after me." Her throat moved up and down and the letter trembled in her hand. It was clear her uncle had loved her, and why shouldn't he? She was sweet and loyal and determined. Walter must have admired those qualities in his niece, a young woman who had stood by him when the rest of his family had deserted him.

"What else does the letter say?" he gently prodded.

She released a shaky breath.

"I knew that after I was gone, you would come to see for yourself what I have left you, and that when you did, you would find this letter. You always believed in me. Now all my years of hard work belong to you. This mine is all I have to give you, but I am certain you will find it to be more than enough. God be with you. Your loving Uncle Walter."

Sabrina turned away but not before Alex saw the tears in her eyes tremble onto her cheeks. He walked toward her, turned her around and drew her into his arms.

"It's all right, love. He's in a better place. And now you know how much he loved you."

She nodded, hung on to him for several moments. She felt soft and feminine in his arms and he was glad he was there when she needed him. After all, he told himself, what were friends for? She clung to him a moment more, then stepped back and wiped away her tears.

"Uncle Walter didn't come right out and say it, but he's telling me there's silver here. I'm not going to fail him, Alex. I'm going to find it."

He reached out and traced a finger down her cheek. He wanted to lean down and kiss her, taste those sweet lips and take away a little of her sadness. Now wasn't the time. And it was a bad idea to even be thinking that way.

He glanced out the window, saw a cloud of dust rolling toward them along the dirt road they had traveled, marking the progress of the mining engineer.

"Looks like your guy is here."

Her glance sliced to the window. They watched the white Ford pickup drive up in front of the cabin, then together walked out to greet him.

Arturo Hernandez was a tall, lean Hispanic man in his early forties, handsome, with his darkly tanned skin and traces of silver in his hair. Sun lines fanned out at the corners of his eyes but it only added an air of ruggedness to his appearance.

"You must be Ms. Eckhart." He smiled, his gaze running over her, taking in her fiery hair and sexy curves. Alex felt an unexpected stab of jealousy.

"It's a pleasure to meet you, Mr. Hernandez," she said, extending her small hand, which Hernandez held a little longer than Alex liked. "This is my friend, Alex Justice."

Alex shook the man's hand.

Hernandez glanced around, taking in the deserted buildings. "There was mining here many years ago," he explained, turning back to Sabrina, "after the turn of the last century, in the early nineteen twenties. The mine never produced much of anything and finally fell into ruin. I did not know it was here until after you called and I started doing some research. I discovered that a man named Walter Eckhart most recently owned the property."

"That's right. He was my uncle. He died six months ago. I own the property now."

Hernandez's dark eyes swung toward some fresh tailings near the opening in the mountainside. "It has been worked fairly recently. Let us see what we have."

The engineer had the gear they needed, which he dispensed from the bed of his pickup. Helmets with lights in the front, several LED flashlights. Apparently Sabrina had arranged for him to bring the equipment when she had spoken to him on the phone.

For more than an hour, they explored the mine and the nearby surrounding area. The interior had been shored up with new timbers and there was a generator to work the lights that hung from the ceiling inside the main shaft, but it was clearly a one-man operation.

"It is well maintained," Hernandez said. "Looks like your uncle did a lot of work."

"For the past seven years, he spent most of his time out here."

Hernandez took samples from various locations inside the mine shaft. "Your uncle must have assay records, information on what he found over the years."

"I haven't seen anything."

"Maybe it'll turn up," Alex suggested.

By the time they walked back out into the light, Arturo and Sabrina were on a first-name basis, and the engineer was smiling.

"I will let you know what these samples show, but I can tell you now this looks very promising. If that is the case, we'll need to drill core samples to determine the extent of the deposit, as well as the purity of the ore. That will also tell us the limits of the deposit or deposits, and the quantity of material present in them."

Sabrina started grinning. "So you're fairly sure there's silver in the mine?"

Hernandez frowned. "I am sorry. I didn't mean to give you the wrong impression. What we are looking at here are deposits of molybdenum and copper."

"Molybdenum?"

"Moly, they call it," Alex said.

"I've heard of it, but I'm afraid I haven't done any research on it," Sabrina said.

"Mainly it is used to make stainless steel," Arturo explained. "Since steel production is down, the price is down, but it is still over thirty thousand a ton."

"That sounds as if a find could be very good."

"Indeed, it could be." Hernandez gave her a slow

smile and Sabrina smiled in return. Alex gritted his teeth.

"I guess Uncle Walter was right," she said, flashing him a look of triumph. "We may not have silver, but the mine is worth something."

Alex flicked a glance at the dark-haired man and hoped for Sabrina's sake the guy was right. "Looks like."

Her attention swung back to the engineer as he returned his equipment to the bed of his pickup. "How soon will I know anything?"

"I should have something for you by the end of the week." His dark eyes slid over her in a way that made the hackles rise at the back of Alex's neck. To hell with just being friends. They were more than that—whether he wanted it that way or not, and he wasn't going to let some slick-talking joker take advantage of her.

"As a matter of fact," Hernandez said, "I'll be in Houston next week for a business meeting. Perhaps we could get together, talk about your project over supper."

Alex's jaw tightened. Hernandez might be good at his job, but he was clearly a ladies' man. And it was also clear he wanted more from Sabrina than just her business.

"Yes, I think that's a good idea," she said in an irritating show of naïveté. Couldn't she see what Hernandez was after?

"If you're right and the deposits are there," she said, "how much would the property be worth?"

Hernandez shrugged. "It depends on what we find. There is a twenty-eight-hundred-acre parcel for sale in this part of Texas with some rich deposits. The asking price is twenty million."

Sabrina's mouth dropped open. "Dollars?"

Hernandez smiled. "That doesn't mean your parcel would be worth that much, but it is possible."

So much for motive. Sabrina's parcel could be worth big bucks. Alex thought of what had happened to the helicopter and how close they had come to dying. Twenty million dollars was more than enough reason to commit murder.

Hernandez handed Sabrina a business card. "I have put your phone number in my cell. Perhaps I should have yours, Alex, as well."

Alex handed him a business card, which Hernandez perused.

"A private investigator?"

"That's right. I also provide personal security." He glanced down at Sabrina in a way that let the guy know he wasn't going to stand by and let some sleazeball take advantage of her.

Hernandez just smiled. "Yes, I can understand that a beautiful woman might need protection traveling all the way out here by herself."

Sabrina actually blushed at the praise. Alex wanted to wring her neck.

"I will let you know what I find out," Hernandez said to her.

Alex felt a sweep of relief when the guy headed back to his truck.

Ten

Dust swirled around them, the hot breeze lifting the sand up off the desert floor, carrying it toward the mountains as the white pickup drove away. As she stood next to Alex on the porch and watched the truck disappear in the distance, Rina couldn't keep a smile off her face.

"Twenty million dollars," she said. "I can't believe it."

"Don't get your hopes too high," Alex said. "He'll need to take more samples and these things can be tricky."

No kidding. The odds were probably a million to one. "You don't have to tell me that. Uncle Walter was up and down, high and low for years. He was sure he was going to be rich, then certain he was doomed to failure."

"Maybe this time he hit the jackpot."

"He never mentioned molybdenum. All he ever talked about was silver."

"You hadn't seen him for a while though, right? Not since Christmas before last."

"That's right. He could have found moly instead of silver and never had the chance to tell me."

"If Hernandez is right, then I guess you'll sell the property. Make a nice tidy sum."

She looked up at him and thought of the letter she had left inside the cabin. It seemed as if it belonged there, waiting for her return, waiting for her to take up where her uncle had left off.

She smiled. "If Hernandez is right, I'm about to go into the mining business."

One of Alex's dark blond eyebrows went up. "You don't even know what it takes to mine molybdenum. Hell, you didn't even know what it was."

"True, but as I said, I'm a fast learner." She stepped off the porch and Alex fell in beside her. "You'd be amazed how much I've learned about mining silver."

He laughed. "No, I really don't think I would. You're a pretty amazing lady."

Her head came up. She looked into his handsome face and her stomach flip-flopped. She'd been doing her best to ignore those gorgeous dimples all day. With the possibility of millions of dollars to keep her distracted, she had managed fairly well.

But now they were alone and her mind kept sliding back to those moments in the cabin and the tender way he had held her. For an instant, she'd thought he was going to kiss her.

She should have known that wouldn't happen. Alex was an extremely virile male, but she wasn't really his type, and neither of them wanted to get involved in a relationship. They were friends, she reminded herself. That was all either of them wanted.

"We never had our lunch," he said as she buckled her seat belt and he started the engine of the Jeep.

"Too hot to eat out here now. Let's wait till we get back to town and find someplace with air-conditioning."

"Amen to that."

They headed for Highway 67, the road that would take them back to the airport and their return trip to Houston. In a few days she would hear from Arturo Hernandez. She would know whether Uncle Walter had been right.

Rina smiled as she leaned back in her seat. The next few days would determine the course of her life.

It was getting late by the time they pulled up in front of Sabrina's apartment. After such a long day, both of them were exhausted. She paused beneath the porch light, waited while Alex took the key from her hand and opened the door.

"Are you really going to have supper with that Hernandez guy?" he asked.

"What do you mean, of course I am. I need to know what I might actually find on my uncle's land. If there's moly there, I'll need to find a mining company to work with. Mr. Hernandez may be able to help me."

"I'm sure he'll be able to help you with something," Alex said sarcastically.

"What's that supposed to mean?"

"It means the guy is interested in a lot more than mining. Surely you can see that."

She blinked up at him, surprised at his words. "You think he's interested in me personally?" She smiled, flattered by the idea. "Well, he certainly seemed like a nice enough man."

A muscle ticked in his cheek. "If you like the slick type."

Rina ignored him. He was just tired. They both were.

"I really appreciate you taking me back there, Alex. I feel like I should at least pay for your time and the gas for your plane."

"I went as a friend," he said tightly.

"Yes, but still, I ought to at least pay—"

"You want to pay me? Fine." She heard the anger in his voice, gasped as he hauled her against him. "I'll take this in payment." His mouth came down over hers and Rina clutched his shoulders to stay on her feet. It was a hot, fierce, wildly erotic kiss that had her senses reeling. Her stomach muscles contracted and her breath whispered out on a moan.

Alex didn't stop, just kissed her until her whole body tingled and she was hot and embarrassingly turned on. She didn't remember her arms going up around his neck, didn't remember kissing him back as wildly as he was kissing her.

It hit her like a splash of cold water when Alex broke away.

"I've been wanting to do that all day. Consider your debt paid." He turned and started walking.

For several long moments, Rina just stood there, her legs quivering, her lips still on fire. She wondered if Alex knew what a kiss like that did to her. Wondered if he knew it made her so weak in the knees she could barely stand up.

She wondered if he'd just done it to put an end to her offer of money. Obviously he didn't need it. She was beginning to realize he had a lot more than she'd thought.

"What...what about the helicopter crash?" she called out to him as he neared his car.

Alex turned and stormed back to the porch. "What about it?"

She forced herself to look at him and not think of the burning kiss that seemed to have no effect on him at all. "We need…need to research the man who owns the helicopter, see if…if he has any enemies, someone who might have reason to destroy it that doesn't have anything to do with us."

"I haven't forgotten what happened. I was the pilot, remember? I'll be checking on everything we talked about."

"That…that's good."

"I went down in that chopper, too, you know. I want to know what happened as much as you do."

She forced herself to concentrate, reminded herself that maybe he was the one they were after. In a way it made more sense.

"I know that. I'm sorry."

He reached out, almost touched her cheek. "Get inside and lock the door," he said instead, then turned and strode away.

Sabrina forced her legs to move, to carry her into the house. She closed the door behind her, turned the lock and leaned against it.

Thank God he's gone, she thought, the taste of him still on her lips, her body still tingling all over. Worse yet, she wished he hadn't stopped, wished he would have kept right on kissing her. Wished he had— She broke off the thought, didn't dare let her mind continue down that road.

One thing she knew—if there was any way to avoid it, she wasn't seeing Alex Justice again.

As he slid behind the wheel of his BMW, Alex softly cursed. Dammit, he hadn't meant to do that. Or maybe he had. He'd been thinking about it all day, remembering the last time he'd kissed her, wondering if it was really as hot and soul-shattering as he imagined.

Unfortunately, this time was even hotter. He was still hard as stone and aching with every heartbeat. Which meant he definitely had to put an end to his fantasies about Sabrina or she was going to wind up in his bed.

Which he could not let happen.

Sabrina deserved more than a quick roll in the hay with a guy like him. True, her last boyfriend had been a dud. It had taken a while, but Sabrina had finally realized what a poor match they were.

But Alex was the guy on the opposite end of the spectrum. Unsettled, unsure what he wanted out of life. Not sure he could ever be happy with just one woman.

She hadn't been dating, she'd said.

Not the way he had, picking and choosing as if he were selecting a puppy to take home for the night, then returning it to the pet store in the morning. Oddly enough, the women he chose didn't seem to mind. They were in the same remote, mindless place he was, living only for the moment, with no thought of the future. Lately, their faces had all begun to blur together.

All but Sabrina. Her pretty, heart-shaped face, glorious red hair and brilliant blue eyes stayed with him day and night.

It's only because you want her and can't have her, he told himself. She was a friend, and friends didn't hurt each other.

Hell, even if he decided to give in to the relentless craving he felt for her, he wasn't sure Sabrina would go for it. Hot kisses were one thing. A roll in the hay was another.

Besides, if she wanted that, she had plenty of guys to choose from. The way Arturo Hernandez had been sizing her up, if she gave him the slightest encouragement, the guy would be all over her.

The image set Alex's teeth on edge.

The good news was Sabrina might be as physically attracted to him as he was to her, but she knew very well the kind of guy he was. She didn't want to get involved with him any more than he wanted to get involved with her.

Alex took a calming breath and started the engine, backed the car out of the parking space and headed for the street. The important thing right now was finding out who had sabotaged the chopper. He couldn't be sure Sabrina would be safe until the question was resolved.

On the other hand, she could very well be right about the target being him instead of her. Anyone in his line of work had enemies. Whether any of them would go as far as sabotaging an aircraft to kill him he didn't know.

While he waited for word from the sheriff, he would do a little digging. Check his files, his client list, see if anyone popped up. If not, and it looked like the target was Sabrina, he was going to need her help to figure out who it was, and at the same time figure a way to keep her safe.

Alex inwardly groaned. Seeing her again was the last thing he wanted.

Alex prayed the sheriff would make an arrest and solve the problem for him.

Sabrina spent the following morning on the computer in her home office, researching molybdenum. Aside from its primary use in making stainless steel, it was also used as a super alloy for automotive parts, aircraft engines, high-speed drills, even in the construction of nuclear power plants. She studied how it was mined, the costs involved, companies who handled that kind of work.

The Desert Mining Company, which employed Arturo Hernandez, was run out of Presidio, the nearest town to the Desert Mine and also the Sabrina Belle. It produced both copper and molybdenum. Being located so near Uncle Walter's property—now hers—Desert Mining could be the perfect company to form a partnership with to extract ore from her mine.

If there was really anything there. When she finished her research for the day, she started going over her finances, seeing how far she could stretch the money she still had in the bank and trying to figure how she might raise more if the mine appeared to be viable.

The phone rang an hour later. It was the call she had been waiting for but hadn't expected quite so soon.

"Good morning, Sabrina. This is Arturo Hernandez."

Her pulse kicked up. "Good morning, Arturo. I'm surprised to hear from you so soon." But now that she had, her nerves were humming with a mix of hope and fear.

"The assay report looks very good," he said, and she shot a fist into the air. "The next step is to arrange for core samples to be drilled. Once we have them, we can determine the extent of the deposit, as well as the purity of the ore."

Her excitement surged. They were moving forward. The samples looked promising enough that they were going to want core samples!

"That's wonderful news, Arturo. I've been reading

up on your company. I wonder if Desert Mining might be able to handle the drilling for me."

"As a matter of fact, that is one of the reasons I called. As I said before, I am going to be in Houston the first of next week. Desert Mining has asked me to speak to you in regard to setting up a meeting to discuss your property and its potential."

She thought of Uncle Walter and how thrilled he would be. "Yes, that sounds good."

"Of course, we won't know exactly what you have until the samples are processed."

Which wouldn't be cheap. "I imagine that's fairly expensive."

"Why don't we discuss the matter in person? Are you available for dinner Monday evening?"

For a chance at millions of dollars, of course she was! "Monday would work very well."

"All right, I'll pick you up...say seven-thirty?"

Rina gave him her address and directions to her apartment then hung up the phone. She found herself grinning. Uncle Walter wasn't just a crazy old man like everyone said. He'd been right all along. Her first impulse was to phone Alex, share the exciting news.

She clamped down on the urge. Alex Justice was her weakness. She had to stay away from him. She'd tell Sage instead, ask her to let Alex know how things were progressing. Rina reached for the phone and punched her best friend's number.

Alex sat behind the desk in his office. He'd been there for hours, making calls, running down information, anything that might give him the answer to why the helicopter in Rio Gordo had been sabotaged. There was nothing he could do about Sabrina's theory that it could have just been vandalism and they just happened to be at the wrong place at the wrong time. He was waiting for word from the sheriff on that.

Instead, he focused on the possibility that it was someone who wanted payback on him. He'd been going through old case files, then running down the whereabouts of guys he'd helped put in jail, the most recent being Edward Bagley, the bastard who had murdered Carrie Wiseman.

Though officially Bagley was innocent until proven guilty, Alex had no doubt the scumball had done it. And the good news was, the guy was locked up.

Which brought him full circle back to Sabrina and stirred the worry that had been riding him since he'd left her last night. Until he knew who was responsible for bringing down the chopper—and why—he had to entertain the possibility Sabrina was the target. That someone wanted what could turn out to be an extremely valuable chunk of land. If that were true, she could still be in danger.

He needed to see Walter Eckhart's will, find out who was next in line for the mine. Sabrina had said she remembered a survivorship clause. That meant if she died prematurely, someone else got the land.

He needed to know who that someone was.

Which meant he needed to see her.

His pulse kicked up at the thought, and inwardly, he cursed. Being around Sabrina was dangerous—for both of them. Only Sabrina didn't seem to know it.

The phone rang, jerking him out of his thoughts. Alex picked it up. "Justice."

"Sheriff Dickens here. Thought ya'll would want to know we've made an arrest."

Alex felt a sweep of relief. "That's welcome news."

"Guy named Martin Gilroy. Worked for Westfield Helicopters, did odd jobs, kept the chopper clean. Westfield fired him a couple months back for being drunk on the job. Gilroy claimed it was bull. He wanted his job back and when they refused, he was pissed. Made no bones he was going to make Westfield pay. Surveillance camera at the airport picked him up three times in the last two weeks. He was out at the airport the day before your chopper went down."

Alex's hand unconsciously fisted. "You got him on video tampering with the chopper?"

"No, but he was there. We're sweatin' him. Odds are, he'll confess. Gilroy's not long on brains, but he's smart enough to foul up the chopper."

"Or he might have had help."

"Could have. We'll find out. Either way, Gilroy's going down for this."

Alex released a slow, relieved breath. "Thanks for the call, Sheriff. I'll let Ms. Eckhart know."

"Good enough." The line went dead and Alex leaned back in his chair. *Wrong place, wrong time, nothing more than that.* He didn't have to worry about Sabrina. He could just call her, tell her the news and put her mind to rest.

He didn't need to see her. Which should have been good but instead made him feel like hell.

Eleven

Sage Cantrell walked into the Atlas Security office looking for Jake. Or at least that was her excuse.

Annie Mayberry glanced up from behind her desk as the bell rang above the door and Sage stepped into the small reception area.

"Your husband's not here," Annie said, stuffing the end of a pencil into her frizzy blond hair. "Had a meeting with a client. You should have called. I could have saved you a trip."

"I was over at the new house. I needed to take some measurements." The big two-story colonial she and Jake had just purchased was in the University District, not far from the office. It was a lovely older home, but it needed some refurbishing. Sage hadn't realized how much she would enjoy the challenge of redecorating the place until she got started.

She glanced past Annie and spotted Alex sitting at his desk. He was the real reason she had stopped by. She had seen his car in the lot and figured he was there.

Alex hung up the phone and stood up as she approached. "Hey, lady, what's up?"

"I was looking for Jake, but I was hoping you'd be here, too. I was wondering if you were going to the Cancer Research Benefit at the country club Saturday night?"

"I made a donation. I wasn't planning to go."

"I'm on the committee so I have to be there. Jake's going with me but he'd have a better time if you came, too."

Alex shook his head. "Sorry, I don't have a date. It's too short notice to ask someone to go."

She glanced away, pretended to agree. "You're probably right. Oh, by the way, I'm supposed to tell you…I got a call from Sabrina this morning. That engineer phoned that you met out in the desert…what was his name?"

Alex's blue eyes darkened. "Hernandez."

"That's right. Apparently, those ore samples from the mine look very promising. Mr. Hernandez is coming to town on Monday. Rina's having a dinner meeting with him that night to discuss going forward with the mine."

Alex's jaw hardened. "Guy's a real ladies' man. He's interested in a helluva lot more than mining. Sabrina's too damn trusting to figure that out."

Sage flashed him a look. "Being a ladies' man yourself, I guess you'd know."

Alex made no comment but a muscle ticked in his cheek.

"Well, Rina wanted me to let you know things were going really well."

"Thanks," he said darkly. "Actually, I was getting ready to call her, let her know they arrested the guy who sabotaged the chopper."

"That's great news, Alex."

"At least now we know she isn't in any danger."

"Rina said you were worried the crash might have had something to do with the mine she inherited. Assuming Mr. Hernandez is right about the value."

His features tightened. "Yeah."

"Listen, I've got to run. Give me a call if you change your mind about the benefit."

"I'll do that." She could see his mind working, thinking about Sabrina with Arturo Hernandez. Alex and Rina did their best to deny the attraction between them, but it was far stronger than Sage had believed.

It wasn't long ago that Sabrina had helped Sage come to grips with her attraction to her big, handsome bodyguard, the man who was now her husband. It was only fair to return the favor.

Sage bit back a grin as she turned and headed for the door. She had no doubt Alex would be going to the benefit and who he would be bringing.

Men could be so much fun.

Alex pressed the doorbell for Sabrina's apartment, then forced himself to wait patiently while she made her way to the door. He had news he needed to relay. Sure, he could have called, but he'd decided to tell her in person.

She opened the door and her eyes widened. She was always surprised to see him. It annoyed him to think how little interest she thought he had in her.

"Hello, Alex. I didn't expect you. Come on in." She stepped back out of the way and he walked into the apartment, noticed how cute she looked in a pair of cut-off shorts and a bright yellow tank top.

"Would you like a Coke or some iced tea or something?"

"Getting hot out there. Iced tea sounds great." He followed her into the kitchen. Frilly yellow curtains, a painting of a Parisian garden filled with yellow spring flowers.

"Place looks like you," he said, glancing around the interior. "Feminine and pretty. Nice antiques. I guess you've been to France."

"*Oui,* M'sieur Justice." She grinned. "I love France. I was a foreign exchange student there for a couple of years." She opened the fridge and pulled out a pitcher, put ice in a couple of glasses and poured them each a drink.

She handed him a glass and they sat down at the white, butcher-block-top kitchen table.

"You did a nice job," he said, liking the cheeriness of the place that seemed to fit her perfectly.

Sabrina started to frown. "What's going on, Alex? You didn't come over here to tell me you liked my apartment."

He took a drink of sweet tea from the icy glass she'd handed him, set the glass down on the table. "Sheriff Dickens called. They've made an arrest. Guy named Martin Gilroy. I figured you'd want to know."

Her small shoulders sagged in relief. "That's really good news. Did the sheriff say why he did it?"

"Apparently he had a beef with the company. They fired him for being drunk. Gilroy wanted payback."

"Seems like killing two people is an awful thing to do because you're mad at your employer."

"Yeah, well, how about those postal workers who

keep going off their bean and shooting everyone they work with? You can't tell what some people will do."

"People without any conscience. We could have been killed, Alex."

He didn't like to think about it. "We weren't. That's what matters." But he'd like to rip Gilroy's head off and stuff it down his neck.

He took another drink of iced tea, set it down and ran a finger through the condensation on the side of the glass. "I was wondering if you might do me a favor."

Her head came up. "Sure. What kind of favor?"

"I…ah…need a date for Saturday night. Sage and Jake are pressing me to go to a benefit at the country club. It's black tie. I know it's short notice. Any chance you could help me out?"

She sat up a little straighter in her chair. "You want me to go out with you…as your date?"

He shrugged. "We're friends, right? I figured you might take pity on me. We'll be sitting with Sage and Jake so it might even be fun."

"I…I don't know, Alex."

"Come on, Red. Who's the guy who flew you all the way to Rio Gordo?" It wasn't a fair tactic, but he was pretty sure it would work.

She bit her lip. "You're right. I owe you. Of course, I'll go. I just…I hope I can find something to wear."

He grinned. "Are you kidding? You're a woman. You have ten things in your closet to wear—you just want an excuse to buy something new."

She laughed. "You're probably right. I'll figure something out."

He took another sip of iced tea, came to the last subject he wanted to discuss. "Sage says those samples from your mine look really good."

She smiled. "That's right. Arturo called. He says we should drill for core samples. I'm hoping his company will want to get involved, maybe work on some kind of a percentage. We're going to talk about it."

His mood darkened. "At dinner Monday night."

"That's right."

He clamped down on his temper. "You realize this guy is trying to get you in bed."

"What? You're crazy. Arturo has no personal interest in me. This meeting is strictly business."

"Bullshit. The guy looked at you like a cream puff he wanted to take a bite of."

Sabrina came out of her chair. "That's not true."

Alex stood up, too. "The hell it isn't!"

"Even if you happened to be right—which you aren't—it's none of your business."

She had him there. But he didn't like Arturo Hernandez and he didn't want her going out with him. Hell, he didn't want her going out with anyone but him.

Son of a bitch. This wasn't good.

"Come on, Red, I just don't want the guy taking advantage."

"I'm a grown woman, Alex."

The words stirred thoughts he was working to ignore. He tried to keep his eyes from straying but they ran over her cutoff jeans, those curvy hips and shapely legs, came back to the plump breasts he itched to cup in his hands. "Afraid I can't argue with that."

Her cheeks turned pink, making the freckles stand out on her nose. "It's just business," she repeated, her chin hiking into the air.

"Yeah, right." Knowing he had better leave before she dumped her iced tea over his head, he started for the door. "I'll see you Saturday. Pick you up at seven."

By the time he had stepped outside the apartment, he had made a decision. Friends or not, when Saturday night came to an end, Sabrina wouldn't have the slightest interest in Arturo Hernandez.

Twelve

The gala at the River Oaks Country Club was a first-class affair. The building, with its row of white columns, sat on a long stretch of brilliant green, perfectly manicured lawn, reigning like a queen over the verdant Houston landscape.

As a child living in a small two-bedroom, one-bath house in a lower-middle-class neighborhood in Uvalde, Sabrina would never have dreamed she'd be attending a dinner with the cream of Houston society.

Or maybe she had always imagined herself here. From grade school on, she'd been driven to succeed. She'd been determined to go to college, graduate and find the kind of job that would pay enough to buy the things her parents couldn't afford.

Uncle Walter had helped her to get through school, but mostly she had done it on her own. Tonight she was dressed in a long, strapless, sequined black gown from Neiman Marcus and a pair of black satin Jimmy Choo heels that cost nearly six hundred dollars. Rhinestone earrings dangled from her ears and the fragrance of

Chanel No. 5 floated up from between her breasts and behind her ears.

She felt feminine and sexy, and pretty enough not to embarrass her stunningly handsome date, Alex Justice.

Dressed in a white dinner jacket with a black tuxedo shirt, Alex's expensive clothes fit his tall frame perfectly. His dark golden hair, crystal-blue eyes and dimples set him apart from every other man in the room. Or at least it seemed so to Rina.

Seated at a table with Sage and Jake, the mayor and his wife, and a congressman accompanied by an older female staffer, she felt more at ease than she had imagined. Of course, as a stockbroker, she had attended these sorts of affairs to build her clientele. But she hadn't been with Alex, hadn't felt him watching her with those hot blue eyes that made her heart beat a little too fast.

She had enjoyed the table conversation through dinner, served in a sumptuous room lit by crystal chandeliers, the decorations for the evening done in shades of rose and ivory. She even made it through several after-dinner speeches without being bored to tears. With Alex sitting next to her, she had drunk a little more champagne than she usually did, which may have helped, because she found herself laughing more easily, heard him laughing back. By the time the dancing started, she thought maybe Alex would be ready to go home.

Instead, he stood up from his chair and offered her his hand. "They're playing a slow song. It's a good way to get started."

Get started? She was only there as a favor. He didn't have to entertain her. Still, the thought of dancing with Alex made her stomach float up and a sigh hover on her lips. Resting her hand in his, she let him lead her onto the parquet dance floor and ease her into his arms.

An eight-piece orchestra was playing, the music soft and romantic. Alex was more than a foot taller than she was, but in her very high heels, dancing with him wasn't awkward.

It was magical.

As the music swelled, swept them into its bluesy rhythm, he drew her closer, his hard body enfolding hers, his white satin lapels brushing against her breast. He was a very good dancer—of course he was—but then she was pretty good herself, and they danced together seamlessly.

One song blended into the next and Rina let herself go, dreamily following his lead. Her eyes slid closed. She let herself drift and simply enjoy. She was so swept up in the feel of his body against hers, the soft beat of the music, she didn't realize the song had ended and they were the only ones still on the dance floor.

He was smiling when she opened her eyes and blinked up at him, felt her face heating up. "You're...umm...a very good dancer," she said lamely.

His gaze held hers. "You look beautiful tonight, Sabrina."

She flushed. She did look good, not really beautiful, but he probably would have said that to whomever he had brought with him. She was saved from a reply when the orchestra began a fast song and they broke apart to start dancing to a different beat. They danced twice more before he led her back to the table.

"You two looked great out there," Sage said, smiling. In an emerald-green gown, her dark hair pulled up in a loosely knotted twist, she looked gorgeous. She nudged her handsome husband with an elbow. "Your turn, big guy."

Jake just smiled. "I hope your toes can stand it."

Sage rolled her eyes. Jake Cantrell could hold his own at just about anything. Rina figured he'd do just fine out there dancing and, as she watched them, saw that he did.

"He's crazy about her," Alex said.

"It goes both ways," Rina said.

Alex's eyes swung to hers. "You never found the right guy?"

She shook her head. "Not so far. I guess you haven't found the right person, either."

"I'm not sure marriage is what I want."

"Ever?"

"I don't know. Hell, most of the time, I feel like I'm still trying to figure things out. Like I'm searching for something, but have no idea what it is. Wouldn't be fair to bring a woman into a situation like that."

Rina made no reply. Alex wasn't the marrying kind. She had known that all along. She had no reason to feel this little pinch in her heart.

He asked her to dance again, and she rose, let him guide her toward the dance floor. They had almost reached it when a familiar figure stepped into their path. Ryan Gosford, her former live-in boyfriend, looked good in his black tuxedo, wavy brown hair neatly groomed.

There was a time she'd been attracted to his good looks and unassuming personality. In the past few months, she had learned that the attraction had only been based on how safe he was. There was never a risk of falling in love with Ryan, never a chance their relationship would deepen into something she couldn't handle.

"Well, well, look who's here?" he said as he stepped into the path they were weaving toward the dance floor.

She ignored the sour note in his voice and managed to smile. "Ryan... It's nice to see you. You remember Alex Justice?" They had met at Sage's wedding. Neither had seemed interested in more than a polite acquaintance.

"How could I forget?" Ryan looked at her with a hint of distaste. "You said you didn't like his type. You thought he was arrogant and overbearing and you had no interest in him at all."

Her face went warm. She could feel Alex's presence behind her, wondered if he were angry or amused to hear what she had said. "I didn't really know him at the time."

"And now you do."

"We're just friends," she said firmly, wishing Ryan would take the hint she was trying to give him and disappear.

"Friends," he scoffed. "I'll just bet you are." He looked past her into Alex's face. "Friends with benefits, right, buddy? I hope she screws you a lot better than she did me."

It happened so fast, she only had time to gasp. One moment, Ryan's face was twisted with righteous disdain, the next, he was doubled over and Alex had an arm over his shoulder and was walking him to a quiet place at the edge of the dance floor.

Oh, my God! Rina's heart thundered as she hurried after them, determined to keep the men from making a scene.

"You had your chance," Alex was saying. "She was yours and you blew it. From now on, you leave her alone or you'll deal with me. You got it?"

Ryan wheezed in a breath, straightened a little and nodded.

Rina stood there frozen, praying no one had seen what had happened. Alex caught Ryan's shoulders, made a point of straightening the lapels of his black tuxedo, turned and walked back to where she stood.

"I think it's time we went home."

She felt a little dizzy, knew her face must be pale and realized she was trembling. "Yes...okay."

They left without saying goodbye, just headed for the car and the trip back to her apartment. She didn't live that far from the country club so it didn't take long to get there.

"I don't know whether I should thank you for what you did, or apologize for what Ryan said."

Alex wheeled his BMW into one of the guest parking spaces. "You mean what *you* said, don't you? That I'm arrogant and overbearing?"

Embarrassment swept through her. "I didn't know you very well at the time."

He sliced her a look. "So I'm not arrogant and overbearing?"

She couldn't stop a grin. "Well, actually you are, but I'm kind of getting used to it."

Alex laughed. "I can't figure out what you ever saw in that guy."

"Well, he *is* good-looking."

"That's it?"

"He's nice. At least he used to be."

"Yeah, that was the problem. You know the old saying, nice guys finish last."

Maybe that was it. Sage had said a number of

times that Rina liked Ryan because he let her walk all over him.

Alex turned off the engine, rounded the car and helped her climb out. All the way to the door, she thought about the good-night kiss he was sure to expect and wished she wasn't looking forward to it so much.

"It's been an interesting evening," she said as they stepped up on the porch. "I have to admit I had fun."

"Even after what happened with good ol' Ryan?"

She smiled because Alex had always called him that. "Even after."

"So did I."

"Thanks for standing up for me."

"You're welcome."

She dug her house key out of her black evening bag and shoved it into the lock. "Good night."

One of his dark blond eyebrows went up. "Aren't you going to invite me in for a nightcap?"

"Well, I... Would you like to come in for a drink?"

"Yes." He reached out and turned the key in the lock, opened the door and they walked inside.

He waited while she silenced the security alarm. When she turned, Alex was right beside her. Before she had time to think, he pulled her into his arms and his mouth came down over hers.

It wasn't the gentle good-night kiss she'd expected, but a hot, wet, plundering kiss that sent her head reeling and set her on fire. His hands slid down to her hips and he drew her solidly against him, into the V between his legs. He was hard, she realized, and the knowledge stirred the desire curling through her, desire she had been fighting since the day she had met him.

Alex deepened the kiss and Rina melted against him,

giving in to the pleasure, losing herself in the moment, as she had always feared she would. Her arms slid up around his neck and she kissed him back, felt the glide of his tongue over hers, felt the hard muscles tighten beneath his crisp black shirt.

"God, I've been wanting to kiss you for hours," he said. She thought he would stop as he always had before, but his lips moved to the side of her neck and his teeth nipped an earlobe. Goose bumps skittered across her skin and her fingers curled around the white satin lapels of his dinner jacket. Moist kisses trailed over her shoulders and along her throat, down to the swell of her breast, and she moaned.

It was time for them to stop. She was sure he would. They were just friends, after all, but instead, she heard the buzz of her zipper, felt the top of her strapless gown fall open.

She gasped at the feel of his mouth on her breast, his tongue circling the pink areola, drawing the hard tip between his teeth.

"Alex...dear God..."

He returned to her mouth, drew her back into another steamy kiss. Her insides were quaking, her breathing ragged.

"It's all right, baby," he said, as if he knew she was about to fall apart. "We'll take it slow and easy." He returned his attention to her breast, nibbling and tasting, making her stomach muscles contract. Her fingers slid into the golden hair at the nape of his neck as he suckled and laved, turned her body liquid and hot. Alex kissed her and kissed her. Deep, drugging, potent kisses that seemed to have no end. Sabrina kissed him back, unable to stop herself, unable to refuse what he was offering. What she had denied herself for so long.

Alex's hands caressed her breasts and her knees went weak. She was trembling. A soft moan escaped from her throat. She might have collapsed onto the floor if he hadn't swept her up in his arms and started down the hall leading to her bedroom.

"We can't...can't do this," she said, but Alex ignored her and deep down she was glad. She wanted this. Wanted him so badly.

He kicked open the bedroom door and carried her inside, stood her on her feet, and his mouth found hers once more. He tasted like champagne and smelled male and sexy, and any reservations she had were rapidly slipping away. Alex finished unzipping her gown and eased it down over her hips till it formed a glittering black pool at her feet.

She wore only a black lace thong and her Jimmy Choo high heels. Unconsciously her hands came up to cover her breasts, but Alex caught her wrists.

"Don't. I want to see you." He tugged her forward, out of the sparkling folds of the dress. Nearly naked, she stood in front of him, his eyes moving over her, burning like the blue tip of a flame.

"Jesus God..." he said, and then he was bending his head to her breasts again, drawing her nipples into his mouth, making them tighten to the point of pain.

"We've got...got to stop," she said, but the heat was building, desire sweeping through her like an onrushing wave. Stopping seemed impossible, and even as she considered it, she was reaching for his jacket, sliding it off his wide shoulders, tugging his tuxedo shirt out of the waistband of his pants.

Bare-chested, his tuxedo pants unbuttoned and riding low on his hips, he was magnificent. In the moonlight streaming in through her bedroom window, all those beautiful muscles she had admired in the desert gleamed, waiting for her to touch them.

She ran her hands over the six-pack ridges on his belly, testing the valleys, the sinews, pressed her mouth against one of the thick pectoral muscles on his chest, felt it bunch against her tongue. A faint trace of yellow remained from the bruises on his ribs. She placed her lips there in a feather-soft kiss, then ringed a flat copper nipple and heard him groan.

His hands slid into her hair. "I need you, Sabrina." Cupping her face, he claimed her lips in another ravaging kiss. "I need you so damned much."

Deep, wet kisses followed. She was breathless and trembling, her hands running all over him, reaching for his zipper, sliding it down.

"Christ," he said. Turning away from her long enough to deal with protection, he reached for her, drew her back into his arms. Sabrina gasped as his fingers curled around the black lace thong. Alex ripped it away, found her soft folds wet and ready and began to stroke her. Another deep kiss and he lifted her up, wrapped her legs around his waist.

"I know I should go slow, but I've waited too long to have you." Rina felt his erection at her core, made a low keening sound as he buried himself to the hilt.

For several long moments, he held himself in check, his forehead bent against hers. "You feel so damned good."

Her eyes burned. "Alex…" She wanted to remember this moment, tuck it away for when this night was over.

Alex began to move, his heavy strokes filling her, deep and penetrating, drawing out the pleasure. He felt thick and hard, his body rock-solid as he moved against her, and heat burned through every cell in her body. Emotion surged through her, and hot, driving need. This was Alex and she had wanted him for so long.

Clinging to his neck, her body responded to the rhythm of his thrusts, the saturating pleasure, and a powerful climax began to build. It hit with hurricane force and rippled like shock waves through her body. She cried out Alex's name, her head falling back, sensation rolling up from deep inside. She hung on, rode through another fierce climax before he allowed himself to reach his own release.

Minutes ticked past and neither of them moved. Limp and sated, Sabrina rested her head against his shoulder, her throat aching and tears burning her eyes. She had never felt anything so wonderful, so intense. She had known Alex would be a skillful lover, but this was far more than that.

She squeezed her eyes shut, blocking the tears and the emotion that pressed down on her chest. Alex's lips moved softly against the top of her head as he carried her over to the bed and settled her in the middle.

She thought he would make some excuse to leave, but he only climbed onto the bed beside her and pulled her into his arms.

She told herself to send him home, that it was too risky to let him stay, but soft heat still hummed through her, remnants of the pleasure they had shared. When he leaned down and kissed her, she reached for him, responding as she always did, and let him sweep her away.

Thirteen

They made love three more times before morning, once in the soft dawn light coming in through the window. Afterward, they fell into a deep, contented sleep. Alex awakened first, looked down at the petite redhead curled against him, and a sweet longing welled inside.

It was new for him, this wanting that wouldn't seem to go away. He wished it were only the sex, but he knew it was more. Knew he felt something for Sabrina he had never felt for a woman before.

She stirred on the bed beside him and her eyes cracked open. In an instant, she was fully awake, shoving herself back against the antique rosewood headboard, pulling the sheet up to cover her pretty breasts.

She stared at him with such a mixture of horror and regret, he wanted to laugh and shake her at the same time. And kiss her and make love to her all over again.

"Oh, my God, Alex, what have we done?"

He shoved himself back until he was propped up beside her, the sheet covering his lap and the hardening in his lower body that seemed out of place at the moment.

"We've done exactly what we wanted to, love. We're mature adults and we've been fighting this for a long time."

"We've...we've ruined our friendship."

One of his eyebrows went up. "Have we?"

"You know it'll never be the same again."

God, he hoped not. He'd suffered enough of wanting and not having. "We'll be fine."

She just shook her head. Reaching down, she grabbed his tuxedo shirt off the floor and pulled it on, slipped out of bed. The shirt came well past her knees and her soft red curls were mussed around her face. She looked adorable.

"I have...I have to go," she said.

His mouth edged up. "In case you've forgotten, this is your house. I'm the one who has to leave."

"Oh. Yes, well, I have some...umm...errands to run. I need to shower and get ready."

He wanted to join her under the fine, warm spray, run his soapy hands all over her sweet little body. He knew better than to push his luck. He started to say he'd leave, but she was already in the bathroom with the door closed. He pulled on his wrinkled black slacks and went in to make coffee, prowled her sunny yellow kitchen looking for something to eat that was more substantial than flax bran or turkey bacon.

He'd make do with what he had. By the time Sabrina came out of the bedroom dressed in navy blue slacks and a no-nonsense white cotton blouse, he had coffee made and turkey bacon set out on the counter next to a jug of orange juice, a carton of Egg Beaters and a loaf of twelve-grain bread.

"Oh. You're still here."

Irritation trickled through him. This was the first time in his life a woman had wanted him out the morning after. "It's Sunday. I'll make us something to eat, then I'll head home."

She bit her lip, glanced away. "I...umm...really have to go."

"Is that so? Where to?"

Her shoulders straightened. "Look, Alex, we both know what's going on here. Last night was a mistake for both of us. It was fun, but it's not going to happen again."

"Why not?"

"Because we just don't fit. You know that as well as I do. By tomorrow you'll be interested in someone else. I'm fine with that—really, I am. I mean, I know the way you are. I knew it before we...before we..."

"Had sex?"

"Yes. But I'm not interested in getting involved in any sort of relationship and neither are you."

He frowned. Those were the kind of words he was usually saying. "Maybe we should let things play out, see where they lead."

She started shaking her head. "It's better if we end things now before they get too complicated."

His temper was building. How could she be talking about complications? About ending things after the incredible night they'd just had? There was no way she was faking all those orgasms. No way in hell.

"You're sure that's the way you want it."

She swallowed, glanced away. "I'm sure."

"Fine." Turning, he strode back to the bedroom to retrieve his shirt and finish getting dressed. By the time he walked back into the kitchen, the food on the counter had all been put away. Hell, he hadn't even had a cup of coffee.

"Thanks for the favor," he said as he walked past.

Sabrina flushed, which made him mad all over again. "Dammit, not that kind of favor. Thanks for going with me last night."

"Oh. You're welcome."

When Sabrina said nothing more, he jerked open the door and stormed out of the apartment.

Women! Who the hell needed them.

But there was one particular female he was afraid he was beginning to need way too much.

Sabrina stood in the kitchen, staring at the place Alex had been. She felt drained and ridiculously depressed. She told herself ending things now was for the best. Neither of them wanted entanglements. Not when it was so completely clear it wouldn't last.

Now that he was gone, there was no need for her to leave. Since she needed to get ready for her meeting with Arturo Hernandez tomorrow night, she sat down at the computer in her study. There was a lot more research that needed to be done on molybdenum. She set to work, but quickly discovered concentrating wasn't that easy.

Not when her mind kept sliding back to Alex and the passionate night they'd shared. She hoped he was right and making love hadn't completely destroyed their friendship. Alex had come to mean a great deal to her, more than she ever should have allowed. She should have controlled the attraction she felt for him, kept things on an even keel.

On the other hand, going to bed with Alex Justice had

been one of the most incredible experiences of her life. There was no way she was going to regret it.

She looked down at the keyboard, at her fingers that sat unmoving on the keys. For the tenth time, she fought to shove thoughts of last night away, along with visions of hot, sweat-slick flesh, burning kisses and a string of orgasms more plentiful than she had believed it was possible to have.

Instead she focused on the business she hoped to start—mining the Sabrina Belle. She looked up *moly* on Google, checking the costs of mining the ore, and its fluctuating value, which was currently thirty-four thousand dollars a ton, but in 2005, had reached a high of over a hundred thousand.

If Uncle Walter was right, the mine could be worth a fortune.

Sunday was a long day and restless night of remembering the night before, so on Monday she decided to give herself a break and go shopping. She would find something new to wear for her dinner with Arturo Hernandez, something that made her look smart and professional yet still feminine and attractive.

Climbing into her blue Toyota Corolla, biting back a wistful sigh that it wasn't her Mercedes convertible and wondering if the mine might one day buy her another one, Sabrina headed for the freeway and the short hop down the 605 to the Galleria.

She had just pulled into traffic, eased over a lane and started to pick up speed when she noticed something odd going on with the steering.

She turned the wheel to adjust the distance between the Toyota and the big 18-wheeler rolling up beside her in the right lane, but her car kept moving in that direction. Her pulse shot up. She cranked the wheel harder, trying to make more of an adjustment, but the Toyota continued at the same angle as before—still drifting into the path of the truck.

She tried to slow, saw a silver Porsche rushing up fast behind her. It all happened in an instant. She heard the truck driver blasting his horn, but the steering wheel no longer controlled the front end of the car. The truck was jammed between two other cars with nowhere to go but on top of her.

The driver of the silver Porsche was talking on his cell phone, oblivious and way too close. The truck was a death sentence. With no other choice, Rina slammed on the brakes. The truck horn blared as the heavy vehicle shot past just inches away, but even with her foot off the brake to lessen the impact, the tailgating Porsche smashed into her with devastating force.

She heard the screech of metal, the crack and shatter of glass. Carried by the car behind, the Toyota slammed into the vehicle in front of her. The wheels of the Toyota skidded over the pavement, the air bags deployed and Rina's head snapped back at a tremendous force that jarred every bone in her body. Then everything went black.

Alex heard the bell ring above the door and looked up to see his sister, Becca, walking into the office. She was wearing jeans and a tank top, her blond hair pulled up in a ponytail. She was grinning as she approached his desk.

"You're in a good mood this afternoon," Alex said. "Where's Ginny?"

She slid into the chair beside him. "Playdate with a friend."

"Why are you grinning?"

"I just heard the gossip. You at the country club Saturday night. Your little tiff with Ryan Gosford. Were you playing white knight again, big brother?"

Irritation trickled through him. "Who the hell told you that?"

"Ilsa Carras. She's on the committee, remember? She was there at the gala that night."

Ilsa was involved in fundraising for cancer research. Since Becca had received the same inheritance from their grandfather Alex had gotten, she was a generous donor.

Which was how she'd met Ilsa, the gossipmonger.

"Apparently Ilsa heard it from Connie Gartner. Connie saw you punch Ryan in the stomach to keep him from harassing his ex-girlfriend, who happened to be your date."

Alex raked a hand through his hair. "I've already taken a ration of crap from Sage and Jake. I'd prefer not to hear it from you."

Rebecca just laughed. "So who is she?"

Alex didn't answer. His attention had shifted, focused on Jake, who had shoved through the front door and was striding toward him with a grim look on his face.

Alex came up out of his chair. "What is it?"

"Rina. She was in a car accident. She's at Houston Memorial Hospital."

The words hit him like a fist in the stomach. "How bad is she?"

"They don't know yet. She's in the emergency room. Sage is with her." The knot in his stomach twisted. "Something happened, Alex. She's asking for you."

"I'm already on my way." Brushing past Jake, he started for the door.

Becca must have sensed his fear and his desperate need to reach her. "I'm going with you," she said as she fell in step beside him. Since he knew that tone of voice, Alex didn't argue.

"I'll meet you there," Jake called after them, heading for his Jeep. Alex shoved open the door and they hurried out to his car. Becca climbed in on the passenger side; Alex slid into the driver's seat and started the engine. His stomach was churning. Worry had his hands sweating on the wheel.

"I have a feeling this is the girl you took to the benefit Saturday night," Becca said.

"That's right."

"The way you're driving, she must really be something."

He slowed because he wouldn't do Sabrina any good if he got pulled over for speeding or was in an accident himself.

"She's a very good friend." He squealed around a corner, shoved the accelerator down again.

"A friend. Yes, I can see that."

He flicked her a sideways glance but made no comment.

"What's her name?"

"Sabrina Eckhart."

"Sage's friend?"

"Yes."

"I thought you said she was a pain in the ass."

"She is a pain in the ass."

"But she's your pain in the ass and she's in trouble, right?"

"Close enough." He just hoped to God she was going to be okay.

Houston Memorial Hospital was in the Medical Center area, not that far away. The complex was a city in itself, with a half-dozen high-rise buildings and thousands of employees. He knew his way to the hospital, having been there a couple of times before. Wheeling into one of the visitor parking spaces, he got out of the car and crossed the lot, Becca beside him, her long legs working to keep pace with his.

As he slammed through the heavy glass doors, acrid hospital smells hit him, but for once didn't slow him down. He strode down the corridor to the emergency room and spotted Sage hurrying toward him.

Alex caught her shoulders. "Is she going to be all right? What do the doctor's say?"

"It was a bad wreck, Alex. The car was totaled, but it could have been a whole lot worse. God must have been riding with her. By some miracle, it looks like she's going to be okay."

Relief made him shaky. He felt his sister's fingers wrap around his arm and was glad she had come with him.

"You okay?" she asked softly.

He took a deep breath, slowly released it. "Just worried, is all." He turned to Sage. "Tell me what happened."

"I don't know the whole story. I know the wreck occurred on the 605 Freeway southbound not far from her apartment. Rina said she was on her way to the Galleria, but that's about all I got."

"Jake said she was asking for me."

"That's right. She's awake. She's battered and bruised. She's got whiplash from being rear-ended, but the air bags did their job and she doesn't have any broken bones.

They did X-rays to see if there were any chest injuries from the bag, but everything looks okay. They're keeping her overnight for observation."

"That's it?"

"She asked me not to call her mom. She doesn't want Florence driving all the way down here from Uvalde again."

"I'll go get her, fly her down."

Sage laid a hand on his shoulder. "Let's wait, Alex, see what Rina wants to do."

He nodded. He wanted to see her. He'd waited long enough. "Where is she?"

"One of the emergency bays. They made me leave. I don't know if they'll let you see her or not."

He thought of the fat donation he had made to the new hospital wing they were building. "Oh, they'll let me see her." Leaving his sister with Sage, he went in search of Sabrina, prepared to call the head of the hospital if he had to.

He lucked out and saw a familiar face, a little black-haired nurse named Heather who had treated Joe McCauley after a run-in with a skill saw.

Alex flashed her a smile that showed his dimples, explained he needed to see one of his clients, a patient named Sabrina Eckhart, and Heather personally led him over to the curtained enclosure.

He braced himself as she drew the curtain aside. Sabrina was lying on a narrow hospital bed, her neck immobilized by a brace, her face scratched and her lip split. Her eyes were closed and seeing her lying there as pale as the sheet, for a moment, he couldn't breathe.

As he approached the bed, her eyelids flickered, then her eyes slowly opened.

Alex forced himself to smile. "Hey, Red."

"You came…"

"Of course, I came."

"I thought you might still be mad at me."

"I am mad at you. You tossed me out without my morning coffee. But that wouldn't keep me away. How're you feeling?"

Her mouth edged up. She had a bruise on her cheek and one on her jaw, myriad cuts and abrasions. "Exactly like I look. Rotten."

He reached over and caught her hand, gave it a gentle squeeze. "You look beautiful."

She glanced away, unconsciously reached up to touch her neck brace. "Alex…something happened out there."

"Yeah, I can see that."

"I mean something like before…with the helicopter."

His hold tightened on her hand. "What are you talking about?"

"The car…I couldn't control it. There was something wrong with the steering wheel." She looked up at him with those big blue eyes. "I think you were right, Alex. I think someone wants the mine."

He made himself argue, though the hair was rising at the back of his neck. "They arrested the guy who sabotaged the chopper. It had nothing to do with either one of us."

"I think it did."

He looked at her and willed her to be wrong, but his instincts had warned him the first time, and now it was happening again. Two near-fatal accidents in less than a month. He had never believed in coincidence and he didn't believe in it now.

"You feeling well enough to tell me the details of what happened?"

She moistened her lips, which were swollen and cracked. "I want to, Alex, while it's fresh in my mind."

For the next few minutes she went over the accident, explaining how all of a sudden the car wouldn't respond, how the front wheel pulled her into the right lane almost beneath the wheels of an onrushing 18-wheeler, how she had stepped on the brake in order to stop the momentum, knowing the car behind would hit her but that it was her only chance.

He thought of what could have happened, imagined her small body crushed and mangled inside the little Toyota, and his mouth went dry.

"I'll find out what went wrong with the car. I don't want you to worry, okay? Right now, the most important thing is for you to get well. Once you're out of here, we'll go through everything step-by-step. We'll figure all of this out, make sure nothing else goes wrong. There won't be any more accidents, Sabrina—I promise you that."

Because the minute she walked out of the hospital until they knew what the hell was going on, Sabrina wouldn't be leaving his side. She might not like it, but that was the way it was going to be.

"You just get well," he said, reaching out to gently touch her cheek. "I'll be here when the doctors say it's okay for you to leave."

She seemed to relax, gave him a weary smile. "Thank you."

"No problem." She was thanking him now. He was pretty sure she wouldn't be thanking him when she found out what he planned to do.

She didn't want things to get complicated between them. Well, they were damn well complicated now.

Fourteen

The curtain swished closed and Sabrina relaxed against the pillow. Alex had come. Everything was going to be okay.

She heard voices outside. The curtain opened again and Jake walked in, all six-foot-five, two-hundred-thirty-plus pounds of mule, accompanied by Sage and a beautiful willowy blonde. For an instant, she thought it was one of the gorgeous models Alex was known to date and her chest clamped down.

"Rina, this is Alex's sister, Rebecca," Sage said.

His sister. Thank God.

"Hello, Sabrina. I know this isn't the best time for us to meet, but I wanted you to know how worried my brother is about you, and how glad we both are you're going to be okay."

"Thank you."

Jake reached down and gently touched her shoulder. "Hey, sweetcheeks, how're you doing?"

She managed a smile but it made her swollen lip hurt. "I knew I shouldn't have sold my Mercedes."

Jake smiled back but she could tell he was worried.

Sage reached over and squeezed her hand. "They want us to leave and Alex's outside waiting for Becca. We're going to say goodbye for now."

"Would you do me a favor?"

"Of course. Anything."

"I'm supposed to have a meeting with Arturo Hernandez, the mining engineer from Presidio. Can you call him, tell him I'll need to reschedule? His card's in my purse…if you can find it."

"I'll track him down one way or another and let him know what's happened. You don't need to worry."

"Thanks."

"They'll be moving you into a private room in a little while. I'll come back tonight during visiting hours."

"You don't have to do that. I'm getting out tomorrow."

"I know. Alex is going to pick you up."

"He is?" He'd said he would be there when she was released. She didn't expect him to drive her home. She started to say so, but Sage and the small group were already leaving.

"I'll see you tonight," Sage said, and then they were gone.

Rina closed her eyes, exhaustion sweeping over her. She wished she were home; she was just so tired. She would be back in her own place tomorrow if they didn't find anything wrong.

Alex planned to drive her there. He believed her. He was worried she might be in danger. Together they would figure things out.

It was possible she was wrong, and the whole thing was just another of life's little misfortunes, but she didn't think so. Alex would find out for sure.

As she drifted to sleep, she wondered what Uncle Walter would say if he knew his good intentions had turned her life upside down.

Alex dropped Becca off at her white Suburban in the parking lot at Atlas Security, then went inside.

"How's Rina?" Annie asked, clearly worried, by now probably knowing more about what had happened than he did. The woman knew everything that went on in the office. Hell, she knew just about everything that went on in the entire city of Houston.

"She's gonna be okay. They're keeping her overnight for observation."

"That's the second time this month," Annie said. "Little gal's sure having a string of bad luck."

"Maybe." Leaving Annie to ponder the remark, he headed for Trace's glass-enclosed office. Ben Slocum stopped him along the way.

"I heard about Rina. She okay?" Ben had met her at Sage and Jake's wedding. Looked like half of Houston was worried about her.

"Yeah, considering. She'll be out of the hospital tomorrow."

"Glad to hear it," Ben said. "Tell her we're all thinking about her."

"Will do." Alex started walking, waved at Sol, sitting at the computer in the office next to Trace's, and went inside to see his boss.

"I just heard," Trace said. The lanky Texan came out of his chair. "Rina gonna be all right?"

"Looks like. She's got whiplash and she's beat all to hell, but they're releasing her tomorrow, if nothing worse crops up."

"That's good news."

"It may not have been an accident, Trace. Sabrina doesn't think so." He filled his friend in on the wreck as briefly as possible, telling him about the way the steering had malfunctioned and how she'd ended up in a rear-end collision crushed between two cars.

"Sounds like she's lucky to be alive," Trace said when Alex finished.

"Damned lucky. I need to have the car gone over, find out what happened. See if it could have been made to malfunction on purpose."

"Son of a bitch, you're thinking this may be connected to the helicopter crash."

"Sabrina thinks so and I'm more than half-convinced myself. That property she inherited may be worth a ton of money. If it is, someone might figure it's worth killing for."

"Any idea who that someone might be?"

"Couple of ideas. Not ready to say just yet. I need to know what happened to her car, but the hell of it is, if I have some mechanic go over it, any evidence, any fingerprints or DNA will be destroyed. You've got that friend in the department, that homicide detective... Sayers?"

"Mark Sayers, yeah."

"I was hoping you could convince him to have his forensic guys take a look. If the steering was tampered with, it's attempted murder. That makes the case fall under his jurisdiction."

"I'll talk to him, see what he can find out."

Jake walked into the office. "What the hell's going on?" Trace and Alex both looked up at him. "This is the second time Rina's been in the hospital in a little over three weeks."

Alex's jaw hardened. "You can believe it isn't going to happen again."

Jake looked relieved. "Why don't you tell me what, for chrissake, is happening to my wife's best friend."

Alex and Trace exchanged glances and Alex launched into the details of the wreck once more.

"You stupid bastard. That's twice you've screwed things up since we started this."

"Look, I hired a specialist to take care of the chopper. It went down just the way he planned. Not his fault if the guy she was with was some kind of superpilot. The chopper went down like a stone and blew sky-high. All of this should be over."

"But it isn't."

"No, but they arrested some yokel for it. That'll keep them from digging any deeper. Guy hasn't got a pot to piss in so he can't afford some fancy lawyer to get his ass out of jail."

"What about the car wreck? That wasn't a great idea to begin with. There was no way to control where she'd be when the steering went south."

"You said it had to look like an accident. A car wreck would have been perfect."

"Yes, if it had worked." A slow, disgusted breath blew over the phone. "Her mother says she's going to pick up where the old man left off and find a way to mine the ore. She's all excited about it."

"The hell you say. She think she's a man, or what?"

"She was always a little too big for her britches, even when she was a kid."

"Yeah," Henry said. "Thought she was better than the rest of us just because she got good grades. Got Walter to help her get through college, went off to study in some la-de-da place in France."

"And conned Walter into leaving her the mine."

"Conniving little bitch."

"Don't worry, she isn't going to get it."

"How do we stop her?" Henry asked.

"I'll give it some thought and let you know what I come up with. Whatever it takes, little Rina will soon be out of the picture—for good."

Henry grinned as dollar signs flashed in his head. He lifted his whiskey glass in salute and shot the contents down his throat.

Rebecca heard pounding in the kitchen downstairs where the remodel was being done, followed by an unintelligible, softly muttered curse, then her daughter's childish giggles.

"You think that's funny?" Joe said. "You think me hitting my thumb is funny?"

"Yes." Ginny giggled again.

"How about I take this hammer and pound on *your* thumb?" Joe teased, eliciting a peal of laughter. Clearly, Ginny wasn't afraid of Joe.

Smiling, Rebecca descended the last few stairs and rounded the corner into the torn-up kitchen. The new window was in, Joe was putting up drywall, getting ready to tape and texture the area he'd expanded.

"What's going on, you two?"

Ginny grinned, exposing the hole where one of her bottom teeth was missing. "Joe pounded his thumb instead of the nail."

"Your kid's got a warped sense of humor," Joe said, dramatically sucking his thumb.

Ginny laughed. "Can I hammer something, Joe? Please?"

Joe's gaze swung to Rebecca. "Okay, Mom?" He was dressed in jeans and a short-sleeved navy blue T-shirt that stretched across his heavily muscled shoulders and barrel chest. Thick biceps bulged beneath the sleeve of the shirt. There was a streak of pale skin across his forehead where the bill cap he usually wore kept the sun from tanning a portion of his face.

He wasn't handsome in the way her ex-husband, Jeremy, had been, but in a rugged sort of way, he was amazingly attractive.

"Please, Mom," Ginny pleaded.

"I guess it's all right."

Joe took a board and hammered a couple of nails into it about halfway. "Take this over there in the corner and pound the nails in the rest of the way." He handed her a tack hammer, far smaller than the heavy hammer he was using. "It'll be good practice for when you grow up and need to fix something."

Ginny grinned, grabbed the board and took the hammer, hurried over and plopped down in the corner. Wild pounding filled the air and Rebecca's smile slid away. Her daughter was already a tomboy. Rebecca did her best to keep her in dresses when Ginny wanted to wear faded jeans and T-shirts, bought her dolls instead of the Lego building set she had wanted for her birthday. Ginny didn't need the influence of a rough man like Joe.

He was hammering again and now so was Ginny, the racket so loud Rebecca could barely think. Joe didn't seem to notice. Rebecca let the racket continue a moment more, then headed for the corner.

"That's enough, honey. Joe's busy." She knelt in front of her daughter. "Why don't you go upstairs and play with Pearl?" Pearl was the baby doll Rebecca had bought her last Christmas. She nursed and drank and wet her diaper just like a real baby. Ginny had played with her for about an hour.

She gave the nail another fierce whack. "I'd rather stay here and hammer with Joe."

Rebecca cast a sharp glance at the brawny man engrossed in nailing up a sheet of wallboard. "Could I speak to you a minute?"

Joe shrugged his thick shoulders, set his hammer on the counter. "Sure."

Rebecca walked out of the kitchen and Joe followed.

"Look, Joe, I don't mean to be an overprotective mother, but Ginny's a little girl, and I don't think it's good for her to be pushed into behaving like a boy."

"It's just a phase she's going through. She's interested in boy stuff right now. I'm sure that'll change. Who knows, maybe she's just interested because she doesn't have a dad around anymore."

The words stiffened Rebecca's spine. "She doesn't need a dad...she has a mother. We do just fine on our own."

Joe made no reply, just looked at her with a trace of pity.

"Fine," Rebecca relented. "I'll let her play down here awhile. But I still think it's better if she sticks with little girl toys."

"I'll make sure she doesn't stay too long."

"Thank you." Rebecca left the kitchen and went back

upstairs to finish the thank-you notes she had been writing. Her shoulders slumped as she sat down at the small writing desk in the corner of her bedroom. What was it about Joe that always made her seem waspish and a bit of a snob?

She wasn't attracted to him. Well, maybe a little. Well, more than a little, but only because Joe looked at her as if she were a pretty, desirable woman. And though she knew she was attractive, it had been a long time since she had allowed herself to respond to any of those kinds of looks from the opposite sex.

She didn't like big, rough men, she told herself. She preferred a man with polish, a man like— Rebecca broke the thought. She didn't want a man like her ex-husband, Jeremy, who was handsome and sophisticated on the surface but underneath the polish, dictatorial, vicious, even physically abusive.

Joe might be different than the men she was used to in Connecticut, but she didn't think he would ever hurt her or Ginny.

That was all that mattered. Besides, as soon as the kitchen was finished, Joe would be gone.

Fifteen

It took almost two hours to get the paperwork completed and Sabrina released from the hospital. Alex waited patiently through it all, anxious to get her home and settled.

His home, that was, where she would be safe.

She was sitting in the passenger seat of his BMW, a thick white padded brace around her neck, her cuts and bruises more purple and pronounced than they had been yesterday. Alex drove more slowly than he usually did, determined not to jostle her battered body and make her feel worse.

"There're a couple of things we need to talk about," he said as he headed toward her uptown apartment.

Sabrina turned a little in her seat so she could look at him. "You want to see a copy of Uncle Walter's will."

"For starters, yes."

"I'll have to run it down. It should be filed with the rest of my legal papers, diplomas, my birth certificate, things like that."

"Should be interesting to see if you're right about the survivorship clause."

"I'm pretty sure there's something like that. I don't know if that's the legal term. If I die, the property goes to someone else. Walter's children, I think. It would make the most sense."

"How many did you say he had?"

"Three. Robert, George and Priscilla."

Alex turned west onto San Felipe and merged into traffic. "There's something else," he said, wanting to get this out of the way before he reached her apartment and she had time to dig in her heels. "You aren't going to like it."

She caught his gaze in the mirror. "What is it?"

"Until we know what's going on, I want you to stay with me."

She frowned. "Stay with you? Where? At your house? Don't be ridiculous. I can't do that."

"I'd stay at your place, but you don't have enough room, you don't have the best security and you're too easy to find. My house is better equipped to handle the two of us and no one will know you're there."

"That's crazy. I'm staying at my house and you're going home."

"That isn't going to happen, Sabrina. I'll get Sage and Jake—hell, I'll call your mother if that's what it takes to convince you. You're going somewhere safe until we sort this out. That someplace is my house."

"I can't believe this. You would actually call my mother?"

"You bet I would. If you're right about the car—and you very well could be—someone wants you dead. I'm not letting that happen." He sliced her a sideways glance, saw uncertainty creep into her features.

"Having a houseguest is a lot of trouble," she hedged.

He smiled. "You won't take up much room."

Sabrina rubbed her forehead, looked back at him in the mirror. "Are you sure, Alex?"

"I've got plenty of space. I don't expect you to spend the night in my bed unless you want to."

"Oh. Well…"

"I've got a pool. It's very private. No one will bother you."

She ran her tongue over her split, puffy lip. "I like to swim. It's very good exercise."

"Then it's settled." And with less haranguing than he'd figured. But then she didn't have her usual energy— she was just recovering from a near-fatal car crash. His jaw tightened as he pulled up in front of her apartment.

"We'll go in and pack what you need. Take a look at the will, then I'll take you home and get you settled." He rounded the car and opened her door. She was shaky on her feet as he helped her climb out of the car.

"If you aren't feeling up to it, I can take you straight to the house and come back with Sage to get your things."

"I'm okay. Besides, I've got to get the will."

He didn't argue. He needed to find out who would benefit by Sabrina's death.

"You don't have a will of your own?" he asked as they stepped into the entry, not wanting to overlook the obvious, that the beneficiary of Sabrina's will might be the person arranging her "accidents." Assuming any of his suspicions were real.

"I suppose I need one, but no. If something happens to me, my mom's the beneficiary on my life insurance policy, which isn't very big, and she also signs on my bank accounts."

He didn't see her mother as a suspect, at least not

at the moment. And from what he'd learned, after the stock market tanked, there wasn't much money left in Sabrina's bank accounts, anyway.

The first thing they did when they got inside the apartment was look for the will. It was right where she'd thought, filed in a small fireproof safe in her study along with the rest of her important papers.

On the third page, he found the clause she'd remembered. If Sabrina died within two years after receiving the inheritance from her uncle and no significant improvements had been made to the property, it went to Walter's three children, Robert, George and Priscilla. Should that happen, a monthly payment was to go to Florence Eckhart for life from the profits of the mine or proceeds of sale from the property.

"You were right," Alex said. "If you die, his kids get the land and your mom gets a monthly stipend for the rest of her life."

"Walter was my dad's older brother. He and my father were close. After Dad died, Walter and Mom stayed in touch as much as possible. He would have trusted me to take care of her from whatever he gave me, but he'd want to make sure she got enough to live on if his kids got the property."

"None of his kids tried to contest the will?"

"Robert did some grumbling about it, but it never went any further than that." She took the document out of his hand, flipped back a couple of pages. "Walter left his children whatever money he had in the bank. If I remember, it came to about fifty thousand. Besides the property, that was all he had left in the world."

She showed him the page. "There's a clause here that says if any person named in the will contests it, that person receives nothing. I guess my cousins didn't want to lose their portion of the money he left them. As far as they were concerned, going to court for what they considered a hunk of worthless desert wasn't worth it. Or at least that's what I figured at the time."

"Or they figured there was a better way to get hold of the land—a way that insured they couldn't lose it in a court battle. They could just get rid of you."

Sabrina started shaking her head. "We're cousins. We grew up together in Uvalde. We were never close, but I can't imagine any of them trying to kill me."

"Twenty million can do funny things to people."

"How would they even know about the mine? I'm sure Walter never told them."

"You said he was convinced there was silver on the land. You think his kids didn't believe him but that might have changed."

She didn't try to argue and he could see she was really getting tired. "I'll make a copy of the will while you pack. I think it's past time we got you home and settled."

Sabrina nodded and headed for her bedroom. He tried not to let his mind wander back to what had happened in that room the last time he'd been in her apartment, but his brain refused to obey. A memory of hot, steamy sex popped into his head and he started getting hard.

Alex cursed.

He wasn't sure what it was about this particular lady that sent him into caveman mode, but it seemed to happen fairly often. Focusing his attention on the will, he walked over to Sabrina's printer and scanned a copy, then returned the recorded document to the fireproof safe.

It took twenty more minutes for Sabrina to pack a

bag, grab her laptop and ask the neighbor, Mrs. Ren-hurst, to water her plants and pick up the morning paper while she was away on an extended trip.

He'd cautioned her not to tell anyone, not even her neighbor, where she was going. Since the last person she remembered talking to about their trip to Rio Gordo be-fore the helicopter crash was her mother, he didn't want even her mom to know.

But that was an argument they'd have later. Right now he just wanted to get her home and settled and take the exhausted look off her face.

From Rina's apartment, Alex drove down San Fe-lipe and turned into a quiet, shady neighborhood in River Oaks. He pulled into a garage attached to a white, single-family residence, not a condo as Rina might have guessed since he was a bachelor.

She waited while he unlocked the door from the ga-rage into the utility room, then came back to help her out of the car. Slinging the strap of her handbag, retrieved from the wreck, over her shoulder, she took his arm as she climbed the two steps into the house.

The kitchen was very upscale, with ultramodern white appliances, lovely honey-colored wood cabinets, and white-and-gold granite countertops. As they moved through the dining room into the living room, she saw it was surprisingly traditional, with a brass chandelier in the entry suspended over white-and-gold marble floors.

The colors in the living room were masculine: cream, brown and gold. The dark brown sofa looked comfort-able. The throw pillows on top matched the chairs be-side it, which were done in a striped fabric of the same gold, cream and brown and appeared to be expensive designer pieces.

The fireplace had a warm maplewood hearth. A gold silkscreen with a slightly Asian flair ran along one wall. The results were sophisticated and expensive. Masculine with class and style.

Sabrina turned to find Alex standing behind her. "It's beautiful, Alex."

He smiled. "If you're going to ask if I did it myself, the answer is no. My sister has a pretty good flair for design, but she wasn't living in Houston when I bought the house."

"Whoever did it did a wonderful job." There was an unspoken question in the remark. *Who was responsible? One of your many female conquests?* But Alex left the question unanswered.

"The family room is more casual," he said. "I spend most of my time in there."

"I'd love to see it."

His eyes ran over her face. "You're looking a little pale. How about a nap then I'll give you a tour?"

A nap sounded wonderful. She realized she had been running on adrenaline and determination since she'd left the hospital. "That might be a good idea."

"Your bedroom's upstairs. I can carry you if your legs are still shaky."

"I'm fine." But as she started up the stairs, her legs began to tremble and Alex carefully scooped her up in his arms.

"I'm not hurting your neck?" he asked as he effortlessly made his way to the top.

"No." But she was suddenly breathless just the same. Since the night they'd made love, she'd thought of him a hundred times, remembered the way his body felt on top of her, inside her, remembered those hard, beautiful muscles that were moving and bunching even now as he carted her down the hall and into in a bedroom done in soft shades of cream and blue.

She glanced around as he set her on the bed. The furniture was expensive, a mahogany four-poster and matching dresser and nightstands, a pale blue silk comforter on the bed. "Whoever she was, she had exquisite taste."

"That was the reason I hired her."

She flicked him a glance. "Not because you wanted to take her to bed?"

He grinned unrepentantly. "That, too, but it was a long time ago."

Sabrina just shook her head. Alex settled her on top of the bed and busied himself removing her sneakers, fluffing the pillows and easing them behind her head, tossing a blanket over her legs.

"I'll get your stuff out of the car and be right back," he said.

Sabrina nodded and relaxed against the pillows. Her eyes felt heavy and she was drifting on the edge of sleep when her cell phone started chiming. Alex had left her purse on the nightstand. She reached for it, dug out her phone and pressed it against her ear. "Hello?"

"Sabrina. This is Arturo. Your friend, Mrs. Cantrell, telephoned yesterday to tell me about the accident. I phoned the hospital this morning, but they said you had already been released. I am so sorry to hear you were injured. I hope you are feeling better."

"Much better, thank you. I appreciate your call, Arturo. We'll need to reschedule—"

With a low curse, Alex dropped her overnight bag, stormed across the room and took the phone out of her hand.

"Ms. Eckhart isn't feeling well enough to talk," Alex said darkly. "She'll have to call you back."

"What are you doing?" Rina demanded. "Arturo and I were involved in a business conversation!" But Alex had already broken the connection.

"No more phone calls. There's a GPS tracking device inside your cell." He pulled out the battery, opened the drawer in the nightstand and dumped the phone and the battery inside. "I'll buy you a disposable at the grocery store then there won't be any way to track you here."

"Don't you think you're being a little paranoid?"

"You're the one who told me you thought your accident wasn't an accident."

She reached up to adjust the uncomfortable collar. "Maybe I was wrong."

Alex tugged her suitcase over and set it up on the dresser. "Why don't we wait and see what the cops find out."

Rina didn't say more, just leaned back against the pillow and closed her eyes, let the exhaustion she was feeling sweep over her.

She didn't hear Alex leave. She had already fallen asleep.

Alex watched her a moment, then quietly left the bedroom. She was sleeping hard, her body trying to recover from the trauma it had undergone. He got to the bottom of the stairs before his iPhone started to ring.

Alex pulled the phone out of his pocket, recognized

the caller ID as belonging to Trace and pressed the phone against his ear. "Hey, buddy, you got something for me?"

"Mark Sayers just called. He says the bolt came off the steering rod. No prints, nothing to say for sure whether it happened by accident or if someone loosened the bolt enough it would eventually work its way off the rod."

Another nonanswer.

"It's a fairly rare occurrence," Trace continued. "Which puts my thinking on the same track as yours."

"Even with the guy in jail for the helo crash, my instincts are telling me there's more happening here than coincidence. I'd rather err on the side of caution and find out if there's someone who wants Sabrina dead."

"You any closer to figuring that out?"

"Maybe. According to her uncle's will, if she dies within two years after she inherits, her three cousins get the property. I've got their names. I may need some help from Sol but I want to dig up a little preliminary information first."

"You got her stashed somewhere safe?"

He didn't hesitate. Trace was a man he trusted with his life—and Sabrina's. "My house. I don't know how long I can convince her to stay without having to lock her up and toss the key, but it gives me a little time."

Trace chuckled. "Sounds as hardheaded as my wife." Alex didn't miss the affection in Trace's voice. "Let me know if there's anything else you need."

"Will do. Thanks, buddy."

The phone went dead.

Since Sabrina was sleeping, he headed for his study, sat down at his desk and turned on his computer. He needed to find out as much as he could about Robert,

George and Priscilla Eckhart. If he turned up anything that looked interesting, he would hand it over to Sol to dig deeper.

Alex set to work.

Sixteen

⟋⟍⟋⟍

Dressed in a clean, lightweight yellow sweatsuit, her hair still damp from the shower she had so desperately needed, Rina walked out of the bathroom next door to the guest bedroom, her neck brace once more in place.

She'd awakened half an hour ago, a little disoriented at first, then remembering that Alex had brought her home with him. After the night of the benefit when she had given in to her weakness and allowed him into her bed, staying in his house was the last thing she wanted. But she wasn't a fool and Alex was right. Until she knew for sure the car accident had been just that, she needed to stay somewhere safe.

Feeling better than she had since the wreck, she wandered downstairs. There was no one in the living room or kitchen.

Continuing down the hall, she found Alex working at the computer in his study. He looked up as she walked in and flashed one of his winning smiles. Rina ignored a little flutter in her stomach when his dimples appeared.

"You look better," he said. "Not so pale."

"The nap helped and the shower felt great. I hope that was okay."

"I invited you here. As long as you stay, it's your home, too."

She arched a russet eyebrow. "Invited? More like demanded."

His smile flashed again. "Demanded in your best interest."

"I suppose." She wandered closer, looked over his shoulder. "What are you doing?"

"Just a little preliminary checking on your cousins. I realize you don't want to believe they have anything to do with the bad luck you've been having, but…"

"But what?"

"Well, let's take your cousin George. He's a high school dropout, moved to San Antonio and took up welding. He makes a decent living but he's got three kids and a wife to support."

"That doesn't make him guilty of attempted murder."

"No, but he could definitely use the money."

"Who couldn't? Oh, that's right, you already have more than you need."

He ignored the remark. "Then there's Priscilla. She still lives in Uvalde. She's had two husbands and she's single again. She's got a couple of kids and she's been picked up twice for drunk driving."

"A person would have to have money to hire someone to sabotage a helicopter or disable the steering on a car. Priscilla's a waitress."

"When enough money's involved, deals can be made. That being said, let's take a look at Robert. Robert lives here in Houston. He owns a company called R. T. Eckhart Development. Before the real estate bubble collapsed, he was extremely successful. He had a big name in construction, built subdivisions and commercial buildings. Now half his properties are in foreclosure and the construction business is on its ass."

"I haven't seen Bob in a couple of years, but he's smart and he could probably figure a way to hire someone to do it. But...I don't know...I just can't imagine him being that ruthless. Or any of the others, for that matter." And she hated the idea that maybe Alex was right and one of them had enticed someone to do the dirty work for a share of the profits. Profits that at this point still had not been confirmed.

Feeling another shot of weariness, she sank down in the chair next to Alex's desk. "The more I think about it, the more I think maybe I was wrong. They arrested that man in Rio Gordo. They said he was a disgruntled employee."

"One of your cousins could have hired him."

"Then hired someone else to sabotage my car?"

"I don't know, maybe. I just know I don't like the way this lines up. Stay here a few days and give me a chance to see what I can come up with."

She didn't want to. She didn't trust herself where Alex was concerned. Tonight she'd be sleeping in a room just down the hall from his. She'd be remembering what it was like making love with him, fighting not to give in to temptation and join him in bed.

She couldn't do that. She couldn't risk getting more deeply involved with him. Couldn't risk falling in love with him. And after the time they'd spent in the desert, after finding out he was a far better man than she had believed, it was a very possible risk.

"Just a few days," he repeated. "If it looks like it's all just coincidence, you can go home."

She thought of the sleepless nights, the hours she'd be spending in his company. Then she remembered how terrified she had been when the chopper went down. How scared she'd been when the eighteen-wheeler nearly crushed her little Toyota beneath its heavy wheels. She remembered the sound of grinding metal and shattering glass. Remembered how close she had come to dying.

Rina closed her eyes, took a deep breath and gathered her resolve. "Fine," she said. "I'll stay."

Sabrina still tired easily. For the next two days, Alex didn't press her to do more than nap and relax on the sofa in the family room. The first night he'd ordered pizza. Last night, he'd called out for Chinese. She had eaten a little better, finishing her egg drop soup and some of the chop suey, but she'd pretty much ignored everything else and gone to bed early.

Alex had stayed up late, trying to tire himself out enough to sleep. With Sabrina just down the hall, the nights were torture.

He'd had a weight room installed in the downstairs bedroom. Yesterday, he'd gone in for a lengthy workout, hit the punching bag until his shoulders ached, worked on the Tai Chi he practiced with a trainer whenever he got the chance, then watched the late, late show before heading up to bed.

Even so, he spent a restless night filled with erotic dreams: heated images of making love to Sabrina. In the morning, he'd awakened with a raging hard-on, swore an oath at women in general and especially the one down the hall, pulled on his swim trunks and headed outside

to the pool. He did laps for half an hour before returning upstairs to shower and dress for the day.

He was grumpy when Sabrina joined him downstairs
in the kitchen. "Sleep okay?" he said a little snidely as
he took in the faint smudges beneath her eyes and her
soft, sleep-rumpled red curls and thought of how soundly
she would have slept if she'd invited him into her bed.

"I don't sleep well in strange places," she said, which
could have been true, but he preferred to think she'd suffered the same fate he had.

As she padded over to the coffeemaker sitting on the
counter and poured coffee into the cup he'd set out for
her, he tried not to notice her small bare feet, the pretty
little toes with their frosted pink polish, the bare legs
that disappeared beneath the hem of her short pink robe,
but a twinge of desire slipped through him.

"I need to go into the office for a while," he said. "You
be all right here if I leave you alone?"

"Of course." She took a sip of coffee, made a little
sighing sound in her throat that made him think of sex
and grit his teeth.

"There's cereal in the pantry, eggs and milk in the
fridge. I'll be back in a couple of hours."

He showed her how to set the alarm after he left then
headed into work, taking the printouts on her cousins
he had made off the computer last night.

Annie was behind the front desk when he stepped
through the door. "You got a call from that sheriff up in
Rio Gordo," she said. "He wants you to call him back."

He took the message Annie handed him. "Thanks."

"You takin' good care of our girl?"

"I'm doing my best." He started walking again.

"You know that property she inherited?"

He stopped and turned. "What about it?"

"You don't think someone's trying to kill her to get it? Stuff like that happens, you know."

Alex smiled. "I think you missed your calling, Annie. Maybe you should have been a P.I."

She grinned. "Maybe so. Think about what I said."

"Oh, I will." He sat down at his desk and phoned the Rio Gordo sheriff's office. One of the deputies put him through to Sheriff Dickens.

"I got your message," Alex said. "What's going on?"

"Got some bad news," Dickens said. "We released Martin Gilroy this morning. Turns out he's got an alibi for the night before the crash."

"You said he was caught on video."

"He was, but that was during the day and he was in a different part of the airport. Gilroy was doing some cleanup work for Mesquite Aviation. He was working with a couple of other guys who swear he never went near the chopper that day."

"Maybe he went back that night."

"Yeah, that's what we figured. Turns out, he was sleepin' with some married gal who finally came forward. Took some punches from her old man over it. He's a long-haul trucker, out of town all week. Gal says Martin was with her all that night."

"You believe her?"

"You'd see her face, you believe she was tellin' the truth. She knew what her husband would do. Says he's the reason she didn't come forward in the first place."

Alex softly cursed. "Which puts us right back to square one."

"That's about it. I'll keep you posted if something else comes up."

"Thanks."

They were back where they'd started. Only now it was possible the same man who had fouled the engine on the chopper had plenty of time to return to Houston and destroy the steering on Sabrina's car. He would have had the mechanical know-how, and if the money was good enough, the motive.

Alex picked up the printouts and headed into Sol's office. Seated behind his desk, the kid took off his dark brown horn-rimmed glasses and set them next to his computer, raked a hand through his too-long hair.

"What can I do for you, Peaceman?" Alex's navy call sign. *Justice of the Peace.* Pilots always came up with some crazy name to call each other. Sol had stumbled across the information on the internet, nosing around where he shouldn't have been the way he usually did. Aside from Joe McCauley, Sol was the only one who called him that anymore.

"I need some info, Sol." Alex set the printouts down on the kid's desk. "Robert Eckhart, his brother, George, and his sister, Priscilla. They're Sabrina's cousins. If something happens to her, they're next in line for the property she inherited."

Sol picked up his glasses and shoved them up on his nose. "Two accidents, both of which could have been fatal. Could be she's got a problem. I'll check it out."

"Thanks, kid." Alex left the office. It was past time they talked to Sabrina's mother, found out who she'd told about the trip her daughter planned to take to Rio Gordo.

He hadn't told Sabrina the cops had come up with nothing conclusive on the car. He hadn't wanted her to use that as an excuse to leave. He'd have to come clean today—at the same time he told her whoever had destroyed the chopper could have taken out the steering on her car.

He wasn't looking forward to the conversation.

It was the middle of the afternoon by the time Alex got home. He wandered through the house looking for Sabrina, but she wasn't in the kitchen or the family room. He started toward the stairs, then spotted her through the sliding glass doors, floating on a blow-up mattress in the swimming pool. Her neck brace was gone, her fiery, chin-length curls wet and gleaming. A pair of sunglasses shaded her eyes, and all she was wearing was a little yellow string bikini.

His groin tightened. He wanted to pull those strings and toss the suit, take a long, slow look at what was underneath, lick the wetness off her skin. He wanted to hear the water lapping against their bodies as he took her right there in the pool.

He inhaled a deep, calming breath. Instead of going outside, stripping naked and joining her in the water, he went upstairs, changed into his swimsuit and shoved on a pair of wraparound shades.

Take it easy, he told himself as he returned downstairs and slid open the sliding glass door leading out to the terrace. *She's probably still hurting.*

She looked up as he approached. He couldn't see her eyes behind her sunglasses, but he could almost feel her gaze sliding over his chest before she smiled. He pulled off the wraparounds, tossed them onto a table beside the pool and dived into the water.

The sun had done its job and the pool was bathtub-warm. He scissor-kicked up from the bottom and surfaced beside the air mattress.

"Enjoying the water?" he asked, running a hand through his hair, slicking it back from his face.

"It's wonderful."

"How are you feeling?"

"Much better. I took off the brace. The doctor said if my neck felt all right, I could."

He must have been staring. She glanced down at her skimpy bathing suit, then slipped a little self-consciously off the air mattress into the pool and sidestroked toward the shallow end.

Alex followed, moving closer, until they were standing face-to-face in the waist-deep pool. She looked so tempting he wanted to eat her up. "So you're feeling okay?"

"Yes, I... Yes..."

It was completely private in his backyard, the high fence, wide, leafy trees and grassy lawn giving him the seclusion he wanted. It was one of the reasons he had bought the place.

Her eyes remained on his. She was breathing a little faster and so was he. He reached out and gently cupped her cheek. "I'm going to kiss you, Sabrina. I really need to." He didn't say more, just pressed his lips to hers and savored the sweetness. She tasted like chocolate, and mint iced tea, smelled like sunshine and fresh air. Her skin was soft and moist beneath his fingers.

For an instant, she kissed him back and he deepened the kiss, his tongue sliding into her mouth to tangle with hers. When her small hands pressed against his chest and she pulled away, it was like a sharp knife slicing his insides.

"Alex, we...we can't."

"I'll stop if I'm hurting you. Am I?"

"No, but—"

He kissed her again, took it slowly, let her get used to the feel of his mouth moving over hers, coaxing at first, then taking. Sabrina clutched his shoulders. Her lips were full and wet as she opened for him, let him sink in, let him taste her more deeply. He could sense the battle she waged with herself, knew the instant she gave in to the needs of her body over the logic of her mind.

"I need you," he said, breathing her in as he deepened the kiss. And it was true. There was something about her, something that satisfied some hollow place inside him that had never quite been filled. He needed her, and whether she realized it or not, he believed she needed him.

She was trembling as he pulled the strings on her yellow bikini top and tossed it up on the pool deck, bent his head and took one of her heavy breasts into his mouth. Her nipples were big and pink, and soft until they tightened under his tongue.

His erection throbbed. The desire burning through him went hotter, deeper, stole some of his control. He pulled the string on her bikini bottoms and tossed the wet fabric up beside her top, lifted her up on the pool deck and moved between her legs.

"We...we can't," she whispered. "Someone will see."

"They can't. I promise." He pressed his mouth over hers and kissed her deeply, then moved to the side of her neck to nibble an earlobe. Her skin was damp beneath his tongue as he rained soft kisses along her throat, her shoulders, moved lower, suckled each of her breasts.

She gasped as he sank down in the water in front of her and fastened his mouth on her sex. Her fingers curled into his hair and a little whimper escaped. She was wet and ready, and the minute his tongue touched her inner flesh, she started to come.

His body tightened, hardened to the point of pain. God, he wanted to be inside her more than he wanted to breathe. She was so damned responsive. He remembered that from before, though he hadn't had the pleasure of tasting her as he did now. It had been a while for her, she'd said, but something told him a lot of this was new to her. It made him feel protective and at the same time wildly possessive.

He kept her on the edge through another jagged climax, then set his hands on the pool deck and hoisted himself up out of the water. Sabrina looked dazed, soft and slightly bewildered.

He wanted her hot for him again, greedy to have him inside her. Reaching down, he lifted her into his arms and carried her under the overhanging roof, into the open cabana. There were wide, orange-striped padded benches along the walls. He settled her on one of the benches and stretched out beside her, leaned over and kissed her again.

He could feel her small body trembling beneath him, feel her breasts pressing into his chest, and lust hit him like a fist. He wanted to plunge himself inside her, pound into her until he had his fill. He wanted to take her and take her until she forgot everything but him.

Instead, he forced himself to go slow, to drive her up again toward the peak. When she started to shift restlessly beneath him, he lifted her, set her astride him and dragged her mouth down to his for another burning kiss.

"Take what you need," he coaxed, sliding his hands over her bottom to hold her in place. "Pleasure us both."

She looked down at him and something shifted in her

features, turned her expression from hesitant to seductive. She bit her lip as she rose and took him inside her, settled deeper and made him groan.

He nearly came when she started to move, easing up, then sliding the length of him. He clamped down hard on his control and let her set the pace, determined to make it good for her. She looked beautiful lost in her pleasure, and his own pleasure built.

His groin tightened. His erection pulsed and throbbed. He couldn't remember wanting a woman the way he did this one.

Alex clenched his jaw against his building need, then Sabrina started to come and he let himself go. Release sucked him under, wouldn't let him go, the pleasure fierce and intense. As he drifted back down, he felt drained and satisfied, content in a way he had rarely known.

Long seconds passed. Sabrina lay slumped against his chest, her body pliant and sated. He smoothed a hand over her damp red curls, enjoying the feel of her snuggled against him. He could feel her heart pounding, matching the thunder of his own.

His chest tightened when he felt her tears.

Worry slid through him. "Don't cry, love. Please don't cry."

He eased her off him, got up and disposed of the condom he had retrieved from a drawer below the padded bench. Grabbing a couple of bath towels from one of the cabinets, he wrapped one around his hips and tied it, walked back and handed the other one to her. She fastened the towel sarong-style around her, tucking the ends in over her pretty breasts. He wanted to strip the towel away and start kissing her all over again.

Instead, he sat down beside her and eased her into his arms. "I didn't hurt you, did I?"

She shook her head. "No."

"Tell me what's wrong."

She looked up at him, her eyes big and blue and luminous with tears. "I can't do this, Alex. I can pretend if you want. I can say that I can handle what's going on between us, that I can deal with it. But the truth is, I know the kind of man you are—we both do. If we keep going, sooner or later, I'm going to get hurt."

His heart was hammering even harder than before. "Maybe you're wrong. Maybe I'm not the man you think I am."

"Can you promise me that?"

Could he? He tried to convince himself he had changed, but the truth was he didn't know who he was now any more than he had four years ago when he'd come out of the navy.

"Can't we just let things play out, see what happens?"

She released a shaky breath. "I don't understand what's going on here, Alex. You date some of the most beautiful women in Houston. What could you possibly see in me that could compare to them?"

Anger sent his temper up a notch. "What the hell are you talking about? You're beautiful and intelligent. You're brave and you're sweet. On top of that, you're sexy as hell. Why wouldn't I want you?"

She seemed surprised by his words. "Those are… very nice things to say, but they don't change anything. You're not the kind of man who can be happy with just one woman—and why should you be when you look the way you do?"

"For chrissake, Sabrina—the way I look doesn't have

a damned thing to do with any of this. I'm not interested in seeing other women. Not as long as we're involved. Does that make my feelings clear?"

She looked even more confused. Clutching the towel a little tighter around her, she stood up and walked away, faced the pool with her back to him.

She turned. "I want to go home, Alex. Unless you've heard from the police, we don't even know for sure if the accidents are connected."

She couldn't go home, dammit. It just wasn't safe. He told himself to take things slowly, give her time to come to that conclusion on her own. He walked over to where she stood and began the conversation he couldn't put off any longer.

"The police weren't able to confirm one way or another exactly what happened with the car. The bolt came off the steering rod. No prints, nothing to confirm whether or not it was tampered with."

"So it could have just been a malfunction."

"It's a pretty uncommon occurrence." He didn't think that's what had happened, but he had no proof. "The thing is, the sheriff in Rio Gordo released Martin Gilroy. He's got an alibi for the time that would have fit the guy who sabotaged the chopper. Dickens believes it's good."

He could see that quick mind of hers at work, coming to the same conclusion he had. "So the person responsible for the crash was someone else, someone who could have come to Houston and sabotaged my car."

"It's possible."

"It's still just speculation. We don't really know."

"That's right. If there weren't such a powerful motive, we could be pretty sure something else happened. As it is—"

"As it is, I need to get those core samples drilled. Then we'll know if the mine is valuable enough for someone to want me dead."

"And you need to call your mother, find out who she told about your trip to Rio Gordo." And he would bet dollars to doughnuts the answer would lead directly to one of her cousins.

Seventeen

Rina raked a hand through her hair, shoving it back from her face. Beneath the towel, the moist Texas heat soaked into her, warming her and washing away some of the regret she felt for giving in to her weakness for Alex.

And now that she was a little more in control, maybe making love with him wasn't such a terrible thing. They were both adults, weren't they? And from what Alex had said, he was as attracted to her as she was to him. Maybe just this once, she should take the chance, live her life to the fullest, take what Alex had to offer for as long as it lasted and worry about the future when it came.

"I should have asked my mother when she came to stay with me after the helicopter crash," she said, picking up the conversation where they had left off. "At the time, I thought the crash was an accident. I talk to her every few days, but after the car wreck, I wanted to wait until I got out of the hospital. I should have called yesterday, but I didn't want her to worry."

"She's your mother. She's bound to worry."

"I suppose. She'll be wondering why she hasn't heard from me. I guess it's time I called."

"Past time," Alex said.

"I need to shower and put on some clothes."

Alex nodded. She could feel his eyes on her as she left him there by the pool and headed into the house. Twenty minutes later, she returned downstairs dressed in lightweight khaki slacks and a yellow print blouse. She found Alex dressed in crisp blue jeans and a polo shirt at work in his study.

She thought of their passionate lovemaking and soft warmth crept into her cheeks. Alex was an amazingly virile man and an incredible lover. Watching him work, she felt a little pinch in her heart.

"I'll...umm...call my mother right now."

He leaned back in his desk chair. "Florence, right?"

"That's right. My dad's name was Mike. Big Mike, they used to call him, but he wasn't really big. I guess he just seemed that way. He was a great dad and a really good husband. When he died, it broke my mother's heart."

"You're lucky to have had parents like that. My family isn't really a family at all."

"What do you mean?"

He just shook his head and got up from his chair, drew her over and urged her down in the seat. Wishing he had opened up to her, Rina sat down and picked up the phone, punched in her mother's number in Uvalde, then settled in to the call.

Her mother answered on the second ring. "Mom, it's me."

"Oh, hi, sweetie. I've been trying to call but you

haven't been home and your phone keeps sending me to the message center."

"It's...umm...on the blink."

"Well, I've been hoping to hear from you. It's been a while since you called. I guess you've been busy."

"Well, sort of." Over the next few minutes, Rina told her mother about the car accident and being in the hospital, but made it clear she was okay.

"I would have come to you," her mother said. "You know that."

"I know. I'm fine, really, Mom. Next time you come to the city for a visit, instead of having to nurse me, we'll do something fun."

They talked a little longer and Rina finally broached the subject of her trip to the mine. "I've been wondering, Mom. I'm curious who knew I was going to Rio Gordo."

"It wasn't a secret, was it?"

"No, not at all. I was just wondering if you'd talked to anyone about it."

"Well, I can't think of anyone special...just Susan and Priscilla." Susan was married to Thomas Eckhart, Uncle Walter's youngest brother. Susan and Flo Eckhart had been friends for years. The bad news was, Susan was an even bigger gossip than Florence.

"I mentioned it to Sill when she came over to pick up her girls. You remember, I babysit for her once a week. The girls are really sweet. I wish Priscilla would pay more attention to them, but you know how busy she is, working two jobs and all."

"I know." Sill tried to be a good mother, but she had always been a little wild, and since Rina didn't have any kids of her own, she had no right to criticize.

"Oh, and Bob called to wish me a belated happy birthday. I might have mentioned it to him."

Sabrina looked at Alex and rolled her eyes. He must have been getting the gist of the conversation because he was frowning.

"What about George?" Rina asked, just to be thorough. "Did he know I was going?"

"Well, I don't know. His mother might have told him. Susan's a friend of Marlene's, so she probably knew." Marlene was Walter's ex-wife, her cousins' mother. "Marlene's a terrible gossip."

Rina felt like screaming. Was there anyone in Texas who didn't know about her trip?

"So I guess most of the family knew I was flying out to look at Uncle Walter's mine."

"Well, I guess. Susan was really excited about the helicopter. She said she'd always wanted to ride in one."

Oh, God, could it get any worse? Alex was going to have a fit.

"You said it wasn't a secret," her mother reminded her after a pause on the phone. "I hope you aren't upset."

"No, I'm not upset. It wasn't a secret." At least not at the time. "I was just curious. Listen, Mom, I've got to run. You take care of yourself, okay?"

"I love you, honey."

"I love you, too, Mom." Rina ended the call and leaned back in the chair behind Alex's desk.

"My mother told half the population of Texas I was going to look at Walter's mine. The whole family knew."

"Including your cousins. Walter's kids—next in line for the property."

She nodded, feeling slightly sick. "Mom said my aunt Susan—she's my uncle Thomas's wife—was really excited about the helicopter. She's always wanted to ride in one."

Alex groaned. He rubbed his forehead. "You realize what this means? Your cousins already have motive—twenty mil isn't chump change."

"Assuming the core samples prove the moly is there."

"That's right. And now we know they had opportunity. They knew when you were leaving and where you were going. Some of them even knew you would be using a helicopter. All we have to do now is find the means. How they managed to get the job done."

"Just because they knew I was going, doesn't mean they hired someone to kill me. It still could have been someone who was after you."

"I've got enemies. None of them looked good for the crash. And there's your car accident to consider."

She didn't want to admit it, didn't even want to think it might be true, but Alex was right. There was a possibility—however slim—that one of her cousins wanted to kill her in order to get the mine.

"So now that you know, are you staying here where you'll be safe?"

Staying with Alex was a long way from safe, but she summoned her courage and nodded. "I'll stay until we figure things out."

"Good. We need to get your buddy Arturo started on those core samples, and I need to talk to your cousins. Bob Eckhart lives here in Houston. I'll start with him."

"If he did it, he isn't going to just come out and say so."

"No, but it'll give me an idea where he's coming from, how he feels about you, how much he knows."

"All right, but I'm going with you. We might get more information if I'm there when you talk to him."

"You can't do that. Bob could put two and two together and figure out you're staying with me."

"Well, I can't sit here all day and do nothing. I've got to go out sooner or later. This is my life we're talking about, Alex. I need to find out what's going on, and if someone's really after me I need to find out who it is and make this end."

"I don't like it. I'd rather no one knew you were staying here."

"I'm going, Alex. If I have to call a cab and go on my own, I will."

A muscle tightened in his jaw. He blew out a frustrated breath. "All right, you can go. I've got the best security system money can buy. Afterward, I'll just have to stay a little closer to home."

Rina blanched. More hours with Alex? Dear God, she hoped she could survive it.

Alex looked at the gold Rolex on his wrist. "Time's slipping away. How about we pay Cousin Bob a little visit right now? You can phone Hernandez on the way."

Sabrina pasted on an overbright smile. "I'm ready when you are. I'll just go get my purse."

Smoke curled up from the ashtray on the glass-topped table on the patio where the two men sat. There was no smoking inside the house.

"The little bitch has completely disappeared," Henry said, reaching down to pick up his cigarette, knocking the ashes off the end.

"Take it easy. I'll find out where she's gone."

"How you gonna manage that?" Henry took a deep

drag, filling his lungs with smoke. He was only thirty-eight but he already had a smoker's hack and yellowed teeth. He rubbed his unshaven chin. He was also a man who was smart enough to go along with what he was told as long as he got paid.

"Florence is a bloodhound. Once she finds out Rina isn't staying in her apartment, she won't be satisfied until she knows where her daughter is. Since she never could keep her mouth shut about anything, getting her to tell me what she knows won't be hard."

"Okay, so once we find her, what's the plan?"

"Same as before—we get rid of her. You said you knew someone who might be able to help."

Henry nodded. "Hector Ortega. Works on Jimmy Wilson's framing crew. He's got friends. For the right price, he can get 'em to take care of whatever we need done."

"This is getting expensive. We can't afford another screwup."

"What you spent so far ain't a gnat's ass compared to what you get if we pull this off."

"True enough."

Henry shoved up from his chair. "Let me know when you find her."

"You just get things ready. I'll call you when I've got the information."

Henry nodded, already anticipating the money. Rubbing the stubble on his jaw, he sauntered off the patio, heading for the gate on the side of the house.

Alex had just settled Sabrina in his car when the roar of a jet screaming down the runway alerted him to an incoming call. Sabrina rolled her eyes.

Alex just grinned and pulled his iPhone out of his pocket. "Justice."

"Alex, this is Josh Reynolds at the district attorney's office. I wanted to let you know Edward Bagley has been released from the county jail."

"What?" Alex's fingers tightened around the phone. "What the hell's going on?"

"Judge Clarksen ruled the DNA evidence you brought in was obtained illegally. Apparently one of the neighbors was watching when you reached through the kitchen window and grabbed that Coke can off the table. That was trespassing, Alex, and without that evidence, the judge had no choice but to let Bagley go."

"That's bullshit and you know it."

"It's the law, Alex. There's nothing we can do until we come up with something new."

"So you're just going to let that murderer loose on the streets? What little girl is he going to rape next, Reynolds?"

"I don't like this any better than you do. The thing is, now that we know Bagley's our man, we'll be watching him night and day. He won't be able to eat in a restaurant for fear we'll get his DNA off something. Soon as we're able to obtain it legally, he'll be back in jail."

"What's to keep him from running?"

"Like I said, we'll be watching him. It shouldn't take long to get what we need."

"I hope to hell you're right."

"I may as well tell you, the D.A. is royally pissed. I'd be expecting a call if I were you."

"Thanks for the heads-up." Alex disconnected and shoved the phone back into his pocket. He slid behind the wheel and started the car, backed it out of the garage. The air conditioner was blasting, working to cool the black leather interior in the roasting Houston heat.

"What's happened?" Sabrina asked.

"Edward Bagley's out of jail."

"You're kidding! What about the DNA evidence you found? It was all over the news that it matched the sperm sample they got from Carrie Wiseman's body."

"The judge said it was illegally obtained."

"Was it?"

"Pretty much. I picked up an empty soda can through an open kitchen window. To do it, I trespassed in his yard. I said I found it in the trash behind his house. I figured with a case like this with so much at stake, no one would push it. Apparently I was wrong. Without that evidence, the D.A. had no choice but to let Bagley go."

"I can't believe this. The man raped and murdered a ten-year-old girl."

"Allegedly raped and murdered."

"He did it. His DNA sample proved it."

"Reynolds says now that they know it's him, it won't take long to get a sample that's legal. Once they find it, he'll be back in jail."

The phone rang again, this time ringing on the hands-free device. Alex picked up the call. "Justice."

"You realize what you've done?" He recognized the District Attorney's husky voice.

"Yeah, I found your killer for you." Richard Kaplan was basically a good man, but he played politics a little much to suit Alex.

"You embarrassed the district attorney's office and cost the department a lot of money," Kaplan said. "You're lucky we don't haul you in on charges."

"But you won't because the public would be up in

arms. They want their children safe. And identifying Bagley as the killer gives them a far better chance of that."

"You realize you'll probably lose your P.I. license over this."

"You better make sure I don't. It won't look good for you if you try to nail me for doing the job your department was supposed to do. Besides, if you play it right, you'll have that bastard back in custody in a couple of days and all the glory that goes with it. This time, you'll be able to put him away for the rest of his miserable life."

A pause on the other end of the line. "Let's hope you're right." Kaplan ended the call and Alex hung up the phone.

"I guess the District Attorney wasn't too happy with you," Sabrina said, having heard the call over the mic.

"He has to play it that way, but the truth is Kaplan wants that bastard nearly as much as I do."

"You and the parents of that little girl."

"That's right." Alex took a deep breath and dialed down his temper. He reached over and touched Sabrina's cheek. "In the meantime, we need to find out if someone is trying to make you dead."

Eighteen

Rina sat back in the passenger seat of Alex's BMW. "I punched Bob's address into your navigation system while you were on the phone." She had called his office at R. T. Eckhart Development before they left the house, found out he had taken a day off and was probably at home. She'd called there and told him she would like to stop by.

Alex drove the car toward Bob's house in the Woodlands, a prestigious neighborhood about twenty-five miles north of downtown. The homes in the area were hidden away among a lush landscape of green foliage and leafy trees, making it an extremely desirable place to live.

Rina had been to Bob's house a couple of times over the years. It wasn't one of the huge mansions in the area, but it was at least thirty-five hundred square feet on a lovely oversize lot with a kidney-shaped pool. When Bob got divorced, his ex-wife had wanted to move to Dallas, so Bob had kept the house, and Linda had gotten enough alimony to live in a fancy high-rise in the city.

They walked up to the door and Alex pressed the bell. Chimes sounded, and a few minutes later, the door swung open. Bob Eckhart stood in the opening, a big man eight years older than Rina, attractive, with thick dark hair beginning to silver at the temples, eyes a light shade of blue and a body that was going to fat.

Bob smiled. "Rina—it's good to see you."

"You, too, Bob." She turned. "Bob, this is Alex Justice."

Alex made a nod. "Bob."

"Nice to meet you, Alex. Any friend of Rina's and all that." The men shook hands. "Come on in."

"Alex is a private investigator," Rina said. "He's investigating the helicopter crash in Rio Gordo."

"And her car wreck on the freeway," Alex added, watching Bob's expression.

Bob frowned. "I heard about the helicopter crash. Glad you're okay. You wrecked your car, too?"

She nodded. "Last week. I've been having some bad luck lately."

"Sorry to hear it."

"Alex wanted to talk to you and I told him you wouldn't mind."

"Not at all." He tipped his head toward the sliding glass doors visible through the great room on the other side of the kitchen. "I was sitting out by the pool. If you don't mind the heat, we can talk out there."

The heat hit them as Bob slid open the heavy glass door and they stepped outside. A blond woman in a navy blue swimsuit reclined in a chaise lounge, the brim of a floppy straw hat tilted over her eyes.

"That's Polly. She's a friend."

Polly waved, a good-looking woman in her thirties.

She took a sip from the tall, frosty glass on the table next to the chaise, and went back to reading her book.

"You guys want a drink or something?"

"We're fine," Alex said.

"So how can I help you, Alex?"

"Well, the thing is, Bob, the sheriff in Rio Gordo says the chopper crash wasn't an accident."

"Really?"

"That's right. Sheriff Dickens says someone purposely fouled the engine. I'm trying to figure out who was responsible. That led me to motive. One possibility stood out. Since you and your siblings are the beneficiaries of your father's property, should something happen to Sabrina, it would seem to me that you three had the most to gain if Sabrina had died in the crash."

"That's crazy. None of us ever wanted that worthless hunk of land. That's the reason my father left it to Rina. She actually believed the ridiculous stories he told."

"So you think the land is worthless?"

"Isn't it?"

"That's something we're trying to find out. What about your brother and sister? They feel the same way?"

"If they'd wanted it, they could have had it. My father would have given it to them. He knew they weren't interested in wasting their lives out in the desert the way he had."

"If you had it, you could always sell it."

"That's not what my father wanted. He thought Rina might be willing to pick up where he left off and try to find the silver he believed was out there."

"And if she does?"

"More power to her."

"So none of you had anything to do with the helicopter crash or her accident on the freeway."

"Hell, no, and if that's what you're trying to prove, I think its time for both of you to leave."

"I'm sorry, Bob," Sabrina said as they made their way toward the door. "But Alex has to explore every possibility."

"I can't believe you think one of us would try to kill you."

"I'm sorry."

"Get out, Rina. You aren't welcome here anymore."

Her chest squeezed. Bob was family. But then she had never really been part of any of her cousins' lives. She was adopted and to them an outsider. On top of that, they had all resented her relationship with their dad. Still, she felt as if she had somehow betrayed them.

Alex's hand settled at her waist as he guided her back through the house and out the front door.

"Well, that got us nowhere," she said as she slid into the passenger seat and Alex closed the car door.

"Maybe, but it gave me a sense of how he feels about you and how much he knows—which is a lot more than he's telling us."

"From what he said, he doesn't know the mine could be valuable."

"That's what he said. He also said their father would have given them the land if they'd wanted it. That true?"

"I think it might be. Walter's attorney told me it was only a few weeks before he died that Walter changed his will. Originally he had left the property to all four of us. A little before he died, he decided to disinherit his kids and leave the property solely to me." Which had so far caused her nothing but trouble.

"Bob and the others didn't know they'd been cut out of the will," she continued, "until the attorney contacted them after Walter's death. They were really upset when they found out. At least that's what my mother said."

"Interesting. Any idea why he changed it?"

"My mom might know something about it."

"Since we need to talk to your cousin Priscilla, we'll ask your mother in person when we get up to Uvalde."

"We're flying up?" She wondered what Alex would think of the simple life her mother lived, the kind of home she had grown up in. It certainly wasn't the estate he must have lived in as the child of a wealthy Connecticut family.

"We'll go tomorrow. In the meantime, I want you to get things rolling with those core samples."

"I'll call Arturo as soon as we get home."

Alex sliced her a glance. "Just don't make any more dinner dates with the guy."

"It wasn't a date. It was business."

One of his dark blond eyebrows went up. "Yeah? Then maybe we can talk a little *business* when we get home."

Rina knew what that hot look meant and her heart skipped a beat.

Alex drove too fast all the way back to his house.

Rebecca walked into the kitchen where Joe McCauley was standing on a ladder installing one of the new oak cabinets she had ordered for the remodel. He looked good. Why a man in jeans and a tight-fitting T-shirt doing manual labor was so appealing she couldn't begin to understand.

Joe looked down at her. "Have you seen the news this morning?"

She smiled. "Why? The world still seems to be turning. Or have I missed some new catastrophe?"

"Edward Bagley's out of jail."

Her smile slid away. "That's impossible. My brother found DNA evidence that matches—"

"Judge tossed it out. I have a feeling Alex played a little too fast and loose with his evidence gathering. Without it, they haven't got a case."

Rebecca sighed. "Sounds just like him. So what are the police going to do? Now they know Bagley's the killer. Surely there's some way to get him off the streets."

"You can bet they'll be doing their best." Joe climbed down off the ladder and walked toward her. She found herself taking a step back.

Joe frowned. "You aren't afraid of me, are you? Because I'd never do anything to hurt you or Ginny."

"I know that."

"I know about your husband. I know he beat the crap out of you. Alex told me. I guess he went down there and had a little chat with him."

Alex had played big brother and done a lot more than chat. Her brother was lucky Jeremy hadn't pressed charges.

"It happened. It's over. Jeremy's not in our lives anymore." Not even in Ginny's. He called a couple of times a year, sent her a birthday present and a couple of presents at Christmas and that was it.

"Maybe not," Joe said, "but it's like he still lives here."

"What does that mean?"

"Do you like me, Becca?"

Alex called her Becca. Since Joe and Alex were friends, she supposed it was all right. And she kind of liked the way it sounded when he said it.

"I like you," she said. "Of course, I like you. You're doing a wonderful job and you're very kind to Ginny."

"I'm not talking about that kind of like. Are you attracted to me? I realize you're used to guys with a lot more money, but I'm not poor. I want to know if you feel anything when you look at me. Because I sure as hell feel plenty when I look at you."

Her insides tightened. She wasn't prepared for this conversation. Hadn't begun to see it coming. She opened her mouth to say something that would calm the situation, but before she got a word out, Joe hauled her into his arms and kissed her.

For an instant, she was too stunned to breathe. Then his arms tightened around her, heat settled low in her stomach, spread out through her limbs and her eyes slid closed. She couldn't stop herself from reaching for him, curling her fingers into his T-shirt, parting her lips, inviting him to deepen the kiss.

Joe groaned and didn't hesitate. The kiss he took wasn't what she would have expected from a gentle man like Joe. It was hot and wet and it turned her insides to honey. She thought he would stop, but he just kept kissing her, as if he had no choice, as if he knew how good he was making her feel. By the time he eased away, she was trembling all over, her lips tingling, her nipples hard beneath her sleeveless top.

His dark eyes burned into her. "I want to see you, Becca. Not just here in the kitchen. I want to take you out—Ginny, too. I want to spend time with you."

She started shaking her head. Her heart was beating too fast and she felt a little light-headed. "I admit I—I find you attractive. You're a very...well, your kind of man has a very potent appeal."

"My kind of man?"

"You know…a…a masculine man like you."

His mouth edged up. He had a very sexy mouth, she noticed, surprised she hadn't realized it before.

"A masculine man like me would like to take out a very sexy woman like you. Say yes, Becca. What have you got to lose? You can always fire me. There's a boat-load of carpenters out there who need jobs."

"Not like you. I mean…you're extremely capable."

"And masculine," he teased. "You said that."

"Well, yes."

"We're going out. All of us or just you and me. What-ever you want. Tomorrow night."

She looked him over top to bottom: wide, heavily muscled shoulders, powerful biceps, flat abdomen. For the first time, she allowed herself to feel the attraction she had been forcing herself to ignore. "I'm not ready for a relationship, Joe."

"Sometimes things happen whether we're ready or not. Tomorrow night. Seven o'clock." Turning, he climbed back up the ladder and went to work as if noth-ing had happened.

But a monumental event had occurred.

Rebecca had just discovered she was coming back to life after her painful divorce and that her tastes in men had changed. She knew she shouldn't go. She and Joe were far too different for anything serious to develop. She'd been raised in East Coast high society, gone to Wellesley College and graduated with honors. Joe was a former naval officer, a carpenter and—

Rebecca frowned, realizing how little she actually knew about him. The truth was, she hadn't wanted to know. She'd been determined to keep her distance. Apparently, that was going to change.

She wouldn't take Ginny. She didn't want her daughter to get her hopes up. Rebecca knew how badly her little girl wanted a father, and Ginny already idolized Joe. She would get a babysitter and go by herself. She knew Joe wouldn't press her for more than she was willing to give, and she was sure she could handle her growing attraction to him.

As Rebecca headed back upstairs, she found herself smiling. Tomorrow night she was going out with Joe.

Nineteen

❧❧❧

The plane landed at Garner Field in Uvalde the next morning. With a population of a little over sixteen thousand, three-quarters of which were of Hispanic descent, Uvalde was the most southerly town in the Texas Hill Country. But the land itself was flat and arid with nary a hill in sight. Lots of trees, though, in the town itself and along the numerous rivers in the area.

It was a nice little town, Alex thought, kind of old-fashioned, with a row of old buildings along the main street downtown. It was hotter than a West Texas bar-becue as they picked up a rental car from Hertz and he followed Sabrina's directions to a small, flat-roofed, single-story house in a 1960s subdivision just outside town.

The yard was well-maintained, with trees spreading thick branches over the lawn and a neatly trimmed ce-ment path that led to the front door.

"It isn't much," Sabrina said as they walked along, "but it's home."

"This where you were raised?"

"That's right. Now it's paid for."

"You paid off the mortgage?"

She shrugged. "I was making a lot of money at the time. Mom loves the house and she wouldn't leave Uvalde for all the money in Texas."

He thought he caught a hint of something in the words, reached over and caught her arm, stopping her before they reached the porch.

"It doesn't matter where you come from, love. It's what you make of yourself, and whether or not you're happy."

She smiled up at him, seemed to relax. Florence Eckhart opened the door before they reached it, spread her arms and gathered her daughter into a welcoming hug.

"I'm so glad to see you!" She turned, beamed a smile at Alex. "And this must be that handsome pilot you told me about. The one who took such good care of you when you got stranded with him out in the desert."

Sabrina's cheeks colored a little, which meant she'd really said that and pleased him more than it should have.

"Hello, Mrs. Eckhart. I'm Alex Justice. It's a pleasure to meet you."

Instead of taking the hand he held out to her, Florence went up on her toes and hugged him, something his own mother would never think of doing to a stranger. Hell, she rarely hugged her own kids.

"It's wonderful to meet you, too. Now you both come on inside where it's cool. I've made some fresh iced tea and ham sandwiches. I figured you'd be hungry by the time you flew all the way out here."

Sabrina cast him a glance. "Mom thinks food is the answer to just about everything."

Which was clear from Florence Eckhart's plump figure. She had dark brown hair and hazel eyes, and when she smiled, which was often, her whole face lit up. Alex liked her immediately.

"A sandwich sounds great," he said.

Passing an overstuffed blue-flowered sofa and chair in the living room, Florence led the way into the kitchen, which had ruffled blue curtains at the windows and was as immaculately clean as the rest of the little house. The furnishings were simple but neat.

They sat down at a round oak table in the kitchen and ate ham sandwiches and drank sweet iced tea while Sabrina and Florence chatted about family and what had been happening in Uvalde.

"We talked to Bob the other day," Sabrina said, easing into the conversation they'd come to have. "Alex is helping the sheriff up in Rio Gordo find out what happened to the helicopter. Bob didn't seem to know anything useful."

Florence started frowning. "I heard you were there. Marlene called yesterday. I don't understand why you would think Bob would know anything about it. Marlene said you thought he was somehow involved. I told her that was ridiculous. You would never believe something like that about your cousin."

"We're just eliminating possibilities," Alex said, having already warned Sabrina to say as little as possible since her mother wasn't very good at keeping secrets. "We're just tying down loose ends."

Florence smiled. "I knew there had to be some other explanation. Bob's a good man, even if he and his father never got along. Bob never fails to call on my birthday or send a gift at Christmas."

"We're going to talk to his sister while we're here," Alex added. "Just to make sure there's no connection."

Florence frowned again. "I still don't understand. Connection to what?"

Sabrina reached over and caught her mother's blunt-fingered hand. "The thing is, Mom, the sheriff says the chopper crash wasn't an accident."

Her eyes widened. "It wasn't?"

"It was made to crash on purpose. We still don't know why. The problem is that if something happens to me, Uncle Walter's mine goes to Bob, George and Priscilla."

"Why, I didn't know that."

"It was in the will. It just didn't seem important until now."

"The crash might have nothing to do with the will," Alex added, "but certain questions have to be asked."

"That's right," Sabrina said. "There could be any number of motives."

"As I said," Alex finished, "we're just eliminating possibilities."

"I see."

"Mom, after Walter's death, his attorney told me he changed his will a few weeks before he died, leaving the property solely to me. Do you have any idea why he might have done that?"

"Well…as I recall, I think he and the kids had some kind of falling-out. You know how they were always belittling poor Walter."

"Do you know what happened?"

"I remember Walter stopped by the house in late October. He told me he'd come to see Priscilla. He planned to visit each of his kids before he went back to the mine. A week or so later, Marlene called. She said his trip hadn't gone well at all—which probably pleased her no end."

"Why is that?" Alex asked.

"Marlene and the kids never forgave Walter for abandoning them to go off hunting treasure. They never got over it, not even after Marlene divorced him and married Cliff Beringer. My guess is that when Walter went to see them they treated him as badly as they usually did."

"Bad enough to cut them out of the will and leave the property entirely to his niece?"

"Maybe. It's the only reason I can think of."

"And a month later Walter died."

Florence set her glass of iced tea back down on the table. "That's right. In a car accident right here in Uvalde. He was on his way over here that night—he always came back for Christmas, even after my husband died."

"I gather your husband and his brother were close," Alex said. Florence hesitated. Something passed over her features, but Alex couldn't tell what it was.

"That's right," she said. "Walter loved Big Mike. They were inseparable as kids. That never changed. They became even closer as Walter and his kids grew further apart. Rina and I were the closest family Walter really had."

Sabrina set her glass back down on the table. "We were waiting for him to get here that night so we could all open our presents together," she said softly.

Florence shook her head. "Poor Walter never arrived. Instead the police came to the door. They said there was a hit-and-run accident in front of the Stop & Shop market. Someone hit Walter when he was walking back to his car after he'd stopped to buy a bottle of champagne. They've never found the person responsible."

Alex looked at Sabrina. *Hit-and-run.* She must have made the same connection he just had, because her eyes were as big as saucers and suddenly they filled with tears.

"Oh, my God," she said.

"What is it, dear?" her mother asked worriedly.

Sabrina shook her head. Digging a Kleenex out of her purse, she wiped the moisture from her eyes. "Nothing, Mom," she bluffed. "It's just…you know, talking about that night always makes me sad." She looked up and Alex read the question in her pretty blue eyes. *Do you think someone killed him?*

And though he wanted to believe it was just another in the string of coincidences that all seemed linked to the mine, he couldn't convince himself.

Alex shoved back his chair. "The lunch was great, Mrs. Eckhart. I wish we could stay, but we'd like to talk to Priscilla before we head home so we haven't got a lot of time."

She rose from her chair. "Of course, and please, just call me Flo like everyone else."

Alex leaned down and hugged her. "Thanks, Flo."

She walked them to the door and he waited while she and Sabrina said last-minute goodbyes.

"We'll talk again soon," Sabrina promised, hugging her mother hard.

Then she and Alex headed for the rental car parked at the curb.

Sabrina blew her nose and blinked against another round of tears. "I don't know why I didn't put it together," she said as he drove the rental car toward Pris-

cilla's apartment on the other side of town. "It's just…
it all seems so impossible. Like something out of an old
Alfred Hitchcock movie."

"We have to be careful not to jump to conclusions, but
I have to tell you, from my point of view, your uncle's
death is just one coincidence too many."

She glanced away, fixed her gaze on the flat land
passing by outside the window. "So what do we do
now?"

"Two things. First, we talk to your cousin Priscilla,
see what she has to say. Then we find out how the Uvalde
police are coming along with their investigation into
your uncle's death."

"How much do we tell them about what might be
going on?"

"Nothing. At least not yet. At this point, we can't do
much more than make unfounded accusations."

"If my cousins believed the mine was worthless, why
would one of them kill him? They had to know or at least
believe it had some kind of value."

"Maybe when he talked to them in October he told
them about the molybdenum. Maybe this time they believed him. By the time he was killed, Walter had already changed the will. Maybe the mistake he made was
in not telling them what he'd done."

"So one of them might have killed him or arranged
for him to be killed believing they were still going to
inherit."

"It's a theory. If the mine turns out to be as valuable
as Hernandez thinks it is, it makes sense."

Sabrina sighed and leaned back in her seat. "According to Arturo, it shouldn't take long to get those core
samples done." Though Alex wasn't too happy about

it, Sabrina had phoned the mining engineer yesterday. Hernandez planned to have his company begin the work within the next few days.

"I wish Uncle Walter hadn't changed the will," she said grimly.

Alex flicked her a glance. "In a way, so do I. You'd definitely be safer. But the land's yours now and making it productive is what your uncle wanted. What he may have died for."

She turned to face him and determination strengthened her features. "If there's something there, I'm going to find it. I'm going to give Uncle Walter his dream."

Alex felt a shot of admiration. She was an amazing woman. But he had learned that when they had crashed and nearly died in the middle of the Texas desert.

Priscilla wasn't home. Rina had phoned her that morning before they'd left Houston and asked if she could stop by. Priscilla had said she would be there.

Instead, a lanky, darkly tanned man with shaggy brown hair and brown eyes met them at the door.

"You Sill's cousin?" he asked, clearly expecting her.

"Yes. I'm Rina and this is Alex Justice. We had a couple of things we wanted to talk to her about."

"I sent her out to fetch some beer. Shouldn't take long. I'm Rusty Jenkins. You wanna wait?"

"Sure." Alex urged her into the apartment. "Good to meet you, Rusty." He stuck out a hand and the two men shook.

"Priscilla mentioned you," Rina said. "I guess you two have been seeing each other for a while?"

"'Bout a year, I guess."

"What kind of work do you do?" she asked.

"I'm a mechanic down at Pete's Garage." Which accounted for the grease under his fingernails and the way his hair stuck to the back of his neck. Of course it could have been remedied with a shower.

Alex picked something up off the table next to the sofa, held it out for Rina to see. It was a framed photo of Rusty wearing coveralls, standing next to an airplane marked with an army insignia. Her pulse kicked into gear.

"Army." Alex studied the photo. "I'm a navy man myself. When'd you get out?"

The guy reached over and took the photo from Alex's hand, set it back down on the table. "Couple of years."

"That where you learned to mechanic? Working on airplanes?"

"Only thing good I got out of it." Unlike her mom's neat, clean home, her cousin's apartment was a shambles. Dirty clothes on the floor, a load of laundry piled on the brown vinyl sofa, a pizza box with a leftover slice sitting on the coffee table next to a couple of empty beer bottles.

"You wanna Pepsi or something? Sill ought to be back pretty soon with the beer."

"We're fine," Rina said.

Rusty turned at the sound of a door opening and Priscilla walked into the living room, a brown paper grocery bag in her arms. She was dark-haired and a little taller than average. She had always had a fabulous figure and beautiful face.

"So you made it," she said, handing a six-pack of Lone Star to Rusty, who grabbed an opener off the breakfast bar and popped the top on one, held the beer out to Alex.

"No, thanks," he said.

Rusty shrugged and upended the bottle, took a hefty swig.

"We flew out to see Mom," Rina explained. "We wanted to stop by and say hello."

Priscilla's full lips flattened out. "Bullshit. I just talked to Bob. He told me you thought he rigged that chopper you were in so it would crash and we could get our hands on Daddy's mine."

"Priscilla, I'm Alex Justice," Alex cut in smoothly, saving Rina from having to make a reply. "I'm a private investigator."

"Shit," Rusty mumbled.

"The sheriff believes the helicopter engine was fouled on purpose. I'm helping him find out who was responsible for the crash. You and your brothers would be the beneficiaries of your father's property if Sabrina had been killed. I'm just trying to eliminate you and your family as possible suspects."

Priscilla jammed her hands on her hips. "So you don't *really* think any of us had anything to do with it," she said sarcastically.

"Sabrina doesn't think so. She says you're family. You wouldn't be involved in something like that." Alex was watching Sill closely, looking for anything in her expression that would give her thoughts away. Rina was beginning to realize how good he was at gauging people, discovering things about them by what they *didn't* say.

"I've got two kids," Silla said. "I don't want any trouble. I didn't have anything to do with that crash."

"Where are the girls?" Rina asked. "Kelly and Heather? I was hoping to see them."

"They're playing next door with a friend. I'll tell them you said hello. Now ask whatever it is you want to know and then get out of here."

Alex turned to the mechanic, who took another swig of beer. "Where were you, Rusty, on Monday the ninth of June?" The date of the car accident, not the date of the helo crash.

"What the hell?"

"You make a little trip to Houston?" Alex pressed.

"Hell, no. I was working at Pete's, like I do five days a week. You can check with my boss."

"But not on Sunday, the day before. You're off on Sundays, right? Not much of a drive, just a little over four hours to Houston. You could have driven down, loosened the nut on the steering rod in Sabrina's car and driven back, still been at work on Monday morning."

"You're crazy. I was with Sill all weekend. Right, baby?"

"That's right. Rusty was here day and night. And don't you dare bother George with this crap. He and Mindy got enough to worry about with Janie bein' so sick."

Rina's heart jerked. "Janie's sick? I hadn't heard. What's wrong with her?"

"Got some kind of cancer. They didn't want anyone to know so keep your mouth shut about it."

"How long has she had it?" Alex asked.

"Got it sometime last year. Now get out."

Rina didn't say anything more. She kept seeing little Janie's face, the turned-up nose, the brown eyes and curly blond hair. Her throat felt tight as they made their way out the door and along the sidewalk, heading back to the rental car.

"I hate what we're doing," she said as they got into the car and Alex started the engine, turned the air conditioner up high to cool down the interior.

"Rusty's a mechanic, Sabrina. He worked on airplane engines in the army. He could have sabotaged the chopper *and* jimmied the steering on your car."

She let her head fall back against the seat rest. "I know."

"He was living with your cousin when your uncle was killed. He could have done that, too."

The lump in her throat went tighter. "She has two little girls, Alex, only a year apart. They're really sweet. You know what will happen to them if it turns out Priscilla was involved."

"If she's involved in murder, they're better off without her."

Maybe they were, but Rina didn't think so. Priscilla might not be the best mother, but she loved those girls and they loved her.

"What about George? If Janie has cancer, I'm not going down to San Antonio and give him the third degree. I just can't do it, Alex."

"If George's daughter is that sick, he's bound to need money. That gives him a powerful motive."

"I don't care. I'm not doing it and I don't want you going there, either. Promise me you won't."

He blew out a breath, raked a hand through his hair. "All right, I'll dig around, find out what I can without seeing him. In the meantime, before we leave town we need to talk to the police."

They needed to get the details of the investigation into Walter's death. But stirring up painful memories was the last thing Rina wanted.

"The building's on West Main," she said, her chest clamping down at the thought of what else they might learn.

"You can wait while I talk to them," Alex said, and she nodded. In the end, she waited in a chair beside the window at the front desk while Alex spoke to the officer who had handled the accident just two days before last Christmas.

She breathed a sigh of relief when she spotted his tall frame walking back across the room. Wordlessly, he escorted her out into the heat, back to the car.

"It happened pretty much the way your mother said," he told her as he drove back toward the airport for the return flight home. "Cops figured the driver was drunk and that's why he didn't stop. A witness said it was a white van, but didn't get a plate number. Cops figured the driver probably lived in the area and they'd find him sooner or later, but so far that hasn't happened."

"So maybe he lives somewhere else. Maybe it wasn't Rusty."

"I mentioned him. One of the officer's knew him, says he drives a brown Chevy pickup."

She felt a sweep of relief. "Maybe Walter's death is completely unrelated to everything that's happened."

"You mean it's just another coincidence?"

Her insides tightened. She knew Alex didn't believe it. Deep down, neither did she. "No," she said.

"Let's go home." Reaching over, he gently brushed his knuckles across her cheek. "I know what a hard day this has been for you."

Rina swallowed, nodded, felt the sting of fresh tears. She might be adopted but these people were her family. The only one she had ever known. She didn't want any of them to be involved in this. She just wanted everything to be back the way it was before Walter had died and she had inherited the mine.

She just wanted to go home, but when she got back, the home she'd be going to wouldn't be her own. It belonged to Alex.

He squeezed her cold hand. "It's all right, love. I won't let anything happen to you. You'll be safe as long as you're with me."

But she wasn't safe with Alex. Because every day she spent with him, she fell a little more in love with him. Sooner or later, Alex was going to break her heart.

And there didn't seem to be a single thing she could do to protect herself.

Twenty

⟨⟨⟨·⟩⟩⟩

The sound of cicadas intruded on the darkness, a thick, steady hum Rebecca found soothing as they walked to her front porch. Joe's big hand wrapped around her fingers and she found herself smiling.

The evening hadn't gone anything at all as she had imagined. Instead of taking her to dinner at one of the better restaurants as she had expected, he had taken her to a place called Johnny Ringo's, a country-Western dance hall. They'd eaten barbecued ribs and drank beer, and Joe had shown her how to Texas two-step.

They had tried a little line dancing, which she discovered after a few tries was harder than it looked. Joe promised to take her back sometime when they were giving lessons. Rebecca couldn't remember a night she'd had more fun.

As they neared the porch, she reached up and tugged on the brim of the white straw cowboy hat he was wearing with jeans and a pair of scuffed boots.

"You look really good in a hat," she said. "You ought to wear one more often."

"Truth is, I'm more of a baseball cap kind of guy. I haven't worn a cowboy hat since I worked out on our ranch."

"Your family has a ranch?"

"Used to. Out on the east side. Our property butted up against the Rawlinses' place. Seth Rawlins was Trace's dad."

Trace was the man her brother worked for at Atlas Security. She knew him and his pretty wife, Maggie, liked them both. "So you left the farm and joined the navy."

"I enlisted after I got out of college. That's where I met Alex. Your brother was one of those cocky SOBs who flew jets off the carrier I was assigned to. I was an officer in the ship's maintenance crew. We butted heads a few times, wound up being friends."

She smiled. "So indirectly, you're responsible for Ginny and me being in Texas."

"If you came because your brother is here, then yeah, I guess I am." They had almost reached the porch when he tugged her off the walkway into the shadows. He ended their discussion by leaning down to kiss her. She'd been expecting a good-night kiss. When his lips brushed hers, then settled in, softened over hers, melded, and he pulled her against him, it turned into something far more.

For an instant, Rebecca's breath stalled and her heart seemed to stop. Joe coaxed her lips apart and his tongue slid in to taste her. He took the kiss deeper and she lost all track of time. Her only thought was of Joe and the erotic feel of his mouth moving hotly over hers.

It was the fiercest, deepest, most wickedly sexy kiss she'd ever known. Rebecca barely realized that his big hands were cupping her breasts, his thumbs running gently over her nipples, turning them into tight little buds beneath her sleeveless, scoop-neck blouse. But the coil of heat in her stomach expanded and the desire burning through her began to spiral out of control.

She knew she should stop him, but after years of being alone, it felt so good to have a man touch her this way, to have him kiss her as if he couldn't get enough. Her arms slid up around his neck and she clung to him, kissed him back as wildly as he was kissing her. She had never felt this way with Jeremy, not even when they were dating. She could feel Joe's arousal and it made her ache to let him take her where the wild kiss was leading.

She was breathing hard, pressing herself against him, her fingers digging into the thick bands of muscle across his shoulders, when Joe pulled away.

"Easy," he said softly, pressing a last kiss to her forehead. "We'll get to this soon enough, just not yet. Not until you're ready."

Embarrassment spread through her. Dear God, she was practically mauling the man on her front lawn!

"I can't…can't believe I did that. I know what you must be thinking, but I'm not…not the kind of woman who…who—"

"Hold it right there. I know exactly the kind of woman you are. You're a beautiful, sensual woman, the mother of a wonderful little girl. You've been treated badly and I have a feeling the sexual attraction between us is new to you. There's nothing wrong with it, honey. It's perfectly normal between a man and a woman."

The endearment washed over her, soothing her a little. "Jeremy and I…we married for other, more practical reasons. Sex wasn't really that important to either one of us."

Joe's mouth edged up. "In that case, I came along at just the right time. When can I see you again?"

She hesitated, shook her head. "I shouldn't, Joe. I've got to think of Ginny."

"What happens between us isn't going to hurt Ginny. I won't let it. I promise you that. How about we all go out for pizza on Sunday?"

She wanted to. She couldn't remember wanting anything for herself in months. Years, maybe. But she wanted to see Joe again. And, as he had said, not just in her kitchen.

She smiled. "All right. Pizza on Sunday."

"Pick you up at six." He leaned down and gave her a final deep kiss then guided her up on the porch and waited while she took out her key and opened the front door.

The light in the hall was on. Mrs. Slotski, the older woman who lived next door, had fallen asleep on the sofa in the living room with the TV on.

Rebecca whispered, "Good night," and watched as Joe walked away. Rebecca closed the front door behind him. Time to be a mother again.

But oh, it had been fun for a little while, just to be a woman.

Golden rays of morning sun seeped into the bedroom. Rina felt the soft brush of lips nibbling the side of her neck, grazing an earlobe. She was sleeping in Alex's bed. Well, pretending to sleep because what he was doing felt so incredibly good she didn't want him to stop. One of his hands found a breast and his thumb slid over her nipple. She couldn't stop a moan.

"Faker," he whispered, pulling the sheet back, replacing his hand with his mouth.

Rina grinned. "I couldn't help it. What you're doing just feels so good."

Alex chuckled, went back to laving her breast. Pleasure sparkled through her, tingled over her skin. Since they'd made love in the pool, she'd been sleeping in his bed every night. She knew it was stupid, knew the consequences would be harsh when they came, but for now she didn't care.

She was smiling, enjoying his attentions and anticipating what was to come when the roar of a jet engine split the air. Alex cursed.

He rolled away from her to the side of the bed and picked up the phone, checked the caller ID. He looked at her over his shoulder. "It's Sol. I'd better take it."

They had things to do and it was getting past time to get up and get dressed. Reluctantly, she left the bed, grabbed her pink silk robe off the chair and headed for the bathroom she was using in the guest room, Alex's hot gaze following her all the way.

He wasn't in his bedroom when she came back dressed in navy capri-length pants and a sleeveless red-and-white top. Heading downstairs, she found him in the kitchen.

"I've noticed you like to eat healthy," he said. "So do I. We're having an egg-white spinach omelet, fruit and multigrain toast. Sound okay?"

"Perfect." She walked over and poured herself a cup of coffee, blew on the top and inhaled the rich aroma. Alex might not be a great cook but he made the world's best coffee. "So what did Sol have to say?"

He finished dishing up the omelet while she set the

table, and they sat down in front of a kitchen window that overlooked the pool.

Alex took a sip of his coffee, set the mug back down. "Sol says your cousin Bob isn't just having financial trouble, he's about to file bankruptcy. He needs a bundle to save his company."

She glanced away, forced herself to take a bite of her toast though her appetite had suddenly waned.

"He also says Rusty Jenkins got a dishonorable discharge from the army."

"What for?"

"Got into a fight with his commanding officer. They discharged him rather than throw him in the brig."

Sabrina shook her head. "Poor Silla. She always seems to pick losers."

"Yeah, well, this loser might have had something to do with your uncle's death."

The bite of omelet she had taken seemed to stick in her throat. "Did Sol tell you that?"

"No, and we don't have any proof to that effect. But I'm not ready to rule him out of the equation just yet. I had Sol email his photo to Sheriff Dickens. I called, asked Dickens to show it around the airport, see if anyone recognizes the face."

"You think someone will?"

"We might get lucky. It's worth a try."

She sipped her coffee, cradling the cup between her palms to warm her suddenly cold hands. "Did Sol have any other little tidbits of good news?"

"I'm afraid so and it isn't good. I hate to be the one to tell you, love, but George's little girl, Janie, needs a bone marrow transplant. The family doesn't have insurance and the procedure costs a small fortune."

She could feel the blood draining out of her face. "Oh, God, I had no idea." She set the mug down on the table, feeling suddenly sick. "You should see her, Alex. She's only five and she's the cutest towhead you've ever seen. I have to help them. Last year I could have. This year—"

Alex reached over and caught her hand. "I'll help them. Whatever George might or might not have done has nothing to do with that little girl. I'll have my people take care of it."

Rina stared at him in amazement. Then started shaking her head. "I can't let you do that. Janie's part of my family. I'm the one who should be helping her. If I can get the mine up and running, maybe I can."

"Listen to me. Even if you find the moly, it's going to take months to get the mine productive. Janie needs help now. I donate to charities who help people like her every day. Helping one more little girl isn't going to break me and that little girl might as well be Janie."

She started crying. She couldn't help it. Inside her chest her heart was beating so hard it hurt. Alex was on his feet in an instant, easing her up from her chair and into his arms.

"It's all right, love. It's only money and I have plenty of it."

She shook her head, unable to find the words, knowing there was nothing she could say that would ever be thanks enough. She wiped a tear from her cheek, fought to control the emotion she felt inside.

"Sometimes I really hate you," she said.

His mouth twitched. "Hate me? Why?"

"Because you're so damned nice and it just makes me like you even more than I do already." *Like* being far too mild a word for her feelings for Alex, but for now it was all she was willing to give.

Alex dipped his head and kissed her. "I'm not nice. Well, I am, but I'm also arrogant and overbearing. I believe that's what you said."

She smiled up at him, her eyes still moist. "You're right. You're nice, but you're also arrogant and overbearing and cocky as hell."

Alex laughed. He kissed her softly, brushed a last tear from her cheek. "This is one problem you don't have to worry about, okay?"

She swallowed, nodded, managed a watery smile. There was no way she could refuse his help when little Janie needed it so badly. They started to sit back down and finish their breakfast when the doorbell rang.

"I'm not expecting anyone." Alex walked over to the kitchen counter, opened a drawer, pulled out a pistol and stuck it into the back of his khaki pants. Rina followed him into the entry, stood back as he looked through the peephole then opened the door.

"Alex! *Cher,* it is so good to see you." The gorgeous brunette who sashayed into the entry and threw her arms around Alex's neck looked vaguely familiar. In her six-inch spike heels, she was even taller than Alex, and her figure in the sleek, formfitting, white-and-blue print sundress she was wearing was stunning to say the least.

"Gabriella." Alex caught her arms and eased them from around his neck, setting her a little away from him. "I didn't know you were in town."

"I am here for *Vogue,*" she said with a soft French accent. "They are doing a feature in Galveston."

Alex turned to look at Sabrina, who couldn't seem to make her feet move toward the stairs.

"Gaby, this is a client of mine, Sabrina Eckhart. Sabrina, this is Gabriella Moreau."

A client? That's all she was to him? She was sleeping in his bed every night and she was nothing more than one of his clients? She swallowed, a hard knot building in her chest.

"A pleasure to meet you," Gabriella said, her cool gaze sliding the length of her aristocratic nose.

"You, as well," Sabrina managed. She turned to Alex. "If you'll excuse me, I have something to do upstairs."

Alex didn't try to stop her, just let her climb the stairs and disappear down the hall. She stopped as soon as she was out of sight, unashamedly eavesdropping, unable to resist hearing what Alex would say.

"It's good to see you, Gaby. Unfortunately, I'm tied up at the moment. You should have called." There was faint censure in his words, but Gabriella seemed not to notice.

"The woman…she is your mistress?"

Rina's whole body went tense.

"I told you she's a client."

"But you are sleeping with her."

"Since when is that your business?"

"You are right, *cher,* of course. It has been some time since we have seen each other. I was hoping we might renew our…friendship…while I am here." She paused. "Apparently, that is not possible."

"I'll walk you out to your car."

"Do not bother. I can find my own way. Enjoy your little…diversion. Call me if you wish to see me. You can find me at Tremont House in Galveston."

Alex made no reply and the door closed solidly, indicating the woman's departure.

Rina continued on to her bedroom, her legs shaky

as she hurried along. She swallowed against the tears lodged in her throat. What in God's name had she been thinking? Staying in his home? Sleeping with him every night? By now, Alex must be bored senseless. He was used to sleeping with a legion of women. To help her, he had put his life on hold—and he wasn't even getting paid!

She fought to keep from crying as she dragged her suitcase out from under the bed and started tossing in clothes. The suitcase was almost packed when Alex showed up in the open doorway.

"What do you think you're doing?"

She glanced up at him, hurt mixed with anger. Anger won out. "What does it look like? I'm leaving. You don't owe me anything, Alex. Not your services as a bodyguard or as a…a stud. I have other friends who can help me. I'm Sage's best friend. Jake won't let anything happen to me. You don't have to feel obligated just because you slept with me."

"Bullshit." He grabbed the suitcase and tossed it away, spilling clothes all over the floor. "You aren't going anywhere. Just because one of my old girlfriends showed up at the door—uninvited—doesn't change things."

"Doesn't it? I knew I recognized her. She's a supermodel, for God's sake. Her arrival reminded me quite clearly that I'm your *client* and nothing more."

"That isn't true and you know it."

"Do I?"

He sighed, ran a hand over his face. "I know I handled that badly. I said the wrong thing and I'm sorry. It's just… This is new to me, too."

"You mean sleeping with one woman instead of a

baker's dozen? I imagine that takes a lot of self-restraint for a man like you."

His jaw hardened. Alex caught her shoulders. "Whatever you think, the fact is you need me. And dammit to hell—I need you."

She gasped as he hauled her close and kissed her, not a sweet, apologetic kiss, but a hot, greedy kiss that turned her inside out.

"It's you I want—can't you see that?" Hot kisses burned along her throat, and little shivers raced over her skin. He grabbed the hem of her red-and-white top and dragged it off over her head, popped the clasp on the front of her white lace bra, tore it off and tossed it away.

She was barefoot. He stripped away her navy blue pants and the white lace bikini panties she wore underneath, then he was kissing her again, running his hands all over her body, stroking, caressing, kindling the arousal he'd stirred that morning.

"Tell me you want me," he demanded, his teeth grazing her neck, biting an earlobe, making her hot and wet. "Say it."

She bit back a moan. "I want you. God, yes, I want you." She was trembling, panting, aching as he filled his hands with her breasts, kneaded, lowered his head and tasted.

Heat roared through her, made it impossible to think. She didn't realize he had backed her up to the bed until her knees hit the mattress, he tumbled her backward and came down on top of her. She only knew she was more than ready for him to relieve the hot, sweet yearning inside her.

She burned for Alex. Never seemed able to get enough. She heard the buzz of his zipper as he freed himself, found her wet and ready, buried himself deep inside. He caught her hands and pulled them over her head, holding her in place while he took her with long, determined strokes, took and took, as greedy for fulfillment as she.

Deep, saturating pleasure washed through her, pulled her toward climax. His fierce need was exactly what she wanted, his body telling her that he truly cared, that she was the woman he desired above all others.

She climaxed, then came again. Moments later, Alex followed her to release. Both of them were breathing hard, their muscles taut, then slowly relaxing. Alex came down next to her on the bed and pulled her on top of him, ran his hands over her back in a gently soothing motion. She could feel his heart racing, the damp heat of his body.

"Don't go," he whispered against her ear. "I don't want you to go." And though she knew the risk she was taking, the yearning in his voice was enough to convince her to stay.

It was insane. The unmistakable road to heartbreak, and yet as she lay there with his arms possessively around her, she couldn't make herself leave.

"I'll stay," she said, and felt his body relax beneath her.

Long seconds passed as they lay together, each taking comfort in the other.

"We didn't finish our breakfast," Alex finally said, nuzzling her ear.

"No, and now I'm really hungry."

He kissed the top of her head and uncoiled his long body from around her. "We could use the microwave to heat it back up."

Rina smiled. "That'll work." She knew she was getting in way too deep with Alex, but there was something about him that called to her, urged her to follow her heart.

Alex scooped her up in his arms and carried her naked down the hall to his bedroom. He stripped off his clothes and they climbed into the shower together. They didn't come out from under the dense, hot spray until he'd made love to her again.

Twenty-One

Henry felt the vibration, dug his cell phone out of his pocket and pressed it against his ear.

"Why haven't you answered your goddamned phone?" said the irritated voice on the other end of the line.

"I was busy. I have a life, too, you know."

"If you want your money, you better put your life on hold and get this done."

Henry took a deep drag on his cigarette, blew out a smoke ring. "You sayin' you found her?"

"It isn't confirmed, but there's more than a good chance she's staying with the guy she was with in the chopper. His name is Alex Justice and he's a private investigator. He's been asking questions, digging up information. She showed up at Flo's with Justice in tow, and they went to see Priscilla. According to Flo, they've got a thing going. I imagine Florence is ecstatic, since the guy's worth a fortune."

"You know where to find him?"

"He lives in River Oaks. Write this down."

Henry wrote the address in the palm of his hand.
"How you'd come up with it?" He figured a private dick
would be careful about letting people know where he
lived.

"Nobody hides from Google. And don't underesti-
mate Justice the way you did the first time. If he's as
good a detective as he is a pilot, you better watch your
ass."

"I'm not stupid."

"That remains to be seen. Have you talked to Ortega?"

"He's ready to go whenever you say the word. I'll
call him, fill him in, give him the address. He'll move
as soon as he can make it work."

"Do it." The line went dead, and Henry closed the
phone. There was big money in this. His old Uvalde high
school buddy knew he could count on Henry the way
he had since they were kids. And this time, the payoff
would be once-in-a-lifetime big.

Henry smiled and opened the phone.

Alex got the call just before dark the next day. For the
past half hour, he'd been listening to Sabrina complain
about getting out of the house. Even keeping her in bed
half the afternoon hadn't worked.

The memory brought him back to his visit from the
tall, statuesque Gabriella Moreau, and he wondered at
his reaction—which was no reaction at all. He had no
desire for Gaby, who had once stirred his blood just by
walking into a room. He couldn't pinpoint the time when
Sabrina had become the focus of his desire. And an important part of his world.

It bothered him a little. He wasn't sure if he was
changing, finding his way through life as he had been

trying to do for years, or if she was just a fresh diversion, a woman unlike the type he had been attracted to for as long as he could recall. Beautiful, svelte and emotionless. The kind of woman who didn't need anything from him except the use of his Platinum American Express card.

He wasn't sure what was happening between him and Sabrina. Whatever it was, he wasn't ready to give her up.

When the call came in, she was upstairs in the guest bedroom, using her laptop to dig up information on Desert Mining, the company she hoped to work with if the molybdenum was actually there.

Alex heard the roar of a jet and dug out his iPhone, pressed it against his ear. "Justice."

"Alex, this is Josh Reynolds." The assistant D.A. who had been keeping him posted on Edward Bagley.

"Hey, Josh, what's up?"

"This is a call I really hated to make, but I figure you deserve to know."

His fingers tightened around the phone. "What is it?"

"Bagley slipped surveillance. He's in the wind, and we have no idea where he'll surface."

Fuck. "Tell me you're kidding."

"I wish I were. Nobody knows exactly how it happened. He was home and we had men watching the house 24/7. We didn't figure out he was gone until one of the undercover officers spotted flames coming out the back windows. The building was nearly destroyed, but the arson guys are sure he wasn't inside."

"I can't believe this. He must have had a way out you didn't know about."

"We got a warrant after you turned in that DNA evidence, searched the place top to bottom but didn't find much of anything. And any DNA resulting from the search was also ruled out because we got the warrant on illegal evidence in the first place."

"Son of a bitch."

"I think you're right. He had some kind of secret passage we didn't find."

"It fits. Could be how he was moving around without getting noticed, and he burned down the house to destroy any other evidence that might have turned up."

"That's the way it looks."

Alex closed his eyes, fought to rein in his temper. "So you've got nothing," he said softly. Too softly. "Not a goddamned single thing—including Bagley."

"Sorry, Alex."

"Yeah, you can say that again." Alex hung up the phone and turned to see Sabrina standing a few feet away.

"What is it?"

"Bagley slipped his tether. He's on the loose and nobody has any idea where he's gone."

She walked over, wrapped her arms around his waist. "I'm so sorry."

"Mr. and Mrs. Wiseman are going to be devastated. They still had hopes we were going to find new evidence that would nail the bastard once and for all."

"It's not your fault. They wouldn't even know who killed their daughter if it weren't for you."

"Maybe. Doesn't help the next little girl Bagley murders." Or the ones before Carrie Wiseman, and Alex was fairly sure there were some. "The son of a bitch was a schoolteacher. Can you believe it?"

"Teacher of the Year, they said on the news."

"*Teacher of the Year.* That's a good one. That's what

kept him out of the spotlight for so long. People just couldn't believe an upstanding guy like that could be capable of such a heinous crime."

"They'll find him. We have to believe that."

Alex released a slow breath. "I wish I were convinced." He rubbed his jaw. He needed a drink, something strong. Hell, he needed a whole damned bottle.

Sabrina gently tugged on his arm. "Come on. It's almost time for supper. I'm going crazy locked up in here every day, and now so are you. Let's get out of here for a while."

She was right. He needed to get out, and he couldn't keep her locked up forever. She was ready to bolt as it was.

"Let me get my weapon." He ignored the Ruger he kept in a drawer in the kitchen and headed upstairs for his S&W .45. Strapping his shoulder holster on over his T-shirt, he slipped a blue flowered short-sleeved shirt over the gun and headed back downstairs.

By the time he reached the bottom of the staircase, Sabrina had changed into a yellow sundress that left her back exposed and barely covered her sweet little ass. He wasn't sure he wanted her flashing that luscious body for anyone but him, but it sure was turning him on.

"I'm ready," she said, slinging the strap of a small white handbag over her shoulder.

He felt more like peeling off the dress and keeping all that sweet femininity to himself, but he figured that wasn't an option—at least not until they got home. Leading her out to the garage, he loaded her into the car, punched in the alarm code and climbed in behind the wheel, backed out and remotely closed the garage door.

"So where are you taking me, flyboy?" she asked as

he drove down the street. "And it better be the kind of place you'd take your friend Gabriella."

Alex just smiled, thinking most of the time he'd just taken Gaby to bed. "How about the Post Oak Grill? If I remember, Jake said it's one you and Sage really like."

Sabrina leaned back in her seat and closed her eyes, gave him a tiny catlike smile. "Purrrfect."

Even in the black mood he was in, Alex couldn't stop a grin.

The atmosphere was elegant and the food delicious, as usual. Rina remembered only too well the last time she had been there with Sage, when Jake Cantrell, her bodyguard at the time, had stormed in to rescue her from a group protesting the oil deal her company was making with a Saudi Arabian sheik.

Tonight was infinitely more relaxing.

She took a sip of the expensive Bordeaux that Alex had ordered. "All right, so now that you know most of my family's dirty little secrets, I want to know something about yours."

Alex's smile slipped away. "Not much to tell. They're rich and they spend a lot of time in Europe."

"That's it? Sorry, not enough. What else?"

Keeping his expression carefully bland, Alex took a drink of his wine. "They're old-money, East Coast high society and they were pretty much lousy parents when Becca and I were growing up."

She had begun to figure that from the little tidbits he'd let slip here and there. "What about now?"

Alex shrugged, his wide shoulders moving beneath the blue-flowered shirt. The color matched his eyes and just looking at him sitting there made her heart beat faster.

"Same deal," he said. "I try to stay away as much as my conscience will allow. I go back about once a year."

Rina studied the blank expression he was working so hard to maintain. Maybe the need she read in him had something to do with his past. "But they loved you, right?"

He lifted his wineglass then returned it to the table without taking a drink. "In their own way, I guess. Mostly we were raised by nannies. A string of them. I don't even remember most of their names."

"Oh, Alex, that's so sad."

His features tightened. He picked up his wineglass and leaned back in his chair. "Beats living in Uvalde."

Rina blanched at the cutting remark, the kind she had never heard him make before. He didn't want her pity. If she hadn't understood that, she might have been angry.

"We didn't have much money, that's for sure."

Alex blew out a slow breath, set his wineglass back on the table. "I'm sorry." He reached over and took hold of her hand. "I didn't mean that. I have a hard time talking about my parents. In a way I'm jealous of the life you lived."

"Jealous?"

"It's obvious how much your mother loves you. And the way you talk about your dad…he must have loved you, too."

She smiled wistfully. "I was lucky. My cousins and I, we didn't even know we were poor until we grew up. That was when things changed."

"That's when you decided to put yourself through college and became a successful stockbroker."

"I worked my way though school, but Uncle Walter helped me."

"What about his own kids? He help them, too?"

"Bob was the only one who went on after high school. He got a two-year degree from community college, but he had no desire to continue. He started working and eventually got his real estate license. He was very successful as a developer."

"Until the recession hit."

"That's right."

They finished their meal, medium-rare steaks and potatoes au gratin for both of them, then shared an extravagant desert of vanilla bean crème brûlée.

So full her ribs were aching by the time they finished and headed outside, Rina noticed the way Alex studied the landscape, keeping an eye out for trouble. He hadn't forgotten the plane crash or the car accident. He had even paid the valet extra to park his BMW in the lights in front of the restaurant so no one could tamper with it.

Rina knew he was good at his job. She smiled to think he was earning every dollar of the money she wasn't paying him.

Alex took the long way back to his house. Once he thought he caught a glimpse of a dark brown sedan that seemed to be following them, but a couple of turns and the car was gone. He made a couple more evasive moves just to be sure they weren't being followed, but the car didn't reappear. A motorcycle turned a corner behind them, appearing for a couple of blocks in his rearview mirror, then it rounded a corner and headed off in another direction.

"We need some milk for breakfast," Sabrina said.

"Would you mind stopping at the minimart? It won't take a minute."

He checked the mirror. No sign of the dark sedan or the cycle. It was safer just to go home, but Sabrina liked granola and milk for breakfast and so far there'd been nothing to indicate anyone even knew where she was. And there was still no conclusive proof she was in danger.

He pulled into the minimart lot, parked up close to the front door and turned off the engine.

Sabrina cracked open her door.

"Hold on...we'll both go in." He wasn't about to leave her in the car alone or let her go into the store without him.

They walked inside, and she headed back to the dairy section. The store was empty except for the bald man behind the counter and a skinny teenager trying unsuccessfully to buy beer. Sabrina grabbed a quart of nonfat milk off a refrigerated shelf and brought it up to the counter. Alex paid for it and they headed out the door.

They were almost back to the car when a movement at the edge of his vision caught his eye. Metal gleamed in the fluorescent light coming out of the store windows as three men ran out of the darkness.

"Run!" He only had time to shove Sabrina out of the way before a big, burly Hispanic man was on him. Sabrina screamed as Alex threw a punch that broke the man's nose and spewed blood all over his black T-shirt. The return punch split Alex's lip; he ducked a jab, and swung another punch as a second man appeared just to his left, knife in hand.

Swearing an oath, Alex brought his knee up hard into the first man's groin, doubling him over, then drove a fist into his face, knocking him down. No time to pull his pistol. The second man, solidly built, iron-jawed and ready for a fight, rammed into him like a freight train, driving him backward, the knife slashing viciously through his shirt and T-shirt, streaking like fire across his skin.

Alex dived forward instead of back, chopping the edge of his hand down hard against side of the second man's neck and sending him sprawling on the ground.

He jerked his pistol, heard Sabrina scream, "Alex!" saw her jump on the first man as he tried to get back on his feet, spotted a third man—lean, solid, do-rag tied around his head. The guy was moving fast, sprinting toward her, the barrel of his semiauto aimed at her heart.

Swinging up his .45, Alex aimed and pulled the trigger, one, two, three shots dead center to the middle of the third man's chest, slamming him backward, up against the side of a car, blood spreading over the gunman's faded black T-shirt as he went down hard on the pavement.

He didn't get up.

The big Hispanic guy ducked another blow from Sabrina's purse, shoved her off him onto the asphalt and started running. The guy with the knife ran after him and both men disappeared around the back of the store into the darkness.

Forcing down the urge to follow, unwilling to leave Sabrina unprotected in case one of them returned, Alex bit back a curse.

"Alex! Oh, my God, Alex!"

He lowered his weapon as she raced toward him, threw herself into his arms. "Alex! Are you...are you all right?" She was shaking all over, her petite frame trembling against him. One of the straps was torn off her pretty yellow sundress, the slim skirt covered with dirt, and her high heels were gone.

His chest clamped down at what might have happened if she had been alone.

The store owner ran to the door. "Police are on the way! They'll be here any minute!"

Alex nodded and shoved his pistol back into his shoulder holster, his arm still tight around Sabrina.

She looked him over, her eyes big and luminous in the harsh lights over the parking lot. "Oh, my God, Alex, you're bleeding!"

The thin slash across his stomach registered as a faintly stinging pain. The wound wasn't deep, thank God. He wiped blood off the corner of his mouth. "I'm all right. This one's not."

She glanced down at the man on the pavement whose eyes stared unseeing into the harsh lights overhead, and her face went pale.

Alex steadied her against him. "It's all right, love. It's over. You're safe."

His gaze went to the darkness at the edge of the parking lot. He hadn't had much doubt before. Now he knew for certain. Someone wanted Sabrina dead.

Twenty-Two

The police arrived, along with half a dozen other official vehicles. The area in front of the minimart was cordoned off with yellow crime scene tape. The paramedics went to work on the gash just below his ribs, deemed it superficial, cleaned the scrapes on his knuckles and taped him up. They cleansed the dirt and grit from the scrapes on Sabrina's hands and knees, and pressed a cold compress on the bruise along her jaw.

Alex drew her back into his arms and just held on. He had almost lost her tonight. A shudder rippled through him at the thought.

Detectives arrived and began asking questions, which seemed to have no end. He relayed in detail what had happened, but purposely left out the part about the previous attempts on Sabrina's life until he could talk to the detectives in the morning. It was getting late and there would be time enough to get the incidents that technically were no more than a series of unfortunate coincidences, into the police report.

They'd been there less than an hour when Alex spotted a rugged black Jeep with chrome wheels and oversize tires pulling up at the edge of the minimart parking lot. He'd phoned Jake and Sage after the shooting, figuring Sabrina might need a woman to talk to, and he could use Jake's take on the situation.

Sage jumped out before the Jeep had rolled to a complete stop and ran to Sabrina, who went into her best friend's arms. The women clung to each other.

"Are you okay?" Sage asked, looping a heavy red curl behind Sabrina's ear. Alex caught the sheen of tears in her eyes before she stoically blinked them away.

"If Alex hadn't been with me, I'd be dead."

His stomach knotted, the scene flashing through his mind all over again: three men appearing out of the darkness, the knife, the gun that would have ended her life if the man had had the chance to fire.

"I don't know about that," he said just to lighten the mood. "You were doing one helluva job on that guy's head with your purse."

She looked down at the little white handbag, saw a trace of blood on the clasp, and managed a wan-looking smile. "I hope I gave him a lot worse headache than I have."

Sage leaned down and hugged her, then held her out at arm's length. "No one's going to kill you. Alex won't let them. Neither will Jake." She looked up at her tall, muscular husband.

"That's not gonna happen, sweetcheeks," Jake said, reaching out to run a gentle hand down Sabrina's cheek. He turned to Alex. "We need to talk."

"Yeah." Leaving the women together, he and Jake walked a few feet away. Alex had told his friend the basics on the phone so Jake already knew most of what had happened.

"You recognize any of them?" Jake asked.

"No. Three Hispanics, gangbangers-for-hire, I figure."

In front of the store, the crime scene guys were at work taking photos and collecting evidence while the detectives interviewed the store owner and anyone who might have seen something.

While Alex kept an eye on Sabrina, Jake walked over and talked to one of the CSIs, then took a look at the body. He returned a few minutes later.

"Word is he isn't carrying ID, but he's got some flashy tats. Trace has a friend in the department, detective named Castillo. He's head of the Houston P.D. gang division. Castillo knows tattoos. The department'll be working that angle but they may not be willing to give you the info right away. Castillo might be able to help."

"I know who he is. Trace mentioned him a couple of times when he was working Maggie's case. Alex held up his iPhone, showed Jake the photo he had taken of the colorful tat on the dead guy's arm. "I'll call Castillo in the morning, see if he'll take a look at this."

"Might hurry things along."

"Yeah, and once we've got an ID, maybe we can tie him to Sabrina's cousins."

"You're sure they're behind this?"

"One of them is. It still isn't confirmed, but it looks like there could be millions involved in that mine she inherited. With Sabrina out of the way, those three are in line for the property. It's the only thing that makes sense."

Alex glanced over at the little redhead standing next

to Sage and felt a tightness in his chest. She'd been amazing tonight. He still couldn't believe she'd squared off with one of them. She was one tough lady when she had to be.

Still, just thinking what might have happened made his stomach feel queasy.

He returned his attention to Jake. "I'm going to need some backup on this. I don't want to leave Sabrina alone, but I need time to work the case."

"Not a problem. She can stay with us as long as you want. I won't let her out of my sight."

He almost smiled, imagining how well that idea was going to go over with Sabrina.

He heard footsteps, glanced up. Over Jake's thick-muscled shoulder, he saw Ben Slocum walking toward them. With his black hair, dark-tanned skin and fierce expression, he looked even more dangerous than the dead guy on the ground. It was those pale, ice-blue eyes that gave him the edge.

"Annie called," Ben said, "told me what happened. She thought you might need some backup. Trace is out of town or he'd be here, too."

"How the hell did Annie know?" Alex asked.

Jake answered. "She was on the phone with Sage when you called on my cell. They're planning your birthday party—which is supposed to be a surprise, so keep quiet about it."

"Are you sure Annie isn't CIA?" Alex grumbled. "That woman seems to know everything that happens two minutes after."

"If she isn't, she should be," Ben said. "At any rate, she figured you'd need help coming up with a way to catch the bastard behind this. She said three heads are better than two, and she's right."

"She usually is," Alex conceded.

Ben walked over to look at the body. One of the uniforms stepped in his way, Ben said something and the officer let him pass. He didn't get too close, just took a look, then walked back.

"How many?"

"Three."

"Two now," Ben said.

"How'd they know you were going to stop at the minimart?" Jake asked.

"They didn't. They must have followed us from the house to the restaurant, then waited for us to come out after we ate. I thought I spotted a dark brown sedan when we left the place, but it disappeared. Cycle trailed me for a couple of blocks. I think they were running a relay."

"And if they followed you from your house to the Grill," Jake said, "they knew you'd be heading back home after supper."

"Which means they knew where to find you in the first place," Ben said.

"Any chance they bugged your car?" Jake asked.

Alex shook his head. "I keep it in the garage. No way to get to it, at least not before we left the house."

"Could have been the GPS in your cell."

"Maybe." He'd disabled Sabrina's phone but not his own. "If it was, it won't happen again." He took the phone apart and pulled out the battery, shoved the phone back into his pocket. "I'll pick up a disposable, use that from now on."

He glanced over at Sabrina. "Wouldn't take much for the cousins to figure she was staying with me. We paid cousin Bob a little visit and went to see Priscilla in Uvalde. With Sabrina's mom thrown into the mix, they've got one helluva grapevine."

"You can't take her back to your house," Ben said. "It's not safe anymore."

"I'll get us a room for the night. I'll have to go home sometime. I need some clothes and Sabrina will need to pack a few things."

Ben scoffed. "She's a woman. She'll need more than a few."

As tired as he was, Alex almost smiled.

"Let me know when you want to go and I'll tag along," Ben said, "make sure the party doesn't get out of hand."

Alex nodded. "I'll take you up on that."

"This ought to throw them off their game for a while," Jake said. "When a plan goes south it takes time to regroup."

"I hope you're right." And chances were Jake was spot-on. These guys were not a professional hit squad. They were lowlifes someone had hired, just the way someone had been hired to sabotage the helo engine and the steering in the Toyota.

"I'll follow you to the hotel," Ben said, "make sure you don't run into any more surprises."

"Thanks. In the morning, I'll bring Sabrina into the office. Annie can keep her entertained while we figure our next move."

And Sabrina would definitely be safe with a former Special Ops Marine sniper and a former Navy SEAL.

One of the detectives approached and led Alex away for another round of questions. It was getting late for all of them, and since the mart owner's story matched the one Alex and Sabrina both told, they were finally released on the condition they come into the station first thing in the morning.

As promised, when they left, Ben followed them in his big black SUV. Alex made a number of turns, just to play it safe, but with Ben behind them in his Denali, he was sure he wasn't being tailed.

He and Sabrina spent the night, what was left of it, at the Westin Hotel near the Galleria.

Morning came way too soon.

Rina was exhausted. Her muscles ached from her fight with the big, brawny man who had attacked them—she couldn't believe she had actually jumped on his back and started whacking him over the head with her purse! But Alex was fighting for his life—fighting for both of their lives—and there wasn't any other choice.

She thought of what had happened and a shiver raced over her skin. Alex had been amazing, a hero in one of those action movies. He'd taken on three men and come out the winner, kept her safe at the risk of his own life.

Her heart squeezed. Dear God, what if Alex had been badly injured or even killed? She tried to feel sorry for the man he'd shot, but the fact was, if Alex hadn't killed him, she would probably be dead. Both of them might be.

She'd awakened a few minutes ago, tired and edgy, her heart pounding from a dream that was bloody and terrifying and a lot like the shooting last night, and found herself alone in the room. Her sundress lay on the floor, torn and dirty, completely unwearable.

She grimaced as she held it up, wondering where Alex had gone and wishing she had something else to put on. Then she heard the sound of a key in the lock and Alex stepped into the room. He had showered last night—they both had—and now wore a new pair of blue jeans and a dark blue T-shirt that covered the bandage across his ribs and had HOUSTON printed in big white letters on the front.

He tossed a plastic shopping bag up on the bed. "These won't be much of a fit, but the stores in the mall aren't open yet, and at least these are clean."

She reached into the bag and pulled out a pair of jeans, a T-shirt with the Texans' football steer-head emblazoned on the front, and a pair of red plastic flip-flops.

"Where on earth did you find this stuff?"

"Gift shop in the lobby. They sell souvenirs and toiletries, T-shirts, things like that. I figured these would do till you could get your own things. I changed in the bathroom downstairs so I wouldn't wake you up."

She reached into the bag and pulled out one of those disposable cell phones.

"Those can't be tracked," Alex said. "That one's for you. I figured you'd want to call your mom."

"That was very thoughtful. Thank you."

She shoved the phone into the purse she had used last night, grimaced at how battered it was, then slipped into the bathroom to brush her teeth and put on the clean clothes. Though the jeans were baggy, the boys' size large T-shirt fit pretty well, and as Alex said, they would do till she could go home and retrieve some of her own clothes.

"I'm ready if you are," she said as she came out of the bathroom.

"One last thing before we go. It's time we told the police what's going on. This is the third time someone has tried to kill you. There's a good chance the attacks involve one or more of your cousins. They may not like the police asking them questions, but that's just too damn bad."

She thought of George and the battle he was waging to keep his little girl alive. "We can't do that, Alex. We don't have a single scrap of evidence that incriminates any of them. All we have is the assumption that someone in my family is willing to commit murder to get their hands on Uncle Walter's mine."

"It's something the cops need to know."

"We both know none of my cousins personally carried out any of the attempts."

"No, but they could have paid someone to do it. That's the same thing."

"We can't prove that. They're my family and we don't have a single shred of proof they're involved. And even if you're right, once the cops start asking questions, whoever it is may just pull in his horns for a few weeks or even months, then come after me again. What do I do then? I'm not willing to live like a rabbit until whoever is after me gives up trying to kill me."

"Once the mine is improved, the property goes to your heirs, not to them—it says that in the will. Your cousins would have no more reason to kill you."

"Assuming the ore is actually there, improving the mine will take months. I need this over with now."

Alex blew out a breath, his eyes a dark, penetrating blue as he weighed her words. "I don't like it. Not one damned bit." He rubbed a hand over his jaw. "Unfortunately, you're right. The cops might scare them off. Which would be even more dangerous for you in the long run."

"Exactly."

"We'll tell the police about the other two incidents, get the information into the report. But we won't mention any names. In the meantime, I'll talk to Jake and Ben, see what we can come up with."

She walked over and caught his arm, went up on her toes and kissed his cheek. "Thank you."

"For chrissake, don't thank me. I'm just trying to keep you alive."

She started to back away, but he caught her shoulders, dragged her up on her toes and kissed her, deep and thoroughly. "We'll get through this, all right?"

She nodded, still feeling the imprint of his mouth over hers. "Okay."

For the first time Alex smiled. "Time to go, Red."

Wishing she didn't have to relive the entire experience again at the police station, she let Alex guide her out of the hotel room down the hall to the elevator. At least they didn't need a bellman.

All she had to carry was her purse.

Rina was edgy and nervous as they drove toward the station. Several times along the way, she caught Alex checking the rearview mirror to see if they were being followed. It was just a precaution, since no one had followed them last night, but in the makeup mirror above her seat, she found herself doing the same. Nothing looked suspicious, just the usual buzz of traffic headed downtown.

"I'd better phone my mother," she said. "I don't think the attack will make the Uvalde news, but it might."

"Whatever you do, don't tell her where to find you. Just give her the disposable number and keep the story simple. A mugging. That's all that happened."

"Got it."

She kept the call brief, explaining about the men and the shooting. "We just happened to be in the wrong place at the wrong time."

"Dear God, Alex shot the man?" her mother said.

"It was self-defense, Mom. The police understand what happened."

"Oh, dear. Is Alex all right?"

Sabrina flicked a glance in his direction, tried not to think of that last hot kiss. "He's fine."

"I'm just so thankful he was with you when it happened. You're sure you're okay?"

"We're both okay." She gave her mother the number on the disposable phone, then signed off.

"Police headquarters are just up ahead," Alex said.

Sabrina took a deep breath, bolstering her courage. When was this ever going to end?

Twenty-Three

The pavement burned the soles of her flip-flops as Rina approached the imposing, multistoried police headquarters building on Travis Street in downtown Houston.

Alex checked in at the front desk, speaking with an attractive blonde police officer, and a few minutes later, a young patrolman came out and led them down a long white hallway into an interview room that held a table and four black vinyl chairs. A mirror covered one wall, which Rina presumed was the see-through kind she had seen on TV cop shows.

The young patrolman brought them each a foam cup of coffee—thank you, God—and a few minutes later, Homicide Detective Colin Murphy arrived, one of the two who had interviewed them last night at the minimart. A freckle-faced man with red hair going to gray, Murphy settled into the chair across from Alex and began asking questions.

"This won't take long," Murphy said. "There's just a few more things we need to go over."

Most of the questions were the same as the ones he had asked last night.

He got the same answers.

Rina had no trouble recalling what had happened. The incident was burned into her brain.

"Depending on where our investigation leads," Murphy said, "you may be asked to come in and look at some mug shots, see if you can pick out the other men who assaulted you."

"That won't be a problem," Alex said.

Murphy skimmed through the pages of the police report. "Anything else either of you want to add?"

Alex flicked her a glance. "Only that this isn't the first attempt on Ms. Eckhart's life."

Murphy's head came up. "That so?"

Rina flicked Alex a warning glance, reminding him of the deal they had made, then listened as he told Detective Murphy about the helo crash, referring them to Sheriff Dickens, and the accident on the freeway.

"And you believe these incidents are all connected?"

"We aren't completely sure," Rina said before Alex could answer, "but it's possible."

"Do you have any idea who might be behind the attacks?"

"At this point," Alex said, "we have nothing more to go on than a string of bad luck. We come up with something you'll be the first to know."

Murphy turned in Rina's direction. "You realize, Ms. Eckhart, even if Justice here is right, we can't offer you police protection. As far as the department's concerned, last night was a mugging gone bad. We don't have anything to tie what happened to you before with what happened at the minimart."

"Ms. Eckhart has private protection," Alex reminded him. "That being you."

"That's right. It's my job to keep her safe."

Murphy's eyes crinkled at the corners. "Seems to me you did a fine job last night."

Alex flicked Rina a glance and his mouth edged up. "That's what I get paid for." A look passed between them, and Alex winked.

If she hadn't been so depressed, Rina would have laughed.

Cell phone pressed to his ear, Henry tipped his recliner forward, folding the footrest out of the way under his feet.

"Jesus Christ, tell me you haven't screwed up again!"

Ignoring the irate voice on the other end of the line, Henry grabbed the remote and turned the volume down on the TV. "The guy's got fucking nine lives."

"What about the man he shot? The news report said he was dead. Can the police connect him to Ortega?"

"I don't think so. Hector knows a lot of people. I don't think he knew the dead guy personally, just paid some bangers to handle it for a price."

"Yeah—ten thousand dollars."

"Hey, you only had to pay the first five since the job didn't get done."

"I don't give a crap. It's money I can't afford. I don't like it, Henry. I'm tired of sticking my neck out."

"Well, I don't like that we still don't get the fucking money!"

"Listen to me. This guy Justice isn't a fool. He knows it's one of us—just not which one. We need to lay low for a while, let all this blow over."

No goddamn way, Henry thought. He needed his
share of the money and he was going to get it. "You got
a shitload of bills. What do you plan to do about that?"

A disgruntled sigh seeped into the phone. "I'll manage. Just let it go. Ending up in jail isn't part of my plan."

It wasn't Henry's plan either, but he wasn't about to
walk away from a deal worth millions. He needed Rina
Eckhart dead, and he was going to make that happen.
Once it was accomplished, his old high school chum
would owe him big-time.

"Listen, Henry, it's just too dangerous. If things
change, I'll give you a call. Till then, it's better if we
don't talk."

Henry reached over and plucked his cigarette out of
the ashtray, took a heavy drag. He blew a smoke ring into
the air, watched it float away. "Whatever you say, boss."

The phone went dead, and Henry smiled. So far he
hadn't been able to get the job done, but neither had he
left any trace that would lead back to him or anyone else.

Still, in a way his boss was right. They needed to wait
for the right opportunity. He had connections of his own.
He'd be able to work something out.

He remembered the old saying. *If you want something
done right, do it yourself.*

Henry leaned back in his recliner and turned the volume up on the TV.

Alex sat next to Sabrina in Detective Danny Castillo's
crowded office, his second stop at police headquarters.
The office was small and unimpressive, with manila files
stacked on the floor and spread all over the metal desk.
A photo of Castillo's wife and three kids sat on top, and
framed commendations hung on the walls.

"Thanks for giving us a hand with this, Detective," Alex said, taking Castillo's measure. Head of the gang division, Castillo was a tall, good-looking Hispanic man with short black hair combed straight back and jet-black eyes.

"Happy to help if I can."

Mentioning Trace's name had gotten him the appointment, since the two men had worked together before. Castillo seated himself, then leaned forward in his chair, propping his forearms on the brown desk pad on top. His shirtsleeves were rolled up and Alex noticed a small blue ink tattoo on his wrist, wondered if he'd gotten it in his youth or from working undercover.

"Let's see what you've got," Castillo said. Over the phone, Alex had told him about the homicide last night, so the detective knew most of what had happened.

Digging out his iPhone, Alex replaced the battery, enabling the phone, then turned it on and brought up the screen. He handed the phone to the detective, showing him the photos he'd taken of the dead man's arm, framed by the cutout sleeves of his faded black T-shirt. The tat ran from wrist to shoulder and wrapped all the way around the arm.

"I need a closer look," Castillo said. "Let's upload the photos onto my computer."

It didn't take long to make the transfer from the cell phone camera into Castillo's machine. iPhones took great pictures and even at night, these were good. Across the monitor, dragons and snakes in red, green and blue crawled up the hard-muscled arm. Openmouthed skulls ate something that looked like a human version of a vampire bat, and snakes wound their way out of the skull's empty eyes.

Castillo fixed his attention on the enlarged photo on the computer screen.

"This wasn't done in any prison. It's really fine work. I'd say it's local. Artist named Leon Crutch does this kind of thing."

Castillo studied the picture, his black eyes going over every line. "Crutch always leaves his initials camouflaged somewhere in the design." He pointed to the screen. "See, here's the *L* and over here's the *C*. Leon Crutch." He looked up. "Even if you don't like the subject matter, the man's a real artist."

Alex made no comment. Tattoos weren't high on his list of good ideas. He kept imagining what the designs would look like when the skin beneath the tat got old and saggy. "Any chance you could print that for me?"

Castillo clicked the mouse and a few seconds later, a copy of the picture came out of the printer. Castillo made a copy for himself and handed one of them to Alex.

He passed Sabrina the photo to hold on to. "I need to talk to Crutch. Where do I find him?"

"He's got a shop on Tetley Street, Living Color. Got an apartment upstairs, so he's usually around most of the day." He slid his own photocopy over to a corner of his desk. "Detectives on the case'll want this information. I'll pass it on to them. They talk to you about Crutch, be better if you don't tell them how you got his name."

"Not a problem."

Castillo stood up from his chair, and Alex and Sabrina rose, as well. "Nice to meet you, Ms. Eckhart."

"You, too, Detective. Thank you for your help."

"If you hear anything," Alex said, "I'd appreciate a call. This goes way deeper than a mugging. Someone wants Sabrina dead and whoever it is isn't going to stop until someone stops them."

One of Castillo's black eyebrows went up. "You tell the detectives that?"

"I told Murphy. He's the lead on the case. We don't have enough proof to name names. Maybe this will help."

He held the door as Sabrina and Castillo walked out into the hallway. The corridor was even busier than it was before, the elevators crowded as Castillo accompanied them back to the main part of the building.

"I'll let you know if anything comes up," the detective said.

"Appreciate it." Alex led Sabrina across the lobby to the thick glass doors, held them open to allow a heavyset woman and her two young boys to walk past. Sabrina was quiet as they moved along the sidewalk toward the police station parking lot, pigeons fluttering out of their way to let them pass.

"How would my cousins even know people like those?" she asked.

"You mean street thugs? They're like gutter rats. Easier to find than you might think. These days, money buys damn near anything. You just have to figure out who to ask."

She just kept walking, looking even more exhausted than she had that morning. He knew she was thinking about her family, wondering if one of them was trying to kill her. She didn't want to believe it. He didn't really blame her.

"Are we going to see this man, Crutch?"

"I am. First we're going to the office. I'm leaving you there with Jake and Ben till I get back."

Sabrina stopped dead in her tracks, whirled and pressed a hand against his chest. "I am not sitting in your office while your friends babysit. I'm going with you, Alex. I want to hear what this man has to say."

"It won't take long and I need you someplace safe."

"I'm safe with you. You proved that last night. I've never felt safer in my life."

He released a slow breath. He'd been careful driving to the hotel last night and leaving again this morning. There had been no opportunity to bug the car and his cell phone was once more disabled. Maybe if he let her go with him to the tattoo parlor, she'd give him less flack when he left her with Ben and Jake.

"It's my life we're talking about," she pressed. "Besides, I might think of something useful."

Alex opened the passenger door. "Fine. But once we get there, I do the talking."

Sabrina just nodded and quietly climbed into the car. He wasn't fooled for a minute. She was pushing her luck and she was smart enough to know it. But Tetley Street wasn't in a bad section of town, and even with Jake and Ben watching out for her, he would worry.

And dammit, when had worrying about Sabrina become way more than a job?

Rebecca listened to the voice on Alex's cell phone, directing her call straight to the messaging center. She glanced back at the TV, at the reporter broadcasting from the minimart parking lot where a vicious mugging had occurred last night. One man was dead in a robbery attempt on Alex Justice and Sabrina Eckhart as they walked out of the store.

The newscaster, a woman in her thirties with short

blond hair, spoke into the microphone as the camera swung toward the convenience mart.

"This is the second time in the past few weeks that Alexander Justice, a private investigator with Atlas Security, has been in the news. The first involved the case of ten-year-old Carrie Wiseman, the little girl who was brutally raped and murdered three years ago."

As the reporter went on to retell the story of Edward Bagley and the accusations of his alleged involvement in the murder, Rebecca heard the thud of heavy boots behind her and turned to see Joe McCauley shoving through the back door into the kitchen. She ignored a little tremor of awareness as he came up behind her.

"God, Joe, have you seen the news? Someone attacked Alex and Sabrina last night on their way home from dinner. Alex killed one of them."

His big hands came to rest gently on her shoulders. "I saw it. It's all right. Both of them are okay."

She could feel the rise and fall of his powerful chest against her back, and her heartbeat quickened. She turned to face him, forced herself to take a step away. "I tried to call him. Alex isn't answering his phone."

"He's turned it off. Probably trying to dodge the media."

She grabbed her purse off the counter. "Something's wrong. I want to know what's going on." She and Alex had always been close. Even as kids, they'd shared a sort of sixth sense that told them when one of them was in trouble. Over the years that hadn't changed.

Rebecca hadn't seen Alex since they'd gone to the hospital together to see Sabrina. He'd been frantic to get to her, terrified she had been badly injured. Though her brother didn't seem to know, it was clear he was at least half in love with the woman. Now something else had happened.

"Where are you going?" Joe asked as she started for the door.

"Ginny's in KinderCare." A preschool for gifted kids her little girl loved. "I'm going down to Alex's office. If he isn't there, Annie or one of the guys will know what's going on."

Joe plucked the keys to the Suburban out of her hand. "Come on, I'll drive you."

Rebecca didn't argue. Joe was a rock, a man she could depend on. After the terrible years with Jeremy, she had told herself depending on another man was the last thing she wanted. But Joe was…well, Joe was different.

Last night they'd had dinner together at the local Pizza Hut, all three of them. It was the closest she had ever come to feeling like part of a family.

It was dangerous to let her feelings deepen so fast. She didn't know Joe that well and she had Ginny to consider.

Still, when Joe reached for her, she didn't hesitate, just let his strong fingers wrap around her hand as he led her out the door.

Twenty-Four

"Thanks for letting me come along," Rina said as Alex drove the car toward the tattoo parlor.

"I didn't exactly let you, but I feel better keeping you with me."

She studied his handsome profile. With a face any Renaissance sculptor would love and those sky-blue eyes, she was amazed he could look so completely male. There was nothing soft about Alex Justice, not in his features, not in his iron-hard body. Just sitting next to him made her wish he hadn't let her sleep in that morning.

"You don't trust Ben and Jake?" she asked, forcing her thoughts back where they belonged.

A smile flickered at the corner of his mouth. "I trust them with my life. With my woman? Not so much." He grinned and his dimples popped out, making her stomach contract. Though he was only teasing, a little coil of warmth spun through her.

Did he really think of her as his woman? He had never said anything like that to her before.

And was that what she wanted? To be Alex Justice's woman?

She was, she supposed. She just wasn't sure how long it would last.

"The shop's up ahead on the right."

She spotted the sign, Living Color, above a narrow brick building wedged between a sleazy bar and a beauty salon advertising cheap haircuts.

Alex grabbed the photo Castillo had printed and they headed for the shop, Rina staying close by his side. He shoved open the door and guided her inside and a strong, soapy smell hit her. Three black vinyl chairs lined the wall but only one was in use.

"I'm looking for Leon Crutch," Alex said to a barrel-chested man carefully inking a heart-shape design on a client's shoulder. "That you?"

A cigarette dangled from the man's thin lips, a thread of smoke curling up beside his ear. He wore a faded tank top, baggy tan shorts and Jesus sandals. He tipped his shaved head toward the ceiling, making the earring glint in his ear.

"Upstairs." His hard gaze ran over Alex's clean-cut appearance in his brand-new jeans and navy blue, souvenir T-shirt. He still wore the Italian loafers he'd worn to dinner at the Grill last night. "You got an appointment?"

Sabrina bit back a laugh as she tried to imagine where Alex would put a tattoo. Certainly no place it would show.

"Maybe later," he said. "For now, I just want to talk to him."

"Take the stairs at the back of the building. Apartment five, down at the end."

"Thanks." Alex led her in that direction and she could

feel the man in the chair and the tattoo artist watching her as they passed through the shop. It was well lit, though the windows were painted black. There was clutter on the counters at each station, and she could see stacks of tattoo needles in a drawer that stood partially open.

They made their way out through the rear of the shop and up the stairs. Alex rapped on the apartment door and a couple of seconds later, it swung open.

"Leon Crutch?"

"Who wants to know?"

"I'm Alex Justice. I'm a private investigator." He flipped open his wallet, showing his badge, stuffed the wallet back into the pocket of his jeans. Behind his back beneath the T-shirt, he was carrying his pistol stuffed into the waistband. "I'd like to ask you a couple of questions."

Crutch hesitated a moment, gave her a long, slow perusal, must have figured Alex wasn't there to cause him any trouble if he had brought her along and stepped back to let them into his living room. The apartment was surprisingly clean, the walls lined with grotesque, wildly colorful contemporary art that mirrored his taste in tattoos.

"What can I do for you?"

Alex handed Crutch the photo of the dead man's arm. "This man was shot and killed last night."

"The guy at the minimart?"

"That's him."

"Yeah, I caught it on the news."

Alex pointed at the design on the arm. "Looks like your work. I'm hoping you can give me a name."

Leon studied the photo. "I did the tat. You can see

my initials right here—" He pointed out the *L* and the *C* camouflaged in the design. "Problem is, that pattern isn't completely exclusive. You look at the flash art on the wall downstairs, you'll see some different variations. My designs are all unique, but still, this is a popular style."

Crutch tried to pass Alex the photo. Alex pushed it back in his direction. "Take another look. Anything in the picture that jumps out at you?"

Crutch stared down at the photo and something moved across his features. Even with her untrained eye, Rina could tell he recognized something.

"The cops'll be following up on this." Alex pointed to the photo. "As you said, your initials are in the pattern. No way for you to skate. Who is he?"

Leon ran his tongue over his lips. "I'm pretty sure it's a guy named Luis Catano. I recognize that little scar near the elbow, just to the right of the skull. I had to work around it."

"What else?"

"Catano runs with a bad bunch down in the barrio. He heard about my work through a buddy of his. I did the tat, and that's the last I've seen of him. That's all I know."

Alex studied Crutch's face, seemed satisfied the man was telling the truth. "I'll have to tell the police. They may have some questions."

"Not a problem. All I did was the tat, man."

Alex nodded. "Thanks for the help, Leon."

They left the shop, and on the way back to his office, Alex called Detective Murphy. He was using one of the throwaways he'd bought in the souvenir shop that morning.

"According to the guy who did the tat," he told Murphy, "the shooter is a guy named Luis Catano."

Murphy's voice came back over the hands-free. "Name rings a bell. I'll check it out."

"Let me know what you find out." Alex ended the call and turned the car toward the office, where he was meeting Ben and Jake to strategize and plan.

Rina suppressed a shiver. Whatever plan they came up with, she prayed that it would work.

It was hot. It was always hot in Houston. Ginny's blouse was sticking to her chest and her hands were sweaty. Still, she liked it better here than when they'd lived with her dad.

She tried not to think of him and wonder if he ever missed her, thought of Joe instead and rushed out onto the playground with the other kids. She headed straight for the jungle gym, wiped her sweaty hands on her blouse, grabbed one of the bars and started swinging, reaching out to pull herself along from bar to bar.

She wished she was wearing jeans instead of a stupid skirt. Then she could swing up high and catch the bars at the top. But her mother insisted she dress like a *little lady.*

Yuck. She didn't want to be a *little lady.* She wanted to run and jump and climb, do handstands in the grass. She was as fast as any of the boys her age, but she felt silly racing them in a skirt with blue ruffles around the hem.

With a sigh, she let go of the bars and wandered over beneath a big leafy tree at the edge of the playground, plopped down on the concrete bench underneath. She loved sports. She even liked to watch football and basketball on TV. She and Joe talked about the games all the time. She didn't know what was wrong with that.

Lots of girls liked to play sports. She didn't know why her mother didn't understand.

"Hello, Ginny. You're looking very pretty today."

She turned at the sound of a man's soft voice coming from the other side of the chain-link fence around the playground. She liked to wear jeans, but she also liked it when someone said she looked pretty.

She stood up from the bench and smoothed her ruffled skirt. "Thank you." Through the fence she saw a thin man with light brown hair and blue eyes. He had on nice clothes, tan slacks and a pullover shirt. There was a funny little brown spot on his neck shaped like a heart. "How did you know my name?"

"I'm a friend of your uncle Alex. He said to say hello."

She brightened. "He did? Uncle Alex is my very favorite uncle."

The man smiled. He had a nice, friendly smile. "I bet he is," the man said.

"He's been working hard lately so we haven't got to see him very much."

"That's too bad. I bet he really misses you."

Ginny nodded. "I miss him, too." The buzzer sounded, signaling recess was over. "I have to go back inside."

"That's okay. I'm sure we'll be seeing each other again. Tell your uncle I said hello."

She saw the kids racing back toward the classroom and worried she would be late.

"What's your name, mister?" she asked.

But when she turned to look at him, the man was already gone.

The mid-June heat was cranking up, the humidity building along with it. Still dressed in the clothes he'd bought in the gift shop that morning, Alex guided Sabrina into the Atlas Security office, the air conditioner pleasantly humming, knocking his body temperature down a couple of degrees.

Seated behind the reception desk, Annie tipped her head toward the beautiful blonde rushing toward him. "You got company."

"Alex! My God, are you all right? I saw the news. I've been calling you for hours. Why aren't you picking up? Joe and I stopped by your house. We thought we might find you there but—"

"Take it easy. Everything's okay." He gave his sister a hug, kept his arm around her as he drew Sabrina in front of him.

"You remember my sister, Becca? She came with me to the hospital."

Sabrina smiled at her warmly. "Of course I do. It's nice to see you, Rebecca. You were very kind that day."

"And this is Joe McCauley, the guy who convinced me to come to Houston." Alex grinned. "He's a pain in the ass, but he's a good man to have on your side when you need him."

"Hey, Peaceman. Heard the news on TV. Glad to see you're still breathing."

Alex reached out and the men shook hands. "Good to see you, Mac."

"I'm glad you're all having a nice little meet and greet," Becca said, "but I want to know what's going on. Alex, why did someone try to kill you last night?"

"Actually, they were trying to get to Sabrina. I just happened to be in the way."

"What?" His sister turned toward the little redhead at his side.

"Alex saved my life last night." Sabrina managed to smile. "He was amazing."

Why it pleased him so much to hear her say that, Alex couldn't say. "I'm her personal security," he said. "That's my job."

Annie spoke up from behind them. "And since you're finally in the office, hotshot, here's your messages. Quite a few since your phone isn't working."

Alex rattled off the number of the disposable. "You can reach me there for the next few days." He shuffled through the messages, found one from Sheriff Dickens that could be important.

"You holdin' up okay, honey?" Annie asked Sabrina.

"I'm all right. Last night was pretty bad. I've never seen a man killed before."

"Maybe not," Alex said, his gaze swinging toward her. "But she's tougher than she looks. She beat the crap out of one of the bastards with her purse."

Annie laughed. "Atta girl!"

"Alex took on all three of those men at once. He was like some kind of James Bond or something. You should have seen him."

One of his sister's eyebrows cocked up. "That's all well and good, Agent 007, but you might not be so lucky next time."

"Look, sis, I'm fine and so is Sabrina. But we need to find out who's behind these attacks."

Rebecca's eyes widened. "You aren't saying the shooting is related to Sabrina's car accident?"

"That's right, and the helo crash. The chopper was meant to go down."

"Oh, my God, why didn't you tell me?"

"In case you haven't noticed, I've been busy. At the

moment, I'm here to talk to Ben and Jake, try to figure our next move." He wrote his cell number on a piece of scratch paper on Annie's desk and handed it to his sister, looked over at his brawny friend. "Take her home, Joe. Make sure she's okay."

Joe flashed a smile and gave a nod of his dark head. "You got it."

Becca kissed Alex's cheek. "Be careful, big brother, okay?"

"I'm always careful."

She reached down and squeezed Sabrina's hand. "Take care of him."

Something moved across Sabrina's features. Alex wished he knew what it was. He flicked a glance at Joe, who settled a big hand at Becca's waist and guided her out the door. When she looked at his friend, there was a trust in his sister's eyes Alex had never seen before.

"Peaceman?" Sabrina's russet eyebrows went up.

"Justice of the peace. That was my call sign when I was flying jets. Joe and Sol are the only ones who still call me that."

"*Peaceman.* I think I like it."

Hearing footsteps, he turned to see Ben walking toward him. "How'd it go?"

"We got the shooter's name," Alex said.

"Who was he?"

"According to the guy who did the tat, name's Luis Catano. Runs with a bad bunch from the barrio."

Apparently following the conversation, Sol stuck his head out his office door. "Luis Catano. I'm on it. I'll let you know what I find."

Everyone wanted to help. Clearly Sabrina was in

grave danger. They needed to know who was responsible for this latest attack and figure a way to stop him.

From the corner of his eye, Alex spotted Jake shoving through the front door. He was relieved to see Sage beside him.

"Why don't you two get a cup of coffee and talk for a while," Alex said to Sabrina, "give me a chance to fill these guys in on what we've learned." Alex bent his head and very softly kissed her. "I think more clearly when you're not around."

She looked up at him in surprise. She hadn't expected a show of affection in his office in front of his friends. Clearly, she still didn't trust his feelings for her. It irritated him a little.

"All right," she said, "but I want to be involved in this. I need to know what you're planning to do."

"I've got a couple of ideas. I'm hoping these guys can help."

Sage reached out and caught Sabrina's hand. "Come on. Let's give the men a little time to brainstorm. Then we'll listen to what they have to say and add our own two cents."

Sabrina just nodded, which told him how worried she was.

"How about that coffee?" Sage asked. "Annie usually keeps a fresh pot."

Alex watched the two women walk toward the employee lounge in the back of the office. Sage was dressed to the nines in a fancy white linen suit and a pair of superhigh heels. Sabrina wore a pair of baggy jeans and a boy's T-shirt.

Crazy thing was, it was Sabrina who held his attention. All he could think of was getting her somewhere he could strip off the ugly clothes and bury himself inside her.

There was something about her that just flat-out turned him on, but more than that, he wanted her safe.

He wasn't supposed to have those kinds of feelings for a woman. He sure as hell hadn't expected it. He never would have believed he'd let himself get in so deep.

And he wasn't sure what the hell he was going to do about it.

Twenty-Five

Sage poured coffee into paper cups and handed one to Rina. "It's strong and it's hot. Annie likes it bracing. That's what she calls it. *Bracing.*"

Rina took a sip and hissed at the taste of the thick brew rolling over her tongue. "Alex makes the best coffee I've ever had."

"Jake likes his so strong you can stand your spoon in it."

Rina grinned, enjoying this short break from the intrigue swirling around her. "Aren't you supposed to be at work?"

"I was there all morning. I'm not working as hard as I did before I got married, and it feels really good." With her dark hair pulled back in a stylish chignon, dressed in a designer suit and very high heels, it was clear Sage had come from her twelfth-floor executive office at Marine Drilling International.

Rina looked down at the baggie jeans and souvenir T-shirt and felt like a lump of coal next to a four-carat diamond.

"I need to go home and get some clothes." She tugged on the T-shirt. "This was the best Alex could come up with this morning."

Sage squeezed her hand. "You look fine." She reached out and gently touched the bruise on Rina's cheek. "You okay?"

"I'm all right. I thought I'd feel worse about the man who got shot, but I just keep thinking what would have happened if Alex hadn't killed him."

Cup in hand, Sage led her over to a small, Formica-topped table. They pulled out chairs and sat down.

"This must be terrible for you. Until they catch whoever it is, you're practically a prisoner. You've never been good at being cooped up."

"If it weren't for Alex, I'd already have gone stir-crazy." She didn't mention he'd been keeping her entertained in bed.

"So how are you two getting along?"

She took a sip of her coffee. "The sex is great, but that's probably no surprise since he's had so much practice. The man is insatiable."

Sage grinned. "Sounds like the one I've got. And aren't we lucky girls?"

Rina laughed. It felt good. Since all of this had started, she had forgotten how to enjoy herself.

"The thing is, Alex is different than I thought. In some ways I wish he were the man I imagined him to be when I first met him."

Sage smiled. "An arrogant macho jerk? Wasn't that what you called him?"

"Among other things. Instead he's brave and kind, and he's generous." She looked at Sage over the rim of her coffee cup. "Did you know he arranged for one of his foundations to take care of my cousin Janie's doctor bills? She's only five years old and she needs a bone marrow transplant. Alex has people helping her family make the arrangements. It's all being handled anonymously. Alex insisted."

Sage sipped her coffee. "I'm not really surprised. Since I've gotten to know him, I've discovered he's got a very big heart."

Rina stared down at her cup. "It can't last, you know. This thing between us? He's still searching, still trying to figure out what he wants out of life. He's not ready to settle down."

"Are you?"

Her gaze swung up to Sage. "I don't...I don't know. Maybe. With the right man."

"Maybe Alex is that man."

She set her cup down on the table. "I don't think so. I'd need someone willing to make a strong commitment to marriage and family. I'd want the kind of relationship my mother and father had. Alex is a playboy. We're having a fling. Both of us understand that."

"Maybe. I suppose time will tell."

But she already knew. Where Alex was concerned, time was her enemy. Once all of this was over, Alex would be ready to move on.

Whether she was ready or not, it would be time for their affair to end.

Sitting at the table in the conference room, all of them sipping cups of the strong black coffee Annie had made, Alex finished going over the events of the morning, relaying his conversation with Detective Castillo and his visit to Leon Crutch. He looked up as Sol rapped on the door and peered into the room.

"Come on in," Alex said. "What have you got?"

Sol shoved his glasses up on his nose and looked down at the printout in his hand. "Luis Catano, aka *El Sapo*. The Toad." He looked up and grinned. "The Toad. Can you believe these guys?"

"What else?" Alex pressed.

"Catano's a low-level drug dealer, has a couple of kids by a woman named Felicity Marquez. Got a rap sheet a mile long, been in and out of prison since he was fourteen—burglary, drugs, assault, pretty much anything you can think of."

"I know who he is," Ben said. "His name came up when I was working a case a couple months back. Catano's a punk with big plans but not enough brains to back them up. Word on the street is he'll hire out to do just about anything, long as the money is good."

"Got an address for him?" Alex asked.

"Got an address for the girlfriend," Sol said, rattling off a street in one of the roughest sections of the city. "That's where he hangs his do-rag—or did." He looked up. "That's all I've got."

"Let's see if we can find a connection between Catano and any of the cousins," Alex said. "Can you find his cell number?"

"Already got it.

"Check the cousins' phone records against the number, see if any of them made a call to Catano in the last few weeks."

"I'm on it." Sol turned and headed out the door.

"We need to talk to this Felicity woman," Ben said.

"That's where I'm going next." Alex took a sip of his

coffee, lukewarm now and bitter. He grimaced. Annie made the kind of coffee you could only stomach when it was hot. "Maybe she'll give us something we can use."

"You're gonna need some backup," Ben said. "Not a place you want to go alone."

Ben was right. Alex turned to Jake. "Okay if I leave Sabrina with you till we get back?"

"You don't need to ask."

Chairs scraped against the floor and the men headed out of the conference room, Alex anxious to get on his way.

Rina and Sage walked out of the back room the same time the men walked into the main part of the office.

Alex caught her shoulders. "Catano had a woman. Ben and I are on our way to talk to her, and no, you can't go with us. You need to stay here with Jake." He started past her, but she grabbed his hand, turning him to face her.

"You don't have to go." She flicked a glance at Sage. She hadn't even told her best friend, but she had been mulling it over for some time and this morning she had made her decision.

"I've thought this through, Alex, and I've...I've decided to sign the mine over to my cousins."

Alex straightened away from her, his features turning hard. "What are you talking about? That's bullshit. If you do that, you're rewarding them for trying to kill you."

"Did you see the worry on your sister's face? You could have been killed last night. You nearly died in the helicopter crash—we both did. I couldn't live with myself if something happened to you because of me."

His gaze ran over her face and his hard look softened. "It isn't time yet to make that kind of decision. There's still a chance your cousins aren't the ones behind the attacks. We need more information."

She closed her eyes. She wanted to believe her family was innocent. It was impossible to believe the kids she'd grown up with wanted to kill her.

Sage reached over and took her hand. "I know you're scared, Rina, but Alex is a professional. So are Jake and Ben. Before you do something you'll regret, give them a chance to do their job."

She swallowed the lump that was building in her throat. "I just...I don't want anyone getting hurt. I just want all this to be over."

"Your uncle gave that land to you," Alex said. "He wanted you to have it, Sabrina. *You.* Not your cousins. And in case you've forgotten, they may have been the ones who killed him."

Her insides tightened. She wanted this to end, but not if it meant Walter's killer would go free.

Alex tipped her chin up, bent his head and very softly kissed her. "Have a little faith in me, okay?"

She had enormous faith in him. More than he would ever know. And she wanted to know the truth. "All right," she said softly. "For now."

His hand moved gently over the bruise on her cheek. "Stay with Sage and Jake. When I get back, we'll go get your things."

Then he and Ben were gone.

As Rina stared at the place they had been, the misery she'd been holding back returned, dragging her down like a soggy blanket.

Sage must have noticed. She turned to Jake. "Okay, big guy. You ready to go into bodyguard mode?"

He looked warily at his beautiful wife. Even in her six-inch spike heels, she was far shorter than Jake's towering frame.

"Rina and I need to do some shopping," Sage said. "Can you handle it?"

The corner of Jake's hard mouth edged up. "I've had a little experience with that. I think I can handle it. And you know how much I love to shop."

Rina grinned. Jake hated shopping with a passion. Sage just rolled her eyes.

"If we're going out," Sabrina said, "there's something I need to get from my house."

"What is it?" Sage asked.

"My gun."

One of Jake's dark eyebrows went up. "You own a gun?"

"I'm a Texan. What do you think?"

"What kind is it?"

"Twenty-five caliber. And I know how to shoot it so you don't have to worry."

"Twenty-five caliber," Jake repeated as if she were talking about a toy. Walking over to his desk, he opened the bottom drawer, lifted out a holstered weapon, pulled out the pistol inside, checked it, walked back and pressed it into her hand.

"Thirty-eight revolver. My ankle gun. Just cock it and pull the trigger. It's loaded so don't point it at anyone unless you intend to shoot them."

The gun felt heavy, but comforting. She looked it over then shoved it back into the holster. "Thank you."

She left the gun with Annie while they went shopping and a few minutes later, Jake was wearing his big semiautomatic clipped to his belt beneath his shirt, and they were heading for the University shopping district, not far away.

It was the best Rina had felt in days.

Since half the gangbangers in the country drove black SUVs, they decided to take Ben's big Denali, which would definitely be less conspicuous than Alex's flashy BMW.

When the traffic slowed, Ben reached behind the backseat and grabbed a faded black T-shirt and a pair of worn jeans with a hole in the knee. "Put these on. You look like a tourist."

Alex grinned, started stripping off his clothes. They were about the same size; though Ben carried ten more pounds, there wasn't an ounce of fat on his hard-muscled frame.

Alex dragged on Ben's well-worn clothes, slid his gun into the back of the jeans, pulled the disposable phone out of his pocket and tossed the new jeans he'd been wearing into the backseat.

"I need to make a call." As the big SUV roared down the freeway, Alex phoned Sheriff Dickens. The deputy who answered put him straight through.

"Dickens here."

"It's Alex Justice. You got something?"

"Showed your picture of that fella, Rusty Jenkins, around. Nobody recognized him. Doesn't look like he's our man. 'Course, could just be he was slick enough to get in and out without being seen."

"Could be. Any new leads?"

"Still working on it."

"Keep me posted." He looked up as Ben exited the 59 Freeway and turned south, heading into the neighborhood where Felicity Marquez lived. Along the street, the walls of the commercial buildings were covered with graffiti, and iron bars protected the doors and windows, some of which were broken and replaced with sheets of plywood.

Kids in ragged clothes played kickball in the middle of the street; others idly milled around looking sullen and angry.

"Nice place to live," Ben said dryly.

"It didn't always look this way." But the gangs had moved in and they had no respect for the people who lived there or their property.

"True enough."

Alex pulled his S&W .45 out from behind his back and checked the load, shoved the clip back in. A patrol car cruised by, slowed, gave them the once-over, kept driving.

Through the dark lenses of his wraparound shades, Ben glanced over at the nav screen on the dash. "GPS shows the address just down the block."

They were in more of a residential area, older two-bedroom, wood-frame houses mixed with seedy apartment buildings. An overturned pink tricycle lay in the front yard of the house. Ben pulled up in front and turned off the engine.

Both of them cracked open their doors, got out and headed for the porch. Alex glanced around, saw no one who seemed interested in their arrival, climbed the steps and rapped on the screen.

The door was open. Behind the screen he could hear movement, someone in the kitchen. A little girl sat on the carpet in the living room, playing with her doll. He knocked again and a woman appeared, started walking toward them. Ben melted away, disappearing somewhere outside, keeping watch for any sign of trouble.

Alex held up his wallet, displaying his P.I. badge. "I'm Alex Justice. I'm a private investigator. I'd like to ask you a couple of questions. Mind if I come in?"

She was a big woman, not fat, just big-boned, with lots of curves and heavy breasts. And pretty, with her long black hair and creamy dark skin. A Hispanic Sophia Loren.

"I know you. I saw you on TV. You're the man who shot Luis."

He should have let Ben talk to her. He'd been hoping she hadn't seen the news. No such luck.

"It was self-defense. If you watched the news, you know Luis and two of his friends attacked me and the woman I was with. Luis tried to kill me. I didn't have any choice."

She scoffed. "Luis is a fool." She surprised him by shoving open the screen, inviting him into the house. "I have been expecting the police."

He stayed alert, wondering if she was planning some kind of revenge, but instead she just shook her head. "That *cabron,* Luis, he has never been any good. I toss him out in the street, but he always comes back. I am a fool and let him in."

"I'm sorry about what happened." It was the truth. He didn't like killing people, not even when they deserved it.

Felicity shrugged. "He was worthless. But the children are his, and he paid the rent."

"Does the name Sabrina Eckhart mean anything to you? Perhaps someone Luis spoke about, something he was being paid to do that involved her?" Alex pressed a hundred-dollar bill into her hand.

Felicity eyed it with appreciation, tucked the money into the front of her low-cut blouse between her full breasts. "Luis tells me nothing. If you want to know something, ask his friends."

He peeled off another hundred, held it out to her. "You know their names?"

She looked at the money and bit her lip, trying to decide how much she should say.

"You'll have to tell the police what you know. If not, they can arrest you as an accomplice."

She snatched the hundred from his hand, stuffed it in with the other. "Jose Garcia and Ricardo Zamora. He left with them last night. They are as worthless as he is, but maybe they know something."

"You know where I can find them?"

"Somewhere in the neighborhood. You must not mention my name."

"No, of course not."

She smiled, reached out and ran a finger down his cheek. "You get lonely, *querido,* you come see Felicity. She will make you feel better."

Alex kept his smile in place. "I'll keep that in mind. Thanks for your help, Ms. Marquez."

Feeling as if he had made a bit of progress, he left the house, retreating down the front steps and along the walkway toward the street. Ben appeared to his left, three swaggering teenage boys gaining on him from behind.

Confrontation was in their every move, the need to prove their manhood. They were young, but they were big and strong and they knew it. They moved between Ben and the car.

"What you got in your pockets, gringo?" the one on the left said, lanky, hard-faced, maybe seventeen.

"If you don't want trouble," Ben said, "I'd advise you to step out of my way."

The kid in front grinned. "We do not mind a little trouble, gringo." His glance shifted left and right. "Do we, amigos?"

The one on the right took up a splay-legged stance. He smiled. "Trouble, she is my middle name."

Alex's hand went to the weapon he carried behind his back, but he held steady. Ben looked like he had this, and interfering might make the situation worse.

"Step aside," Ben said. "Do it now, or you're going to regret it."

The leader gave a laugh that turned into a grunt of pain as Ben's knee shot into the kid's groin, doubling him over. Ben spun, threw a quick jab to the jaw of the boy on the left, sending him sprawling. Steadied himself to face the third.

The wide-eyed teen glanced from one of his friends to the other, both lying on the ground, making little groaning noises. The kid started trembling.

Ben ignored him and started walking. He didn't stop till he reached the Denali. They both climbed in and he fired up the powerful V-8 engine.

"Nice work," Alex said.

Ben's hands tightened on the wheel. "They're just kids. They'll be dead or in prison by the time they're twenty."

"It's a lousy deal. But a lot of it's the choices they make. You've got to want out to get out."

"Trouble is, it's usually too late by the time they figure that out."

Ben was right. Some of the money Alex donated went to groups like Big Brothers Big Sisters, and other inner-city programs helping teens change their lives. Sometimes they actually worked.

"I got the names of the two men Catano was with last night. Trick's going to be finding them."

As the Denali rolled toward the freeway, Ben flicked him a sideways glance. "Might be good to give that info to the cops, let them do the hound-dogging."

Alex nodded. "Let the police bring them in, we'll get Murphy to find out what they know about Sabrina."

"Meantime, I've got a couple of contacts in the neighborhood. One of them might be able to give you a lead on them."

"Sounds good."

"Unless Catano was the connection to the cousins. Then we're shit out of luck."

"Unless Sol finds something."

"Yeah. Meantime, you're gonna need a safe place to keep your lady. My place would work. I've got a friend I can stay with for a while."

Ben lived in a small house in Rice Village, nice little place with a yard. Good security, easy to defend. Being an ex-SEAL, Ben was just naturally cautious.

"This friend of yours…she a lady friend?" Alex asked.

"Female acquaintance."

He cocked an eyebrow. "With benefits?"

The corner of Ben's mouth edged up. "Hell, yeah."

Ben didn't go long without a woman. And at the same time he was never really involved with one. Just the way

Alex used to be before he'd met Sabrina, only Ben didn't usually stay friends with the women he dated. Maybe they fell too hard.

"Cleaning lady was there today. You've even got clean sheets."

"Appreciate it," Alex said. He liked being in a place he knew, a neighborhood he was familiar with, a layout he could control. "Thanks."

"No problem. Just be sure and feed my cat."

Alex smiled. His friend was as softhearted with animals as he was hard-hearted with women.

Ben stepped on the gas, picking up speed, matching Alex's anxiousness to get back to the office. He felt better when Sabrina was close by where he could protect her.

The bad news was, when they walked inside, Sabrina wasn't there.

Twenty-Six

Rina breezed back into the office laughing. Oh, it felt good to get away from all of this for just a little while. After they had raided enough stores to outfit her for at least a few days and bought the necessary makeup and toiletries, Sage had insisted they stop for a late lunch at a little out-of-the-way Italian place where she and Jake liked to eat.

At the last store they'd visited, Rina had changed into a pair of black capri pants and a sleeveless black-and-white-print top, put on a pair of dangling silver earrings she had purchased and slipped her feet into inexpensive low-heeled silver sandals.

Full of antipasto, lasagna and a glass of Chianti, she climbed into the backseat of Sage's Mercedes, and Jake drove them back to the office.

Since she hadn't gotten any phone calls, she figured Alex wasn't back yet.

Which worried her a little. Alex was in a dangerous neighborhood asking dangerous questions, and after last night, she knew the kind of violence he could be facing.

As Jake pulled into the parking lot, she spotted the black SUV Ben had been driving and breathed a sigh of relief. They climbed out of the car. Sage hugged her goodbye and headed back to work, and Jake carried her shopping bags into the office.

She smiled as Alex approached, happy to see him until she saw the black look on his face.

"Where the hell have you been?"

Sabrina opened her mouth to explain, but Jake answered for her.

"Take it easy. She needed some clothes. I didn't want her going back to her apartment or to your place, so Sage and I took her shopping."

Alex blew out a breath. He raked a hand through his hair, mussing the golden strands a little. "We just got back. I should have known you had things under control. Sorry." He looked over at Sabrina. "I was worried, okay? No big deal."

Feeling a little catch in her chest at the concern in his face, she slid her arms around his neck and kissed him full on the lips. "Thanks for being worried."

He held on to her for a moment before he let her go and she thought how good it felt when a man you cared about cared in return.

"Come up with anything?" Jake asked Alex.

"Got the names of the two men who were with Catano last night. I called Murphy on the way back, fed him the info."

"Good idea. Cops'll have a better chance of tracking them down."

"I'm hoping they'll know something that will give us a lead on who hired them." Alex started to say something more when the bell rang above the door.

Sabrina recognized the handsome man she had met at the mine, Arturo Hernandez, the engineer from the Desert Mining Company.

"I'm looking for Alex Justice," he said to Annie, then spotted her standing there and started walking toward her.

"Sabrina… I have been trying to reach you. I called your home number and your cell. I left messages but got no answer."

"I'm sorry, Arturo. I didn't mean to cause you so much trouble. Some things have been happening. I didn't expect to hear from you so soon."

"I came to Houston to find you. I had your friend's card. I hoped he would be able to put me in touch with you."

"I guess I should have called."

Eyes the color of melted chocolate ran over her and Arturo smiled. "You look as lovely as ever."

Beside her Alex stiffened, but Rina didn't mind the compliment. She was a woman, after all. She enjoyed a little flattery once in a while. She just thanked God she had changed out of her baggy jeans.

"That's kind of you, Arturo. You remember Alex."

"Of course."

"Hernandez," Alex said brusquely. The men made cursory nods but didn't shake hands.

Arturo's attention returned to her and his smile widened. "I have news. Most exciting news." He reached over and caught her hand. "Is there someplace we might speak?"

Alex pulled her away from him, back against his side. "You can use the conference room," he said tightly, clearly unhappy that Arturo was there.

Rina reached for Alex's hand. "I'd like you to come with me."

Some of his tension eased. "All right."

Alex urged her ahead of him and Arturo fell in behind. Alex closed the conference room door and they sat down at the long oak table.

"Since you're here," Sabrina said to Arturo, "I presume the core samples have come in."

He nodded. "Indeed they have. I am pleased to tell you that they surpassed my highest expectations." He set his leather briefcase up on the table and popped the brass latches, pulled out a folder and pushed it in front of her.

"Desert Mining has done a thorough chemical analysis of the ore. That is what determines the composition." He reached over, opened the folder, flipped through to one of the pages and pointed to the columns of numbers.

Which meant nothing to Rina, but looked impressive.

"We've also determined the limits of the deposit, which are quite vast." He turned the page, showed her more charts and numbers.

He turned back to his briefcase, took out a photograph and placed it in front of her. "This is an aerial view of the property. The area outlined in yellow marks the land where the open pit mining will be done."

She followed the outline. "It appears to be quite large."

"Yes, it is. In this presentation, you will find an in-depth analysis of the project. It includes a feasibility study examining the cost of initial capital investment, the optimal method of extraction, the operating costs and the estimated length of time before we can expect a return."

"What about gross revenue projections?" Sabrina asked. "Have those been done?"

Arturo looked surprised and impressed. Flipping through several more pages, he showed her the revenue projections.

"And net profit margins?"

"Those are calculated here." He turned to another page, and Rina studied the numbers. Finance was an area she understood.

"You will also find the projected life of the reserve," Arturo said, "the value of that reserve and the residual value of the land for possible resale." He looked up, smiled. "As you can see, Desert Mining has been extremely thorough."

She studied the information they had put together for her review, a large number of pages. "I'll need time to go over all this, and of course my attorney will need to review it." Assuming she could find one willing to wait for his fees. "But the research I've done indicates your company has a very good reputation for honesty and fairness."

She glanced over at Alex, saw a faint smile of approval on his lips.

"Should you decide to partner with us in this project," Arturo continued, "we will also take care of environmental impact studies, reclamation, possible legal ramifications and of course, the necessary government permitting."

She tapped the file. "It looks as if I have the information I need. Assuming we go forward, what's our next step?"

"You must come back to the desert. You must look at our mining operation, observe our equipment at work.

The board would like to set up a meeting at our offices in Presidio as soon as it can be arranged."

She flicked a glance at Alex, saw him frowning. "Yes, of course. Let me go over the information and I'll get back to you as quickly as I can."

"The nearest airport is Odessa. I will be happy to make hotel arrangements, pick you up and drive you to Presidio."

"Sabrina has her own transportation," Alex put in before she could reply. "Should she decide to make the trip, she'll arrange her own accommodations."

A little thread of annoyance slid through her. She was perfectly capable of making those decisions for herself. She pasted on a bland smile, cast Alex a warning glance and hoped he got the subtle message, which he must have because he was looking amused and a little too pleased with himself.

Rina stood up from the table, signaling the end of the meeting, and the men stood up, as well. "One last question. Was your initial assessment of the property value correct? Twenty million?"

Arturo smiled. He was a very handsome man, confident, and under different circumstances, would have been extremely appealing.

"That estimate would now be somewhat low. Of course, once the actual mining operation begins, the land will be worth a great deal more."

She kept her smile in place though her heart was pounding like a hammer in her chest. "Thank you, Arturo. Let me give you a number where I can be reached." She gave him the disposable cell number. "I'll be in touch very soon."

They made their way out of the conference room. Rina walked Arturo to the door.

"I look forward to our working together," he said, holding the hand she held out to him a little longer than necessary.

"You, as well," Rina said. As the bell rang signaling Arturo's departure, she turned and grinned, took a couple of steps toward Alex and threw herself into his arms.

"Oh, my God—did you hear that?" She mimicked Arturo's Spanish accent. "'Twenty million would be *somewhat low.*'"

Alex didn't laugh. "I don't like him. But that doesn't mean he isn't good at his job. And I'm really glad for you." He bent his head and kissed her, drawing it out, making her stomach float up beneath her ribs. "Congratulations."

Behind them, Ben and Jake were grinning. "Guess our little treasure hunter hit the jackpot. Congratulations."

Rina grinned. "Thanks."

"I don't know about you," Alex said, still keeping an arm around her, "but it's been a damn long day and I'm ready to go home."

She looked up at him. "Which one, yours or mine?"

"Neither. We have new accommodations for a while. I'll fill you in on the way."

Gathering up the bags of clothing she'd bought, Alex started for the door, but Rina stopped at Annie's desk.

"I need my gun."

Alex scowled. "What the hell?"

Annie smiled and handed Sabrina the holstered weapon. "Jake's loaning it to me," she said, "and yes, I know how to shoot it."

Alex cast a dark look at his friend, who grinned unrepentantly. "I hope you know what you're doing," Alex said to him.

"You better hope *she* does."

Ben laughed.

Alex frowned. "You don't have a concealed-carry permit, do you?"

"No, this is just for when I'm in the house."

Alex plucked the weapon out of her hand. "Fine, I'll take care of it till we get there."

Rina fought not to smile. "Thanks." Breezing past him, she sailed out the door.

"Do you really know how to shoot that thing?" Alex asked her as he drove his BMW the short distance to Ben's house.

"My dad taught me. I have a .25 caliber at my place, but Jake seemed to think that was a popgun, not a real gun, and besides he didn't want me going back there."

"Probably not a good idea at the moment."

"So where are we staying?"

"Ben's place. It's not far from the office and the security's good."

"If they found us at your place, what makes you think they won't find us there?"

"These guys are not professionals, love. Think about it. The helicopter was a damned good bet, but the car wreck was a long shot. And the guys last night were right off the street. They knew where to find us because your family figured we were sleeping together, which meant we'd probably be at your place or mine. It was a guess that panned out."

Rina looked down at the hands in her lap. "You're that sure it's them."

"Aren't you?"

"If it's one of them, they must be desperate."

"Or greedy. All they had to do was be nice to their old man. They sure as hell didn't have to kill him."

He didn't miss the tremor that ran through her. She didn't say anything more until they walked into Ben's small, single-story, wood-frame house. He tossed her shopping bags onto the dark brown leather sofa, then reset the alarm by the door.

"Definitely a man's place," Sabrina said, trailing a hand over the sturdy oak end table where a beige pottery lamp shed light into the room. She checked out the big-screen TV and the outdoor magazines on the coffee table. "He keeps it nice and clean, though."

"He's ex-military. Old habits, you know?"

Just then a big gray tabby walked out of the kitchen, his attitude haughty, as if they were intruding on his domain.

"Ben has a cat?"

"Believe it or not, he's a real animal lover."

"What's its name?"

"Hercules. Ben calls him Herc."

Sabrina knelt and extended her hand. "Hello, Herc. Aren't you a big pretty kitty?"

Herc seemed to preen. He wandered toward Sabrina, ducked under her hand for a little stroking. When he butted his head against her, she scratched his ears and rubbed his chin. For the first time in his life, Alex was jealous of a cat.

She came to her feet as Herc meandered away, her

expression once more serious. "I have to go back to the desert, Alex."

"I know that. In a couple of weeks, this'll be over. I'll fly you back and—"

"Not a couple of weeks—a couple of days. You don't want me to sign over the mine to my cousins. The only other way for us to stay safe is for me to improve the property as quickly as possible. That means I need to get things started."

"And you will. But right now, your immediate safety is what's important."

"I'm going, Alex. I have to. You don't have to go with me. I'm a grown woman. I can handle this. I won't tell anyone except Arturo I'm coming, and I'll fly commercial. No one will even know I've left Houston."

Alex's jaw tightened, clamped so tight he could barely force out the word. He felt like the top of his head was about to blow off. "No."

She blinked. "No? You think you can just say *no* and I'll toss away all my plans? Do you really think—"

"Don't you understand?" He caught her shoulders, drew her so close she had to tip her head back to look at him. "I'm responsible for you, Sabrina. I'm trying to keep you safe!"

"But—"

He bent his head and kissed her, cutting off her words. He tipped her chin up with his fingers. "I'm crazy about you, baby. Someone wants to kill you and I can't— *won't*—let that happen."

Her gaze found his, held. "You're…you're crazy about me?"

He smiled. "What did you think?" He kissed her again, a long, slow, unhurried kiss that had her molded against him and made him hard. "You think I work free for all my clients?"

Her lips edged up but tears brimmed in her eyes. "Alex…" Her arms slipped around his neck and it felt so good just to hold her.

It was crazy, insane to feel this way when his life was still so unsettled, so undetermined. Hell, he didn't even know if he planned to stay in Houston.

His arms tightened around her. Surely the day would come when this hard knot in his chest that formed when he looked at her would loosen, when the passion between them would fade and they would go their separate ways. They'd be friends, of course. That's all he'd ever meant for them to be.

He tangled his hands in her hair, pulled her back to him and kissed her, the thought of their parting making his stomach burn. He refused to worry about it now. For now, she was his and the important thing was keeping her safe.

He pressed moist kisses along her throat, heard a soft purr that sounded a lot like Herc and reminded him of a sexy little kitten.

"Ben says the sheets are clean." He nuzzled the side of her neck.

Sabrina gave him a teasing smile. "I bet a guy as hot as Ben has a great big comfortable bed."

Alex nipped an earlobe, not sure he liked the sound of that. "A guy as hot as Ben?"

"Well, he's not as hot as you, of course, but still…"

He grinned. "Why don't we find out just how comfortable it is?"

She looked up at him with those big blue eyes that

wreaked havoc on his senses. "I have to go to Presidio, Alex. But I won't go without you."

He sighed. He should have known he couldn't win. "Stubborn, hardheaded little wench." She yelped as he swept her off her feet and up against his chest. He couldn't help admiring her. But then he always had. "All right, I'll take you. But we do it my way, okay?" She started kissing his neck as he carried her into the bedroom, his erection throbbing with urgency.

"Whatever you say." They both recognized the complete and utter lie.

"Fine, but you owe me." He tossed back the covers and settled her in the middle of the bed.

Sabrina eyed him warily. "What do you want in return?"

Alex just smiled. There were some places he was still the boss. The bedroom was one of them. "Why don't I show you?"

Reaching down, he started peeling off her clothes.

Twenty-Seven

When a man like Alex Justice made love to a woman, said woman just hung on and enjoyed the ride.

Inwardly, Rina grinned at the unexpected pun. Alex was all man and he was in charge and she loved every minute of it. More today because of what Alex had said. He didn't just like her. She wasn't just a friend with benefits. He was *crazy* about her. That's what he'd said.

And God knew she was crazy about him. Crazy in love with him, a fact she had tried very hard to deny but was finally forced to admit. But that was a whole different subject, one she wasn't willing to think about right now.

It didn't take long before both of them were naked, the ceiling fan slowly revolving above them, moving the cool air over their bare skin. Late-afternoon sun poured through the curtained windows, lighting the darkened room just enough to give it a golden glow.

Her nipples were hard and tight from the feel of Alex's mouth moving over them, suckling and tasting, making her shift restlessly beneath him.

He returned to ravishing her mouth. Alex loved to kiss and he was amazingly good at it. He could almost make her come just by moving his tongue in a certain erotic pattern over hers.

She shivered, trembled, tangled her fingers in his dark gold hair and kissed him back as thoroughly and hotly as he was kissing her. Damp kisses rained over her body. He kissed the flat spot beneath her navel, the insides of her thighs, stroked her just to the point of climax.

She whimpered when he stopped, had to force herself not to beg him to continue.

"Time to pay," he said, returning to her breasts, then nipping the side of her neck. He lifted her, turned her onto her stomach and pulled her knees up beneath her.

"I don't think we've made love quite this way." He trailed kisses along her shoulders, left a hot, moist trail down her spine, massaged the muscles over her ribs, her hips. "I think you'll like it."

She was going to like anything that brought relief from the heat burning through her body. She was hot and wet and ready. Moving behind her, Alex set his hands at her waist and entered her slowly, buried himself deep, then started to move. It felt naughty and erotic, and the thick, hard length of him seemed to short-circuit her brain, leaving her senses in control and her body completely at his mercy.

Her heart rate quickened. Her breath came in short little pants. She was slick and hot, her skin on fire. She arched her back to take him deeper, heard him hiss in a breath as he fought for control.

Faster, deeper, harder. The world spun away, sucked her into climax. Fierce, saturating pleasure washed through her and she tightened around him like a fist.

Alex groaned as he followed her to release.

They collapsed together on the bed, skin moist, bodies pressed together. Still joined, Alex rolled them onto their sides, pressed a soft kiss to the back of her neck.

"I meant what I said," he whispered. "I'm crazy about you."

She smiled. "I'm crazy about you, too." She didn't say more. She didn't want to ruin things between them and she knew telling him she loved him would do exactly that. For now, she was with Alex and it was enough.

They made love twice more that night, then slept the sleep of the dead till seven in the morning when Alex's disposable cell phone rang.

He rubbed his face, rolled to the side of the bed and picked it up. "Justice."

"Alex, I need to talk to you."

He recognized his sister's voice. "Becca…what is it?"

"Something's happened, Alex. I'm not sure it's any big deal, but there was a man at Ginny's school…out near the playground. It's probably nothing but Ginny said he was a friend of yours. He wanted her to tell you hello."

Alex went cold all over. He forced a note of calm into his voice. "Where's Ginny now?"

"She's here. I wanted to talk to you before I sent her off to school. She's furious I wouldn't let her go, but I just…something just didn't feel right."

"Don't let her leave. I'm on my way." He was up and reaching for his jeans, the same worn pair he'd borrowed from Ben yesterday, pulled on the same faded black T-shirt.

"Alex?"

"You need to get dressed. I've got to see my sister and I'm not leaving you here."

She came up off the bed, shoving back her glossy red curls. "What is it?"

"Just hurry. I'll tell you on the way."

They were dressed and out of the house in minutes, driving too fast toward his sister's house.

"All right, tell me," Sabrina said as the car raced along.

He went over the conversation he'd had with Rebecca about the man near the playground.

"You're worried. You're thinking it could be Bagley."

"I need to talk to Ginny, get more information, hopefully a description. But it's possible it's him, and that scares the living hell out of me."

Sabrina didn't say more, just leaned back in her seat until the car pulled up in front of a two-story, turn-of-the-century house in Houston Heights. A fresh coat of white paint gleamed in the morning sun. A turret sprang up from one corner, cornflower-blue shutters bracketed the windows, and a covered porch wrapped all the way around the house.

The former owner had added bathrooms and done some preliminary remodeling. Joe was helping Rebecca remodel the kitchen.

Both of them were waiting when he walked into the entry, guiding Sabrina in front of him.

"I know you're busy," Becca said apologetically, walking toward him. "This is probably silly."

"It isn't silly," Joe said firmly.

"Where's Ginny?" Alex asked. "I need to talk to her."

Rebecca glanced upward, as if she could see through

the ceiling. "She's upstairs pouting. They were assigning school projects today and she didn't want to be left out."

"I'll be right back." He started for the stairs, heard Sabrina behind him talking to his sister.

"Alex is really worried. You did the right thing."

He didn't hear Becca's reply. He headed down the hall to Ginny's room and knocked on the door that had a red finger painting pinned to the front.

"Ginny? It's your uncle Alex. Can we talk a minute?"

He heard her small feet on the carpet as she walked over and opened the door. "Hi," she said dejectedly.

"What? No hug for your favorite uncle?"

She brightened a little. Put her arms around his neck when he leaned down to her height, squeezed.

Alex scooped her up in his arms. "That's better." He carried her over to her pretty little pink-ruffled princess bed and they both sat down.

"I hear you had a visitor at school yesterday."

She nodded. "He was nice. He said he was your friend. He said to say hello, but I wish I didn't tell my mom about him."

Alex caught her hand. "You should always tell your mother things like that. It's really important."

She looked up at him. "It is?"

"That's right. That's the way you stay safe. Next time, you should also tell your teachers."

She stared down at her lap. "Okay."

He caught her chin, gently regaining her attention. "Where did you see this man, Ginny?"

"Out on the playground. I was on the jungle gym but it's hard to swing on the bars in a skirt so I went over and sat on the bench. The man said my name. When I turned, I saw him on the other side of the fence."

"He called you Ginny?"

She nodded. "Uh-huh."

"Can you tell me what this man looked like?"

She pursed her lips, squinted, trying to recall. "Well, he wasn't fat. He had brown hair and nice eyes. Oh, and a nice smile."

"What color eyes, do you remember?"

She bit her lip. "Blue, I think, but I'm not sure."

A knot formed in his stomach. Edward Bagley had light brown hair and blue eyes. "Anything else?"

She started shaking her head, then brightened. "Oh, he had a funny little mark on his neck. It looked like a heart."

The knot twisted tighter. He felt a rush of anger so strong it made him dizzy.

Ginny looked up at him from beneath her pale lashes. "Are you mad at me, Uncle Alex?"

He scooped her up again, kissed the top of her head. "No, sweetheart. Everything's okay. But you're gonna have to miss a few days of school."

Her face puckered up. He could see she was on the verge of crying. "I don't want to miss school!"

Hearing a sound in the open doorway, Alex looked up to see Joe standing in the hall.

"Tell you what, buttercup," Joe said, walking into the bedroom. "You stay home a couple of days and you can work downstairs with me. Your mom already said it was okay."

"She did?"

"That's right. I'll show you how to use a screwdriver."

Alex almost grinned. Rebecca was going to have a fit. He handed Ginny to Joe, who settled her against his hip.

"I gotta go, sweetheart." He leaned over and kissed

her cheek. "Do what Joe and your mama tell you, okay?" While Ginny talked to Joe about how to use a screwdriver, Alex slipped quietly out of the room.

He found the women sitting in the kitchen, drinking cups of coffee.

His sister rose from her chair. "Was it…was it him?"

Alex's jaw hardened. "It was him. No mistake."

"Oh, God."

"I've got to talk to the police, fill them in. You'll have to keep Ginny home until they catch the bastard."

Joe came walking in, Ginny's small hand gripped in his big one. She grinned and ran off to play in the family room. From his scowl, Joe had heard the conversation.

"You don't have to worry," he said to Rebecca. "I'm staying here till this is over. You've got the best alarm system money can buy and you've got me. Bagley gives us any trouble, he's going to be one sorry son of a bitch."

Alex felt a sweep of relief. Joe was tough as nails and loyal to a fault. He was afraid his sister would argue, but she just looked gravely up at Joe and nodded. "Thanks."

Interesting, Alex thought. "I'll be right back." Pulling out his phone, he headed into the study to make the necessary calls.

"What did the police say?" Sabrina asked as Alex drove away from the house, the muscles across his shoulders still vibrating with tension.

"They've put out a BOLO on Bagley as a person of interest in an attempted child abduction. It won't hold up, since all he did was talk to Ginny through the fence, but it'll put him back where the cops can keep him pinned down."

"That's good."

"Yeah, if they can find him. They're also putting extra cars in the area. They'll be watching for him round the clock."

Rina studied Alex's profile. His jaw looked as hard as steel. His hands gripped the wheel as if he wanted to tear it off the steering column. "This isn't your fault, you know."

He rubbed his unshaven jaw where a night's growth of dark gold beard made him look a little like a Viking. "It's Bagley's fault. But I'm the reason the bastard went after Ginny."

"If you feel like you should stay with your sister, I'm sure I can stay with Sage and Jake."

"Joe's there and I trust him. And I can do everyone more good if I'm on the job. That means finding Bagley." He cast her a sideways glance. "Which doesn't mean I'm abandoning you. Ben's got men trying to run down Garcia and Zamora. Once they're in custody, we may be able to find a link between them and one of your cousins."

"What about Bagley?"

His eyes remained on the road. "We're headed down to my office. I'm going to put Sol in action, see if there's something new we can come up with that might tell us where Bagley's hiding. I thought we'd go by Ben's, pick up that Desert Mining portfolio you wanted to study. That'll give you something to do."

"And keep me out of your hair."

He grinned, his dimples showing for the first time in days. "Yeah."

"You're in luck. I brought it with me." She dug into the big silver bag she'd bought when she'd gone shopping with Sage and Jake, drew out the folder Arturo had given her. "I figured you might need a way to keep me entertained—aside from erotic sex."

Alex's gaze turned a scorching shade of blue. "Lady, you never cease to amaze."

She flashed him a grin. "Neither do you, flyboy."

Alex walked into the Atlas Security office to see Ben on the phone, Trace in his office leaning back in his chair with his cowboy boots propped on the desk. In the office next to his, Sol was hard at work behind his computer.

Alex left Sabrina in the waiting area, studying her mining portfolio, and went in to talk to Trace.

"Welcome back," Alex said to his friend.

"Good to be back. I hear all hell broke loose while we were gone."

"Yeah, you could say that. How was the trip?"

Trace's mouth curved up in a lazy smile. "We holed up out at the ranch for a few days. Real nice out there even when it's hot."

"Which means you didn't go outside much, just stayed in bed under the air-conditioning."

"We rode in the mornings."

Alex grinned. "I'll just bet you did."

Trace laughed.

Newlyweds. You'd think after the months they'd been married, Trace would have settled back into his regular work routine, but the man was in love.

"Ben's brought me pretty much up to speed on Rina,"

Trace said. "Told me about the shooting. You should have called. I'd have come back sooner."

"I know you would have. Ben and Jake were there and Sage has been great."

"I guess you talked to Catano's girlfriend."

"Felicity Marquez, that's right. She gave up the guys Catano was with at the minimart—Jose Garcia and Ricardo Zamora."

Trace pondered the names. "Doesn't ring any bells."

"Ben's got a couple of snitches he thinks might be able to help us find them. Better yet if the cops bring them in. We need a connection to Sabrina's cousins. Garcia and Zamora don't give us something, we're going to need a way to flush them out."

"Bait?"

"Maybe. Policewoman who's petite and red-haired, somebody trained for that kind of work." Whoever it was, it wasn't going to be Sabrina. No way was he going to let that happen. "We aren't at that point yet. Unfortunately, this morning another problem came up."

Trace raked a hand through his thick dark brown hair. There was a faint crease beside his temple from the cowboy hat he'd hung on the rack beside the door. "Never rains it doesn't pour."

Alex briefly filled Trace in on Bagley and the threat he posed to Ginny. When he finished, his friend's expression looked tense.

"So what's your play?"

"Joe McCauley's staying with Becca round the clock. He's a good man. Tough and smart. Bagley's a worm. I don't think he'll want any kind of physical confrontation. In the meantime, I need to talk to Sol, see if we can come up with something that might help the police figure out where the bastard's hiding."

"Let me know if there's anything I can do to help."

"Will do."

From Trace's desk, Alex headed into Sol Greenway's computer-lined office. Sol rolled his chair back from his desk.

"Hey, Peaceman, what's up?"

"Bagley's zeroed in on my sister's little girl."

"Shit."

"Yeah. She's staying at home till the cops can find him. I thought maybe we'd brainstorm, see what we can come up with that could help them figure out where he's hiding."

"You're thinking a friend, maybe?"

"Once he was arrested, his so-called friends scurried like roaches in the opposite direction. I can't think of anyone who'd welcome him with open arms, but I guess it could happen. I'm thinking real estate, too, someplace he might own under an alias."

"Okay. Let me take a look at his file, see if something jumps out at me. Since we're starting with zip, it might take me a while."

Alex nodded. "Appreciate it."

He left Sol pounding away on his keyboard and went back to where Sabrina was immersed in reviewing her mining portfolio.

She looked up and saw him, cast him a brilliant smile. Alex's chest squeezed. Damn, he didn't get it. She was just a woman. Over the years, how many had he known? His mind strayed to Melissa Carlyle, then the beautiful French model, Gabriella Moreau.

The truth was, Sabrina was nothing like the others.

She was beautiful in a completely different way and somehow more real.

He took a deep breath, waited for his heartbeat to slow. He wasn't sure what was going on with his over-the-top attraction. And he wasn't sure he wanted to find out.

Twenty-Eight

Rina tucked the Desert Mining portfolio under her arm. She'd made good inroads into understanding the information in the packet and she liked what the company was proposing. Next she needed to go to Presidio and see the mining operation at work.

Far more important, she needed to find out who was behind the attempts on her life.

"How did it go?" she asked Alex as he walked toward her. Before he could answer, the disposable phone in her purse started ringing. Very few people had the number. Aside from Alex, only her mother, Sage, Jake and Arturo. She dug out the phone and pressed it against her ear.

To her surprise, her cousin Priscilla's voice came over the line. "Priscilla?"

"Hello, Rina. I'm sorry to bother you but I'm at the hospital with your mom."

"Oh, God, what happened? Is she okay?"

"She's had an allergic reaction. I don't know what happened. We were having our usual Tuesday lunch at

Pete's Café and suddenly she started wheezing, couldn't catch her breath. The owner called 911 but before the ambulance could get there, her face turned blue and she passed out."

"She's not…she's not…"

"No, no. She's doing better, but she's going to be here at least overnight. I found your number on her cell. I knew you'd want to know."

"Tell her I'm coming, will you? I can be there by tonight."

"Good. That's good. I've been really worried. Aunt Flo is…you know, really great. She's always been good to me."

Sabrina felt a catch in her throat. Priscilla loved Sabrina's mother, and her mother loved Sill and her two girls. "I'm on my way. Thanks, Sill, for calling."

She tucked the phone away and looked into Alex's worried face.

"You're white as a sheet. What's happened?"

"That was Priscilla. Mom's had an allergic reaction. She's in the hospital."

"Bee sting?"

"Peanuts. We used to laugh about it, since we're not blood related. It's life-threatening, Alex. I have to go to Uvalde."

Alex rubbed a hand over his unshaven jaw. "Jesus, what next?"

"It's okay. I'll rent a car. I know you don't want me going by myself, but your sister needs you."

"Bullshit. Can't you see? This could be a trap. Maybe Priscilla wants you down there so she and her boyfriend can get another shot at killing you."

Was it possible? It all sounded so completely wrong.

Sabrina's attention snapped toward the sound of heavy footfalls and she saw Ben Slocum striding toward them.

"More problems?" He always looked so dark and forbidding. And yet he seemed to care very much about his friends. She wondered what his story was.

"Sabrina's mother's in the hospital," Alex said to him. "I told her she can't go to Uvalde—that it could be a trap, but—"

"I'm going, Alex. This is my mother."

"Okay, hold it," Ben said. "I'll take Rina where she needs to go and you can stay here, keep an eye on your sister, work on finding Zamora and Garcia. Or you can take her and I'll keep an eye on your sister and keep things moving here. Whichever you want."

Sabrina's throat closed up. Everyone was trying to help but the nicer they were, the more helpless she felt. She tried to hold back the tears burning her eyes, but it was all just too much. A sob escaped and the dam burst, her body shaking as she turned away and started to cry, wishing she was anywhere but there.

Alex caught her shoulders and eased her into his arms. "It's okay, baby." He rested his cheek on the top of her head, held her close against him. "Things happen. We'll handle it. We'll make it work."

She leaned into him, wished she could burrow right under his skin. "I'm sorry. I'm usually tougher than this."

His hold tightened around her. "You're plenty tough. I've already found that out."

Her throat ached. The shooting at the minimart. Edward Bagley and little Ginny. Now her mother. She took a shaky breath, determined to regain control.

"I'm okay." She wiped the tears from her cheeks. "I'll go with Ben. You stay with your sister."

Alex shook his head. "The cops are all over Bagley, and Joe's there. Sol's working on it, but it's bound to take some time. I'll fly us down and we'll rent a car. It's less than three hundred miles. We can be there in a couple of hours. While we're gone, Ben can take care of things here."

She was too weary to fight him. She simply nodded.

"We'll swing by Ben's and pick up some clothes in case we need to stay overnight. Then head out."

He turned away from her, spoke to Ben for a couple more minutes about Bagley, Zamora and Garcia.

"Keep me posted, will you?" Alex said to him.

"You got it."

An hour later, after a quick stop to pick up fresh clothes, they were in the air, headed for the hospital in Uvalde.

Rina prayed that Alex was wrong, that it wasn't any sort of trap. She prayed they would be safe.

The flight was smooth all the way to Uvalde. Heat rolled up from the tarmac as the plane dropped down and made a low, gliding descent onto the runway, then taxied to a stop in front of the executive terminal.

Alex had phoned ahead and had a rental car waiting. As soon as the paperwork was completed, he guided Sabrina out to the compact silver-gray Nissan SUV parked in the lot and they headed for the Uvalde Memorial Hospital on Garner Field Road.

The air was hot and dry, dust blowing up along the side of the road as they passed. The hospital wasn't far from the airport. Before they'd left Houston, Sabrina had called the floor nurse and been given an update on her mother. Florence was breathing better, resting peacefully. Sabrina had told the nurse to tell her mother they would be there very soon.

As the automatic doors to the lobby swung open, hitting them with a blast of cold air, doctors and nurses in scrubs hurried past them. Alex guided Sabrina toward the information desk, wishing he could wipe away the worried look on her face.

"We're here to see Mrs. Eckhart," she said to the dark-haired woman behind the counter. "I don't know her room number."

Peering through a pair of half-glasses, the woman checked her computer. "That would be room 321." She pointed across the lobby. "The elevators are right over there."

"Thank you."

As they walked in that direction, Alex scanned their surroundings, checking for anything out of the ordinary, any sign of danger. His senses were running on high alert and had been since they'd left his Houston office, the semiautomatic pistol in the shoulder holster beneath his short-sleeved shirt within easy reach if he needed it.

They arrived on the third floor without a problem. Halfway down the hall, Sabrina saw her cousin Priscilla standing outside the door to room 321. In a hard, tired sort of way, Priscilla was a beautiful woman. Long, dark brown hair, smooth skin, full lips shiny with a layer of pink lip gloss. Her low-cut red tank top and tight-fitting jeans showed off a dynamite figure.

Didn't make him trust her any more than he had before.

He watched the two women. They didn't hug as he suspected they would have before all of this started. But the smile Priscilla gave Sabrina was filled with relief.

"I'm glad you came. I've really been worried."

"How is she?" Sabrina asked.

"Sleeping. The doctor says she's improving. She really scared me at the restaurant."

"What happened?" Alex asked.

Priscilla wiped the palms of her hands on her jeans. "I don't know. We each ordered a salad. The next thing I knew, Aunt Flo was wheezing, trying to catch her breath. Her face turned blue and she passed out. I caught her before she hit the floor."

"You said it was a reaction to peanuts. Were there peanuts in the salad?"

"No. We had the Cobb Salad, the Tuesday special. We order it a lot."

"Is the doctor sure peanuts are what caused the reaction?" Alex asked.

"Apparently so. They gave her some kind of test or something."

Alex's gaze swung to Sabrina. "We'll talk to the people at the restaurant, find out how this could have happened. In the meantime, why don't you go on in and see your mom?"

She shot him a grateful smile and headed for the door, pushed through and disappeared inside. Priscilla didn't follow her in.

"I...umm...I've been wanting to thank you."

"Why is that?"

"I heard about the help George and Millie are getting with Janie. I heard rumors it was you. Was it?"

"I work with a couple of different charities. The little girl needed care. I'm glad I could help."

Priscilla's dark eyes misted. "It was really nice of you." She dashed a tear from her cheek. "Aunt Flo told me about the shooting. She said you saved Sabrina's life. I guess you were right. Someone is trying to kill her."

"That's the way it looks."

"I…umm…I want you to know it isn't me. I don't know anything about any of it."

He kept his gaze steady on her face, looking for the lie, or confirmation of the truth. "What about your brothers? They both need money. Are they hungry enough to kill for it?"

Priscilla closed her eyes and shook her head. "I don't know. I can't imagine it. You said if Rina dies we inherit the property but none of us knows anything about mining. That's the reason Dad left the land to her instead of us."

"That the only reason? Because he thought she'd be interested in mining the property?"

Priscilla's gaze dropped to her red high-heeled sandals. "Dad was a terrible father. He never had time for any of us and we hated him for it. Then he and Mom got divorced. She was never happy, not even after she remarried. We blamed him for it. By the time we grew up, it was too late to fix things."

"But your father didn't have those kinds of problems with Sabrina."

"My dad and his brother were close. Rina was his niece, the youngest girl in the family, and Dad doted on her. She believed all the crap he told her. It just made things worse for the rest of us."

Sabrina pushed through the door just then, returning to the hallway. "Mom's awake. She was glad to see me. I think she feels better just knowing I'm here."

"Then it's good you came."

She smiled, seemed relieved. "She's sleepy, but she's got a great attitude. She's already wanting to leave."

The doctor walked up just then, an Asian man with smooth skin and black hair, wearing a pair of wire-rimmed glasses. "I'm Dr. Wong. You're Florence's daughter?"

"Yes, I'm Sabrina, and this is my friend…Alex Justice."

Friend. They were a helluva lot more than friends. The word put his teeth on edge.

"Your mother is going to be okay," the doctor said. "We're still trying to piece together how she ingested the nuts. It was her niece's quick thinking in recognizing the symptoms and getting the ambulance there that kept the situation from being far more severe."

"She's always had to be very careful."

"So you think it was an accident," Alex said, and saw Sabrina's gaze shoot to his.

"I would presume so."

Alex wished to hell he believed that, but the way things were going it was hard to swallow.

"The good news is, she's going to be fine." The doctor scanned his chart. "I'm planning to release her in the morning."

"That's very good news, Dr. Wong," Sabrina said. "We appreciate all you've done."

The doctor nodded, smiled and walked away, his mind on his next patient.

"We'll get a room somewhere," Alex said, "stay till morning, take your mom home and get her settled."

"What about your sister?"

"I'll call Joe, see what's happening, check with the police, see if they've found any trace of Bagley. Sol hasn't called, so he hasn't come up with anything. Whether we're here or in Houston probably won't matter."

She worried her bottom lip, made him want to settle his mouth there, taste her. Not appropriate thinking at the moment.

"All right, if you think it's okay."

Once the plan was set, Priscilla went home to take care of her kids. Alex made the necessary phone calls but got no new information, ducked into the room for a brief hello to Flo, then waited while Sabrina went back inside to sit with her a little longer.

When visiting hours were over, a heavyset nurse with iron-gray hair and a thick Texas drawl shooed her out of the room. "Your mama needs her rest. Ya'll come back in the mornin'. If Doc Wong says it's okay, you can take her home then."

Sabrina waited for the door to close on her mother's room then Alex guided her toward the elevator. It was dark outside now, the dry night air much cooler. Alex checked the rental car, saw no evidence of tampering, scanned the parking lot and surrounding area, led Sabrina over to the car and settled her inside.

"The Sunset Motel is a few blocks away," she said as he slid behind the wheel. "It isn't too old and it's clean. There's nothing fancy in Uvalde."

"I don't need fancy," Alex said. Leaning over, he pressed a soft kiss on her mouth. "I just need you."

Her mood seemed to lighten. She gave him a slow, sexy smile. "That's good to know, flyboy. Her gaze drifted down to the bulge at the front of his jeans. "Looks like you've got exactly what *I* need."

Alex grinned. "How far did you say it was to that motel?"

* * *

Night had finally settled in, the cooler air drying the sweat that had his faded brown T-shirt sticking to his skin. Henry was damned sick of sitting in the frying heat. Nearly half a damned day wasted waiting in the van, watching for the bastard to get there.

He'd known they would come. Rina and her mother were tight. Something happened to Flo, she'd bust her sweet little ass to get to Uvalde.

He'd known the family since they were kids, knew all about the old lady's allergy to nuts. Knew Florence babysat for Sill and that the two women had a standing Tuesday lunch date at Pete's Café. Had for the past three or four years.

All he'd had to do was threaten to bring the ICE boys down on one of the illegals working in the kitchen, then sweeten the deal with a crisp hundred-dollar bill. He'd given the guy a bag of finely ground peanuts and told him to sprinkle them in whatever Mrs. Eckhart ordered. The guy knew who she was and reluctantly agreed.

Sitting on his motorcycle out of sight behind the van, Henry smiled as he watched Justice and Rina climb into the rental car. The idea had been sheer genius if he did say so himself. Lure the little bitch to Uvalde and get rid of her. Do what the rest of the dumbasses had tried to do and failed.

He'd done old Walt Eckhart without a hitch right here in Uvalde. Bob had known his dad would be coming home for Christmas, the way he always did. The hit-and-run had played out perfectly. The hell of it was by the time the old man was dead, the prick had changed the will.

Henry had no intention of killing the old woman.

Whenever he'd hung around the house with the other kids, Mrs. Eckhart had always been nice to him. But a night in the hospital was no big deal.

Henry watched the small rented Nissan pull out of the hospital parking lot and started the engine on his motorcycle. He hadn't ridden his Yamaha dirt bike in years, just left it sitting in his garage in Houston. But it still ran good and it would do the job.

So far, he'd had things pretty well figured. Rina was keeping Justice happy in bed. In return he was playing bodyguard. Henry figured as long as she kept putting out, the guy would fly her anywhere she wanted to go. It was a no-brainer he'd bring her here to see her ailing mom.

Henry waited till the car disappeared into the darkness, gunned the engine and roared after them. This time, he'd finish the job. And once again, there'd be no goddamn way to trace anything back to him or anyone else.

Twenty-Nine

By the time they left the hospital, darkness had settled over the flat Texas landscape. The air was quiet, no hint of a breeze. Still thinking about Sabrina and the way he planned to take her mind off her worries, Alex checked the rearview mirror for any sign of trouble. No other cars on the road, just a single headlight in the distance.

He checked again as they rolled along, saw a motorcycle moving up fast. He expected the bike to pass on the left and go around, but instead, at the last minute, the driver swerved to the right and roared up on the passenger side of the car.

"Get down!" Alex shouted, shoving Sabrina's head down an instant before the glass on her side of the car exploded. The next instant, he felt the jolt of a bullet slamming into his side.

"Alex!" Sabrina cried.

"Stay down!" Jamming his foot hard on the gas, the little SUV shot forward after the motorcycle. His side was burning. He could feel the blood seeping into his shirt as he jerked his .45 out of its holster and ratcheted back the slide.

"You're bleeding!" Sabrina cried. "What are you doing!"

He clenched his jaw. "I'm ending this."

He was almost on top of the motorcycle, an older model dirt bike, the rider crouched low over the handlebars. Moving fast, just inches from the rear fender. Then the bastard swerved and shot out into the desert.

Alex didn't slow, just cranked the wheel to the right and flew off the paved road after him. The SUV jolted over the hard-packed earth, throwing him against his seat belt, then slid sideways, the wheels spinning in an area of sandy soil. Alex corrected, throwing up a wall of dirt and dust as they rocketed out into the desert after the bike.

He heard Sabrina dialing 911, filling the dispatcher in on where they were and what was happening. "We need an ambulance! Hurry!"

Her eyes flashed toward him and she must have seen the blood dripping onto his seat. "Oh, my God, you have to stop! You need help!"

Alex just kept driving, swerving to avoid a deep ravine then slamming down on the gas pedal again. In the twin beams of the headlights, the motorcycle hit a pothole and the front wheel wobbled, forcing the driver to slow as he fought to regain control. Alex hit the pothole at sixty miles an hour, the wheels lifting off the ground, then slamming back to earth.

The car surged ahead, gaining on the bike, which was revved full-tilt, trying to reach its former speed. Alex was right on top of him.

The driver tried to evade, but Alex stayed with him.

Catching up to him again, he rammed the back of the bike, once, twice, determined to force the driver to stop. The third time, the machine went airborne, careening end over end, the driver flying off the seat into the air. The bike landed in the middle of a spiny cactus. The driver's body hit the ground, rolled a couple of times and came to a stop at the base of a mesquite tree.

Slamming on the brakes, the SUV sliding, Alex leaped out of the car. "Stay inside!" Weapon in hand, he charged toward the man lying faceup in the dirt, illuminated clearly by the rental car headlights.

Alex prayed to God the bastard wasn't dead.

A wave of dizziness hit him. He was losing too much blood. He hoped to hell the ambulance was on its way. Kneeling in the dirt next to the driver, he checked for weapons, saw none, figured the shooter's pistol was somewhere out in the desert.

One of the man's legs was bent at an odd angle and so was a hand, his wrist clearly broken. He made no move but he was breathing. Once Alex was sure he was unconscious, he pulled the chin strap and lifted off the helmet.

Late thirties. Dull brown hair. Unshaven face and heavily weathered skin. Between the first and second digit of the guy's right hand, he noticed the telltale nicotine marks of a smoker.

He heard footsteps running toward him, saw Sabrina kneeling beside him. She was shaking as she caught his shoulders, leaned over him.

"Oh, God, Alex, where are you hit?"

"Side," he grunted. "I can't tell how bad it is."

She took a deep breath, released it slowly. "Take your shirt off. Here, let me help you."

He didn't argue as she gently helped him unbutton

and slip out of the shirt, then stuffed it against the wound and held it there to stop the bleeding.

"Just hang on, okay? They're coming. I hear sirens. I told them where we turned off the road and about how far we've driven. I hope they can see the headlights."

He managed a smile. "You did good."

For the first time, she turned toward the man lying in the dirt in front of the headlights. "Oh, my God, it's Henry Mullins."

"You know him?"

"Yes…he's…he's a longtime family friend. He's older than I am." She looked up at him, her eyes wide. "He went to school with my cousins."

In that moment, it all fell together. Alex's mouth edged up. "I guess we found our link." He tried to stand but a second wave of dizziness hit him and he wavered. He heard Sabrina scream as he collapsed face-first into the sand.

Rina sat at Alex's bedside at Uvalde Memorial Hospital. He was recovering well from the gunshot wound he had suffered. According to the doctors, the bullet hit a rib and bounced off, cracking the rib and tearing through muscle and skin, but doing no damage to any internal organs.

He'd been extremely lucky. Still, he had lost a great deal of blood.

Rina glanced down to where he lay sleeping and her heart squeezed. She could have lost him. Guilt slid through her. The mine and the money weren't worth Alex's life. She should have given it up when all of this started.

Her eyes filled. She brushed at the wetness with the tips of her fingers.

"Hey…" Alex said softly, and she realized he was awake and watching her. "Those tears for me?"

She reached for a Kleenex, blew her nose, then took hold of his hand. She wanted to tell him how much she loved him, that nothing was worth more to her than he was. But Alex wouldn't want to hear the words. Instead she said, "You could have been killed."

He brought her hand to his lips and kissed the back of it. "I wasn't. And from what the police are saying, there's a good chance we've found your uncle's killer."

She managed a wobbly smile. In that way, maybe it had been worth it. "They're pretty sure it was Henry. The van they found was brown but it was white before it was painted. They found some fairly recent bodywork on the front and there were still traces of blood in some of the crevices on the bumper. They aren't sure they can match the DNA to Walter, but they're trying."

"Maybe they'll be able to get Henry to confess. He's in deep shit and once he wakes up, he'll know it. Texas has the death penalty and your uncle's murder was as premeditated as it gets. If he confesses to the murder and rolls over on the cousins, he might be able to make a deal."

The police had found the van parked near the hospital parking lot, apparently the vehicle Henry had used to transport his motorcycle from Houston to Uvalde. His plan had very nearly worked.

"How's he doing?" Alex asked.

"He's still unconscious. They don't know for sure when he's going to wake up, but they're optimistic."

"You said he was a family friend. Not much of a friend to you."

"Henry never liked me. He said I was *uppity*. That's what he called me. Said I thought I was too good for the rest of them." She leaned down and gently kissed his lips. "How are you feeling?"

"Grouchy." But he was smiling, his dimples showing, tugging at her heartstrings. "I want out of here. How about putting in a good word for me? Get me out early?"

She just shook her head. "No way. They're releasing you tomorrow. I'm not about to intervene. You lost a lot of blood. You need to rest and recover your strength."

He made a grumbling sound. "I ask you for one little favor and what do I get?"

She smiled and so did he.

"Sage and Jake have been calling. Trace and Maggie, too. Oh, and Annie called. So did Ben. They've all been worried. Jake and Sage wanted to drive down, but I told them you'd be getting out sometime tomorrow."

"They're good friends."

"Yes, they are."

"You able to get your mother home and settled?"

Her mother had been released yesterday. At Alex's insistence, Sabrina had declined Priscilla's offer to help and taken her mother home herself. An investigation was ongoing into this latest attempt on Sabrina's life and all of the cousins were under suspicion.

Sabrina's heart pinched. Her mother hadn't taken the news very well.

"I just can't believe it," Florence had said from her place beneath a light throw blanket on the sofa in her living room. "Henry always seemed so nice." She took a sip of the sweet tea Rina had made for her. "Your

Alex thinks this all has something to do with Walter and the mine?"

"The police think Henry might have killed him, Mom."

Her eyes widened. She took a shaky breath, shook her head. "I don't understand any of this. Why would Henry kill Walter?"

"Because the mine Uncle Walter left me turned out to be worth a lot of money. If I die, Walter's kids are next in line. Henry was a friend of theirs."

"Henry was Bob's best friend in high school."

"I know."

Her mother closed her eyes. "You think Bob and Henry made some kind of deal to kill you and get the mine?"

"It looks that way. Though no one knows for sure which of them it might be." *Or if all of them were involved.*

"Oh, honey, I feel so guilty for making you come here and putting you in danger. And that sweet man of yours is in the hospital...I still just can't believe it."

That sweet man of yours. The words cut like a knife. Alex didn't belong to her and once this was over, their relationship would be over, as well.

Today, as she sat beside his bed, Alex still holding her hand, Sabrina pushed the thought away. Even now the police were questioning her cousins. She believed they would find out the truth.

Alex's voice drew her back to the moment. "Hey, baby... Where'd you go? I'm right here beside you."

She looked into his dear, handsome face, her heart beating softy. "I'm sorry. Mom's doing great, completely back to normal. She likes having me stay with her. I was just thinking…going over everything that's happened."

He squeezed her hand. "It's almost over. If we get lucky, Henry will come out of his coma, turn state's evidence and roll over on whoever's behind the attacks. I think he was the linchpin, the cousins' go-to guy. With him out of the picture, you should be a whole lot safer."

Still, until an arrest was made, Rina and her mother were under twenty-four-hour police protection. This was Uvalde. Everyone knew and loved Florence Eckhart. Sabrina was her daughter. It didn't matter that she'd moved away. The town took care of its own.

She looked over at Alex, saw that he had fallen asleep but didn't let go of his hand. She loved him so much. He was the best man she had ever known and until he walked away, she belonged to him, body and soul.

Sabrina ignored the painful squeezing of her heart that told her how much it was going to hurt when she lost him.

They were back in Houston. Alex's side hurt like bloody hell, but he was healing. He and Sabrina were alive, and the police were making progress on the case.

They had interviewed each of the cousins. So far none had admitted any involvement in Walter's death or the attempts on Sabrina's life, but the police were leaning heavily toward cousin Bob. And all three of them were now aware that if anything happened to Sabrina, they'd be arrested for murder.

Alex had no doubt Bob and his siblings were shaking in their boots.

Sabrina was probably safe, but still, he was determined not to let her move back into her apartment. She'd argued a little, not as strongly as he'd figured, but he'd convinced her to stay with him at his house until Henry awakened from his coma. Even if that never happened, the police were working day and night to track down calls and any communication between the cousins and Henry Mullins.

Seated at his desk in the Atlas office, catching up on his email and messages, Alex glanced across to where Sabrina sat behind a computer at one of the empty desks doing the same thing. He was trying to keep her busy and out of trouble until the cops could get all the evidence they needed to nail down their case.

In the meantime, he was working to locate Edward Bagley. Shoving away from his desk, he winced at the jolt of pain that shot up from his injured side and walked toward Sol's office for his second morning update.

He knocked on the door frame, then walked in. "Hey, Sol, sorry to bug you again. Anything new?"

"No problem. Just be somebody else if it wasn't you."

"Where are we?"

"I've gone over every possible combination of names that Bagley might own property under. I've checked his banking records, looked for monthly payments on a mortgage or trust deed. I got zip. I also tried looking at some of his friends to see if maybe they were somehow helping him. Still zip."

"What about his parents? His mother's dead, but his dad's still alive."

"Near as I could find out, he and his dad haven't communicated for years. His dad was a real loser. Maybe even abusive. Could be how Bagley got so fucked-up in the first place."

Alex blew out a frustrated breath. "So we're whistling in the wind."

"I did find something interesting. Found a reference
to a hospital stay by Bagley's mother a few years before he was born. Turns out, the guy's got a half brother.
His mom gave the kid up for adoption before she married Bagley's dad. I don't know if Bagley even knows
he exists. The records were buried pretty deep. I had
to hack—"

Alex held up a hand. "I don't want to know."

Sol just grinned.

"So where's this half brother now?"

"I haven't been able to find him, but I'm on it. I'll let
you know if I get a location. Like I said, I'm not sure
Bagley knows anything about him."

It was something, not much. "Thanks, kid."

Sol nodded and went back to work. Alex headed for
Sabrina, who stood up as he approached.

"You're hurting," she said. "You need to go home
and go to bed."

He hadn't realized he was pressing a hand against the
ache in his side. Since he'd looked as pale as a vampire
in the mirror this morning, he figured that explained
the worry in her eyes.

"I'm definitely interested in hitting the bed, if you'll
join me." His gaze slid over her T-shirt, jeans and sneakers. She looked like a red-haired pixie, which shouldn't
have turned him on but did.

"You can't be thinking of sex. You're recovering from
a bullet wound, for heaven's sake."

"So we'll take it slow and easy." He grinned, trying
not to get a hard-on. "I'll let you do all the work."

Sabrina propped her hands on her hips. "You're incorrigible."

"Guilty," he admitted.

Her eyes slowly ran over him head to foot, sending a fresh jolt of heat to his groin. "You may change your tune, flyboy, once I get started."

He just laughed and tried to ignore the suddenly tight fit of his jeans. "Before we leave, I need to call Becca, make sure everything's okay."

"I'll be ready whenever you are." There was a suggestive note in her voice. He liked a woman who knew what she wanted.

He made the call, found out Joe and Ginny were out in the yard building a tree house, much to his sister's chagrin. He told Becca that Sol was still hard at work trying to locate Bagley, then hung up and collected Sabrina for the trip to his house.

It didn't take long to get there. When he walked into the entry, he was surprised to discover how good it felt to be back in his own home again. As he turned off the alarm and closed the garage door, he looked down at the little spitfire beside him and realized how much he liked having her there with him.

Some of his enthusiasm faded.

He'd told her how much he cared and he'd meant it. But he wasn't ready for a permanent relationship. It just wasn't part of his plans for the future. Hell, he didn't have any plans for the future, which was exactly the problem.

Which meant this thing with Sabrina was going to have to end.

Alex ignored the ache in his chest that hurt nearly as much as the wound in his side. He'd worry about all of that later. Right now he wanted her and she wanted him. That was all that mattered. Alex reached for her hand and they started up the stairs.

Thirty

Through the new kitchen window that looked into her shady backyard, Rebecca watched Joe and Ginny. Joe was building a tree house among the thick branches of the big sycamore in the corner. Ginny squealed with delight as she handed him the various tools he asked for and he showed her how to use each one.

It was all Rebecca could do not to walk outside and put an immediate stop to it. Little girls didn't wear coveralls and pound nails into sawed-off pieces of wood. It just wasn't the proper way to behave.

She tried to imagine herself at Ginny's age wanting to wear a T-shirt and jeans and learn how to use a screwdriver. But Rebecca had been nothing at all like that. Her mother had kept her in frilly little dresses from the most expensive shops in Guildford. She'd taken ballet lessons and cotillion and played with dolls.

She'd done everything her mother told her to do in every part of her life. From as far back as she could remember, Rebecca had never questioned whether her mother was right or wrong. She just wanted to please her.

She still did.

The realization hit her like a slap in the face. Virginia Justice had been a strict, demanding mother. She had commanded every aspect of Rebecca's life, how she dressed, what she studied, which college she would attend, even whom she should date and ultimately marry.

What she hadn't been was a caring, loving mother.

Rebecca thought of Jeremy, her mother's idea of the perfect husband. Virginia had chosen him as surely as she had chosen everything else in Rebecca's life. Her mother was the reason she had stayed with him even after he had become abusive. If it hadn't been for Alex, she might never have left him.

She might never have come to Houston. Might never have met a wonderful man like Joe.

Her heart warmed at the thought of the days they'd spent together since he had moved into the house. Wonderful days filled with warmth, laughter and kindness. And a smoldering attraction that burned so hot it seemed to scorch the very air they breathed.

They hadn't done anything about it. Not with Ginny's life in danger.

At least her brother was back in his home and healing. She'd panicked when she'd received the call from Sabrina that he had been shot. But Joe had been there to help her get through those first hours of waiting, and the doctor's report had been good.

And it looked as if he was very close to ending the threat against Sabrina's life.

Which meant he was back to work finding Edward Bagley. Alex called every day to report on the progress he was making, which wasn't much, but he was good at his job and she believed that with him and the police all working to find the man, soon this would be over.

She looked back out the window and saw her daughter smiling up at Joe. Funny, Rebecca couldn't ever remember being a happy little girl. Not like Ginny.

Her mother wouldn't approve of Joe McCauley, she knew. She'd say he wasn't refined enough. But Rebecca wasn't a child anymore. She could live the life she wanted. Love whatever man she wanted.

It was past time Rebecca realized that neither she nor Ginny ever had to please Virginia Justice again.

She looked out the window at two of the people she loved most in the world and felt as if a heavy weight had suddenly been lifted off her shoulders.

As she started for the door to see how the tree house was coming along, she smiled.

Several days passed and Alex was on the mend. Rina awakened to the feel of the sun warming the room through the curtains across his bedroom window, Alex nibbling her earlobe. She rolled toward him, looped her arms around his neck.

"You're not only incorrigible, you're insatiable."

He grinned. "That's what you love about me." He started kissing his way down her neck.

Rina slid a hand into his hair, her mood switching from light to serious. "I love everything about you, Alex. I'm in love with you." The words spilled out as if a dam had broken. She had held back her feelings so long; she just couldn't do it anymore. "I didn't mean for it to happen...it just did."

He stopped kissing her and rolled onto his back, staring up at the ceiling.

"I'm sorry. I know that isn't something you wanted to hear. But it's the truth and I can't hide it any longer."

He blew out a slow breath. "It's been good between us, Sabrina. Can't we just leave things the way they are?"

She leaned over him, kissed his mouth. "We can. For now. I don't know for how long."

His eyes searched her face. He reached up and looped a stray curl behind an ear. "I don't know what to say. I love being with you. I don't want to give you up, but I can't offer you anything permanent. My life is too unsettled. It just wouldn't work."

Her throat tightened. She had known he would say something like that. "I had to tell you. I've wanted to for a long time. I wish you could have said it back, but I didn't expect it."

"You know how much I care."

She leaned down, softly kissed him. He had been there for her when she needed him. He still was. "I know."

They made love with a ferocity she hadn't expected, a sort of wild desperation, Alex coming up over her, burying his hands in her hair, dragging her mouth up to his for a fierce, taking kiss, then spreading her legs with his knee and driving hard inside her. They moved together, Sabrina arching to take more of him, Alex thrusting deep, claiming more of her, demanding a response.

They reached their peak in a frenzy of heat and need, a powerful climax that spoke of love and loss. From the moment she had said she loved him, both of them had known it was time for their affair to end.

It wasn't what she wanted. She loved him so much. She wanted to stay with him forever.

But Alex was the man he was and she was the

woman she was. From the start, she had known how it would end.

Afterward they lay together, spent and exhausted. She leaned down, pressed a soft kiss on the bandage over his stitches. "Your wound... We shouldn't have done that. Are you okay?"

Alex just nodded. They might have talked, might have tried to breach the silence that settled over them, if the phone hadn't started ringing.

At first, neither of them could figure out whose phone it was, since both of them were still carrying the disposables Alex had bought. He slid on his jeans as she grabbed her robe, fished hers out of her purse and pressed it against her ear.

"Yes?"

"Rina, it's Priscilla." Her cousin started crying and Rina felt a jolt of fear.

"Sill, what is it? Is it Mom?"

"No, no, Aunt Flo is...is fine. It's...it's Rusty."

Alex came up beside her and Sabrina held the phone so he could hear.

"Rusty...?

"Yes. Oh, God, Rina, Rusty's the one who screwed up the engine on the helicopter. He rigged the steering on your car." She started crying again.

"It's all right, Sill." She flicked a glance at Alex. "Where's Rusty now?"

"I kicked him out. After the police were here asking questions about Henry, I started thinking. I dug through some of his stuff while he was at work. He kept a metal box with his papers under the bed. I picked the lock with a hairpin and I found..." She took a shaky breath. "I found his bank statements. There was a five-thousand-dollar deposit made just before the helicopter crash. Then a three-thousand-dollar deposit right before your car accident."

Alex took the phone from her hand. "Where are your girls, Priscilla?"

"They're with me. Rusty would never hurt them, but—"

"Do you have any idea where Rusty is now?"

"Probably down at Casey's Bar. He loves me. He'll figure I'll forgive him. He'll want to come home."

"I'm calling the police, Priscilla. Lock your door and stay inside. Don't let Rusty in no matter what he says, all right?"

There was a long pause on the other end of the line.

"You need to think of your girls, Priscilla."

"I won't…won't let him in."

He handed the phone back to Sabrina, went to phone the Uvalde police.

"You did the right thing calling, Sill. A man like that is dangerous."

"I know that now. But not to me or…or the girls. I think he did it for us. He's been buying me stuff lately, buying stuff for the girls." She sobbed into the phone. "I'm sorry, Rina. I didn't know, I swear."

Rina's eyes welled. "I believe you." She wiped a tear from her cheek. "Everything's going to be okay, you hear me? I promise. Alex will take care of everything."

"He's a good man, Rina."

"I know. We'll let you know when they've got Rusty in custody."

Priscilla started crying again and the phone went dead.

Rina hurriedly dressed and joined Alex in his study just as he hung up the phone.

"They'll call when they pick him up," Alex said, "assuming he's still in town."

"I feel sorry for her."

"You think she's telling the truth? You don't think she had any part in it?"

"No. Do you?"

"My gut says no. I hope for her sake and yours she's telling the truth."

Rina said nothing, just went into the kitchen and started making coffee. They were on the second pot when the police called.

They arrested Rusty Jenkins at Casey's Bar, where Priscilla had said they would find him. He confessed to sabotaging the chopper and destroying the steering on the Toyota. He said he needed the money. He said he loved Priscilla and he was sorry.

He said Henry Mullins paid him to do it.

Another day passed and still the police hadn't located Edward Bagley. The day had been a long one. Rebecca was grateful when it was finally time for bed. But as the hours ticked past, sleep did not come. Still wearing her blue silk robe, she lay on top of the covers, staring up at the ceiling. Ginny slept in the room across the hall and Joe was sleeping in the guest room.

She thought of him lying there beneath the ceiling fan, his big body sprawled on the mattress. She wondered if he slept in the nude, imagined that he did. She remembered the way he looked when he worked with his shirt off, the thick slabs of muscle across his shoulders, the heavy biceps, the wide, muscled chest with its curly dark chest hair.

Just thinking about him turned her body liquid and

warm. Every night since he'd moved into the house, after Ginny had gone to sleep, he had walked Rebecca up to her room and kissed her good-night. A long, simmering, erotic kiss that had her heart pounding and her body pulsing. Joe was usually the one to pull away.

Tonight had been the same and yet different. She had felt his hesitation, felt his burning need for her, his desire to step through the bedroom door, sweep her off her feet and make love to her. She had fought her need for him.

Why hadn't she taken that single step back and invited him into her room? Why hadn't she taken what he offered, given them both what they so badly wanted? Ginny was a sound sleeper. She never woke up before morning. And both of them had waited long enough.

As if he read her thoughts, she heard the creak of hinges, saw the door slowly open, recognized the outline of Joe's solid body as he stepped into the room in only a pair of jeans.

His eyes found hers through the darkness illuminated by a faint sliver of moon coming in through the windows.

"I want you," he said. "I ache with wanting you, Becca. I want to spend the night in your bed more than I want to breathe, but I'll leave if that's what you want."

Her eyes burned. She came up off the bed and went to him, walked straight into his arms. "Don't go. Stay with me. Make love to me, Joe."

He closed the door behind him, bent his dark head and kissed her, a hot, fierce, burning kiss that loosened every bone and muscle in her body. The kiss went on and on, teasing then taking, demanding then giving. His tongue slid over hers and she could taste the maleness of him, the coppery tang of his desire.

Her bones turned to butter and she completely melted against him, felt his hard muscles bunch as he lifted her into his arms and carried her over to the bed.

She thought he would rush, that he would take her in the same fierce way he had kissed her, but instead his movements slowed.

"I won't rush you. No matter how much I want to be inside you, I won't hurry. Not tonight."

The tears in her eyes rolled down her cheeks. She felt cherished, worshipped. "Joe…"

He took her mouth in another ravishing kiss. Rebecca didn't resist when he peeled off her robe, then unzipped his jeans and slid them down over his hips. Her gaze ran over him, saw that the rest of his body was as strong and hard as she had imagined.

She found herself glancing away from his powerful erection as he joined her on the bed, for the first time feeling shy.

"I know it's been a while for you," he said, coming up over her. "We'll take it easy. You can trust me to make this right for us, Becca."

She swallowed past the lump in her throat. "I know. I trust you, Joe."

He kissed her again, began to caress her breasts, first one and then the other, kissed his way down her body then returned to her mouth. As he stroked and teased and tasted, as the pleasure built until she thought she couldn't stand it a moment more, she knew he would keep his word.

When he took her with such gentleness and skill, with such iron control, Rebecca gave herself up to him, let his deep strokes carry her to fulfillment. When the first climax hit her, the pleasure was sweeter than anything she had ever known.

And in that moment, Rebecca understood what the power of love could do. Understood that she was deeply in love with Joe McCauley.

It was nearly two in the morning. Rina lay awake, staring at the ceiling above the bed. At Alex's insistence, she was still staying at his house, but the police were working hard to solve her case. In the meantime, they went on as if nothing had changed. She loved him. She would stay these few more precious days.

She closed her eyes, but sleep wouldn't come. She tried to lie still so she wouldn't disturb him, but somehow he knew she wasn't asleep.

"What is it?" he asked into the quiet darkness.

She moved her head on the pillow. "I don't know. My mind just seems to be working overtime."

Alex reached for her, drew her against his side. She nestled her head on his shoulder. "You thinking about Priscilla?"

Along with thoughts of Alex, she had thought of her cousin a dozen times since Rusty had been arrested. "I keep remembering what it was like when we were kids. Uncle Walter was never there for them. I remember how much Priscilla missed him. George, too. George was the misfit of the family. He used to sit out on the front porch and watch for his dad to come home."

"I hope he isn't involved."

"I called him today. I know I probably shouldn't have, but I was worried about Janie. George says she's doing great. He cried, Alex. He feels terrible about what's happened to me. He said to thank you for saving his daughter."

Alex made no reply. She knew he didn't want her talking to any of them. Until Henry Mullins awakened, the cousins were still not in the clear.

"I remember Aunt Marlene telling George what a rotten guy his dad was. How he never cared about any of his kids. How he only cared about himself. I never believed it. I thought Walter was the freest, most interesting man I'd ever known. I tried to tell my cousins their dad loved them, that he was just different, but they never really believed me."

Alex leaned down and kissed her. "They resented you because you had a loving family and their father loved you, too."

"I was lucky."

"Maybe, but it wasn't all luck. People choose their own paths."

She turned onto her side so she could see his profile, appreciate the beauty of his face, the strength of character in the sculpted valleys and planes. "Yes, they do. Maybe someday you'll find the right path for you."

His eyes found hers and even in the darkness, she could see the turmoil there. "Maybe I'm on the right path now."

Hope flared. Maybe he would finally find his way and the path would lead to her. "Are you?"

He looked away, off toward the window, though he couldn't see outside. "I don't know. I just...I know right now what I need is you." He turned back to her, leaned over and kissed her. Sabrina slid her arms around his neck and kissed him back.

He was everything to her. She had tried not to love

him, but he was more irresistible to her now than when she'd first met him. She wondered if there was the slightest hope for them. She reached up and touched his face as he came up over her, made a place for himself inside her.

It was a gentle taking, a sharing on some new and different level, as if he gave her some small part of himself he had never given her before.

When they reached their peak and drifted back to earth, she was torn between the hollow ache that reminded her she would have to give him up, and the soft pulsing of hope that maybe in time he would come to love her as much as she loved him.

Joe wasn't certain what awakened him. The neon numbers on the clock read 2:45 a.m. Nestled against his side, Rebecca slept deeply. He kissed her cheek and rolled from the bed to check the house and make sure everything was okay.

It hit him as he stood up, the harsh smell of smoke drifting up from the floor below. An instant later, the fire alarms began going off and Rebecca jerked upright in bed, her stunned gaze shooting to the window.

"Oh, my, God, the house is on fire!"

Joe tossed her the pretty silk robe she'd been wearing when he'd walked into the bedroom and started pulling on his jeans. Through the front windows, flames climbed the outside walls above the porch, their bright orange glow filling the black night sky.

Rebecca ran to the door. "I've got to get Ginny!"

"Wait! I'll get her!" He zipped his fly and ran for the door, laid a hand on the wood to make sure the fire wasn't right outside. The door was still cool.

"Come on, let's go!" He swung the door open,

grabbed Rebecca's hand and pulled her out into the hall behind him.

"It's already reached the roof!" Rebecca shouted, looking back through the bedroom window. The flames were chewing their way up the side of the house, burning into the turret in the front.

Joe jerked open Ginny's door, ran over and shook her awake, lifted her into his arms. "Honey, it's Joe. There's a fire. We have to get out of the house."

"A fire?"

He carried her into the hall.

"It's okay, sweetheart," Rebecca said, squeezing the little girl's hand. "We're going out the back."

"Where's the fire department?" Ginny asked.

"The alarm system's already called them," Joe said, urging Rebecca down the hall toward the old servants' stairs leading to the kitchen. He had worked on them himself, made sure they were safe.

The burglar alarm was also blasting now, the sound deafening as they hurried through the thick black smoke toward the door that led out to the yard. The fire crackled overhead, burning into the upstairs floor, the smoke leaking through, filling the kitchen.

"Keep your head down so you can breathe!" He set Ginny on her feet where the air was less smoky, grabbed her hand and urged Rebecca toward the door. "We're almost there!"

A wooden deck stretched across the back of the house, then three steps down to the grass. Joe waited for Ginny and Rebecca to run out of the house, then stepped out behind them. He heard Rebecca scream the instant before he caught movement in the shadows, something hard slammed into the side of his head and he crashed to his knees.

"Joe!" Rebecca cried as the man who'd been waiting swung the baseball bat again.

Joe tried to block the blow, but the bat made contact like a thousand-pound brick smashing into his skull. He went down like a sack of wheat, his mind spinning into darkness.

"Step back and you won't get hurt." The baseball bat was gone. Ed Bagley had an arm wrapped around Ginny's waist and a gun pressed against the side of her head. Her little girl was crying.

Shaking all over, fear clawing at her insides, Rebecca stood her ground. "Let her go."

"Mommy!"

"I know who you are," Rebecca said. "The fire trucks will be here any minute. You can't get away with this."

Bagley's smile seemed almost kindly. How could he look so harmless?

"Actually, I can." Moving before she realized his intent, he swung a blow with the hand that held the pistol, his fist smashing into her cheek. Pain exploded in her face and she went down.

"Mommy!"

Bagley started walking. "Tell your brother I said hello."

Through a haze of pain, she struggled to remain conscious. "Don't take her...please..." Darkness hovered at the edge of her vision. She tried to move but she couldn't seem to make her body work. Her vision dimmed. As blackness descended, she saw Edward Bagley running away from the house, her little girl no longer fighting, just lying limp in his arms.

Thirty-One

Red lights flashed, bright scarlet reflected in the puddles left from the fire hoses. So many fire trucks and police cars filled the cul-de-sac in front of his sister's house Alex had to park down the block.

Next to him, Sabrina sat tensely in the passenger seat as he turned off the engine, then they both got out of the car.

"Oh, God, Alex." Her voice shook as she stared at the wood-framed house. The porch that wrapped around the structure still smoldered. The front was burned clear into the living room and the second story, the roof was partly destroyed, but the flames were mostly out. Only a few tongues of red and orange licked up to where firefighters still worked on the roof.

"Fucking bastard set fire to the front porch and drove them out the back. He was lying in wait for them. They didn't stand a chance."

Joe had called just minutes after he had regained consciousness. Bagley had taken him down with a baseball bat before he'd had time to recognize the threat. Joe was riddled with guilt for having failed Becca and Ginny.

Alex spotted them sitting behind the ambulance in a pair of lawn chairs one of the neighbors must have supplied. Though both had refused to go to the hospital, Joe was being treated for a concussion. From what Joe had said, Rebecca was mostly just battered and bruised.

It was her heart that was in peril. Her little girl had been abducted by a child killer.

Alex's gut churned. As he walked toward the ambulance where Joe and his sister were waiting, his hand unconsciously fisted. It wasn't Joe's fault. Alex was the one who had led the bastard to Ginny.

His sister was on her feet and running the minute she spotted him, hurling herself against him. Alex gathered her into his arms, felt her trembling.

"He took her, Alex. Bagley took…took Ginny. I tried to stop him but there was nothing I could…could do." She started crying and Alex just held her, helpless rage burning through him.

"We're going to get her back," he said. "I promise." But there was no way to know if he'd be able to keep his word.

Joe walked up beside her, a white gauze bandage wrapped around his head. Alex noticed he didn't touch her.

"I should have seen it coming," he said, guilt evident in the slump of his shoulders. "I should have realized what was going on."

Alex shook his head. "There was no way you could have figured this. The guy's smart, maybe brilliant. He had it all worked out."

Rebecca stepped away from him, wiped the tears

from her cheeks. "We've got to find her, Alex. She's alone and she's scared. Oh, God, what if he—"

"Stop it!" Alex gripped her shoulders. "You can't think that way. You need to focus on finding Ginny."

Rebecca made a sad little sound in her throat. She swallowed and nodded.

"You have to be strong." Sabrina leaned over and hugged her. "We're going to find her. Bagley may be smart, but your brother's smarter. He caught Bagley before—he can do it again."

Alex reached for Sabrina's hand, gave it a squeeze. She never doubted him, never lost confidence in him. She had said she loved him. Women had said it before, but none had really meant it.

"I called Josh Reynolds with the D.A.'s office," he said. "Shook him out of bed. Reynolds says the D.A.'s worried about reelection, says by the time I got here, the department would be all over this. By now half of Houston P.D. is looking for Bagley."

"They've put out an Amber Alert," Joe said, "and set up a perimeter around the neighborhood. They're trying to stop him before he gets away."

"I called Sol, woke him up, told him what happened. He's trying some other angles, seeing if he might have missed something."

Joe stared back at the smoldering remains of the house. "I said I'd take care of them. I'm bigger than Bagley. I should have been able to handle him."

Rebecca saw the defeat in his eyes, and Alex saw something shift in her features. "He was waiting for you, Joe. He hit you with a baseball bat. He could have killed you." She swallowed. "It wasn't your fault."

Joe's gaze locked with hers. There was something in

her face that Alex could only call love, and his friend's broad shoulders straightened as if the life had just returned to his body. When he opened his arms, Rebecca went into them and he just held on.

"We'll find her, honey. I swear it. I won't let you down again."

Rebecca started crying, but she didn't leave Joe's arms. Watching them, Alex's chest felt tight. He thought of the words Sabrina had said, knew that she had meant them. Knew that he would never find another woman like her.

She looked up at him. "What can we do?"

Alex drew her into his arms. "Hope to God the cops get lucky. Sol's meeting us at the office. We're going to brainstorm. In the meantime, we just have to wait and pray."

No one slept. Joe's head was pounding. Off and on, he felt dizzy. They were sitting in Rebecca's next-door neighbor's kitchen. Mrs. Slotski lived in a big, older colonial home with an oversize backyard and shady oak trees in front. She was a widow, a sweet, slightly stoop-shouldered older woman who made chocolate chip cookies for Ginny, babysat once in a while and was devastated at the news the little girl had been abducted.

"There's plenty of room in the house," she'd said to Rebecca. "You and Joe can stay right here as long as you like. The police need a place to work and you need a place to wait for your Ginny to come home."

Becca had started crying and Joe pulled her back into his arms. "It's all right, honey. Your brother's working hard to find her and so are the police. We just have to believe they'll bring her home."

Rebecca dragged in a shaky breath and fought to pull herself together. She wiped tears from her cheeks. "Thank you, Mrs. Slotski. That's terribly kind of you."

"I think it's time you called me Frances," the woman said.

Rebecca managed to smile. "All right…Frances."

And so the police, working with a lieutenant named Gleason, had set up headquarters in the kitchen of the Slotski home, a cozy atmosphere with old-fashioned ruffled curtains at the windows and a round maple table and chairs in the breakfast nook.

Joe was resting in one of them as Becca had insisted, wishing he was out on the streets, banging on doors, rousting passersby, doing something. Anything that might bring little Ginny home. Instead, he sat there waiting for Alex to call, waiting for the police to find some clue to where Bagley had disappeared.

Praying as he had never prayed before.

Standing against the wall in Sol's office, Rina looked out through the glass windows to see Jake and Sage walking in. It was only 5:00 a.m.

"What can we do to help?" Jake asked as he strode into the room, his powerful presence making the office seem smaller.

"Sol and I are brainstorming," Alex said, "trying to come up with something that'll tell us where the bastard's hiding. He has to have a place. He hasn't had that much time to plan. I'm thinking it's somewhere he's taken girls before. I never believed Carrie Wiseman was his first victim."

The men began tossing ideas around, going through the file, picking out names of people Bagley had known throughout his life, people he worked with at school, people who were once his friends.

Sage walked over to where Rina stood against the wall, reached out and took hold of her hand, gave it a squeeze.

"How's he holding up?" Sage asked, tipping her head toward Alex.

"He's worried sick, but he won't let it stop him from doing his job. How did you know where to find us?"

"Annie called. She must have seen something on the news."

"What was she doing up in the middle of the night?"

"Jake says she has a police scanner in her bedroom. She has fantasies of being a detective."

Rina couldn't help a smile. "She's pretty amazing."

"You don't know the half of it."

Rina's smile slid away. "They've got to find her. Alex loves that little girl. He loves his sister. Losing her child will destroy Rebecca."

"I know." Sage tugged on her hand, pulling her toward the door. "Let's get some coffee. You can fill me in on what the police are doing."

"I could use a cup. We'll make a fresh pot for the guys."

Sage nodded and they started for the employee lounge in the back of the office.

At 6:00 a.m., Alex spotted Ben walking toward Sol's office, where he and Jake hovered over the computer as the kid pounded on the keyboard. In jeans and a black T-shirt, dark hair rumpled, Ben looked as if he'd rolled out of bed and hadn't taken time to shower.

"Annie?" Alex guessed with a raised eyebrow as Ben walked in.

He nodded. "She called me right after she talked to Jake. I've been doing some legwork. I know some people. I told them any info that would help us locate Bagley would be worth big money. They're lowlifes but none of them are high on child molesters. I'm hoping they'll come up with something we can use."

"Thanks, buddy. We need all the help we can get."

"Anything look promising?" Ben asked.

"Not so far." The words made Alex's stomach burn.

"Actually, maybe I've found something that does." Sol pointed to the screen. "Take a look at that."

Alex leaned closer. "You found intel on the brother?" They'd been working that angle off and on since they'd gotten to the office.

"Bagley has a brother?" Ben asked.

"Half brother," Jake corrected.

"I went back to the hospital records," Sol said, "took another look at what happened to the baby after he was born. At first, I wasn't able to get into the adoption records. Then I got an idea. I went around a back way and finally got in. The kid was adopted by a couple named Ella and Thomas Bartholomew. His adopted name is Jason Bartholomew." Sol started typing away, pulling up one screen and then the next.

Another screen popped up and Sol shot a fist into the air. "All right! Now that's what I'm talkin' about!"

Alex's pulse raced. "What is it?"

"Jason Bartholomew, born at First General Hospital in Dallas in 1963. Still lives there. His adoptive parents passed away ten years ago, but here's the interesting part. They left him a piece of property—out at Lake Houston."

Alex's fatigue fell away beneath a shot of adrenaline. "That's only forty miles from here."

"Let's see what it looks like." Sol's fingers flew over the keyboard. He plugged the address of the lake property into Google Maps, clicked up the street view. "Looks like there's a house there." He went to the satellite photos. "Huge yard, lots of open space around it."

"Maybe Bagley knows Bartholomew," Alex said. "Maybe his brother lets him use the house. Hell, maybe he's even involved."

"What's the address?" Jake asked.

Sol rattled off a number on Sand Springs Trail. "It's on the east side of the lake. Looks like the best way to get there is out I-90."

"I'll call the cops." Alex took out his cell and started dialing 911. When the dispatcher came on the line, he gave the woman his name and asked for Lieutenant Gleason, who was still working the crime scene, and she patched him right through.

"We've tracked down Bagley's half brother," Alex told him. "Jason Bartholomew owns a house at Lake Houston." Alex gave him the address of the property. "There's a chance he may have taken Ginny there."

"We're rolling on it. I'll keep you posted."

"Time to go," Jake said as Alex ended the call, and all three men headed out of Sol's office.

"We've got a lead," Alex called out to Sabrina. "We've got to go." He stopped. "Dammit, I can't leave you here by yourself. It's still not safe. And I sure as hell can't take you with me."

Jake walked out of the back just then, carrying his

M4 sniper rifle. "You can't go, either," he said to Sage. "We have no idea what might be coming down."

Ben sighed. "As much as I'd like to take that bastard down myself, looks like I'm the one who's going to have to stay."

Alex slapped him on the back. "Thanks, Ice Man." He turned to Sabrina. "I'll let you know if we find Ginny."

Before the women's angry looks could turn into actual protests, the men were out the door, the Jeep fired up and pulling out of the parking lot.

"I wish we had time to check the place out before the cops get there," Jake said darkly.

"So do I. If there's gunfire, Ginny could get hurt. Thing is, we can't take the risk. If that's where Bagley was headed, he's got her there by now. The sheriff'll have units close by and we need them there ASAP."

Alex figured Gleason would withhold the information from Rebecca until they were certain. False hope was sometimes worse than not knowing anything at all.

As the Jeep roared along the road, Alex popped the clip on his .45 and checked the load, shoved the clip back in. He prayed little Ginny would be there when they got there, prayed she was alive and unharmed, and that he would soon be bringing her home.

Thirty-Two

The house on Sand Spring Trail, a two-story beige stucco with dark brown trim and thick-trunked trees branching over the front yard, was crawling with sheriff's cruisers, white-and-blue patrol cars and a dozen other official vehicles. Jake pulled off to the side, double-parking next to an empty patrol car, jumped out with Alex and headed for the officer in charge.

SWAT wasn't yet there. But the house was completely surrounded by uniformed police and sheriff's officers. Clearly, they'd confirmed Edward Bagley was inside.

Alex reined in the fury burning through him. He wanted to rip the bastard apart limb by limb, wanted to see him lying dead in a pool of blood where he couldn't hurt a child ever again.

Alex took a calming breath. Ginny needed him. He had to keep a cool head.

Recognizing Detective Pete Devlin, the officer he had worked with on the Carrie Wiseman case, Alex strode toward him. Devlin was approaching fifty, big, tough and capable. He'd been an outspoken opponent of the judge's decision to throw out the DNA that had incriminated Edward Bagley.

Devlin spotted Alex, met him halfway. "Good call," he said. "Bagley's inside. Unfortunately, he's using the little girl as a hostage. Lieutenant Gleason's en route. Negotiator's setting up. SWAT's on the way."

Alex tipped his head toward Jake. "You know Cantrell?"

"By reputation." Devlin extended a hand. "Nice to meet you, Cantrell."

"Same here."

"Jake's former Special Forces," Alex said. "Marine sniper. He's the best marksman I've ever seen."

"My rifle's in the Jeep," Jake said. "I'd like your permission to set up somewhere, cover the house at least until SWAT arrives."

"Officially, I can't do that," Devlin said. "Unofficially, you're licensed to carry, right?"

"That's right."

"He's trained for this," Alex said. "He won't take the shot unless it's safe and there's no other choice."

Devlin was wearing a mic and earbuds. He let his people know that Jake Cantrell was in the area, that he was a sniper and he would be positioning himself to cover the house. As Jake headed back to his Jeep, another officer approached.

"Bagley's on the line with the hostage negotiator," the young officer said.

"That'd be Sergeant Norris," Devlin told Alex as they walked toward the white communications van parked to the right of the house. A stocky guy with a crew cut sat at a card table next to the truck, a mobile phone in his hand.

"We can work this out, Edward. You said the girl was

okay. You said you didn't hurt her. Let her come out of the house. Give yourself up and we'll find a peaceful way to resolve this."

The negotiator listened to Bagley's response and shook his head, telling them it was a no-go. "All right, tell us what we can do for you. What is it you want? Here's the deal. We get you whatever you need and you let the girl go. That's the way it works."

Bagley said something.

"Just a minute." The negotiator put the phone on hold. "He's talking about some guy named Justice. Any idea who that is?"

Alex's jaw hardened. "That would be me," he said, the angry heat returning to the back of his neck.

"Sergeant, this is Alex Justice," Devlin said. "Alex is the guy who brought in the DNA that led us to Bagley in the first place."

"Nice work. Too bad it didn't stick."

"You got that right," Alex said. "What's the bastard want?"

The negotiator went back on the line and the conversation resumed. "I'm afraid we can't allow that. You need to come out, Edward. All you have to do is cooperate and no one gets hurt."

Norris listened again, put the phone back on hold and turned to Alex. "He wants to talk to you. Can you handle it?"

"Oh, yeah, I can handle it."

"Ginny's Alex's niece," Devlin explained as Alex took the phone and pressed it against his ear. Norris lifted a second receiver to listen in on the conversation.

"Hello, Edward," Alex said as if he was a friend instead of someone he'd like to see dead. "You know, my sister's a little upset with you. Setting her house on fire and hitting her boyfriend in the head with a baseball bat? I have to give you credit, that was a pretty smart move. Though it doesn't look like it's going to work out exactly the way you planned."

"You don't think so?" Bagley's lilting voice floated over the line. "How about this? You want Ginny, you can have her. All you have to do is come inside and get her."

Alex's fingers tightened around the receiver. "Count on it."

The phone line went dead.

They had almost reached the address on Sand Spring Trail. Ben was driving his big black Denali, his jaw set in a hard, angry line, Sage riding next to him, Rina buckled into the backseat.

Ben wasn't happy with either one of them.

Twenty minutes after Alex and Jake had left, Annie had called the office. The media had uncovered the story of Edward Bagley and Ginny Wyatt, the five-year-old he'd abducted. The broadcast said Bagley was involved in a hostage situation out at Lake Houston.

Rina, Sage, Sol and Ben had all scrambled into the conference room and turned on the flat-screen TV, tuned in the news and seen the chaos going on out at the lake. There was no sign of Alex or Jake, who hadn't had time to get there, but Rina was no longer willing to sit and wait.

Instead, she and Sage had staged a coup, demanding Ben take them out there.

"I'm going, Ben," Rina said as the argument progressed. "Aside from tying me up, there's no way you can stop me."

"Don't tempt me," he'd said darkly.

"Please, Ben," Sage pressed. "We'll go by ourselves if we have to but we'd be a lot safer if we went with you."

Ben shook his head. "No fucking way. Alex will kill me if Jake doesn't get to me first. You need to stay here where it's safe."

"What if something happens to that little girl?" Rina said. "Alex will be devastated. I have to be there in case he needs me."

"We'll stay out of the way," Sage promised. "Please, Ben?"

He blew out a frustrated breath, raked a hand through his thick black hair. "Get in the goddamn car and once we get there, you do exactly what I tell you—got it?"

"We will," Rina said meekly, but she couldn't suppress a grin that they had won.

"You're the best, Ben," Sage said, gliding past him toward the door.

Ben cast Sol a disgruntled look, grumbled something about pain-in-the-ass women and followed them outside.

They had run into traffic crossing town, which slowed them down a little, but Ben seemed to know all the shortcuts and soon they were back on the freeway.

He turned the SUV onto Crosby Huffman Road, heading north, then turned and began winding through the neighborhoods that bordered the lake. Overhead, the *whop, whop, whop* of a chopper signaled they were near their destination.

Rina's heart kicked up another notch.

Sergeant Norris cursed. "I don't like this. We need to wait for SWAT, let them get into position to cover you."

"I want Ginny out of there," Alex said. "Once she's

safe, you can deal with Bagley, figure out a way to bring me out, too." Or he'd take the bastard down himself.

"Bagley's got a real hard-on for you, Justice. There's no way to know what he's got planned."

Alex pulled his shirt back on over the borrowed flak vest he was wearing. His .45 rode in the waistband of his jeans at the small of his back. He had an ankle gun strapped to his leg and a knife in his low-topped boot.

He'd have to give at least some of the weapons up. Bagley wasn't a fool. But he didn't know how the scenario might play out and he wanted to go in prepared.

"You ready?" Devlin asked.

"I've been ready for this since the day I found out Edward Bagley murdered that little girl."

The negotiator picked up the bullhorn. "He's coming in."

Beneath the roar and spotlight of a media helicopter overhead, Alex crossed the lawn in front of the house. He knew Jake was out there, looking for a clear shot. If the negotiations went south and either Alex or Ginny was in danger, he knew his friend wouldn't hesitate to pull the trigger.

Alex took comfort in that. And the fact that one way or another, Bagley was going down.

In the meantime, he had to get Ginny out and safe.

As he reached the steps leading up to the porch, Bagley opened the door and walked out with Ginny propped against his hip, an arm around her waist. His other hand held a cocked revolver pressed against the side of her head.

"Uncle Alex…" Ginny was as pale as cotton, her blue eyes huge. He could see tears on her cheeks and when he looked at Edward Bagley, a blind, nearly uncontrollable rage seared through him. If the prick had touched her…

He forced himself under control.

Bagley smiled, enjoying himself. "I know you're armed. Get rid of the gun."

He took it out from behind his back, set it on the porch at Bagley's feet. "I'm here the way you wanted. Now let her go."

Bagley kicked the gun away and laughed. It wasn't the soft, oddly gentle laughter Alex remembered, but a grating lunatic laugh that said Bagley had slipped over the edge.

"I'm sorry if that's what you thought, but it isn't going to happen. We have a destiny, you and I. That destiny includes your little Ginny."

Alex's pulse took a leap. He fought for control. "Let her go and we'll go inside, talk things out. You can do whatever you want with me."

Bagley turned his head and kissed Ginny's soft, pale cheek. Fresh tears sprang into her eyes and Alex felt a surge of fury so thick it nearly blinded him.

His jaw hardened. "Let her go, Bagley. Do it or I swear to God I'll take you apart piece by piece."

Bagley just smiled. "Yes, I think we should all go inside where we can talk. You first, Alex."

He clenched his jaw. He was weighing his options, trying to decide his next move, when Bagley made a mistake. Enjoying his moment of power, he swung the weapon away from Ginny and pointed it at Alex. A split second. That's all he had.

Alex sprang forward, knocking Bagley off his feet and sweeping Ginny out of his grasp. Two shots rang out almost simultaneously. Alex felt the impact of the bullet like a punch in the chest, and Bagley dropped like a stone.

Alex hit the ground hard, turning at the last moment to keep his weight off Ginny, jarring the gunshot wound in his side. He clamped his jaw against a jolt of pain, looked over to see Bagley lying a few feet away, blood spurting from a hole in the middle of his forehead.

"Uncle Alex!" Ginny cried, clinging to his neck, sobbing against him as a swarm of police officers rushed up on the porch.

"I'm all right, honey. We're both okay." He kept her head turned away from Bagley and kissed her cheek, damned grateful for the vest, even if the whack from the bullet hurt like hell and his side was burning. "Everything's gonna be fine."

Devlin strode toward him, leaned down and lifted Ginny out of his arms, turned and handed her to Becca and Joe, who appeared out of nowhere.

"You okay?" the detective asked Alex, giving him a hand as he climbed to his feet. He could hear his sister crying, hugging her precious daughter, and relief hit him hard.

"I'm okay." Alex rubbed the center of his chest as they walked off the porch. "Glad I was wearing the vest." The adrenal rush began to fade and he started shaking, his fear for Ginny dissipating, leaving him light-headed.

He spotted Jake, standing at the side of the yard, his rifle beside him, and gave him a grateful wave.

Jake waved back.

"You were right about Cantrell," Devlin said. "Guy's one helluva shot."

"Lucky for Ginny and me."

"I'm glad you're both okay." Devlin walked away as

Joe strode toward him, grabbed his shoulder and pulled him into a fierce man-hug.

"Thanks, Peaceman. You okay?"

"I'm all right." Alex unbuttoned his shirt, took off the vest and handed it to a passing patrolman, surveyed the growing bruise in the middle of his chest, then pulled the shirt back on. "Good thing the little prick wasn't carrying a .45."

Joe glanced toward the porch where the police were taping off the crime scene. His worried gaze swung back to Alex. "You don't think he hurt her?"

"I'm praying he didn't. I figure that's what he intended until the cops showed up. That forced him to change his plans. I think he was aiming to do something pretty gruesome once he got me in there to watch."

Still holding Ginny, Becca walked toward him, tears in her eyes. She opened her arms and drew Alex into a hug. "Thank you, big brother. Oh, Alex, thank you so much."

He worked to keep the emotion out of his voice. "I'm just glad she's safe." He hung on to the two of them a moment, then stepped back to let Joe take his sister and Ginny over to the ambulance to have Ginny checked out.

Feeling suddenly drained, Alex sank down in the grass, exhausted clear to his bones. He heard Sabrina's voice as if it came from a long way away, and then she was there, falling to her knees on the grass beside him, gathering him into her arms.

"Alex…" She just held on to him and he found himself holding on to her, his heart beating softly, a strange ache settling in his chest.

"Oh, Alex. When I saw you up there with Ginny and Bagley, I just…oh, God, I was terrified. For a moment when the gun went off, I thought he'd killed you." She rested her head on his shoulder and he could feel her trembling.

"I'm okay, baby. Jake did his job and both of us are safe. I'm a little bruised, but I'm fine."

He saw Sage had found Jake, whose arms were tightly around her. Everyone was okay.

Everyone but Edward Bagley. By now he was burning in hell.

Alex blew out a tired breath and rolled to his feet, took Sabrina's hand and brought her up with him. He thought of how she had disobeyed him again by coming to the lake, and tried to summon a little anger.

"I thought I told you to stay at the office."

She went up on her toes and pressed a gentle kiss on his mouth. Yeah, he was mad, all right. Hell, he was damned glad she was there.

"I had to come," she said. "I was afraid you might need me. Please don't be mad at Ben."

He lifted an eyebrow. "Are you kidding? I can't expect Ben to control you when I can't manage to do it myself." And then he kissed her. If he didn't he thought he might die for real.

"I love you," she said, pressing soft little butterfly kisses at the corners of his mouth. "I love you so much."

His throat tightened. He wanted to say those words back to her. She meant so damned much to him. But the words seemed to stick in his throat. The promise those words held was more than he could offer. The promise of a loving husband, a home and family, the kind of future he couldn't guarantee.

Instead he just held her and felt grateful that she was there. Grateful that a woman as fine as Sabrina Eckhart could find it in her heart to love him.

Thirty-Three

Two things happened that next week. At his home in a suburb of Dallas, the police located Jason Bartholomew, Bagley's half brother. Bartholomew told them he knew he had a younger brother. The two of them had met once about five years ago. Bagley was a teacher, single and well-respected, but Bartholomew hadn't felt any sort of connection, and since then, there had been no communication.

Bartholomew had no idea Bagley was using the house he owned at Lake Houston, a place he hadn't visited in years. Once a month, a gardener stopped by to take care of the yard, but aside from that the house had been closed up. The police were satisfied the brother was telling the truth.

Jason Bartholomew hadn't been out to the lake, but Edward Bagley had. How the man had found out about the property was a mystery. But clearly little Ginny wasn't the first child he had taken there. The police found the remains of two other young girls, neither of whom had yet been identified.

Alex thought of the man who had destroyed the lives of so many people. And how lucky it was that Ginny was home, untouched, the doctors said, by Bagley and his evil.

The second thing that happened was that Henry Mullins awakened from his coma.

Detective Colin Murphy, the officer in charge of Sabrina's case, had called on Alex's cell phone. He'd been working out in his gym, then gone upstairs to shower and put on fresh clothes.

"Henry Mullins is awake and singing like a bird," Murphy had said. "Now that he's figured out his goose is cooked, he can't talk fast enough." As Murphy filled in the details, including the fact neither of the other cousins was involved, Alex felt a sweep of relief. It was over.

"Thanks for calling," he said. "I'll let Sabrina know."

There'd be loose ends to tie up, statements to make, but basically the case was closed. Robert Eckhart had been arrested in connection with the attempts on Sabrina's life. She was safe at last.

Feeling lighter than he had in days, Alex headed back downstairs.

"Hey, baby, where are you? I've got great news!"

He found her seated behind the computer in his study, tapping away on the keyboard, more research, he was sure, on the mining project she was more than eager to begin.

"Sorry, I didn't hear you calling." She came up out of her chair. "You're smiling. What's going on?"

Alex scooped her into his arms, swung her around. "It's over, love. Henry Mullins came out of his coma this morning. As soon as he realized the game was up, he started talking. Cut a deal with the D.A.'s office. Henry says he and your cousin Bob came up with the scheme to kill your uncle so that Bob and his brother and sister could inherit the mine. Henry was in for a fat cut of Bob's portion of the deal. They planned to buy the other two out of their shares, figured they'd sell cheap. Henry's willing to testify against him."

"I can't believe it."

"Believe it."

"So George and Silla weren't involved?"

"Not according to Henry."

She sank back down in the chair. "Thank God for that."

"The police found a laptop at Bob's house. There were a dozen different email exchanges between him and Henry. They also found a disposable phone with Henry's number on it. Good ol' Bob seemed to forget it was called *disposable* because it was meant to be thrown away."

Sabrina came back up from her chair and he could almost see her mind working.

"How did Bob know about the molybdenum?"

"According to Henry, when Walter came to Houston last October to see his son, he was so convinced there was silver on the property that Bob followed him back to the mine."

"That's what Walter always believed. At least Bob was right about the land being valuable." Sabrina went into his arms and for a moment, he just held her.

"It's over, baby." He kissed the top of her head, thought how good she always made him feel.

Sabrina hugged him one last time, took a shaky breath and eased away. When she looked up at him, there was something in her features. Despair, resignation, whatever it was, it suddenly made him wary.

"So it's finally happened," she said. "It's all finally over. Bagley. The threats against my life. Even you and me."

Unease slid through him. "What are you talking about?"

"I came to you for help. You did everything in your power to protect me. You were wonderful, Alex. You risked your life for me. But I don't need your protection anymore. I need your love and that's something you just aren't able to give me."

He swallowed. His chest felt as if a band was tightening around it. "I don't see why we can't go on the way we are now. We're good together. Surely you can see that."

She reached up and cupped his cheek. "I wish I could do it. I wish I could keep pretending it doesn't matter. But it does. I'll never be able to repay you, Alex, for everything you've done. But it's over and it's time for me to leave."

"Just like that?"

"We both knew it wouldn't last forever."

The band was constricting, making it hard to breathe. "We can still see each other, right? We can still be friends?"

A sad smile touched her lips. "I'm not like your other women, Alex. I can't be happy with a part-time lover." She went up on her toes and pressed a kiss on his lips. For an instant, he couldn't speak.

"Please don't call me," she said. "Don't stop by to see me. Just let me go."

Alex just stood there as she walked out of the study and down the hall, heading upstairs to pack her things.

He wanted to go after her, talk to her, convince her to change her mind.

It wouldn't be fair and he knew it. He couldn't make promises he wasn't sure he could keep. He didn't know himself well enough to know his own feelings.

He was standing in the entry when she came back down the stairs with her overnight bag. "I'll ask Sage to come by and get the rest of my things." She set the holstered pistol Jake had loaned her on the entry table. "Thank him for me."

Alex shook his head. "You can't just leave, not like this. You don't even have a car."

She smiled sadly. "I called a taxi. It'll be here any minute."

"That's crazy. Last night you were sleeping in my bed and now you're just going to disappear?"

A horn honked outside the door.

"The cab's here. I have to go."

He felt on the edge of panic. He wanted to haul her back inside and slam the door. He wanted to carry her upstairs and chain her to his bed.

"Goodbye, Alex. I'll never forget you."

He didn't know what to say. Where was that smooth tongue he'd used to charm women all over the world? Where were the glib words when he needed them?

The door closed in his face and Alex just stood there. What in the hell had just happened? All he knew was that he felt like he was drowning and didn't know how to swim.

With a long, shuddering breath, he headed for the bar. Alex poured himself a scotch with a hand that wasn't quite steady. He couldn't remember ever needing a drink so badly.

* * *

As though she were sleepwalking, Rina rolled her carry-on into her apartment. The place smelled musty and damp, and as she rolled the bag toward her bedroom, she noticed some of the plants were drooping, badly in need of water. Obviously, Mrs. Renhurst hadn't been in to check on them in a while.

She left the bag in the hall, filled a pitcher with water and began making the rounds, taking extra care with the philodendron and the ficus, giving herself something to do, trying to keep her mind off Alex.

Dear God, she hadn't expected it to come to an end so quickly. She'd thought things would taper off, that she'd have time to adjust to being without him.

But once she'd gotten started, said the words she couldn't call back, once she'd said that she was leaving, she had realized she was doing exactly the right thing. Better to amputate, cut him cleanly out of her heart, deal with the pain all at once, than to be with him and die inside by inches.

She finished with the plants and rolled her suitcase into the bedroom to unpack. She needed to keep busy. Work always helped her stay focused. She'd call Arturo tomorrow, finally get that meeting set up in Presidio. Begin to deal with the problems of developing the Sabrina Belle.

She wouldn't think about Alex. She would stay so busy that in time she would forget him. She said it over and over again, repeated it like a mantra. *You'll forget him. It's just a matter of time.*

Then she looked around her empty apartment, the place she had decorated herself, been so proud of and had always loved. It seemed desolate now, a place to hang her clothes, nothing more.

Rina sank down on the edge of the bed, her mind going back to Alex for the hundredth time. Emotion clogged her chest. She felt as if her heart were crumbling inside her. Rina buried her face in the pillow and started to weep.

Thirty-Four

Heat waves rolled up off the pavement. July in Houston felt like a tropical jungle, the thick wet air making it difficult to breathe. *Damned summer weather,* Alex thought, his mood grim as it had been all week. Made him wonder why he didn't live in Connecticut.

He scoffed. Could be the months of ice and snow, the frozen roads and bad memories. His childhood was a part of his life he'd been glad to escape. And Houston wasn't so bad. He loved the sunshine, the ocean being not too far away. And the people here were great.

Didn't make his mood any better.

He shoved through the office door, ringing the bell. He hadn't been there in days, not since Sabrina had made her sudden exit from his life. This morning he'd gotten a business call at home. John Mitchum, a friend who owned a research laboratory in the Medical District, was having security problems. John needed to know who was leaking information to his competitors. Desperate to get out of the house and keep himself busy, Alex had taken the job.

Anything to keep from thinking of Sabrina and the hole she had left in his heart.

He sat down at his desk and turned on the computer, began to search through his email. Maybe she had sent him a message. Maybe she had changed her mind and wanted to see him.

But there was no message there. Then again, he knew her well enough to know once she had made that kind of decision there was no way she would change her mind.

Disappointment slid through him, making him feel raw inside. Forcing his mind back to business, he started searching for information on Mitchum Laboratories. He'd get more specific intel from John at their meeting tomorrow morning. As the laboratory website popped up, Alex caught movement in the corner of his eye and recognized Jake's tall, powerful frame striding toward him.

Alex leaned back in his chair, dreading the conversation he'd been avoiding for days.

"Mind if I sit a minute?"

"Help yourself."

Jake sat down, so big the chair creaked beneath his weight. "Sage says it's over between you and Rina."

A weight seemed to settle on his chest. "It was her idea to end it. I liked things the way they were."

"Her emotions got involved. That happens. How are you feeling? You okay with it?"

Alex looked at his friend. "If you want the truth, I miss her like hell. She was the best thing that's ever happened to me, but it just wouldn't work."

"Why not?"

"Because I'm not ready for the kind of life she wants."

"What kind is that?"

"Marriage. Kids. Settling down."

"She say that's what she wants?"

"That's what all women want."

"Not Sage. At least not right away. Neither of us is ready for that. We want those things eventually. When both of us are ready."

If it were only that easy. It wasn't. No matter what Jake said. "You know the way I am. The way I always have been."

"You mean the women? I've been there. People change. You aren't the same man you were and neither am I. I think deep down you know that."

"Look, I know you're trying to help, but this is personal, okay?"

"So you aren't in love with her?"

His stomach knotted. He hadn't expected his friend to come right out and ask. To make him admit to something that didn't have a damned thing to do with anything.

"That's a yes or no question," Jake pressed when he didn't answer. "Either you are or you aren't in love with Sabrina."

"And it's your business because?"

"Because I'm your friend."

Alex came up out of his chair. "All right. Fuck it. I'm in love with her, okay? Probably been in love with her since she called me an arrogant jet jockey and went on to tell me all the reasons she wasn't interested in a guy like me. Satisfied?"

Jake just shook his head. "I don't get it. If you love her, why don't you just go get her?"

"Because for me it doesn't work that way. I need to know where I'm going. I need to have my future worked out. Until that happens, I can't ask a woman to marry me, and especially not Sabrina. I care about her too much." Translation—*I love her too much.*

Jake stood up, too. "I guess we all approach life differently. The thing is, even when we think we've got everything figured out, it doesn't happen that way. Life is a series of choices. You never get to figure them all out ahead of time."

Alex said nothing.

"You need anything, you just let me know."

Alex nodded. "Thanks." He had good friends, people who cared about him. He wished things were different. Wished he were different.

As Jake walked away, he sat back down at his desk.

But when he looked into the computer screen, all he saw was Sabrina's pretty face smiling up at him, telling him how much she loved him.

At Sage's familiar knock, Rina opened the door to invite her inside. The curtains were still drawn, though it was after ten in the morning. She'd been up for a couple of hours, but she hadn't pulled them open yet. The plants were beginning to droop again.

"So...how's it going?" Sage asked, her gaze going around the dimly lit apartment.

"All right, I guess. I'd hoped I'd be feeling better by now."

Sage walked over and opened the curtains. The bright light coming so unexpectedly hurt Rina's eyes.

Sage walked back to where she stood still dressed in the old cotton robe she'd put on that morning. "If you don't mind my saying, kiddo, you look like hell." Sage reached up and lifted a lock of limp, faded red hair, let it fall back into place. She picked up one of Rina's hands and studied the nails, saw that the polish was worn off and she had bitten a couple of them down to the quick.

"That's it—we're getting out of here. I'm taking you to the spa and don't even think about arguing." It was Saturday and Sage wasn't working. Usually she spent the day with Jake.

"I—I can't go right now. I'm expecting a call from Arturo. We're setting up that meeting in Presidio."

"Too bad. Arturo will have to wait. Now go put on a pair of jeans and a T-shirt and let's go."

She wanted to refuse. She needed to get the mining operation going. She needed to accomplish *something* instead of sitting around her apartment pining for Alex. She'd told herself that in time she'd get over him. So far that hadn't even begun to happen. She thought of him every hour, every minute. She hadn't even had the energy to wash her hair or polish her nails.

Or go to the bank and apply for the loan Arturo had assured her she'd be able to get against the property, a piece of land valued in the millions of dollars.

Sage tugged on her hand. "Come on, Rina. You need this and you know it."

She needed a complete makeover for sure—one that included getting Alex out of her head. "You're right, Obi-Wan. I'll follow wherever you lead. Let me put on some clothes."

They left the Buick she had rented in the parking lot and climbed into Sage's silver Mercedes. She felt better the moment she closed the door. There was something about riding in a sexy automobile that lifted a girl's spirits.

They headed for the Trellis, the luxury spa at the Houstonian Hotel just off the 610 Freeway, and immersed themselves in a day of pleasure. God, it felt good to be thinking of something besides her broken heart.

She was still riding high at the end of the day when Sage brought her home after a facial and massage, her hair freshly colored a lush shade of auburn, her nails and toes polished a saucy red—just to boost her spirits.

They'd had a late lunch at the spa restaurant and enjoyed a glass of Pouilly-Fuissé, Rina's favorite French wine.

"You gonna be okay?" Sage asked when the afternoon came to a close and she pulled the Mercedes into the parking lot in front of Rina's apartment.

"Today was great." Rina smiled. "You were right, I really needed a day away from it all. I'll be fine now."

Sage leaned over and hugged her. "Call me if you need me, okay?"

"I will." She flourished a last wide smile, slipped out of the car and went into her apartment. In the gilded mirror in the entry, she looked like her old self again, maybe even better. It wasn't until she walked into the empty bedroom and glanced at the bed that her throat closed up and tears hit her again.

Dammit, she wasn't going to cry. If Alex didn't want her, that was his loss. She wasn't going to mourn for him any longer. First thing Monday morning, she was going to call Arturo and set up that meeting. If he still showed an interest in her as a woman, she was going to go out with him.

Her lips trembled. And she wasn't going to think of Alex Justice ever again.

Monday morning, Alex walked into the office. Over the weekend, he had tried to convince himself to call one of his lady friends—any one of the forgettable women he had dated over the years. One of them was bound to be up for a good time in bed. The notion made his stomach burn.

The bell rang as he pushed through the office door. Seated behind the reception desk, Annie's head came up.

"Well now, aren't we just the lucky ones?" she said. "Glad you found time to make it into work."

"Leave me alone, Annie. I'm not in the mood for your crap today." He'd been dreading the moment he'd have to face Annie Mayberry. He'd dodged her half a dozen times, but it looked like the moment had finally arrived.

She was frowning, he noticed, as she rose from behind her desk and walked toward him, followed him back to his desk.

"You don't look so good. I figured a guy who just skated the marriage trap would be grinning ear to ear."

"I told you to leave me alone."

She reached out and caught his chin, turned his face one way and then another. "You've lost weight and your tan is fading."

He had to look away.

"Lord help me, Jesus! So that's the way it is. You're in love with her. But hey! The big, bad ladies' man, Alex Justice, is afraid to tell a sweet little thing like Rina he loves her."

"I'm not afraid. It just wouldn't work."

"Why not? Can't give up all those women you got chasing after you?"

He shook his head, released a slow breath. "I don't even remember their names."

"What then?"

He didn't know why he was telling her this. But then

she was Annie and it just seemed okay. "I don't know what I want to do with my life, Annie. I'm not even sure I want to stay in Houston. How can I expect a woman to settle for a life that's still so uncertain?"

Annie's gruff voice softened. "Rina isn't just any woman, Alex. If she married you, she wouldn't expect you to stop living your life. She'd want you to be happy. If that meant moving somewhere else, I think she'd be just fine with it. She's always had an adventurous nature."

He swallowed past the tightness in his throat. "What about kids, Annie? What about settling down? I'm still finding my way."

"Kids can wait. They got a way of comin' when the time is right. In the meantime, there's no reason the two of you can't explore your options. You got plenty of money. It's not like you couldn't take care of her."

"I don't even know what I want out of life."

Annie eyed him with speculation. "Looking at you now, I got a feeling there's one thing you know you want."

He stared into those canny old eyes and his heart began to thud in a soft, painful rhythm. He thought of Sabrina and how much he loved her, thought of how dreary his life had been since the day she'd walked away. Suddenly everything seemed to fall into place.

"I want her," he said. "I want Sabrina."

Annie grinned. "Now you're getting it. Loving the right person makes your life easier, honey, not harder. Sharing those tough decisions, finding answers. You ask her. You tell her those things that worry you and see what she says. I think she'll go along with whatever

you want. I think that woman would follow you to the
ends of the earth."

The weight on his chest seemed to lift away. "I'm in
love with her. I need her. I want her with me. God, I've
been an idiot, haven't I?"

Annie shrugged. "You're a man. Sometimes, that's
just the way men are."

Alex laughed for the first time in days. Cupping Annie's wrinkled face between his hands, he gave her a
smacking kiss on the lips. "You're the best, sweetheart."

And then he was heading for the door. It all seemed
so simple now. So clear. Sabrina was part of what he'd
been searching for. The love she offered was the very
thing that had eluded him.

Now all he had to do was convince Sabrina to marry
him. His steps slowed as he reached his BMW. There
was a time that would have been easy.

Alex was pretty sure it wasn't going to be easy this
time.

Dressed in a yellow business suit and a pair of high
heels, Rina headed for the door. She was meeting Arturo
Hernandez for lunch at a small café near the Galleria.
He had flown into town to finalize plans for her meeting with the company bigwigs in Presidio.

She was still a little early, fidgeting and checking her
makeup, watching the hands on the clock crawl past.
When the doorbell chimed, she wondered who it could
be, walked over and looked through the peephole.

Alex. Her chin went up. She had told him not to come.
When she opened the door and saw him on the threshold
it was all she could do not to slam the door in his face.

"I asked you to leave me alone."

Instead, he walked in without permission and closed the door behind him. "I need to talk to you."

God, he looked so good. A little thinner, maybe, not quite as perfect as he usually did. Still. "I don't want to talk, and besides I don't have time. I have a meeting I have to go to."

He ignored her, of course, and started toward her. Rina held up a hand. "Stay right where you are."

"Why?"

Because with his blond good looks and Alex Justice charm, he was just as appealing to her as he was the first time she had seen him. And as much as she wished it weren't so, she was still in love with him.

"I have a lunch date, Alex. What do you want?"

"A lunch date? Tell me it isn't with that slick-talking Hernandez."

"You're one to be casting stones. And anyway, it's none of your business. Tell me why you're here or leave."

"It's kind of involved. Why don't we go into the living room and sit down?"

"I'm not going anywhere with you, Alex."

Something shifted in his features. "Annie said you would."

"Annie? What's Annie got to do with this?"

His eyes darkened. She had only seen that look on his face a couple of times and never known exactly what it meant.

"Annie said it wouldn't matter to you if my future was still unsettled. She said if I wanted to do something different, change jobs, maybe even leave Houston, you'd be okay with it. She said you liked adventure."

"I like adventure...I mean sometimes I like adventure. Not that time out in the desert. That was more like survival than— Wait a minute. What are you getting at, Alex?"

"Annie said you'd take me just the way I am. She said if I asked, you'd follow me to the ends of the earth."

The floor seemed to be tilting. Maybe sitting down wasn't such a bad idea. "I don't… I'm not sure what…"

"Would you? If I told you I was in love with you, would you go with me no matter where life might lead us?"

Her throat closed up. If Alex loved her… Oh, God, she couldn't stand this. She was going to cry and she refused to let him see. "Please leave, Alex. Please, I can't take any more. I don't know what you want from me."

Instead he moved toward her, drew her into his arms, held her as if she were the most precious thing in the world.

"I want you to marry me. That's what I want more than anything in the world. I'm telling you I love you and I want you to be my wife. I'm asking, begging you to marry me."

Her knees buckled. If Alex hadn't been holding her up, she would have slid bonelessly to the floor. "Alex… Oh, God, Alex."

"Will you? God, please don't say no."

Her heart was beating, throbbing so hard it hurt. He was asking her to marry him. She wanted to say yes more than she wanted the next breath of air. Tears sprang into her eyes. "I love you, but… Oh, Alex, are you sure about this?"

He kissed her mouth, her nose, her eyes. "I was an idiot to let you leave. I screwed things up. I couldn't figure things out, but now I have. I love you. Marry me."

The wetness in her eyes rolled down her cheeks. She

smiled at him through her tears. "Of course I'll marry you. Annie was right. I'll follow you to the ends of the earth if that's where you want to go."

And then he kissed her and she kissed him back, and she knew at last he was finding his way or at least some part of it. He loved her. Deep down, she had known that all along. Felt it every time he had held her, kissed her, made love to her. He loved her and they were going to be married.

It looked like Arturo Hernandez would have to find another date for lunch.

Thirty-Five

Rina was packing her clothes, putting her furniture in storage, at least for a while, giving up her apartment and moving in with Alex.

He'd asked her to marry him only last week and already he wanted to set a date. Fall, he'd said. Or sooner, if she wanted. Fall, she'd agreed was perfect. A backyard wedding, maybe around the pool at Sage and Jake's new place. They'd have the landscaping finished by then. Alex thought it was a great idea. By then the weather would be cool enough for the guests to be outside.

Thinking of the days they had spent together since he'd come for her, Rina went around with a perpetual smile on her face. She couldn't remember ever being so happy. She loved him and he loved her. It just didn't get any better than that.

She was in the kitchen, packing her good dishes into a box, humming as she worked. Alex had persuaded her to hire a moving company, which she had agreed to do for the furniture, but the personal items she wanted to pack herself.

She heard someone coming up the walkway to the front door of the apartment. Alex was due any minute, on his way to help her. Of course, once he got there they'd get sidetracked and wind up in the bedroom.

Rina grinned.

The doorbell chimed. Not Alex. Alex had a key. She peered through the peephole, felt a jolt of surprise to see her aunt Marlene on the doorstep.

Not good, since her son, Bob, was in jail for murder, attempted murder, conspiracy to commit murder, destruction of property, at least a dozen charges. With the repeated attempts on Rina's life, bail had been denied. Bob was sure to cut a deal, but even if he did, he wouldn't get out of prison for years.

At least Silla and George weren't involved, she thought as she pasted on a smile and opened the door. In some strange way, this had brought her and her two cousins closer than they had ever been before.

Maybe her aunt was there to set things right between them, as well. Still, Bob was her son. This wouldn't be an easy conversation.

As the door swung open, Rina took a deep breath and stepped back out of the way. "Aunt Marlene. It's good to see you. Please come in."

"Thank you." At fifty-seven, Marlene Eckhart Beringer was an attractive woman, light brown hair, green eyes, nice figure. She had always had expensive taste, and it showed in the tailored pale blue pants suit she wore with a cream silk blouse, the low-heeled shoes that were clearly designer quality. With her hair swept into a stylish chignon, she could have passed for forty-five.

"I'm afraid you'll have to excuse the mess," Rina said,

leading her into the kitchen. "I'm moving." This time her smile came easily. "I'm getting married."

Aunt Marlene followed. "So I heard." Her gaze slid over the half-full packing boxes. "The millionaire playboy. Congratulations."

Backhanded good wishes. Apparently, her aunt hadn't changed. "Thank you. Would you like some iced tea? I have a pitcher just made in the fridge. I've got Coke if you'd rather."

"I didn't come here for iced tea, Sabrina."

Rina's eyes widened as her aunt pulled a thirty-eight revolver out of the handbag slung over her shoulder.

"I came here to kill you." Marlene leveled the weapon at Rina's chest.

Time seemed to slow. "So it was you all along," Rina said, trying to think of a way to get the gun out of Marlene's hand. "You and Bob and Henry."

"Not exactly. It was Bob's plan. His company was going broke. When Walter came to Houston that fall for a visit, he bragged about the silver he'd found out in the desert. Bob didn't believe him at first, but this time Walter seemed so certain. Bob followed him back to the mine to see if it could be true. And there it was—just like Walter said."

"It was molybdenum, not silver," Rina corrected, just to keep her talking. Alex would be there any minute. His arrival might be enough of a distraction that she could get control of the gun.

Marlene scoffed. "What does it matter? It's valuable, isn't it?"

Rina didn't answer. She was trying to judge the distance between them, inching closer a little at a time.

"So Bob decided to kill his father," she said to distract Marlene.

"That's right. He figured with Walter out of the way, the land would go to him, Silla and George. He figured you'd get cut in for a share, but there was plenty to go around."

"Bob convinced Henry to kill his dad."

"You always were a smart one. But it didn't work out the way Bob planned because Walter changed his will and left the mine completely to you—his daughter."

"What?"

Marlene's lips flattened out. "You never knew, did you? Florence and Mike promised Walter they'd never tell you about him and his little whore, the waitress he knocked up in El Paso. Sherry...that was her name. She wanted to get rid of you, have you sucked right out of her womb, but Walter promised her money. He convinced her that if she'd have his baby, he'd find a home for it. He knew his brother and Flo wanted kids and couldn't have them. He knew they'd take you."

Rina's chest was squeezing, her heart pumping. Surely it wasn't true. She tried to imagine that the man she'd thought was her uncle was actually her father. He was red-haired like she was. He was a dreamer, a risk taker. An adventurer. More like she was than the steady, hardworking man who had raised her.

"Bob needed you out of the way but after the first try failed he didn't have enough money left to get it done, so he came to me." Marlene smiled, enjoying her moment of triumph. "My second husband left me more than comfortable when he died. I could afford to help my son and I relished it." She sneered. "Walter's little princess. His illegitimate kid."

"That's why you hated Walter so much. That's why you always hated me."

"He cheated on me! He was never there for me or his kids! He deserved to die and so do you!" Marlene lifted the gun. It trembled in her hand.

Rina steeled herself. "Put the gun down, Marlene. You don't want to go to prison." Why she wasn't more afraid she didn't know. Maybe after everything that had happened, she had finally just had enough. "Put it down and this will all go away."

"You little fool—I don't care what happens to me. You ruined my son's life! You ruined my life! I want you dead!"

The gun shook as Marlene used both hands to cock the hammer. It was now or never. Rina leaped, grabbed the wrist that held the weapon and shoved it upward. Marlene pulled the trigger, a deafening roar next to Rina's ear. Using her weight, she tripped and shoved at the same time, and Marlene went down hard on the ceramic tile kitchen floor. Plaster rained from the hole in the ceiling.

Rina steadied her grip and aimed the weapon at Marlene.

She didn't hear the lock being turned or the door swinging open. She was pointing the gun at the woman on the floor when Alex rushed into the apartment, a terrified, murderous look on his face.

"Jesus! What the hell's going on?"

Marlene's green eyes stared at her with hatred. "You won't shoot, you don't have the guts for it."

Rina pulled the trigger and Marlene screamed as the bullet slammed into the tile a few inches from her foot.

"Jesus!" Alex said again, awe in his voice.

"It's okay. I've got it under control." The pistol in her hand remained on Marlene, whose perfect chignon had come undone, her hair hanging down around her shoulders.

Alex grinned and his dimples popped out. "Yeah, I guess you do. Looks like you really do know how to handle a pistol."

"I was always Big Mike's little girl."

"Mine now," he said. Taking the gun from her hand, he kept it aimed at Marlene while Rina grabbed her cell and dialed 911.

"You gonna tell me what's happening here?" Alex asked calmly as she ended the call.

"That's my aunt Marlene. She financed Bob's murder attempts." She thought of the secret Marlene had told her, thought of the parents who had loved her even though she wasn't really their child, and her heart squeezed. "Walter's my dad."

Alex's dark blond eyebrows shot up. "Wow, I didn't see that one coming."

"Neither did I. I'm not sure how I feel about it."

Alex moved closer, slid an arm around her waist and drew her against him. "Walter loved you, sweetheart. So did Big Mike. That's all that matters."

He returned his gaze to Marlene. "Bob wouldn't give up his own mother. I should have realized something was missing."

"This time it really is over."

"Yeah."

A lump swelled in her throat. "You sure you want to marry into a family as screwed up as mine?"

Alex scoffed. "They're all a little screwed up, love, take it from me."

"Most of them aren't murderers, though."

He stared at Marlene and his jaw hardened. "There is that." He turned back to Rina, gave her a smile. "One thing for sure, married to you, there'll never be a dull moment."

And then to the tune of wailing sirens, a smoking gun still in his hand, Alex leaned down and kissed her.

Epilogue

They were driving through the West Texas desert on the two-track road leading out to the Sabrina Belle. It was still burning hot, dust rolling up from beneath the wheels of the rented pickup. Alex had tried to talk Sabrina into waiting for a change in the weather but she was determined to get the mining operation under way.

He glanced at her sitting in the seat beside him, couldn't stop a grin at the perfect, brilliant-cut, three-carat diamond she was wearing on her left hand.

She'd wanted something smaller, less ostentatious. He'd wanted something even bigger, something that would keep guys like Arturo Hernandez away. The solitaire rising up from a platinum band was a compromise, and he could tell she loved it, even if it did look like a headlight on her small hand.

His sister was wearing a ring now, too. The diamond was smaller, but Becca treasured the engagement ring that had belonged to Joe's mother.

Alex's gaze went to the dusty Ford pickup barreling down the dirt road ahead of them. Hernandez was a helluva lot more reserved around Sabrina these days, now that he knew she was engaged. Which was lucky for him if he wanted to keep all the pretty white teeth in his head.

They had come for the meeting with Desert Mining. The lawyers were flying into Presidio to sign the contracts, but Hernandez wanted to show them something first. When they came to the old wooden cabin Walter had lived in while he worked the mine, Hernandez kept driving, the dirt track narrowing even more, the vehicles bouncing over cactus and flinging rocks out of the way.

Another mile passed before the engineer pulled up in front of a long rocky rift that rose up from the sandy floor and ran for miles across the desert.

"Look, Alex! There's an opening in the hillside. It looks like another mine."

Braving the brutal heat, drier out here than in Houston but still plenty vicious, they walked up to Hernandez, who stood in front of the man-made tunnel that had been shored up with timbers in the mountain.

"This is it," Arturo said. "I wanted you to see it before you sign the contracts."

"Walter was working two locations?" Alex asked.

"Yes, and as it turns out, both were productive."

"More moly?" Sabrina asked.

Hernandez grinned, a flash of white in a face even more suntanned than before. "Not moly, my friends. Silver."

"Silver?" they both said in unison.

"That is correct." He smiled. "Walter Eckhart was right. As well as the molybdenum, there is a large deposit of silver on the property."

Sabrina looked at Alex. "Oh, my God—Bob must have followed him here."

"Looks that way."

"This strike makes the land even more valuable than our first estimation," Hernandez said. "You are a very wealthy young woman, Sabrina Eckhart."

"Soon to be Sabrina Justice," Alex pointedly reminded him.

"He found silver, Alex." Sabrina smiled up at him. "Half his life, he worked morning to night, barely eking out a living, searching for treasure. I'm glad he finally found it."

Alex pulled her into his arms. "So am I." Over her shoulder, he drilled Hernandez with a look that said, *you're too late, buddy,* leaned down and kissed her.

"Let's get going," he said, grinning at the pink in her cheeks that had nothing to do with the sun. "It's hotter than seven levels of Hades out here and I've got plans for you when we get home." Alex winked and her cheeks went even pinker.

He thought of all that had happened, of the unexpected twists and turns that kept life interesting and had led him to Sabrina. Thought how lucky he was to love a woman willing to travel life's uncertain paths along with him.

Alex took her hand and started walking, looking forward to the journey ahead.

* * * * *

Author's Note

I hope you enjoyed Alex and Sabrina in *Against the Odds*. They were characters I hated to leave when the book was over. I'm thrilled to tell you there are more books in the *Raines of Wind Canyon* series to come. In *Against the Edge,* Ben Slocum goes on the hunt for the son he never knew he had, and along the way meets a woman he just can't resist. Then back to Los Angeles for *Against the Mark,* where Johnnie Riggs's friend, former marine Tyler Brodie, searches for a killer and finds a woman who perfectly suits him.

If you haven't read the first books in the series, look for the Raines brothers in *Against the Wind, Against the Fire* and *Against the Law,* as well as Trace Rawlin's story, *Against the Storm,* Johnnie Riggs in *Against the Night,* and Jake Cantrell's adventures in *Against the Sun.*

Until then, very best wishes and happy reading.

Kat